I0610074

A GEOFFREY PEACE THRILLER

PER
FINE
OUNCE

PETER VOLLMER

LUME BOOKS

LUΜE BOOKS

This edition published in 2020 by Lume Books
30 Great Guildford Street,
Borough, SE1 0HS

ISBN 978-1-83901-207-5

Typeset using Atomik ePublisher from Easypress Technologies

www.lumebooks.co.uk

Original version of *Per Fine Ounce* by Geoffrey Jenkins

Historical Background and Two-Page Extract of "missing" James Bond novel

Glidrose Productions (now Ian Fleming Publications) planned for a series of James Bond novels to be published under the pseudonym of Robert Markham. Celebrated South African novelist and award-winning Sunday Times correspondent Geoffrey Jenkins was asked to write an original James Bond 007 novel by Glidrose in 1966, following on from *The Man with the Golden Gun*.

Ian Fleming wrote at the time, "Geoffrey Jenkins has the supreme gift of originality. *A Twist of Sand* is a literate, imaginative first novel in the tradition of high and original adventure."

Jenkins and Fleming had talked about a diamond-smuggling storyline based in South Africa, which Jenkins later penned for Glidrose entitled *Per Fine Ounce*. Despite the promising Bond storyline and the fact that Jenkins was a best-selling thriller writer in the Fleming mould, along with being a friend and colleague of Fleming's, Glidrose rejected Jenkins' draft manuscript after Fleming passed away. Much speculation has ensued over the years about the reasons for this rejection, and why the manuscript was never published and seemingly "lost" by Glidrose.

However, it later emerged that the original manuscript for Jenkins' *Per*

Fine Ounce had not been lost, as extracts, in fact, remained in the possession of Geoffrey's son, David, who then gave his consent for the following two pages to be published from the original *Per Fine Ounce* novel, and for Peter Vollmer's version to be published, which shares the same title and is written in the same style, taking its lead from the original manuscript and endorsed by the Jenkins Estate.

The author, Peter Vollmer, has removed any references to the Bond characters to differentiate this version from the Ian Fleming Publications, and hopes this version will further encourage the Ian Fleming Foundation to publish the original version of *Per Fine Ounce* as written by Geoffrey Jenkins, or to give the Jenkins estate the right to do so for James Bond readers around the world to decide for themselves whether the original version of *Per Fine Ounce* merited publication nearly 50 years ago.

Author's Note

The next two pages are original extracts (pgs. 86 & 87) from the "missing" James Bond 007 novel PER FINE OUNCE by Geoffrey Jenkins (printed with full permission from the Jenkins family estate).

159

"Expensive powder-puff-- £137-millions," said M.
— WASN'T BIG ENOUGH TO KILL THE

Bond argued on. "This gas cylinder business/was bound POUND .7

to be discovered. I say it was meant to be discovered so that

we would start a wild-choose chase after an agent who is probably

sitting safely in this moment in Moscow. The trail will be so

cold now that it will be impossible to follow up."

"Out with it, 007," snapped M. "What are you driving at?"

"The South African gold flights," answered Bond slowly.
THEM.
"Someone is trying to make us take our eyes from that."

At Bond's words, Sir Benjamin glanced uneasily round the

room as if he was afraid someone might overhear.

M gave a short, explosive bark. "The gold flights is ARE
PROVINCE OF THE
outside the/OO Section, 007.What you say is nonsense, in the

light of what is being done to ensure its safe arrival. "

"And what is that?"

M paused for a moment, glancing at the financier,

then he said abruptly. "The Americans are in on it, of course.

Information from the CIA, who is reponsible for the coverage.

The flights goes from Luanda in Angola via Las Palmas to London.

The South Africans will provide a fighter escortess far as Luanda.

After that the Shackletons will home in one chain of American

PANGLOSS and British nuclear subs at waiting at 1,000-mile intervals.

GIVE
NAMES
ON. anyzinterference The flight will keep tight radio touch with

the sub ahead and the sub behind. Any interference--" he shrugged.

AGATE
LEFAY "They're all carrying surface to air missiles. Latest."

"Finger-on-the-tit stuff," murumured Bond.

"Long-range United States fighters will escort them from
the Ascension Island base," added Sir Benjamin. "Likewise both
south and north of Las Palmas."

"There'll only be one leg over the sea between Luanda
and Ascension where they will not have a fighter screen," added
M. "No,007. This bullion broker business is not related to the
gold flight."

Bond "You said, Sir Benjamin, that it would take
a tap on the chin to send sterling for the count.Would you
consider the loss of the gold flight to be that tap?"

Th e colour drained from the financier's face. "Yes," he
replied. "But God forbid that it should be so. Not only for England'
sake, but the West's."

M was impatient. "The two things are unrelated, 007. Go
and find out who put these damn things in the flags."

Bond stood up, looking down from across the desk into
the old sailor's face. "I'm sorry, sir."

M put down his pipe. "Sorry about what, 007?" The
voice was ominous.

"In just over two months this department won't exist,"
he said.X As he did so, he regretted the pain he saw in the
face of the man whom he admired above anyone he knew. "You recalled
me because the Treasury wanted help. Fair enough. But do you think
that you'll get anything more than an appreictaive minute for
what today's discovery? Do you really think they'll repirve
your department because of a couple of piddling things like
soda-water syphon cylinders?"

Preface

I remain in awe of those who have control in fulfilling their aspirations — this usually from a young age and already evident during the senior school years. This is reflected by those who devoted time to their studies and made the necessary sacrifices to attain their goals with the resultant excellent marks and acceptance to a tertiary education. Looking back, my scholarly career progressed in uncontrolled fits and starts, peppered with moments of outright brilliance offset by many others that are so shameful, that at the thought, I still cringe today. I can now only nostalgically think of those golden moments, of which there were surely many, that I let slip through my fingers.

I started reading prolifically from an early age, losing myself in John Buchanan, Elleston Trevor, Wilbur Smith, Ian Fleming and a near endless list of others. Each subsequent book hinting to me that I too needed to write something. But as the years went by, and I led a life filled with career-building, sports, various hobbies, then boating, and flying, there was never a dull moment and seemingly not a minute to spare either. Eventually, now in my later years, the desire became overwhelming, and I sat down and finally put pen to paper and wrote a book, which is, in itself, an achievement I'm proud of. The idea and story that came from it I thought good, but I was truly not prepared for what came after the actual writing. Suffice it to say that since then, I've written a few more!

At the time, a number of people inspired me, but in particular, Ron Payne, a literary agent in the USA, a novelist, and past war and political correspondent who had seen it all. He inspired me to write this novel, although I never precisely followed the storyline he proposed. However, I have included certain aspects and names he did suggest. Sadly, Ron Payne passed on a few years ago, but I will forever remain indebted to him.

The story takes place during a time of great change in South Africa, and I have relied extensively thereon for the background to my novel — the story itself is a work of fiction, as are the characters. While an effort was made to keep the actual historical timeline as accurate as possible, slight creative liberties were taken and all obvious inaccuracies are mine.

I wish to express my gratitude to my wife Elaine, who I would continuously interrupt with the questions *give me another word for* or *please buy*, or *please pay* — all related to writing and publishing a novel. To Jacqui Corn-Uys, my editor who literally worked wonders with my stilted dialogue and German-influenced grammar; to my agent, Tom Cull, whose persistence, patience, and belief in me are *'par extraordinaire';* and to my friend, George Carter, who would read my first drafts and produce reams of pencil-filled notes of discovered errors and sometimes hilarious inaccuracies. There are many more and to all, I give my heartfelt thanks.

Prologue

Shrouded in the utmost secrecy, the mission was planned to keep pace with the demarcation between night and day as it rushed its way westwards. The high-altitude spy plane was in a race with the rotation of the earth and would attempt to close in on its targets out of the darkness of the approaching night sky.

The aircraft had departed the U.S. Indian Ocean rapid deployment military base and climbed swiftly to seventy-five thousand feet, where it levelled off and accelerated to its cruising speed of Mach 1.6. It flew due west from the island of Diego Garcia, the largest of sixty small islands comprising the Chagos Archipelago, a thousand miles to the south of India.

It passed over the Seychelles, remaining well out over the Indian Ocean detouring north of the huge island of Madagascar. With Madagascar behind, it changed course southwest over the Mozambique Channel, where it descended to forty thousand feet to rendezvous and refuel.

Sitting in the tail of the TriStar, the fuel-boom operator stared intently into the night sky looking for the expected reconnaissance plane.

Suddenly, the operator's earphones crackled. "Boomer-2, Boomer-2, this is Shadow-1 approaching. We are a thousand feet behind you and fifty feet below your current altitude."

Against the black velvet of the night sky, the boom operator seated in the tail of the U.S. Air Force Lockheed TriStar K. Mk.1 tanker could not see the Blackbird as it slowly approached. The recon aircraft's matt fuselage and wings merged with the night sky, the still-secret matt black titanium, and carbon-fibre skin of the hypersonic SR71 designed to absorb most light and all radar waves, rendering it invisible against the dark backdrop. However, the hypersonic spy plane's proximity radarscope clearly revealed the tanker.

The operator jerked upright in his seat, immediately fully attentive, and began to flick various switches on his small instrument panel. Suddenly, a brilliant cone of light bored through the darkness from below the tanker's tail, illuminating the dark shape that approached. Still, the reconnaissance aircraft was difficult to see as it closed to about a hundred and fifty feet, where it slowed to match the tanker's speed of almost 500 m.p.h. In the cold night air, now free of the usual daytime tropical turbulence, the two aircraft were vague shapes against the stars, seemingly stationary and joined by some invisible force.

With the slightest of movements of a small joystick, the operator guided the long refuelling boom into the refuelling slot above the recon aircraft's cockpit. He felt a slight shudder as the connection locked.

"Contact… coupling confirmed. Lights green — commence pumping," the Blackbird pilot said.

No small talk ensued. The black ops aircrews who flew the SR71 and U2 high-altitude reconnaissance aircraft never said more than was absolutely necessary. They were not inclined to friendly banter and were all business, cocooned in their airtight suits and full-face helmets. They appeared to live in a world of their own.

The operator was a skilled technician who knew his job. He activated the high-speed electric pumps and hundreds of gallons of jet fuel swiftly flowed through the boom into the large wing tanks of the recon aircraft, filling them in mere minutes as the spy plane kept meticulous station behind the air-tanker.

The moment the tanks were full, the boom operator disengaged and retracted the flying boom. Briefly, a vaporised cloud of fuel appeared, only to be instantly swept back over the spy plane's fuselage. A moment later, the Blackbird started to fall behind. When well clear of the tanker, the commander advanced the throttles of the two turbojet engines to full power, leaving a string of pale-blue transparent doughnut rings of fire strung out behind each engine as the afterburners were ignited. The aircraft's nose lifted towards the stars as it climbed, disappearing rapidly from view.

With Mozambique now in sight, it turned west towards the country and soon crossed the coastline, heading for the border with South Africa.

The spy plane chased the setting sun before it, slowly gaining on the day-night separation as the aircraft overtook the speed of the Earth's rotation. The plan was to penetrate South Africa just before the close of day, the aircraft approaching out of the fading darkness from the east, making both the plane and any possible contrail from the aircraft's engines difficult to detect.

The spy plane crossed Mozambique and entered South African airspace, heading towards the industrial complex of the Witwatersrand. Its mission was to photograph the nuclear research facility at Pelindaba, constructed among the foothills of the Magaliesberg Mountains on the outskirts of Pretoria, the nation's capital. From there it would continue westwards towards Vastrap, an arid flat area measuring thousands of square miles on the fringes of the Kalahari Desert. The previous inhabitants had long been displaced, the area now a restricted military training site and weapons range where the South African government tested its latest weaponry far from prying eyes. It was also here that the CIA believed the South African Atomic Energy Board, together with the South African Defence Force, was sinking a vertical shaft deep into the desert to be used to carry out an underground atomic test blast. South Africa had yet to test-fire any nuclear armaments on land, something scientists considered essential before the development of these weapons could be deemed a success. British Intelligence had it that a test firing was due to be carried out with South Africa's secret partners, the Israelis, which of course both countries vehemently denied. Besides, the South African and Israeli governments were not signatories to the Nuclear Non-Proliferation Treaty.

US Intelligence had been informed by reliable sources that the Israelis and South Africans had cooperated in the development of a gun-type firing device required to detonate a weapons-grade uranium core. They had also learned that the South Africans proposed to arm Israeli Jericho-2 missiles with nuclear warheads. It was rumoured other bombs were also being designed, to be delivered by high-altitude English Electric Canberra bombers or Blackburn Buccaneers, along with others that would be fitted to the RSA-3 medium-range ballistic missiles developed in South Africa.

In recent years, the onslaught against the South African apartheid regime had gained momentum, and the country now faced threats on more than one front as it took on several enemies. These terrorist groups, or freedom fighters as they preferred to be called, were financed and armed by the Russians and Chinese. In the north, on the border of South West Africa (now Namibia) and Angola, Black guerrilla movements backed by Cuban Communist forces threatened to overrun the country.

With its apartheid policy, South Africa was a pariah nation, and Western countries faced the choice of which was the lesser evil — a nuclear-armed pro-Western South Africa, hated and ostracised by the world, or a country overrun by Black and Cuban forces who subscribed to Communist ideology. Neither idea was pleasant.

South Africa had built a sophisticated radar network, which monitored and controlled its northern borders and was supported by a ring of airfields on which French Mirage F1 and IIIc interceptor aircraft stood ready to scramble at a moment's notice.

However, for some inexplicable reason, no interception had been ordered against the intruder that now streaked across the southern skies at sixty-thousand feet. The SR71 Blackbird's warning systems remained silent. Were the South African forces even aware of the high-altitude intruder? It did not seem so.

The plane flew over Pelindaba, its instruments registering the complex as a source of atomic radiation. It was generally known that the South Africans had two pilot nuclear reactors for research and *peaceful* use, but it was rumoured that the newly developed nuclear bombs were assembled and stored here. The Blackbird's high-definition cameras took hundreds of photographs, many in infrared. The aircraft then slightly adjusted its course for Vastrap, a new military base in the Kalahari Desert. It was here, far from civilisation, that high-resolution photographs would reveal that a mineshaft was being sunk, the workings surrounded by military vehicles and temporary buildings.

Finally, the aircraft turned south and within minutes was flying high over its ultimate target, a small town not yet revealed on any map. At their briefing, the crew had been told by the chief of the CIA's South Africa desk that this was a mining town in the middle of the Kalahari Desert. It was also said that the town had sprung up virtually overnight. Even from this altitude, a runway of unusual length was clearly discernible. Satellite surveillance had put its length at ten-thousand feet, sufficient to accommodate the biggest aircraft in the world. What purpose then could this possibly serve in a sparsely inhabited desert? It was now up to the CIA to decipher these photographs and come up with an answer to this question.

Its covert task now finished, the spy plane sped high over the Namib Desert towards the Atlantic Ocean, where it rendezvoused three times with U.S. refuelling tankers before it finally entered United States airspace.

Mission complete.

Chapter One

It was a miserable morning. Low cloud rolled in from the west and cloaked the city of London in a drab ominous grey, streaked with dark bands, heralding rain. Cars drove with their lights on and pedestrians scurried along the pavements with their umbrellas handy, clearly expecting the deluge to start at any moment.

The black London cab drew up alongside the kerb. A tall man in his late thirties alighted, fished in his back pocket, and withdrew a folded clip of banknotes. He peeled off a few and thrust them at the driver. He looked slightly out of place among the other people on the street, many of whom were in black pinstripe suits, one or two still wearing bowler hats. He appeared more up to date — his Saville Row tailored suit was of modern cut with slim-fit trousers, though he did not wear the usual waistcoat. The collar of his light-blue shirt was buttoned down and his Gordonstoun Old Boy's tie swung free. A fawn mackintosh was draped over his forearm from which a dark umbrella also swung. He glanced down to check the shine on his expensive black slip-on moccasins. This was no city executive employed by a bank or firm of stockbrokers. Yes, perhaps the tie did reveal some loyalty to his past — but, in truth, a misconception as he only wore it because he liked its design. He wasn't tied to his past in any way; he was a modern man who saw little value in things old.

The cab had drawn up outside the fortress-like SIS building at 85 Albert Embankment in Vauxhall Cross, London. Its drab, slightly sooty appearance belied the building's importance as the headquarters of the SIS, more commonly known as MI6.

He entered through the main access area and approached the battery of arched stiles and x-ray boxes with his security access card in hand. All personnel and visitors, whether entering the complex from the underground parking or through the main entrance, had to endure this ritual; there were no exceptions.

A Regimental Sergeant-Major, one of the many army and civilian personnel in attendance approached him, smiled in recognition, and saluted smartly.

"Good morning, Commander," he said.

"Good to see you again, Jim," Peace said and grinned in return. "You know it should actually be Mr Peace. Goodness, we don't want to remind eavesdroppers of my rank, do we? This is an intelligence establishment. VA would have a bloody fit!" It was obvious this was said in jest, though there was a hint of gravity in the man's deep voice. "Bloody ridiculous, really, they probably all know who I am by now anyway." He looked around as if the enemy could be seen in the passing crowd. Both men laughed.

The RSM and Peace had known each other for years and these short conversations, which usually took place after Peace was off on some clandestine mission, had become a ritual between the two of them. The RSM, a battle-hardened veteran, had participated in his own fair share of black ops and knew where Peace fitted within MI6. The young man also made sure he always exchanged a few words with the RSM.

"Well, in that case, tell me, Guv, how was the holiday?" the RSM asked. The same scene was repeated every time the Commander returned from a mission, with a few comments about his supposed sexual conquests before he entered the precincts.

The young man's eyes flashed, the corners crinkling. "Smashing, as our chaps would put it. Jim, believe me — there's nothing like those hot-blooded Brazilian women. My God, man, those tangas! But then again, I only looked — never had time to test the water."

Peace stood six foot two inches tall, his sandy hair parted on one side, cut short back and sides and shaped by a West End barber. Piercing silver-grey eyes with laugh lines radiating from the corners were set in a chiselled face, his features revealing nothing soft, while under his suit his body was lean and muscled. When he laughed, he revealed a set of straight perfect teeth, with no indication he had recently undergone some major dental work paid for by the British Crown. Chipped teeth, smashed jaws, broken bones and the occasional bullet or knife wound were accepted injuries — merely an occupational hazard.

"How is our illustrious leader, Sir John, this morning?" Peace enquired.

The sergeant rolled his eyes in mock horror. "Awful, Guv, but that's not unusual. I was told by Sir John's office to speed up your arrival were I to see you. The Vice Admiral has some important bigwigs with him. I recognised the Governor of the bank, would you believe."

The young man frowned.

"That's ominous. Well, I best hurry. I'll see you later."

He passed through the security checkpoint, where he looked into the iris-recognition device and then had every personal item in his possession scanned. This done, he strode towards the bank of elevators.

Many might expect the Section Chief, in recognition of his exalted position, to be accommodated in an office near the top floor, overlooking the Thames. However, Vice Admiral Sir John Whitehead, generally referred to as VA when not in his presence, would have none of this. Instead, he and his staff were housed in a lower basement that never saw the light of day, but this was more than made up for by the fancy interior décor which made it appear like just another floor. Other than the absence of sunlight, there was no indication the walls were constructed from solid reinforced concrete, or that there were no apertures to accommodate windows, the lack of which was deftly concealed behind drapes, panelling and paintings. Air was circulated through ducts in the ceiling at a constant 20°C. The furnishings were modern and intended to create a relaxed atmosphere, further enhanced by the deep carpets and recessed lighting.

Peace continued to the end of the corridor. Along the way he passed through a general office and an open-plan area with a dozen or so desks separated by shoulder-high room dividers, giving the occupants at their desks a small degree of privacy — a layout cribbed from the Americans. He was greeted by those at the desks who noticed him.

Sir John preferred the confines of the basement which prevented any long-range eavesdropping with sophisticated acoustic equipment, while the sole entrance via the elevators and the emergency stairway made any unauthorised entry impossible. He had a phobia about security, being forever aware of the embarrassment that Burgess and other Soviet spies had heaped on the British Intelligence Services — a fact that had never been forgotten by their American allies.

Peace entered a door marked *Vice Admiral Sir John Whitehead*, and smiled at the middle-aged woman seated behind her desk.

"Geoffrey, what a pleasant surprise," Jenny Damsby said with a smile. "Need I tell you that Sir John is not happy?" she added, her way of telling him that he was late.

"Really?" Peace replied, raising his eyebrows. He had long since immunised himself against his boss's mood swings.

"Don't let him hear you, he has — "

This was interrupted by a loud crackle from the intercom on her desk. "No chit-chat, please. Send him in immediately."

Peace rolled his eyes, and she smiled at him, shrugging her shoulders.

"He's inclined to eavesdrop, isn't he?" Peace murmured.

Miss Damsby's eyes widened in alarm and she brought her finger to her lips, emitting a faint *shhhh*. She was obviously terrified that Sir John could hear them.

Peace was well aware she knew of his private and professional exploits. MI6 was paranoid when it came to the lives and doings of its top operatives and staff. How many times had she not sent him a bottle of Glenfiddich, courtesy of Sir John, to some hospital where he was recuperating? Peace also knew that she realised he and the VA were forever at a game of one-upmanship to which neither would ever admit. On occasion, Peace would refer to the VA as a member of the Y-front brigade, emphasising that he himself wore skants.

"Bunch of bloody pansies, the Y-fronts," he had once said. He was ex-SAS and would have been slighted were anyone to cast him in the same mould as those known as the *Cambridge Five*, who were Soviet spies and an embarrassment to the British Intelligence Services. Their legacy seemed destined to stay around, since the Soviets had even recently commemorated Kim Philby on a Soviet postage stamp!

Leaving his mackintosh and umbrella hanging from the hat rack in the corner, Peace opened the door and strode into Sir John's office. Here he was surprised to see other occupants in the room seated around the small conference table.

"Come in, Peace. You're late," the Vice Admiral barked. "I'm sure you know the others, but let me introduce you just in case. There's no need to stand on formality. Sit, we have serious matters to discuss."

He'd received no welcoming smile, but he wasn't surprised. VA, in his opinion, was an emotionless mental bully. How could he be late? He had just returned from holiday, after all.

It was 9:08 a.m. Hell, that wasn't late! This was London!

Sir John went on with the introductions. Peace had immediately recognised the Governor of the Bank of England, Sir Ian Douglas; unmistakable with his straight combed-back white hair, and Thomas Fulton, the Exchequer's assistant and right-hand man. *What the hell is going on?* This looked extremely serious.

Sir John studied Peace carefully. "Brazil seems to have agreed with you," he finally remarked. "Well, you'll probably be off to a land of sunshine soon again, but first I need to tell you a rather involved story. Listen carefully, Commander."

Sir John nodded at the Governor and Sir Ian cleared his throat.

"Commander, for all intents and purposes, and certainly as far as the rest of the world is concerned, it appears that we have distanced ourselves from the South African government because of their abhorrent apartheid policy. Actually, this is no more than a façade. In reality, we are still close — the Communists remain a common enemy. The South Africans are the biggest gold producers in the world, the world's largest supplier of strategic metals, and the most powerful country on the African continent. The Western world also needs them to protect the sea route around the tip of southern Africa. Need I say more?"

"You could say we still need each other for a good number of reasons," the Exchequer's man interposed, the only representative of the elected government present.

The Governor frowned at Fulton as he continued. "To the problem. A rather large bullion shipment en route to us from South Africa has been hijacked. In physical terms, this was eight tons of gold ingots. Unbelievable, isn't it?"

When was gold ever expressed in terms of tons? Peace did a quick mental calculation: that was roughly £21,000,000 at the current gold price.

"How were the bullion containers hijacked?" he asked.

"Well, that's the point. They arrived at their destination at London Heathrow, but when the containers were opened, they contained only lead bars. The containers were the original steel ones from the gold refinery in Germiston, South Africa. Of course, we've carried out an extensive investigation together with the Gold Branch of the South African Police. I should add that the Gold Branch is staffed by the very best the South African Police has to offer. Those chaps know what they're doing, in particular a Mr Desmond Carruthers, a Colonel who held the rank of Chief Superintendent when he was with Scotland Yard. Sadly, he was made an offer he could not ignore by the South Africans a few years ago, if you know what I mean. Putting it bluntly, they stole him. However, his presence has ensured good cooperation. Fortunately, he still has some loyalty to the Crown," the Governor said smugly.

Sir John intervened. "Of course, Peace, everything is still under wraps. The disappearance has not been leaked to anyone; neither Fleet Street nor any other international news agencies have an inkling of what has happened. We want to keep it that way. The South African Gold Branch is playing the same game. A loss of this dimension would impact heavily on the mining sector of the stock market, here and in South Africa. This would not bode well. Also, no one has come forward to take responsibility."

Sir Ian nodded in agreement before continuing.

"Naturally, we're in constant communication with South Africa. To add to this, a number of other disturbing events have taken place during the last few months. An abnormally high number of gold shares on the Johannesburg and London Stock Exchange have changed hands. Whether this is merely business as usual has been impossible to establish. The current political situation in South Africa, as you can well imagine, has had a profound influence on South African shares quoted on both the London and Johannesburg Stock Exchanges."

Sir Ian brought his cup to his lips and sipped. He continued, "There are simply too many front companies and investment houses involved. During the past year or so, the gold mines have been plagued by wildcat strikes and other unexplainable disruptions — explosions, mechanical breakdowns, a whole series of incidents; certainly a good many more than is usual. Nobody seems to know whether this is subtle sabotage by the underground Black Nationalist movements, or no more than a spate of unusual events. Some have even suggested that these disruptions have been instigated from within in order to manipulate the share price." Sir Ian smiled. "I never trust stockbrokers. As you can imagine, this has driven the share prices down, with many shareholders disposing of their shares before they plunge further. There are always ready buyers in the wings — there still are, and they are holding the price artificially high as they take up these shares, otherwise, prices would have fallen appreciably more."

"How much do you know about the gold industry?" VA asked Peace.

"Not much, I'm not interested in the stock market. I've never been a gambling man and buying shares is no more than gambling, is it not? I leave it to my brokers to do any investing; they know a lot more than I do."

A look of disdain crossed the Vice Admiral's face, clearly not happy with Peace's reply. Sir John's love for the tables was no secret among his staff.

Peace noticed VA's expression. *He thinks I'm an insolent bastard trying to upstage or embarrass him.*

Sir John indicated to Sir Ian that he should continue.

"Well, let me tell you this — the bulk of the gold industry in South Africa is controlled by five large mining houses. The one that interests us is an Afrikaner group called Afrikaner Goudeiendomme — Gold Properties, if you want a translation. It's chaired by Anton Van Rhyn. He's a late arrival in the industry, but he's amassed a colossal fortune in a relatively short period. He's said to be brilliant, ruthless and an ardent Afrikaner nationalist. He was a firebrand when still young, a follower of the Afrikaner diehards who were sympathetic towards the Nazis and who took over the government from General Smuts in '48. Like many other young Afrikaners, he joined the Afrikaner national youth movement a few years after Smuts' downfall in 1948. He has two daughters, who were or are still both at Oxford. His elder daughter is Janet Van Rhyn and, like her father, is said to be ultra-right-wing. Apparently, she dislikes the Blacks intensely. She's never married. She's also on the board of Afrikaner Goudeiendomme. Her mother, Van Rhyn's first wife, died of cancer and he remarried. He later wedded Lady Jocelyn Langton — ring a bell? She has a daughter, Margaret, whom Van Rhyn adopted; she's now known as Margaret Langton-Van Rhyn."

Peace arched his eyebrows. "Lady Jocelyn Langton? Yes, I do recall her — did she not, even before her husband's death, openly consort with this Van Rhyn chap, causing a scandal? I hear she's quite a bombshell, if you know what I mean?"

VA frowned at Peace's description.

The bastard thinks I've no subtlety whatsoever, Peace thought, as Sir John made no effort to hide his disdain.

For a moment, Peace's directness appeared to have also embarrassed Fulton.

"Oh well… yes, you could say that… you're right. Anyway, she and Van Rhyn married three years ago. Her inherited fortune, combined with his, probably places them among those whose wealth borders on the astronomical. Need I say more?" Fulton said, and then continued, "We believe Van Rhyn is behind the manipulations of the gold shares, particularly as these relate to the five large mining houses. In this, he is supported by Lady Jocelyn. They're both outspoken about our government and the manner in which we have mismanaged our African mining interests, allowing them to be nationalised with little compensation for the original shareholders. Naturally, they're also most unhappy about the alacrity with which we've granted independence to our various colonies in Africa. If I were to wear an industrialist's hat, I would have to concede that they may have a point. They have tremendous support from right-wing quarters." He shook his head in mock disbelief. "Believe me, there is no shortage of right-wing fanatics out there."

Sir John, who had attentively leaned forward in his chair, sighed again and leaned back. All sat in silence, digesting the information.

"You've told me little of the gold hijack. Any idea how this was pulled off?" Peace asked. Sir Ian's faint smile vanished and his face was serious again.

"Unbeknownst to many, Afrikaner Goudeiendomme holds a majority shareholding in the gold refining industry in South Africa. That would be Consortium Gold Refiners Limited. Most gold mined in the country passes through Consortium; they are the largest gold refiners in the world. This shipment was supposedly taken directly from their premises on the outskirts of Johannesburg, in proper bullion containers, to Jan Smuts Airport, a few miles away. However, we have no doubt that the gold never left the refinery. Clearly, this was an inside job, though at this stage, this remains speculation. Mr Van Rhyn is being obstructive and prefers to carry out his own internal investigation. I do not need to tell you that he is under tremendous pressure from the South African government. They're not all diehard fanatics, and our friend is certainly not liked by the new enlightened supporters of President de Klerk. However, there's a rumour, it really being nothing more than a whisper, and without any substantiation at all as of now."

Sir John leaned forward in his chair and rested his elbows on the armrests, his hands clasped in front of him. He silently appraised Peace for a few seconds. Peace knew that another surprise was coming.

VA continued, "It is said that a subversive Afrikaner movement — ultra-right-wing of course, is behind this. The most tantalising piece of information is that Van Rhyn of Goudeiendomme is involved. Remember, this is just speculation but good to bear in mind."

Peace remained silent but pursed his lips and continued to stare at VA whose expression now became particularly sombre as he said, "And now for the really bad news. Several of us believe the South Africans have their hands on a neutron bomb. A bloody enhanced radiation weapon, or ERW as it's referred to. It's not capable of the structural damage an ordinary nuclear bomb can inflict, although its explosive yield is still in the kiloton range. It's the radiation release that's the real killer — armour, dugouts, and so forth, aren't able to protect the occupants. What it does is destroy life indiscriminately by intense radiation. It permeates through everything."

He paused to light a cigarette.

"The Russians have done their utmost to hush things up, but we have reason to believe that a bomb has gone missing from their previous Strategic

Rocket Forces, from a nuclear base in the Ukraine. It may well have found its way to South Africa. We know it's not part of the South African nuclear arsenal, around which the strictest of security is maintained. As you know, their nuclear weapons are now in the process of being decommissioned. We think Van Rhyn has it, along with four missing South African nuclear bombs, all stashed in Copperton." He tapped a photograph on the table as if to lend significance to his statement.

"Intelligence sources have revealed that South Africa never disclosed the correct number of bombs it had, but left all with the impression that those being decommissioned were the total number they possess. However, this was not so. Ultra-right factions in the highest echelons of the military spirited these away in some ingenious manner. The bombs simply disappeared. Well, can you imagine the embarrassment to the South African government? The disappearance of the four bombs is still a secret known to very few."

Sir John added a few more aerial surveillance photographs to those on the table and pushed these across towards Peace.

"That's Copperton." He tapped one of the large prints with a fingernail. "Clearly, these photographs were taken by a high-flying aircraft."

Peace was aware of the American reconnaissance flights over South Africa.

Sir John continued, "We believe this is Van Rhyn's hideaway, but more of this later. We have little to substantiate this tale, though it definitely demands investigation. That's where you come in."

"What about the gold bullion theft and Van Rhyn?" Peace asked.

Sir John pulled a face as he pondered the question for a moment. "I don't know… we still know too little, but keep your eyes open. If we hear more, you'll be informed immediately. Rather concentrate on Copperton for now," he replied.

Peace had the feeling that he'd soon be leaving on the sunny trip VA had alluded to.

Chapter Two

"Peace, we're giving you a new identity. You will be taking on the role of Lord Digby Brentwood." The Vice Admiral spoke bluntly, indicating that the subject was not debatable.

Peace jerked his head up and stared at his boss.

"Lord Digby Brentwood! Good God, the man lost his marbles years ago! Nobody even knows what he looks like, he's been hiding himself on his *estado* in Paraguay for so long. He's a bloody raving fanatic. He never consorts with the coloured locals and only employs Whites on his plantations. What's more, he gives support to extreme right-wing groups in this country! Hell, why would I want to take on his identity? He's a bloody fascist! God, he probably has a few ex-Nazis in his employ — you know, the worst kind."

"You've hit the nail on the head — I agree," Sir John replied. "The whole point of you impersonating him is so you can infiltrate Van Rhyn and his organisation. Hopefully, they'll see you as one of them; white supremacy and all that."

What the hell does that mean? Peace wondered, astounded by this unexpected proposition. "What about the real Lord Digby? Won't he have something to say?"

The Vice Admiral chuckled. "Strangely enough, the recluse officially left his massive rancho on a protracted world cruise, not to be seen or heard of for at least six months. He is, in fact, a guest of Her Majesty's government, although somewhat reluctantly, I might add."

Again, Peace found himself wondering what the hell *that* was supposed to mean.

"What about being recognised?"

Sir John *harrumphed*, and then smiled.

"Unlikely. Actually, the man vaguely resembles you. Maybe somewhat older, but he is a fitness fanatic and doesn't look his age. He's blond, but our chaps will sort out your looks. You needn't resemble him closely; nobody but his most trusted servants know what he looks like, and you'll not be going anywhere near South America. Years back, while in the army, the man had a horrendous accident requiring surgery. His appearance is now different, and few people have actually seen how different. You won't be seeing his fascist cronies either; they'll remain no more than an association. You'll be in South Africa."

Clearly the bugger's happy with the arrangements he's made!

"Who the hell thought this lark up?" he asked, knowing it had to be a VA tactic. The remark certainly had the desired effect; it wiped the smile off the Vice Admiral's face. Peace grinned when he saw his boss flinch. The VA chose not to respond.

"Your first job is to make contact with Van Rhyn," said Fulton. "We can't prescribe how you should do this, but we believe you should target the daughters. Lord Digby is said to be a very wealthy man."

Sir John chuckled. "Peace, the expenditure revealed by your expense account over the years indicates that you were born to play the part. You should enjoy this. However, your supposed wealth alone won't attract these women. In fact, you'll have to be a little more ingenious. Also, Brentwood has, let's say, a penchant for loose women, which shouldn't be difficult for you to emulate."

Bastard, Peace thought, but ignored the sarcastic statement; this was not the time to get into a verbal wrangle with his boss. Inevitably, the man would pull rank.

"How am I to make this unexpected public appearance?"

"Lord Digby has maintained his Military and Naval Club membership in St. James'. He was once a captain in the Royal Fusiliers, and when in London still visits his club. It assures him a degree of seclusion, as club members and staff are very sensitive to their fellow members' needs, and loose talk about fellow members is not tolerated. That's where you will discreetly enter the public limelight. The club has reciprocal arrangements with the Rand Club in Johannesburg, apparently the haunt of most gold mine magnates in South Africa. It's extremely exclusive."

Sir John took a sip of his tea.

"South Africa is in a state of disarray, what with the wave of enlightenment this de Klerk fellow has brought with him. Unbanning the ANC, releasing Nelson Mandela, and with the majority of Whites voting overwhelmingly in favour of free and fair elections. Contrary to general belief, most everyday Afrikaners are peace-loving people. Yes, they're afraid of the Blacks, not as individuals, but of their numbers — *die swart gevaar*[1]." Sir John's attempt at an Afrikaans pronunciation was atrocious even to the untrained ear. Luckily Peace had worked amongst these accents before. He permitted himself to smile, but listened intently.

"They believe they'll eventually be overwhelmed by the sheer weight of numbers and will be side-lined. It's the fanatics who need watching. That includes some of their politicians, those out-and-out supremacists, a few in the top brass in the military, a smattering of industrialists, and of course, our friend Van Rhyn."

There was a pause.

"Here's another shocker. We all know the South Africans have developed the bomb, as have the Israelis; in fact, this appears to have been a combined project. They've manufactured several of these, but no one knows how many. With the cauldron rapidly approaching a boil, we're wondering to ourselves, as are the Americans, what's going to happen to the bombs? Imagine if the fanatics got hold of these — they could hold the world to ransom! They've also developed chemical weapons; they're even assisting Saddam Hussein in this field in order to ensure that South Africa's oil imports from Iraq will never be embargoed.

"Intelligence has it, from what source I don't know, that Van Rhyn has established his own secret base. He proposes to launch strikes at various key targets in the event of de Klerk handing over the government

---

1. The black peril — an Afrikaans reference to the overwhelming number of Blacks in the country who are by far in the majority

to Black majority rule. The man even had the audacity to state publicly that this will not happen in his lifetime. He's even set up a private aircraft museum, and guess what — he has retired Air Force aircraft that are able to deliver nuclear bombs, all in flying condition and maintained at considerable expense. Can you imagine the man's bargaining power if he has the bomb?

"Furthermore, their RSA-3 is an orbital missile capable of carrying an explosive to anywhere on this planet. Fortunately, we don't believe they have the technology to manufacture a nuclear weapon light enough to be carried by this missile. But believe me, the South Africans do not lack ingenuity; they'll overcome this problem soon enough!"

Peace was dumbstruck at hearing this information. With that kind of influence behind them, the fanatics could start a full-blown war. *Jesus, intercontinental missiles with nuclear warheads!*

Sir John's features softened for a moment.

"Geoffrey, I'm sorry I can't give you more, but we don't know much more than what I've just told you. Also, we haven't yet decided quite how you should proceed. This information and the operation are highly confidential, and the more people we throw at it, the leakier it becomes." He paused for a moment.

"You're on a fact-finding mission, you're not being sent to intervene. Have you got that? I'm not giving you backup at this stage. Well, not yet, but I'm working on something that could add to your cover. I've a female agent. She'll help you blend in; you know what I mean. She knows the country well. In fact, she grew up there."

"The last woman you sent got killed!" Peace exclaimed.

"I know. I'm afraid that's one of the risks." Sir John shrugged.

"I've a conscience, although you may not believe it," Peace said, clearly unhappy with this arrangement.

VA ignored his comment.

"You are to use the usual modus operandi when approaching any of our embassies around the world, and you'll be given immediate assistance. If suspicions are raised regarding your identity, we'll see that you get help. We need to know what their grand plan is, Geoffrey." He said this in a kinder tone now, but still with sufficient emphasis to make his intention clear.

Peace nodded. Sir John's use of his first name was not lost on him. The old man was concerned. He just hoped this wasn't going to turn out to be a suicide mission.

Chapter Three

More than three weeks had passed since the meeting in Sir John's office.

Peace, in the guise of Lord Digby, had used the reciprocal arrangements between the Military and Naval Club in London and the Rand Club in Johannesburg to stay overnight at the exclusive Johannesburg club for two days, after which he moved into a small estate on the fringes of Johannesburg's northern suburbs. The grounds were huge, affording him absolute privacy. Little did anyone know, but it was actually a British Intelligence safe house.

By this time, he had become a familiar figure at the Club through frequenting it daily. As was expected within its hallowed walls, his arrival was without fanfare. However, word soon got around that he was on a fact-finding mission looking for investment opportunities and was particularly interested in the gold mining sector. The story was that he wanted a stake in the industry during this time of political turmoil when share prices were soundly depressed, as this would ensure him a handsome return. Furthermore, it was rumoured he believed that the Afrikaner would not simply allow the country to be handed to the Black majority without safeguards to ensure that the Whites remained the champions of industry and commerce for a long while to come.

Peace's chauffeured Mercedes 500SE drew up outside the porte-cochère entrance to the club in the heart of the business centre of the city; the imposing multi-storey building taking up a large portion of a Johannesburg city block. The doorman opened the car's rear door for him.

"Good day, Lord Digby," the doorman greeted him quietly. Peace nodded.

It was already seven in the evening, the summer sun close to setting and the city centre empty of traffic. The usual afternoon thunderstorm had come and gone, the streets were still wet and glistening in the fading light and the air smelling clean and fresh. Already the cordoned-off area of private parking in front of the Club was lined with cars, the chauffeurs congregating in small groups smoking and chatting, their owners already within, having their first evening drink.

Peace's pinstripe suit, black brogue shoes and snow-white shirt were enhanced by a silver-blue tie. He had dispensed with the waistcoat — these were not fashionable in South Africa, which pleased him immensely. He detested them.

The foyer was dominated by a huge carpeted staircase to the next floor, being wide enough to accommodate rush-hour traffic on the London Underground. He ascended the stairs.

Peace was pleased with himself. He had slipped into his new role easily, deftly handling the surprise at his sudden emergence into public life. He hoped to create the impression that although he may abhor the public and was a loner, he had no alternative but to visit the country in person, in order to establish first-hand what developments were taking place there if he were to make the investments he proposed. He needed to be accepted as a frequent visitor and his arrival not unexpected. Already, during previous visits to the club, he had been drawn into conversation by one or two of the members, clearly curious about him, his reputation as an ultra-right-winger preceding him. Since Van Rhyn visited the club when in the city to rub shoulders with his peers, the idea was to bump into him and be acknowledged as one of them.

Peace recognised the man immediately. Van Rhyn was sitting in a leather chair next to a large mahogany coffee table, a glass of what had to be very old Cape brandy next to him. He looked up and lowered the copy of the *Financial Mail* he was reading as Peace entered. This surprised Peace. The newspaper was definitely not right-wing but considered liberal. In the flesh, he appeared larger than in the photographs. He was tall; it was hard to tell when sitting, but he guessed at least six foot three, with a barrel chest that strained slightly against his pristine white, monogrammed shirt. His maroon silk tie was neatly knotted. His hair was dark with streaks of grey, cut short against his scalp and his ears were close against his head.

Peace took a chair at a coffee table no more than ten feet away from him. Van Rhyn glanced up briefly and then returned to his paper; he made no attempt at a greeting. Peace had an impression of eyes that were almost black and unfathomable. A thin moustache covered thin lips, and his narrow aristocratic face had high cheekbones atop a strong jaw.

A steward approached.

"Good evening, Lord Digby. A pleasure to see you again. Is there anything I can get you?"

Van Rhyn swung his head up and gave Peace an appraising look, a touch of amusement on his face.

"A single malt whisky with ice — Glenfiddich?" Peace asked the steward.

"I've got it, Lord Digby," the steward replied, keen to please. Lord Digby's tips were known to be more than generous.

"That's fine. Thank you."

Out of the corner of his eye, he saw Van Rhyn looking at him.

"I've no intention of being presumptuous, but surely not *the* Lord Digby Brentwood?" Van Rhyn asked, his eyebrows lifted.

Peace smiled. "Unfortunately, the one and only. Please keep that between us." Van Rhyn rose, his hand outstretched.

"Certainly, no word will pass my lips. I'm truly glad to meet you. I'm Anton Van Rhyn, chairman of Afrikaner Goudeiendomme. I had heard you were in town — you can imagine my surprise! It is said you shun publicity and the public. It is, therefore, indeed a pleasure to meet you in person, Lord Digby. From what the rumours say, it seems we share the same political sentiments."

Peace withdrew his hand from the huge fist.

"Of course, and I have heard of you. Your country and its politics currently dominate the English tabloids. I've found your utterances on the proposed handing over of this marvellous country to the Blacks interesting. I must say, you express my views entirely." Peace gave him a conspiratorial smile.

"I'm glad to hear that," Van Rhyn replied, looking intently into Peace's eyes as if seeking to read his thoughts. Seemingly satisfied, he continued.

"There aren't many who'd openly side with me. It seems we're a dying breed. I believe some were born to lead and others to serve. As I recall, you said something similar in the past. Who would have ever believed that we'd succumb to the pressures of the world, with the British leading the charge for enlightenment? Would you care to join me?"

Peace took the proffered chair at Van Rhyn's table. He was pleased with developments, never having thought he'd be able to meet his quarry so easily. *The man may be an Afrikaner, but his English is impeccable.* This was often the case where the sons of successful Afrikaners had been sent to English-speaking private schools. The Afrikaners were a resilient breed, staunch Calvinists with a clear distinction between right and wrong, and champions of industry. They were also very pragmatic and understood the benefits of an English-speaking education for their children.

"I'm honoured. Who could better advise me on investments related to the gold mining industry in South Africa?" Peace said, while thinking to himself, *thank God for Englishmen and their damn men's clubs.* He briefly lifted his eyes to the ceiling — the good Lord certainly did work in mysterious ways. Hopefully, the same Lord would also look after him.

Chapter Four

Over the next few weeks, Peace and Van Rhyn met on a few occasions. These all seemed to be chance meetings, and all confined to the Rand Club.

Peace was impatient and found the intervals between their meetings tiresome but doggedly endured them, hoping for at least some form of business friendship to blossom.

He soon realised that the Afrikaner appeared quite taken with this English aristocrat who seemed to despise the proletariat, be they whatever denomination, colour, or creed. The gold-mining magnate commented that he liked the fact that Digby maintained a low profile and shunned any publicity, almost going to extremes to avoid any notoriety. From the gist of their discussions, it was obvious to Peace that Van Rhyn thought Lord Digby could be an asset who may be able to open doors for him in the British capital among those whose fortunes relied on old money, and who shared his views on the African continent. Several of their conversations touched on those Englishmen, they of the upper echelons of finance, industry, and society, who had voiced their misgivings regarding recent events in colonial Africa.

A few weeks after their initial meeting, Van Rhyn extended an invitation to Peace and his partner to join him and his associates for a black-tie dinner at his home in Waterkloof, Pretoria. Peace accepted, but declined the invitation to bring a companion.

Peace's chauffeur-driven car stopped at the security gate in the upmarket suburb at exactly seven-thirty. The huge property was surrounded by a high wall which bore a seven-tier electric fence strung above it to deter any potential intruder. He was also not surprised to find two security guards manning the gates, dressed smartly in khaki uniforms, and obviously Afrikaners. They made no attempt to hide the holstered weapons on their hips. One approached the car with a clipboard in his hand. Peace glanced at the surveillance camera mounted on a pole facing the side of the car and realised that his photograph was being taken.

His name was checked against the list, and only when properly identified was he allowed entry. No doubt this would be run through some database to confirm his credentials. His chauffeur drove slowly along a well-maintained gravel road, which wound through large expanses of lush lawn, flowerbeds, and tall trees. The vehicle was finally halted in front of the house's main entrance, which was already surrounded by a cluster of parked cars and limousines. A dozen steps led up to a large open veranda partially enclosed in glass which overlooked the front of the property. The manorial house, with its gables and oak-framed colonial Dutch windows, vaguely conformed to Cape Dutch architecture. White rose creepers and vines wound their way along the walls, latticed wooden arches that spread over pathways, as well as the many trellises.

As Peace stepped into the foyer, which was carpeted with a number of beautiful Kurdistan rugs, he noticed a large man approaching, dressed in a dinner jacket. Peace saw the radio earplug in the man's ear and the thin white plastic-coated cable that disappeared into his collar. He also didn't miss the slight bulge below the man's armpit. *Serious security*.

"Your name, sir?" the man inquired.

"Digby Brentwood." He purposely dispensed with his title.

"Please follow me."

The man whispered into a microphone hidden in his jacket's lapel and then led Peace through the main entrance into an arrival hall and finally into a vast lounge, which was already occupied by about two dozen other guests.

Peace did not expect to find so many others. The request that he wear black-tie had left him with the impression that this was to be an intimate dinner party, but he was surprised to see that it was more than that.

In a voice louder than the general level of conversation, the guard announced, *"Dames en Here*[2], Lord Digby Brentwood."

Clearly, the guard had been briefed on his title. If this was intended to impress him, it did. This surely had to be the height of Afrikaner society in their mother city in South Africa.

At the mention of his name, a hush descended on the small crowd as all turned to look at him, curious about the man who was known to be a recluse. Clearly, as an ardent supporter of ultra-right-wing politics, his ideals were well known to these Afrikaners.

Peace soon picked out Van Rhyn, resplendent in his black-tie and dinner jacket. The huge Afrikaner broke from the couple he was standing next to, and with hand outstretched, approached Peace.

"Lord Digby, we are delighted that you were able to come. Please let me introduce you to a few of my friends and colleagues. There are a few dying to meet you... how should I put it — a member of the British aristocracy who believes in the Afrikaner ideology." Again, he smiled. "Indeed, a rarity in these times."

Peace returned the smile. "Just *Digby* will be fine, please, I must insist."

"In that case, I'm Anton."

Peace let his eyes sweep across the room. Most attendees seemed to be with a partner — whether male or female. No one struck him as being on their own like he was. Van Rhyn then slowly led Peace from couple to couple and introduced him. Two of the men he met were members of the Afrikaner Goudeiendomme board. All were Afrikaans but greeted him politely in English.

Finally, they approached two women standing alone — obviously mother and daughter.

"My wife and daughter," Van Rhyn said, unwittingly answering Peace's surmise.

Lady Jocelyn was a statuesque blonde in a black evening dress; Peace knew her to be in her mid-forties. They shook hands, and she gave him the briefest of smiles. Van Rhyn then gestured to the beautiful woman he

---

2. Ladies and Gentlemen

guessed to be in her early twenties, who stood next to the other woman. She was clad in a sculpted red evening dress, the low neckline revealing the swell of her breasts. Her blonde hair cascaded to her shoulders while slightly chubby cheekbones still revealed a hint of retreating adolescence. She appeared to be wearing only a touch of makeup, but her most striking feature was her dark-blue eyes.

"This is my daughter, Margaret Langton-Van Rhyn."

Peace took her hand. The woman smiled, revealing dazzling white teeth. He guessed her to be Van Rhyn's stepdaughter, the only child from Lady Jocelyn's previous marriage who had been mentioned during his London briefing. She bore no resemblance to Van Rhyn whatsoever.

The stepdaughter took her time looking him over, and as the seconds passed, the look bordered on becoming rude.

"Lord Digby, please excuse my directness, but is there truth in the rumour that you support fascist groups in England? I would have thought it to be un-English, not to mention narrow-minded?" she asked abruptly, staring fixedly into his eyes.

This directness gave Peace an inkling into what he had heard about her — she was certainly her own person.

"Margaret, that's uncalled for," her mother hissed, clearly disappointed by her daughter's opening remark.

Peace smiled coolly, but inwardly the woman's directness surprised him. From her speech and mannerisms, it was apparent that she had been the recipient of the best education England offered, and could probably trace her aristocratic roots back a good few hundred years. While no radiant beauty, her fortitude in speaking her own mind more than surpassed what one saw from the outside and certainly added to her mystique.

"It is true. I believe we have to ensure that a degree of discipline returns to the world. Current crime statistics are unacceptable, drugs pervade society, and wrongdoers generally get off too lightly. The peasants, workers, blue-collar labour, Blacks, whatever you wish to call them, should follow, not lead. A government run by workers is doomed to failure. You need only to look at the U.S.S.R."

He was surprised at how easily the words tripped off his tongue. Was this how the real Lord Digby would have replied?

Margaret stared at him, her eyes round. He did not miss the distaste in her expression. She pursed her lips into a thin line and looked away.

Lady Jocelyn decided to intervene. "You and my husband certainly appear to share the same sentiments," she said, clearly unconcerned by his reply and by her daughter's reaction. "My stepdaughter Janet is sure to find you interesting. She's an anglicised socialite who believes in White supremacy. In fact, I should warn you she conforms to a far-right political orientation and certainly disagrees with the changes that are happening in our country. I imagine that's not an oddity. Let's find her."

He was now alone with Lady Jocelyn, who led him by the hand, weaving through the couples, introducing him on the way to General Pieter Booyens, a member of the South African General Staff. This was a clear indication that Van Rhyn had friends in the right places. Peace did not doubt that there had to be many in the top echelons of the military that were reluctant to relinquish the enormous power they wielded. He also met more of the top brass in industry and mining on Jocelyn's tour.

Eventually, they reached a woman sitting on a stool at a Steinbach grand piano, who was tinkling softly on the keys.

"Janet, I've somebody here I'm sure you'll be pleased to meet. You share the same sentiments. You should get on well."

Lady Joyce turned to Peace. "Lord Digby, meet Janet Van Rhyn. She's a cum laude graduate from Oxford — and that with an Afrikaans accent, I may add. Rather amazing, isn't it?"

The woman lifted her face and turned her head to look at him. He found himself staring into a pair of dark, unfathomable eyes that reflected the light from the chandelier above the piano. Only after carefully appraising him did she offer her hand. Her fingers were elegantly long and cool to the touch.

"*Enchante*," he said, bowing his head as he brought her fingers to his lips.

A slight smile played at the corners of her mouth. She rose from the piano stool. "British chivalry — how pleasant," she murmured.

She was an astounding beauty. Her hair was black and shoulder-length; it shimmered in the light. The neck of her royal blue silk dress, although quite high, gaped fashionably, luring his eyes to her breasts. She was tall, surely six foot in her high-heeled shoes. The dress hugged her torso, accentuating her slim waist.

"I've placed you next to Janet at the table, seeing as you are both without partners." Lady Joyce pouted, a slight frown of disapproval on her face. "What's the matter with you? Good gracious, coming to a dinner party without escorts... Really?"

"It's all a matter of finding the right one," said Peace.

"I agree," the young woman said.

They both laughed, and Lady Joyce, still clearly unhappy, shook her head and left them to get acquainted.

Having secured his usual whisky from a waiter and a vodka screwdriver for her, they made formal small talk while sitting on a sofa slightly apart from the rest of the crowd. She seemed to consider it taken as read that she should stay close to him. Was this Van Rhyn's instruction, he wondered, but then dismissed this. She did not strike him as the type to take instructions from just anybody. This woman was strong-willed. He soon gathered that Janet was ultra-conservative, clearly believing Blacks to be inferior, and unappreciative of what the Whites had done for them.

"The Lancaster House peace agreement was no more than the British selling out the white Rhodesians, their own kith and kin, without a backward glance, knowing full well there could not be a peaceful transition. Your government knew that Mugabe could not be trusted, and what did you do when things went wrong? Nothing!" she said fiercely.

"Of course," he agreed with suitable fervour, and added his own thoughts concerning the dangers of the new liberalism that was sweeping the world.

"My father mentioned you to me. He said that you're looking to invest. I think he said you're actually looking at mining?" she said.

"That's right. I'm interested in buying gold shares — a substantial purchase. I believe that they'll be the most stable of all in the event of unrest here or elsewhere. After all, even before the great discoveries in the Americas and Southern Africa, it was revered for its value. That's reason enough to invest in gold. But not only that, the fluctuations of the share price, which are sure to come, will provide an opportunity for quick profits.

In fact, the unease that will be generated once South Africa goes to its first so-called democratic general election must put upward pressure on gold shares. Everyone will seek to protect their wealth, fearing a civil war. No matter what prevails in your country, I believe we can be rest assured that gold will ultimately triumph. It would do well to buy now and sell later, or so I believe," Peace said.

"I can give you the names of a few mining houses whose shares are bound to be an excellent buy. My father's been buying large parcels of these, without being too obtrusive." She laid a hand on his arm. "Don't look so shocked. It's not insider trading, it's just that we all know each other so well, it's difficult to keep secrets. Come, it's time to sit down to dinner."

Peace was appalled. Clearly, Van Rhyn had no scruples. Insider trading going on within upper Afrikaner establishment circles! You needed friends in the right places to get away with that.

"You've had your fair share of political upheavals in Paraguay," Janet said to him as they took their seats.

The woman was clearly well-read and politically informed.

Peace was grateful for the time he'd spent reading up on Lord Digby's life. He mentioned that Paraguay had changed little even with a new president and thought his financial interests in the country were still secure.

"It'll take decades before the peasants get a real foothold in the government. I don't believe this will happen in my lifetime. No matter who governs, in Paraguay the elitists still rule and will do so for years to come," he said believing he needed to make some remark that related to his newly chosen home country.

A slight frown crossed her brow. "Unfortunately, we are unable to say the same. Our President de Klerk is hell-bent on changing the course of our future and has released Mandela and put the future of this government to a general vote. This will be disastrous for the Whites," she said solemnly.

"Lord Digby." A loud voice interrupted their conversation, and Peace turned to look at the speaker. It was General Booyens, to his left, who was leaning across his wife to address Peace.

"I heard your remarks concerning Paraguay. I must tell you the same applies here, no matter who is in government. Even if Nelson Mandela's party should represent the government, we will, how should I say, control industry and finance for years to come. You will agree that if you control those sectors, you control the country. De Klerk cannot accomplish anything without us. We'll make certain it remains so for many years," the General said. "Don't underestimate the strength of the South African Armed Forces. And remember, it's a white military force. We'll ensure that it stays that way, no matter what. We have a few tricks of our own up our sleeves."

The man sounded so confident Peace wouldn't have been surprised had the General given him a conspiratorial wink. He did not doubt the man's words for a moment. He couldn't help thinking of the A-bomb. At their meeting at MI6, VA had briefly touched on American SR-71 reconnaissance flights. Within the last few weeks, the world press had made mention of what was termed *The Vela Incident* — a place in the South Indian Ocean from which a double flash had been detected by American satellites and was confirmed to be a nuclear explosion. South Africa had vehemently denied knowledge of this. Although this had occurred in years past, the world and in particular, the Americans and their press had regurgitated the incident time and again.

He gave a brief laugh. "General, thanks for that reassuring piece of information."

The General nodded, seemingly content with Peace's cheerful response.

He was amazed. These people, and specifically this woman, accepted him as an ultra-conservative. The groundwork had been laid. Janet had relaxed; she was no longer stiff and formal. He followed her lead, putting on the charm. They talked their way through the entrée and main course, both having their glasses repeatedly refilled with an excellent wine.

"Lord Digby, tell me, where are you staying?" she asked suddenly.

"Please, I must insist you call me Digby," he said. "Initially, I stayed at the Rand Club, but I needed more privacy, so I found myself a small but secluded place in the northern suburbs of Johannesburg."

"And do you live there on your own?" she asked.

That was direct!

"Yes, completely, except, of course, for the servants that came with the property."

42

He sipped nonchalantly at the excellent Nederburg Private Bin Cabernet Sauvignon wine and then asked, "Would you care to join me for dinner sometime? Of course, you must choose the restaurant, just so long as it's secluded. I don't know the city that well, and I'm no friend of crowds."

"I'd be delighted. I myself hate being noticed and avoid crowds, in particular the press," she replied.

*

Later in the evening, he sought out Van Rhyn's stepdaughter, Margaret, and found her with the General's aide-de-camp, a young Army lieutenant. She appeared to be bored, making desultory conversation, and seemed relieved by his interruption. *Could the young lieutenant's company be that bad*, he thought?

"Ah, Margaret Langton-Van Rhyn is rather long, don't you think? But at last I have found you," Peace said, a smile on his face. "Forgive my use of your first name. I merely wish to apologise for the manner in which I voiced my sentiments on politics. I had no intention of offending you."

"Rest assured, Lord Digby, surrounded as I am by my sister, mother and stepfather and not to forget, the military top brass, your views could not shock me," she replied, returning the smile. "However, there is a difference. At least you appear to be apologetic about your beliefs." With that, she laughed again, the sternness disappearing from her face, her features softening.

The lieutenant had overheard the discussion, and it appeared to dawn on him that he'd suddenly become an intruder on a private discussion. He made a discreet withdrawal.

"Thank you for rescuing me from a truly dull evening. I had to listen enthralled as he lectured me on the invincibility of the South African Armed Forces. I hope you have no such similar intentions?" she asked.

Once again, it was time to turn on the charm, Peace thought.

He laughed. "No, you needn't fear. Other men's exploits don't interest me. I see you have the impression I would suppress the aspirations of lesser men in their quest for equality and freedom." He paused to take a sip of his whisky. "That's not true. What I do believe is that the populace should not be ruled by inadequate men placed in positions of power by no more than a scrawled *X* on a ballot paper just because they'd once been good bush warfare commanders. That doesn't make sense to me. To be qualified to assume a position of power requires, I believe, an educated background, evidence of entrepreneurship, and astute leadership qualities. Also, should it not also include a degree of breeding?" *Dammit, Peace*, he thought to himself, *you're really laying it on now*! He continued, "I don't believe that the successful rebel leaders who suddenly find themselves as presidents and cabinet ministers necessarily have the capacity for good governance. You need only look at Cuba and a few of the emerging African countries north of us." *Now, that was a mouthful.*

She looked at him appraisingly from under lowered eyebrows. "That was quite a dissertation. I accept that you've a point, but you don't have to come across like some of these *verkramptes*[3] and power-mongers." She looked pointedly at the others in the room.

"Let's not argue about that right now — I hope you'll one day find that I'm not what you think I am. I do have compassion for the human race," he said quietly.

The guests were slowly taking their leave and Peace decided to follow.

"Delighted that you and my daughter got on so well," Van Rhyn said as all made their farewells at the entrance.

Presumably, he meant his eldest daughter, Peace thought. Janet must have already said something to him. Again, he wondered whether the rapport between them was a result of her father's urging.

"Ah, glad you mentioned that. It reminds me, I need to say goodbye to Janet."

He found her alone on the porch with a drink in her hand. As he approached, she turned and smiled.

"There you are. I've already been reprimanded by the lady of the house for not taking care of you."

---

3. An Afrikaner expression that refers to those who are considered politically ultra-right-wing — no mixed marriages, no shared politics and segregated housing, schools and public transport.

"Not to worry, I found your sister."

"*Hmmm*, that should have been interesting — is she not too *verkrampte* for you English?"

"It was — she's certainly not you," he remarked.

"No, she isn't. Are you leaving? Will we see each other again?"

"I hope so. Well, until then. Good night." And with that, he pecked her on the cheek.

Peace's chauffeur-driven car left the Van Rhyn grounds just after midnight to commence the thirty-mile drive to his rented estate. The car had been hired to Lord Digby Brentwood through an international car rental business and the booking made from London. The same applied to the rental of the house. Peace had employed the chauffeur from an employment bureau providing temporary staff to overseas tourists and businessmen visiting the country. Martin, the chauffeur, was a Coloured. He wore a suit, not a uniform and cap, so as not to appear ostentatious. This suited Peace; he did not want to attract too much attention, though he was still aware that he needed to play the part of Lord Digby.

They had driven no more than fifteen minutes when Martin spoke quietly, in strongly accented English.

"Sir, I believe there is a car following us. I've noticed that it has been behind us for quite a while now," he said, his eyes catching Peace's in the rear-view mirror.

"Are you sure?" Peace turned to look out of the rear window. There was a car behind; he couldn't make out the model.

"Yes, it's been behind us since we left the Van Rhyn estate."

At this time of the night? *The driver had to be right*, Peace thought. Was Van Rhyn checking on him or was he out to establish precisely where he lived?

"Speed up, but don't make it too obvious."

He felt the car accelerate, the distance between the two cars widening. They were on the turnpike heading in the general direction of his estate.

"Take the next off-ramp and pull into the first service station that has an overnight one-stop shop on the premises," said Peace.

The car followed the slip road and pulled up at a service station with an all-night convenience store leading off the forecourt.

"Stop here." Peace pulled a banknote from his money-clip. "Go in and buy anything you want, meanwhile I'll watch," he said, keeping an eye on the road. A car passed, travelling quite slowly, the occupants trying to look unobtrusively at the garage forecourt. It was the same car, a white Toyota Camry.

Damn! What to do now? He didn't want to arouse suspicion, but he needed to ensure that he was not under continuous surveillance.

He watched as the car pulled up next to the curb about fifty yards beyond the driveway to the service station. He knew that they would have seen that the chauffeur was not in the driving seat, and would probably have assumed that the man was in the convenience shop. He had no doubt that the two men in the car were Van Rhyn's henchmen. Nobody else would have had reason to put a tail on him. It was time he let them know that he did not take kindly to that.

He opened the door and climbed out on the street side of the car, knowing that he was being observed. He walked nonchalantly towards the Toyota, approaching it on the driver's side. He knew that the tactic would cause some consternation in the car. As he was drawing abreast of the door, he noticed it was ajar. He reached into his jacket and withdrew a Smith and Wesson MXP 9mm automatic, a compact handgun, which nestled below his armpit in its suede leather holster, and then grabbed the door handle and jerked it open. Before the driver had a chance to react, Peace pressed the silencer on the end of the barrel hard against the man's temple. The man froze.

"Tell your friend that if he moves, you're dead!" Peace spat, applying a little more pressure to the man's head. "You've been following me — what's the interest?"

"We weren't following you."

Peace swiped the barrel of the automatic across the man's skull. Blood immediately flowed. "Don't insult my intelligence."

The other occupant seemed about ready to make a move. "I wouldn't if I were you. Put your hands on top of the dashboard and keep them there."

"I swear we weren't following you," the man said in guttural English. He cringed, as if expecting to be struck again.

46

Out of the corner of his eye, Peace saw his chauffeur returning to his car.

"Give my compliments to your boss, whoever he may be, and tell him that I don't like being followed. Understand?"

The man, evidently dazed, gave a barely perceptible nod.

Peace took two steps backwards. The silenced automatic coughed twice, the sound no louder than a dog's bark. Air hissed out of the front roadside tyre and the vehicle settled closer to the ground. "That'll keep you," he added, and then carefully backed towards his car.

He climbed into the rear of the Mercedes, still keeping a sharp eye on the Camry. "Okay, Martin, just take us home, but at a sedate pace."

The expression on Martin's face said it all. He was obviously amazed at the sudden turn of events.

"I need you to listen carefully. I don't want this repeated to any others — not your employer or colleagues. Not a word. Is that understood?"

"Sir, my employer expects me to be discreet. Absolute discretion is one of his mottos. I give you my word."

"In that case, you'll get a good bonus when I leave the country, so long as you realise that this is conditional."

"But, sir, if they report the shooting, the police will investigate."

"No, they won't."

"As you say, sir."

Why had he been followed? What could have made them mistrust him? He didn't understand it — surely no one knew his real identity.

He decided he would just let it be for a while.

Chapter Five

The harsh treatment of the two in the Camry did not serve as a deterrent. Peace soon realised that his every movement was being observed. The moment his vehicle left the estate, a tail would materialise and follow, keeping a discreet distance.

He ran into Van Rhyn several times at the Rand Club, and they invariably sat together. They were often joined by other members — friends of the magnate who were also involved in the gold mining industry. In time, Lord Digby was accepted as one of them and listened, without objection, to their discussions about the movement of gold shares and their current volatility.

Guided by Van Rhyn, he had made substantial purchases of gold mining shares over the weeks, and the magnate's suggestions had noticeably increased the worth of his script holdings. Peace wondered what VA thought of this, the enemy adding profit to Her Majesty's coffers! *Rather amusing*, he thought. He might not be a gambling man, but this was not an opportunity to be ignored. He realised that this was illegal, no more than was insider trading, but who was to report them?

About a week or so after the dinner at the Van Rhyn estate, he phoned Janet. She sounded genuinely pleased to hear from him.

"What took you so long?" she teased. Her familiarity surprised him.

"I got caught up in a number of things," he offered.

"So I gathered from my father. You've been following his advice on the stock market and making a substantial profit, it seems. I can excuse you for that."

He asked her out to dinner, reiterating that she needed to choose the restaurant as she had better local knowledge.

"When do you propose we do this?"

"How about Friday?"

"Now, if I were a lady, I would have to decline and tell you that I wasn't free until sometime next week," she replied, laughing. "But to be honest, Friday is fine. You can collect me at my father's Riverside home in northern Johannesburg round eight." She gave him the address. "Casual dress will be fine. Don't bother with a tie."

Peace replaced the phone, pleased with himself. The date was sooner than he'd hoped.

He left the Rand Club later than he expected that night, and it was eight-thirty when his car entered the estate's driveway. His house was in darkness. He recalled it was Wednesday, the staff's day off. Well, it was going to have to be a light snack — that was the arrangement. He did his own thing in the kitchen on a Wednesday.

"Martin, that's it for today. I'll see you in the morning," he said to the driver.

He watched the car's lights disappear down the driveway and climbed the few steps to the front door. As he stepped inside, his nose caught a fragrance he knew he had smelled before, but couldn't place it. Somebody — he was certain it was a woman — had been or was in the house. He was unarmed; carrying a weapon could have given his cover away. During the day he had visited a number of mining houses and with the prevalent tense political situation, many businesses had installed metal detectors.

He moved slowly towards a table in the corner of the foyer near the front door and quietly slid open the single drawer in its side. Out of habit, he ensured a weapon was always close by the front door when taking up a new residence. It was a form of insurance — you never know who could arrive at the door. He had also ensured the drawer would slide open and close silently when he had placed the Heckler and Koch automatic in it. He withdrew the weapon and silently slipped the safety catch off. There was only the faintest click.

Standing in the centre of the foyer, he waited as his eyes adjusted to the dark, fully alert for anybody trying to rush him from the shadows. He stood there for a full minute before moving towards the sitting room to his left. He could now vaguely make out the furniture and windows. The curtains were drawn, letting in no light. Fortunately, the house was carpeted wall to wall and he was able to move silently. He passed through the double door entrance and reached for the main light switch. He flicked it on and immediately the two chandeliers bathed the room in bright light.

Janet sat on the sofa, one leg crossed over the other, a glass of what he guessed to be vodka and orange juice in her hand. A black cocktail dress left little to the imagination, the plunging neckline affording him a generous view of a curve of her breast. The skirt was short and the hem rode high on her thighs, exposing long, crossed legs. From the toe of one dangled a black pointed stiletto. At the sight of the automatic pointing at her, she merely raised her eyebrows questioningly.

"My, my, a gun? I was hoping you'd be pleasantly surprised," she said, with the faintest of smiles.

The barrel never wavered as he let his eyes roam slowly over her.

"How the hell did you get in? The place was locked," he said, still staring at her. He slowly lowered the automatic.

"Your cook, or whatever she is, let me in. Are you sure she's no more than a cook? Anyway, I persuaded her that I wished to surprise you. It took a while, but she finally agreed. Confidentially, she told me that you did not appear to like women, as you've never brought one home. I must say I found that rather difficult to believe. You didn't strike me as being… you know."

Peace saw she was finding it difficult not to laugh.

"God, I'm going to have to do something about security," he said.

"Don't be hard on her. Her intentions were good."

"Okay, I won't, but only because you've asked. What are you doing here?"

"Why are you still holding that damn thing? It makes me nervous. You can put it down. I'll remove my clothes if you insist; you don't need the gun to persuade me." She smiled again, this time seductively. "To be honest, I couldn't see the point of waiting until Friday, and I knew you'd finally agree. I'm known to be quite persuasive."

He chuckled and placed the automatic on a nearby side table. "I may take you up on that offer, but I think we should eat first."

"Oh, I've even thought of that. I remembered you'd said you're fond of lobster, so I brought tails in mayonnaise, plus a salad and a chilled Riesling to go with it." She indicated a large wicker picnic basket that rested on the floor next to the sofa. "Before you change, please open the wine."

She handed him the corkscrew. He extracted the cork and poured the wine, then climbed the stairs to the master bedroom and quickly changed.

When he returned to the sitting room, she'd already found plates and cutlery and was dishing up the tails and salad. She handed him a plate to which she added a freshly buttered roll. The food was exquisite, and for a few minutes, neither of them spoke.

"Digby, you're an enigma." She hesitated for a moment. "No, that's not quite right, let me put it differently... oh, by the way, you did say I should call you Digby, didn't you?"

He nodded his head. "And you, woman, are unfathomable."

"Unfathomable? That's how it should be. Now, just imagine how I see it. You step into your own home with a gun in your hand. Were you expecting trouble?"

Again, he just shook his head. He was still wary. What was she up to?

"Men with guns intrigue me. It's so masculine, and that gun is large, not a little peashooter like that British fellow we see in the movies," she laughed, the ambiguity of her comments not lost on him. "Come, sit next to me. You know, the way you addressed me as woman, it conjures up something wanton."

Janet sounds triumphant — as if we are playing some sort of game and she is winning.

He placed his wineglass on the coffee table and sat down next to her. Her scent drifted to him and a sideways glance allowed him a glimpse into the deep vee of her dress. He could clearly see her breast, not constrained by a bra, the areola visible, and the nipple just hidden. He drew in his breath involuntarily. A slight tingling sensation, that prelude to a sexual encounter, flowed through him.

"I'm watching you, you're getting distracted," she said, her voice throaty. She leaned towards him and he responded immediately, their tongues probing each other in a passionate kiss as she fell back, her head resting on the sofa's armrest. He slid his hand into her neckline and pushed the material aside, lowering his head to take the erect nipple in his mouth. She moaned and arched her back, thrusting up at him. Her cocktail dress had ridden up, the hem now barely covering her. He let his hands drop between her thighs, immediately aware of the warmth that radiated from her even before his fingers slid into her.

"Oh my God," she whispered.

Clothing crumpled to the floor. He ran his lips over her as she groped for him, her fingers finding his hardness.

"Please, my Lawd," she mimicked a Cockney accent, "don't dawdle." She thrust her tongue in his ear and ran her nails down his back.

Suddenly she drew her head back.

"My God, what are all these scars? They look like bullet wounds." She moved her hands over the skin of his chest.

"Sorry about them. I know they're ugly. Occupational hazard, I'm afraid. I was in the army, the Royal Fusiliers. I did time in Malaya — had a bad experience there."

She raised her pelvis to receive him and he entered her. Within minutes, they were bathed in sweat, her breath rasping in his ear as her hands clawed his back, evidently consumed by some urgent primal need, which seemed to flow from her as though she wanted it to devour him as well. It was not long before he rolled off her, drawing in deep gulps of air.

She too was breathing heavily, the magnificent swathe of hair covering part of her face. "My God," she whispered, "you do that well."

They said no more, but just lay there and he felt himself getting drowsy. *God*, he thought just seconds before they both fell asleep, *this woman has everything — wealth, power, brains, and a degree of rampant sexuality seldom encountered.*

Sometime during the night after a post-coitus drink and snack, they retired to the bedroom — the sofa not conducive to a good night's sleep for two.

He awoke to the deep growl of a sports car's exhaust coming from the back of the house. It struck him that she must have hidden her car well. He had not noticed it when he returned the night before.

The bed was empty; she had deserted his lair. It crossed his mind that he had just bedded a fiercely independent woman with a mind of her own. Somehow, he also knew that she was deadly dangerous, like a cornered leopard. She was one who always had to be in control. He couldn't imagine life ever being boring in her company.

The cook and maid had already arrived. He carefully inspected his personal items, the cupboards in the dressing room, his briefcase, and desk drawers. He smiled to himself. His possessions had been meticulously examined and professionally replaced, exactly as they had been. Clearly, the Van Rhyns were taking no chances. They were still establishing his bona fides — they trusted no one and still wondered whether he was the person his public reputation made him out to be.

At around nine, the phone rang.

"Sorry about my sudden departure, but I'm not a morning person. However, I had a wonderful evening. We must do it again," she said.

"When do you propose we do that?" he asked, realising that just the sound of her voice had aroused him.

"I'm sorry, but I'm going away with my father for a few days — a week or more actually, but I'll be in touch."

"I take it our dinner date is off?"

"I'm afraid so. Business. My father's call."

"Phone me on your return," he replied casually, silently noting that she had not indicated where she was going.

His breakfast was interrupted once again by a call from his broker confirming the purchase of a particular bundle of shares. This was a coded message from MI6 telling him that he was to call on the British Embassy in Pretoria as soon as possible.

Chapter Six

The British High Commission office was housed in an imposing building situated behind the Union Buildings in Pretoria. The country was experiencing the last heat of summer as winter approached. The famous jacaranda trees of Pretoria had long lost their purple-blossomed glory, which heralded the arrival of spring.

Peace presented himself at the information counter and slid Lord Digby's passport across to the clerk. The clerk studied it wordlessly and then called a security man standing in the hall and asked that he show Peace to an office on the first floor. He was led through this office to another behind it. Unlike the areas frequented by the public, it was austerely furnished with only a steel desk with a high-backed swivel chair and a few steel cabinets. Other than a cheap calendar, there were no pictures. The single large window overlooked the back of the Embassy grounds. It was evident that this was double-paned one-way glass.

A man in his shirtsleeves rose from behind the desk and stretched out his hand. His red braces and colourful bow tie seemed very casual, but this was perhaps merely to enhance his cover. It certainly seemed out of character, but the colours matched his ruddy complexion and the mass of unruly red hair.

"I'm Thompson, your liaison man here. How do you do?"

Peace took the proffered hand and merely nodded in greeting. "Why am I here?" he asked abruptly, still annoyed at having to travel all the way to Pretoria.

"I'm afraid that's the Vice Admiral's doing. He insisted that you have some form of backup. They've assigned Sergeant Cherry Boxx, previously of Scotland Yard and now of MI6, to be your assistant. She'll be with us in a few minutes; she's been waiting for you. Actually, she arrived from London a few days ago."

"Cherry Boxx! A woman?" Peace raised his eyebrows. *This has to be a stage name.* "Where did she work before, Melissa's House of Pleasure?"

"Please, Commander, she's a respectable woman," Thompson admonished him, clearly shocked at Peace's retort.

Peace merely chuckled, shaking his head.

"God, do I pick 'em!" he said as if to himself, wondering what Ms Boxx looked like. He knew it was futile to argue. What VA demanded had to be carried out to the letter.

Thompson slid a copy of *The Times* across his desk towards Peace. "It's the latest edition. Make yourself comfortable. Like some tea?"

Peace shook his head. "Make it coffee, black, and I'll take you up on the offer."

He was still engrossed in the paper when the door opened and a woman entered with Thompson just behind her. She was tall and dressed in a black two-piece suit with the skirt ending just above the knees. This was complemented by a white silk blouse and black high-heeled pumps. What struck him first was her long legs — they were shapely and tantalisingly well-proportioned. She was not conventionally beautiful, but had the allure of an attractive athlete; she radiated an aura of strength and stamina. Her suit buttons strained slightly, a sure sign of ample breasts beneath them. She had short black hair, and dark eyes that seemed to have a touch of Asian in them — they slanted slightly upwards and were hooded by artfully plucked black eyebrows.

Peace rose from his chair.

"Cherry Boxx, I presume?" he said, his hand outstretched. He could not disguise the smile on his lips as he fought the desire to laugh.

She obviously did not miss this as there was no reciprocal smile on her strong mouth. Her full lips turned down and her dark eyes flashed as she turned to Thompson. "Tell the Commander that I'll take none of his flippant disingenuous crap." She had not taken Peace's proffered hand.

Peace spoke before Thompson could answer.

"Cherry, I was merely being polite. Your remarks are inappropriate. You don't mind me calling you Cherry, do you? No discourtesy was intended."

She harrumphed. "I don't believe it, Commander. Your love of innuendo and your reputation precedes you. Be warned — I know your type. I didn't volunteer to assist you; I was ordered to. That should give you some idea of my feelings." However, she did eventually take his hand.

What did she mean by that? Before he could say anything, she continued.

"I've been properly briefed — ad infinitum, in fact."

Ad infinitum, what did that imply? Had his private life formed part of her briefing?

"I'm to portray myself as your personal assistant and accompany you most of the time. The real Lord Digby always has a personal assistant at his side as you no doubt were made aware of by VA." He recalled this was mentioned. "We are to play the part of employer and employee, and at all times the relationship must be strictly business." This he also remembered, but still, VA's insistence that it be a woman infuriated him.

"You'll do," he replied tersely. What else was there to say? VA could be such an uncompromising, bull-headed prig, always doing things like this without consulting with his agents. He was probably trying to get even! However, he had no choice — VA was the boss.

She shook her head slowly as she stared at him.

"God, yes. You are the self-centred, heartless bastard they say you are." She swung round and strode out of the room.

"I don't think you're going to bed that one!" Thompson spluttered out and his eyebrows rose as the door closed forcefully behind her.

"Bloody hell, do you think I'd want to? She'd probably assume she's the boss and want to tell me how to do it," Peace retorted.

Thompson grimaced at the retort and refrained from further comment.

"Is there anything else?" Peace asked.

"Yes, there is," he said and turned to a steel cabinet behind him, which he unlocked and withdrew from it a grey file with SECRET embossed diagonally on its cover. "This arrived yesterday with the request from VA that you read it. Thereafter, you are to contact the Vice Admiral on the phone. You can use my secure phone. I'm required elsewhere, but by all means use my office — make yourself comfortable, you won't be disturbed."

Thompson left soon after and Peace settled down behind the desk. He opened the file and immediately noticed from the contents it was a copy file, the original obviously still with VA.

There were a number of sharply defined photographs, clearly taken by a high-altitude recon flight since they were more distinct than the usual satellite images. These bore a USAAF stamp. The photographs showed a small town and with them a detailed description of Copperton, a mining town in the north of the Cape Province in South Africa and a short distance from Prieska on the Orange River. It was situated on the edge of the Kalahari Desert amongst a collection of saltpans — some of which were huge, and one made famous by Donald Campbell during an attempt on the world land speed record. What was immediately evident, and even more so surprising, was the enormously long and wide runway. VA had recorded that it was asphalted and capable of handling the very largest of aircraft. This was truly an oddity and begged the question — to what end?

Before Van Rhyn acquired the mine, this had been mothballed on and off for years. Van Rhyn resurrected it and introduced earthmoving and mining equipment and the personnel to operate this equipment. The people he used were from all over South Africa, but were mostly white Afrikaners he invariably employed on a fixed long-term contract basis. All the houses, town administrative buildings, and business premises belonged to the mine — no one was allowed to own any property. Van Rhyn attracted the people by offering good salaries and accommodation, with school, sport facilities, and goods and services at particularly low bargain prices, although the report said the applicants were subjected to a thorough and stringent vetting process. Copperton was, so to say, a self-contained economic world solely controlled by Van Rhyn.

Miles of security fencing enclosed the mine, airfield, and town, and a strong, well-armed security contingent monitored all arrivals and departures. Copperton was a hot, dusty, and drab town without any tourist attractions and had no appeal for visitors. As it was situated in the most sparsely populated and near inhospitable area of the country, any persons

57

arriving unannounced would immediately draw attention and be viewed with suspicion.

While no definite proof existed, the British and Americans believed the stolen Russian neutron bomb had been acquired by a group of Afrikaner reactionaries who may have also usurped a few nuclear bombs from the S.A. Government's arsenal. Nobody appeared to know how many bombs the South Africans had manufactured and the figure varied between six and eleven. The South Africans had yet to confirm a figure.

Meanwhile, Thompson had returned unexpectedly early. Peace needed to speak to VA privately, so Thompson told him to use the scrambler phone in the adjoining office.

He was soon connected with VA.

"I've just read the Copperton file," he said.

"Hah, so I need not fill you in — you now know what I know. You will appreciate that it is of paramount importance we establish what Van Rhyn has secreted away in his hideaway. You need to go there, but please — try not to kill anyone in the process. That could only pre-empt matters."

Peace realised the Vice Admiral was not joking.

VA continued. "I don't know whether this can be done discreetly, but if they were to be suspicious, I'd rather they did not think it was us or the CIA. I've a feeling any strangers are going to stick out like a sore thumb."

"I know what you mean. Is that why you've assigned Cherry Boxx to me?" Peace asked.

VA revealed a brief moment of humour as Peace heard a chuckle over the line. "I did think the name would intrigue you. Maybe you should masquerade as a married couple — what do you think?"

Peace snorted, but did not take the bait.

"All right, we'll take a look, but I will need to have a satellite phone to stay in touch with you. You know, something secure. Can Pretoria assist?"

"I'll arrange it. Take it up with Thompson. He'll provide everything you need — it has been so ordered."

"Oh, by the way, I thought it wise that you disappear for a while. I suggest you both assume new identities. Maybe a British tourist couple? We'll have to think of a reason as to why you find yourselves in what is surely the arse-end of the world. Anyway, there's time for that — you have a few days. Meanwhile, you can begin to prepare for the trip. Remember, it's a desert and can get bloody hot. Actually, I've just realised Ms Boxx should look quite good in shorts." VA chuckled.

Peace sat there silently fuming. *Bugger him! Always playing these damn I'm-one-up-on-you games. I will not give him the satisfaction of a response.*

VA continued. "Also, Thompson has arranged accommodation in Pretoria at some decent country hotel — quite upmarket, I gather. Oh, with a casino, I hear. That should suit you."

Oh, the bastard, trying to rub his nose in it! Amongst his peers, VA was known as a discreet, compulsive tables gambler, with roulette his speciality, but also a lousy loser. Peace did not play often, but when he did, he usually struck it lucky and was known to have a windfall or two — even when on assignment. This, he had heard, infuriated the Vice Admiral.

"Good and thank you," he replied. "I should be able to add to my fortune."

VA mumbled something about not using government funds and then ended the call.

Smiling, Peace returned to Thompson's office. He felt he had made a point.

He was surprised to see Cherry had returned. "What's so funny?" she asked.

Bloody inquisitive you are. I'm not going to let you get to me. "We're to play a married couple and first spend a few days as tourists in some fancy hotel-spa-casino setup. Do some shopping, and spend some money — you know, be man and wife," he said with a slight leer.

She stared at him intently for a moment.

He was sure she was formulating what she thought was the desired response to put him in his place and then seemed to think better of it, leaving him disappointed.

Thompson interjected at that point. "I've already made the reservations and am starting the groundwork to have Peace's, that is Lord Digby's, whereabouts broadcast that he has returned to London on business for a while. That would be the Rand Club, his home, cook, housekeeper, chauffeur etc. — so I imagine all bases are properly covered."

Chapter Seven

Peace asked Thompson that he rent a Toyota Prado four-wheel-drive station wagon under Peace's new alias they would assume while on this trip. This was rented to ensure that nothing suspicious would be revealed should its origin be tracked. A slight modification was made and a compartment hidden in the dashboard where a small satellite phone was concealed. The only other equipment they acquired for him was a Heckler and Koch USP9 and for her a 9mm Sig. Both were automatics with removable silencers, the weapons specially provided by Thompson. After all, the idea was only to observe, not confront anyone. They also had a pair of 207 night binoculars and night-vision glasses.

*

Almost a week had passed.

In possession of new identities, they left Pretoria in the early hours of the morning, ostensibly on their way to Cape Town via the Richtersveld in the Northern Cape, where Cherry — now playing the part of his wife — had been born in Britstown. Her father had been the South African Police station commander there. The family had immigrated to the UK in the late fifties when her father was overlooked for promotion, something he believed was due to his English ancestry. The Boxx family could trace their South African roots back to the MacDonalds, Williams, and Smiths — all British sailors who were shipwrecked on the hostile, northwest desert coast of South Africa. There were now many families in the Northwest who could trace their origins to these castaways. Surprisingly, there was an element of truth in this, as Britstown was her actual place of birth and her great-great-grandmother had married a shipwrecked British sailor.

They drove the five hundred miles to Upington — the largest town in the western region of the country. It was located on the banks of the Orange River, which had its source in the highlands of Lesotho, a land-locked country, but close to the warm Indian Ocean. Although hundreds of miles from the highlands and situated in a vast semi-desert, Upington and the lands on the banks of the river, were extensively irrigated, and a double, mile-wide green band of fruit trees and vines shadowed every bend of the river.

From Upington, they followed the road south until they eventually arrived in Prieska. From there they took a secondary road that led southwest into the Richtersveld, an area of sun-bleached stone and gravel interspersed with low scrub and small patches of dry desert grass, a flat landscape broken by kopjes[4], and sun-blackened rocky hillocks. The road had been built to connect Copperton with the main arterial highways. The only indication that there was a town at the end of the road was a forlorn sign on a shoulder-high pole with *Copperton* scrawled on it.

"Not very exciting," said Peace, in an attempt to make conversation. She ignored him, as she had done for the past twenty-four hours. He pulled onto the gravel verge, removed a twenty-litre container from the rear of the vehicle, and proceeded to pour the contents into the tank.

"What on earth are you doing?" she asked. "We still have ample fuel."

"I'm adding some diesel to the petrol. It'll make the engine misfire and smoke. I need to create a breakdown situation."

It obviously dawned on her what he was up to and she smiled. He noticed this — it was the first time she'd smiled during the entire journey.

"Hmm, a good idea — even more surprising when coming from you," she reluctantly conceded.

The landscape around them was flat and with the sun blazing down relentlessly from a cloudless sky it was stiflingly hot, causing mirages dancing

---

4. A sharp hill usually with boulders, grass, and shrubs.

on the horizon. Although the vehicle was air-conditioned, it could barely keep the scorching heat from overwhelming them.

Moments after they'd started again, the vehicle developed a slight misfire which progressively worsened. Soon it misfired continuously, losing power and trailing a cloud of blue smoke as it moved at a decreasing speed. Finally, the town appeared on the horizon — a scattering of buildings, and most painted white with silver corrugated iron roofs. Were it not for the mine, the town would never have come into existence. There was little else that could draw people to this location.

The road through the centre was lined on each side by various retail establishments including a service station, a bank with a name indicating that it was an Afrikaner establishment, various small shops, and general dealers. A recently built school complete with dirt rugby field adjoined the main street. That the town had only recently come into being again was obvious — there were no tall trees. Peace noticed a small workshop that adjoined the service station, and from the number of pickup trucks in the yard, it appeared to have a large clientele.

He swung the Prado onto the workshop's concrete apron and stopped. Both of them then stepped out into the mid-afternoon heat. Normally, he would have expected to see Blacks and Coloureds, but was not surprised to see only the odd person as he recalled it being mentioned that the idea was to create a haven for Whites. He mentioned this to Cherry.

She just shrugged her shoulders and shook her head. "Who could believe such a thing in this country," she said.

They were both dressed in shorts, the colour chosen to blend in with the terrain. She wore ankle-high hiking boots with short socks, the top of which could just be seen peeking out of the boots. This had the effect of adding to the length of her tanned legs. She wore a simple beige T-shirt with a round-cut neck, low enough to reveal a hint of her breasts, and a khaki baseball cap from which her short-trimmed hair peeked. The overall effect, Peace thought, was admirable.

He too was dressed in khaki shorts and shirt, with a slouch hat. His shoes were proper hiking boots, reaching to mid-calf. His tanned, well-muscled legs revealed a few white scars under the down of near-blond hair.

He stepped into the shade of the petrol-pump forecourt overhang, his eyes needing a few seconds to adjust from the strong sunlight. A middle-aged man approached, wiping his hands on his sleeveless dirty green overall. Although he pretended to give Cherry an innocuous glance, Peace saw him take in her somewhat sexy attire. He pursed his lips so as not to smile.

"*Wat kan ek vir jou doen, Meneer?*[5]" he asked.

"Good afternoon. There's something wrong with my car. It keeps misfiring and cutting out for no reason at all," said Peace.

For a few seconds, the man just stared at the car, his hands on his hips. In guttural broken English but with a hint of amusement, he then asked, "What the hell are you doing here in Copperton?" Again, he gave Cherry a quick glance.

Peace just chuckled. "Doing here? Good God, man, I'd prefer not to be in this Godforsaken place. I'm on my way to the Richtersveld."

"Hey, you don't need to blaspheme! You're on the wrong road for the Richtersveld," he said, a look of distaste now on his face.

Peace remembered that Afrikaners were often extremely religious. "Sorry about that. I know this isn't the right road. I turned onto it for help."

"Okay, I'll look at it, but you'll have to leave it here. There's a hotel," he pointed vaguely down the road that split the town, "and they'll have a room for you if you need one. You won't get the car back today."

He thanked the man who then walked back into his workshop. There was no chance that those working on the vehicle would find the satellite phone, it had been ingeniously hidden. Anyway, why would they look for something? The two of them were obviously tourists, and their reason for being in the town was harmless enough.

"How on Earth does a dump like Copperton have a hotel?" Peace asked.

She laughed. "This is South Africa. If you want a bottle store in a town, you've got to establish a hotel. That's the only way you'll get a liquor license. Good God, man, can you imagine this lot without a liquor store? It's probably the best private business in town if it doesn't belong to the mine — who knows, might even belong to Van Rhyn."

---

5. What can I do for you, sir?

"Makes sense," he replied and started removing their valises from the car. They trudged the short distance to the hotel where a large sign over the entrance read *Copperton Hotel*. They were relieved to find that the interior was air-conditioned. Whether they liked it or not, it would have to be a double room, as they had to go through the pretence of being a couple. He signed the register as Mr and Mrs Sedgewick but they were not asked to produce any form of identification. However, they were asked what had brought them to Copperton and Peace offered up the sad story of their vehicle.

Their room was on the first floor.

"God, I suppose I can't have my own room?" Cherry hissed once they had closed the door behind them.

He ignored her remark and strode to the window and stared out. The room being on a corner of the building gave him an excellent view of the town and mine. From the activity at the mine it was evident it was in full production, what with the trucks, smoke and dust. There were shallow mine dumps where waste ore was discarded, and vast sheds where the copper ore was partially processed. The mine property was an intricate collection of buildings and sheds between which moved the occasional large dumper truck or pickup.

He wedged a chair in the darker shadows of a corner and sat down; no one from outside would be able to see him. He slowly swept the binoculars over the mine and the adjoining airfield. The airfield was situated within the double perimeter fence of the mine and was an integral part of the mine — it also clearly shared the same security. The outer fence was about nine feet high with masses of rolled razor wire at its base, and at the top were further rolls supported in a huge wire Y-troughs. Between that and the inner fence of steel mesh, was a cleared area about thirty feet wide.

The long runway shimmered in the sun and Peace could see a South African Air Force Transall, a large French-built turbo-prop twin-engine cargo plane, parked on the apron. Its rear ramp was lowered and two forklifts were loading steel crates. He estimated their dimensions each to be about a foot by a foot-and-a-half. Whatever was being loaded was exceptionally heavy, for the rear wheels of the forklifts lifted slightly when burdened. It then struck Peace that they were similar in size to the bullion boxes in the photographs that Sir John had produced in London. The men who encircled the plane were clearly armed; there was no mistaking their automatic weapons. A fuel-truck was drawn up next to the aircraft, with thick hoses connecting it to the plane. The aircraft was obviously being refuelled and he wondered if it was about to depart on a long flight.

Still staring through the glasses, he said, "I wonder what they're loading? If I didn't know better, I'd say those could be the bullion we're also looking for. What's an Air Force plane doing here anyway? This is mine property, or rather, private property."

Cherry seemed to have forgotten her resolve to ignore him. "Let me take a look," she said.

He handed her the binoculars. She peered through them for a few minutes.

"I don't know whether this is mere pure luck or coincidental, but I think you're right — that's the missing gold. However, you did say VA had said there was a remote possibility our friend Van Rhyn could be involved," she said.

"Christ… this is really astounding. I'd be willing to bet anything that's the gold. Of course, now it all makes sense. Where better to hide it?" He breathed an expletive. "Well, if it is, then we're too damn late," he sighed.

"I must say," she said, "if I wanted to hide a shipment of gold and have the security to go with it, then this has to be as good a place as any. It's got all the facilities to get it here and out again by air."

Hallelujah, he thought, *she finally mellowed or certainly seems to have forgotten to be an antagonistic wretch.* He smiled at her but she did not respond.

Just then he saw a Land Rover, open to the elements, making its way along the outer fence, three armed men seated in it and with two dogs in the rear, their forelegs on the side sills, staring intently at the passing scenery. She swung the glasses round to look at it.

"They're not taking any chances, are they?" she said. "My God! Those aren't dogs, they're hyenas."

"You can't tame hyenas, well, not the South African ones," he replied, thinking she didn't know the difference between a large dog and a hyena.

"I know it's unbelievable, but they definitely are. Here…" she said and returned the binoculars.

The open rear-deck Land Rover could not have been more than three hundred yards away. He peered through the glasses again — they were hyenas! There was no mistaking the colouring — a mottled brown that appeared mangy with faint large spots visible on the coat. Their heads were large with massive snouts, and the strange unmistakable slope of their backs towards their hind legs was obvious even at this distance.

"Getting in and out of there isn't going to be easy," he said.

"I know, but they told me I'd be working with the best," she muttered.

Was that a hint of warmth? After some deliberation, they reluctantly agreed that the only way was to go through the fence in the dark. Not that night, since their arrival might be too much of a coincidence, but the night after. Tonight, they would keep the area under observation. If they intended to avoid the guards and hyenas, they would need to devise a plan to divert their attention while they made their entry.

"For a mine, the security here is intense. This has to be a sort of hideaway," she said. "It's too remote for intruders; something sinister has to be going on here. This will be dangerous."

Peace took a closer look at the town and carefully studied the few houses he could see from the window. He would have preferred to see more but the small window restricted his vision. He soon noticed not all the houses were occupied — some were clearly empty and neglected, the gardens overgrown with long dry grass. He assumed that most of the inhabitants that lived in the town had connections with the mine. The town was so small that it probably only provided work for the members of the families not directly involved in the mine itself. Peace thought back to the dossier on the town and recalled how it was stated that the occupants were carefully vetted. Van Rhyn was obviously vigilant of who was employed and it was evident that the workers shared in his separatist policies. He could just imagine how the right-wing Afrikaners in the town maintained their *verkrampte* and isolated lifestyles. He would place a bet that the Whites in this town even did the menial jobs themselves, which was unheard of elsewhere in the country, so that they didn't have to interact with others.

He hoped that even though they would immediately be recognised as outsiders, that it didn't place too much of a burden on the mission.

*

That evening they maintained their charade and after a very short stroll round the hotel to get the lie of the land, they decided it was time for dinner. Although they appeared to be the only guests at the hotel, a fair number of tables were occupied, the hotel obviously serving as the town's eating-house. Those they encountered in passing or in the dining room initially gave them enquiring looks, be it that they spoke English or appeared different, obviously recognising them as strangers, but this soon passed.

They projected the image of a typical, young holiday couple — comfortable with each other, given to small-talk interspersed with the occasional smile and him touching her hand on occasion while in conversation. Every now and then she would gaze at him for a short while; a look of contentment crossing her face.

Of course, they had chosen to sit where they could not be overheard, which made it easier for Peace to bring up his misgivings about her impression of him.

Cherry's occasional ambiguous but baseless remarks implying her low opinion of him had irritated him for a while now.

"Cherry, I'd like us to discuss something I find deeply disturbing," he said, aware that she could not react in a manner that would draw attention.

"Really? Now what could that be?" she said in reply, her tone laced with a trace of sarcasm completely opposite to the adoring look she was currently lavishing on him.

"See — that's what I mean. Your demeaning attitude towards me. I don't deserve it or those comments you made when we initially met in Pretoria. I have never in my life used any woman for personal gratification. Christ, I know that must sound corny. Certainly, there have been a few women in my life, but my God, these were relationships of the heart and always with the degree of respect a woman deserves."

She stared at him from across the table with her eyebrows slightly raised. No doubt this sudden personal disclosure had come as surprise.

"Geoffrey, what can I say? I didn't expect this. Not from you. I was led to believe you've no heart." For the first time the detest was missing from her tone.

He raised his hands off the table as if he wished to ward off something. "Enough. Sorry, I did not want to open up like this. I just thought it would make working with me under these circumstances easier for you. It's important that we communicate openly — no holds barred, if you know what I mean." He was clearly embarrassed at having opened up like that.

Her features softened and she slid a hand forward to touch his. "I'm glad you opened up to me and I believe you. Corridor gossip is always exaggerated. However, you should not worry about me — being a female undercover agent has its truly bad moments." She winced for a moment and closed her eyes. "I didn't mean it that way. Don't take offence. Believe me, of all the people I could have been partnered with on this assignment, I'd have chosen you. Truthfully, I actually feel safe with you."

Peace gauged her reaction. *She sounds sincere.* "Thank you for being open and honest too. Before it gets too far, let's just leave it there. I take it we now have a new working relationship?"

"We do."

The atmosphere during the rest of the dinner was now more amicable. They enjoyed the meal with a bottle of wine and while the conversation stayed light, it touched on more personal topics, giving some insight as to who they really were.

The food was typical rural hotel fare with soup, grilled Cape salmon, which was excellent, and roast Karoo lamb with rice and potatoes. Finally, they had a local pudding with custard as dessert.

After dinner they decided to explore further and found a short passage that led off to a bar which was also directly accessible from the street through a separate entrance. This now did a brisk trade, and in typical South African style, the drinks on offer were predominantly bottled beer, brandy and rum. Most of the clientele were rugged and burly, and clearly miners.

Although loud, the atmosphere was cheerful and similar to that after-work vibe with the odd bar game of darts and snooker being played — much the same as would be seen in any establishment around the country. A private lounge with vinyl-covered easy chairs and low coffee tables adjoined the bar, where those with wives and even the occasional child could sit, away from the more raucous crowd in the bar.

They decided not to stop for a drink, but instead, retired to the private lounge in the hotel, which boasted the only TV set in the building. The atmosphere here was more formal than in the bar and most of the channels available were politically charged. They settled down to watch the news where it was evident that de Klerk was trying to persuade his fellow citizens that change was long overdue and it was time to accept majority rule. However, the banners at the bottom of the screen also indicated that this scenario was by no means accepted by many Whites; there were rumours of civil war and some families were already hoarding foodstuffs and other essential items.

A little later Peace and Cherry decided to investigate the town further in the guise of a nightly stroll. Out on the streets, several people were enjoying the cool breeze that blew in from the east. The two wandered along the main road and as it left the town, it led to the main gate of the mine, which was bathed in harsh light from a battery of lamps attached to an overhead gantry that spanned the road. Steel booms, from which chains hung, barred the access for people and vehicles. Pedestrians made their entrance or exit through a turnstile system, and it looked as though security personnel checked everyone going through for identification. The security guards all openly wore side arms and a few were even accompanied by Alsatian dogs on leashes. He realised that there was no way they were going to bluff their way into the mine.

When they couldn't look around anymore and not draw attention to themselves, they went back to the hotel and spent the best part of the night in the darkened room using the binoculars to observe any activity that might occur. After ten, the town was dead — not even patrolled. Only once did they see the blue lights of a police van somewhere near the main road. However, the airport and mine were another matter — the airfield perimeter was patrolled by Land Rovers continuously on the move. Dark shapes, probably dogs, moved in the area among the fences, the area between floodlit by powerful lights atop high standards.

Initially, he sat there alone studying the town and mine from the darkness of the open window. After a while she brought a chair, placed it next to his, and would from time to time ask for the binoculars.

"Well, maestro," she asked, "what do you think? Is it impenetrable?"

She again slowly traversed the night before them with the binoculars and he became aware of her shoulder touching his and the hint of her perfume in the air. For a brief second, he was reminded that she was a woman, the reminder bringing with it a strong sexual connotation.

She had definitely mellowed! Gone was the irritation and sarcasm. "With the right preparation, planning and tools, nothing is impenetrable. We go through the fence where it is darkest. There's a considerable gap in the security patrols — enough time to get through and camouflage where we've made the cut," he said.

As they watched they timed the patrols, and carefully observed those areas where the lights appeared less effective, as some areas were left in near shadow. It would be there that they would attempt to breach the fence.

*

Midnight had passed before they finally decided to call it a night. Fortunately, the room contained separate beds, although these were pushed together. They parted them, leaving a chaste gap in between. Peace had no qualms about his skants being on display before he jumped into the bed. Her reaction was a mixture of surprise and slight annoyance, and he noticed that she was about to comment but then chose not to, abruptly gathered her things and utilised the bathroom to change.

At one point in the early hours, Peace was woken by the sound of loud aircraft engines; he recognised them to be multiple turbo-props. He stumbled out of bed, followed by Cherry who had also been woken, and looked out of the window through his binoculars. The Air Force Transall was slowly trundling towards the main runway which was now lit. The engines' roar rose to a crescendo and slowly the aircraft gained speed, having to cover a long portion of the runway before it slowly rose into the air.

"I'm pretty sure there goes our gold," Cherry said wryly.

She was probably right, Peace thought. He was sure Van Rhyn was getting rid of it. He wondered what he'd be getting in exchange — arms, bombs, and favours from other despotic regimes? Whatever it was, wouldn't be good.

*

The next day Peace called at the garage. The owner told him that whoever had refuelled the vehicle had put diesel in the tank by mistake. He held up a small bottle, which contained a small quantity of liquid. It was supposed to indicate a mixture of diesel and petrol but didn't look any different to Peace. He made a comment anyway.

"I believe you," he said with an expression of surprise and disappointment. "Damn idiots!" He hoped the anger looked legitimate.

"I'll have to remove the tank to drain all the fuel," the owner said. "To just siphon it off would leave a residue of contaminated petrol."

"Will it be ready today?"

"No, but by tomorrow morning. The workshop opens at seven o'clock."

Peace accepted this with pretended reluctance when, in fact, it suited him down to the ground.

Chapter Eight

During the course of the following day, other than the necessary visit to the garage, they mostly confined themselves to their room, only venturing out for their meals. They agreed the less noticeable they were, the less likelihood of any suspicions being raised.

Just after eleven that evening found them lying on their stomachs on the hard ground, which was still slightly warm from the sun of the day. A soft cool breeze blew over them. A half-moon hung in the clear sky; the Milky Way strung across it from horizon to horizon. However, in the distance towards the east, Peace discerned faint flashes of lightning — the first signs of a thunderstorm. But here in the desert, these storms often only threatened rain. There was plenty of wind, thunder, and lightning, but the rain clouds were inevitably blown away by the wind. Proper rain in this area was an event. He had learnt this piece of information from Cherry.

A security-manned Land Rover had just passed and the dust that trailed it wafted over them. The main fence was no more than thirty feet from them. Cherry had told him to keep a sharp lookout for puff adders, which emerged at night from under the rocks and bushes to hunt rats and mice. This made him particularly wary. Peace held a medium-sized bolt cutter and Cherry carried two long steel hooks with wooden handles at their ends. They'd need these to pull aside the coils of razor wire once the wire had been cut. Once through, they'd need to pull the coils together again to conceal where they'd entered. Fortunately, the ground was rough and it would be difficult to see any trace of their tracks.

"Okay, let's go!" he whispered. It took a number of attempts to sever the wire and the snap of the blades as they bit through the strands was loud in the quiet night. They hooked the coils and pulled them apart. Once they'd clambered through, they closed the gap as best they could, the repair good enough to pass normal inspection at night.

They had just managed to do this when they heard a whooping sound. It was nearby.

"God, what's that?" said Cherry, grabbing his arm.

"It's those hyenas. I hope to God they haven't let the damn things loose in the corridors. They didn't last night."

The hyenas continued to whoop as they crossed the cleared area to the inner fence. It consisted of closely knit steel mesh, which required only a few minutes to cut into, leaving a three feet square gap. They peeled the wire mesh back, climbed through, and then closed the cut with a few small pieces of soft wire. Peace made a mental note of the exact location of the breach in the fence.

They now found themselves on the airfield itself. Crouched down so as not to be silhouetted against the light and keeping a sharp lookout, they made their way through the scrub towards the airfield's buildings. Most lights around the airfield other than the perimeter lights had been doused; obviously, no air traffic was expected that night. Keeping to the shadows, they neared a large hangar.

"Down!" he hissed suddenly and pulled her to the ground next to him. The sound of gravel on concrete echoed through the night, which was steadily increasing in volume as whoever was making it drew near. Peace lifted his head slightly and saw a guard. Fortunately, he had no dog with him. He did, however, carry an assault rifle, an R5, a formidable close-quarter weapon.

The guard passed no more than twenty feet from their position. Had the man been more alert, he would have seen them. As he passed, Peace rose and silently moved towards him, approaching diagonally from the side. At the last moment, some sixth sense must have warned the man, for he spun round bringing up his rifle. He was too slow. Peace dodged past the rifle, came up close to the man's chest, and thrust his long SAS knife up under the man's ribs and into his heart. He slammed his other hand over the man's mouth, reducing the man's death scream to a muffled cry. The guard began to collapse and Peace had to let go of the knife to grab him as he crumpled into his arms. With the knife's hilt still rammed in his chest, the man jerked feebly in his final death throes, his heels drumming a brief tattoo on the hard soil. The body eventually went limp. Peace slowly lowered it to the ground, his clothes splattered with the victim's blood. He wiped the blood from his hands on some dry grass.

"VA won't like this," he remarked, recalling VA's request that none should die and then turned to face Cherry.

She just stared at him; her face expressionless. At first he thought she was probably shocked by the surgical manner in which he had killed the man.

"Cherry, there wasn't anything else I could do," he murmured placatingly.

"I know, but it's always a bit of a shock when you watch the first one go down — it's never pleasant. After that, I'm fine until the next mission. And you? No regrets?"

"No," he replied.

She did not respond.

Part of the hangar cast a long shadow over the concrete, providing excellent cover. They dashed across it and flung themselves against the hangar's corrugated metal side, trying to merge with the darkness of the wall. They could still hear the intermittent whooping of the hyenas; other guards could not be far away. What was going on? Staying in the shadows, they slid with their backs pressed against the metal wall while looking for an entrance. Cherry was leading the way when suddenly she stopped and turned, and he bumped into her.

"Quiet!" she whispered in his ear.

He stood still with Cherry close up against him. Over her shoulder, he saw a man who had just rounded the far corner of the hangar, with a dog pulling on a leash and whimpering in its efforts to drag its handler forward. The man shouted at the animal, trying to control it. Peace slowly drew the Heckler and Koch strapped to his leg. He lifted the automatic high to get the silencer to clear the canvas holster. He flicked off the safety catch; the man had still not seen them. The automatic barked twice, the first bullet hitting the man in the mouth, and he immediately collapsed to the ground.

The dog reared up on hind legs in its effort to get at them, but the leash wrapped around the guard's wrist restrained it. It took Peace's second bullet to the chest, yelped loudly, and then it too collapsed to the ground. He removed his arm with the automatic from over her shoulder and let it hang next to his side. She spun round, hard up against him. He stepped back.

"Well, if we are trying not to announce ourselves, we haven't done very well, have we? You realise that was a hyena? Probably one of Van Rhyn's trained-to-kill hyenas. That's enough reason to allow us to shoot anything," he said.

She didn't reply but now started moving along the wall looking for an entrance.

"Here," she called softly.

He crossed to her and saw the door in the wall. She tried the handle, and the door opened. The interior was dark apart from a faint light visible on the far side of the hangar. The hangar contained two aircraft, one of which was a Beechcraft King Air 90 — a twin-engine turbo-prop executive aircraft with Van Rhyn's Afrikaner Goudeiendomme's logo on its tail. At first, Peace didn't recognise the other aircraft, as it was hard to identify in the dark and was painted black. Then he recognised it — a Dornier twin-engine STOL high-wing aircraft, ideal for short field take-offs and landings. The cockpit doors were open, so he peered inside and saw keys to the Dornier hanging from the magneto switches.

He pulled her close, his lips brushing her ear.

"God, we're lucky, the bloody keys are in it," he whispered. "Maybe we can use it if we need to make a break for it."

Although in hindsight he wasn't entirely convinced as it would take a while to pull the aircraft out of the hangar.

She squeezed his arm and pointed in the direction of the interior darkness of the cavernous hangar. He could vaguely make out the shape of two other aircraft.

"Jesus!" he whispered. "That's a bloody Canberra bomber, and the other's a Blackburn Buccaneer. Those aircraft can be used to deliver nuclear weapons! I thought they'd given all their Canberras to the Rhodesians."

As he stared at them, he was just able to make out the outline of the

Dutch Cape Castle emblem with the spread-winged eagle in the centre, the South African Air Force recognition marking. These had once been, or were, South African military aircraft. Clearly, Van Rhyn had friends in the right places. All this would have required massive amounts of capital, not to mention attracting and arming a ragtag group of predominantly Afrikaners and maybe moulding them into a professional fighting force if civil war was ever envisaged. From every newspaper report, including those from the Afrikaner press, it was clear that most intelligentsia in the nation saw the benefits of a new South Africa. He knew that the more enlightened in the country would be appalled if they could see what he was looking at. He also knew that most Afrikaners desperately wanted peace. They realised that the world was smaller; its vast distances reduced by technology, and that it was no longer possible to live in self-imposed isolation and exile.

Suddenly, they heard loud shouts, the banging of steel doors, and the revving of vehicle engines. The whooping of the hyenas had increased.

"I think they've stumbled on the bodies," Cherry said.

He indicated she should follow him and led her towards the light on the other side of the hangar nearest to the mine. They needed to get closer to the mine and investigate it. Why had a mine, previously thought to be uneconomical, suddenly been resurrected? The town had been deserted until about two years ago when Van Rhyn began to employ people to restart the mine, or so it was believed. This had to be Van Rhyn's main operational base. It was perfectly situated geographically and in the middle of staunch Afrikaner territory.

Their boots were crepe-soled and made no noise as they crossed the hangar floor towards the light. The bark of the dogs had subsided, and the vehicles had evidently been driven off. When they reached the other side, they saw it was lined with prefabricated offices, some in darkness, others with lights. All appeared to be vacant. The long line of offices along the opposite wall was broken by a gap revealing a lit passage, and a pedestrian tunnel which disappeared into the darkness. He hoped it would lead outside the hangar and to the mine. As he steered Cherry towards the passageway, he had no idea whether it was deserted but they'd have to just chance it. The problem was that anybody approaching from the other end would immediately see them.

"This feels dangerous," Cherry said.

He agreed. He could not shake off a premonition of impending disaster. Of course, the guards would be looking for the intruders who had killed their companions and they now surely knew their security had been compromised.

They walked along the tunnel but kept to one side, still uncertain what was at the end of it. They soon found their approach barred by a wall of steel bars but with a one-man-sized door within the barrier. This grille door was locked. Against the tunnel wall was a numbered keypad, which had to be accessed to activate the lock. Beyond the grille was the exit. A few small prefabricated buildings were visible in the weak moonlight. But how were they to get out? The steel barrier prevented any further progress and without the code to the keypad they would be stuck.

"*Wat die fok gaan hier aan?*[6]" was suddenly shouted at them.

Peace's head jerked around at the sound and he stared at the man behind them who had materialised seemingly out of nowhere. He appeared to be unarmed. Out of the corner of his eye, he saw Cherry had raised her silenced automatic and had it pointed at the man's chest. Suddenly the man realised it was a gun she had pointed at him. His eyes widened in shock and his jaw dropped.

"*Maak die deur oop!*[7]" Cherry barked. For a few seconds the man seemed paralysed, not moving.

"*Doen dit nou of ek skiet!*[8]" she yelled at him.

Clearly convinced that she meant every word, he slowly walked past them with arms raised and then pressed his finger to the keypad buttons and entered the code. There was a loud click and the door snapped open.

"Thank God you speak Afrikaans," Peace mumbled quietly.

"VA did say he thought it would come in handy." She smiled briefly.

Peace pushed the grille open and they stepped through. Although the man had already raised his hands in surrender again, Peace swung his

---

6. What the fuck is going on here?

7. Open the door!

8. Do it now or I'll shoot!

automatic and brought it down on the man's head with a sickening thud. The man fell to the ground.

"I think you've killed him," said Cherry with a sharp intake of breath.

"Does it matter? Come on."

He knew the man was just badly concussed and certainly wouldn't be speaking to anybody for a while.

They stepped outside into the cool night air.

"That was obviously a quick access tunnel from the mine to the airport. It could be that those arriving by air don't have to use the main gate," Peace remarked.

She shrugged her shoulders. "Who knows — it seems there are a number of hidden agendas here."

Before them, a wide concrete road sloped down and disappeared into a massive excavation similar in size to those found in a large opencast mining operation. Sheer cliffs demarcated the opposite side of the depression, about two-hundred feet deep and impossible to climb. At the bottom of the excavation's cliff-face, two tunnels that bored into the granite could be seen, one larger than the other.

A sunken area directly in front of the tunnels was well lit by floodlights affixed to the granite face of the massive excavation and Peace could see people in hardhats, gumboots, and reflector vests milling about. A stairway adjacent to the road led, in levels, to the tunnels' entrances.

A huge dumper truck laden with large chunks of broken ore suddenly exited the larger tunnel with a roar. The crescendo of noise from its exhaust hammered their eardrums as it approached the ramp's incline. Two massive headlamps bored through the mist of grey dust being created by the people milling around, lighting the way for the behemoth. Green and red lights were also were affixed to the vehicle, making it look like a Christmas tree.

Peace bent towards Cherry's ear and shouted, "This is a helluva operation they've got here. He's definitely resurrected the mining operation. I thought it was just a cover, but it seems to be the real thing."

"I think you're right," she shouted back, and then added as an afterthought, "that's where we've got to enter and take a look." She pointed at the smaller tunnel.

He agreed but didn't like it; they had to assume there was only one entrance. The surveillance photographs didn't show another — and there'd be no escape if things went wrong.

"If we are going to blend in, we've got to find hats, boots, and those reflector vests they are all wearing," he whispered urgently.

There were more of the prefabricated huts to one side and some were lit from within. They quickly walked over and peered into a few, until in one, they discovered what they wanted. It contained various pieces of equipment hanging from racks and coat hooks. They even saw a row of helmet-lamps on a bench, all connected to chargers. This was evidently a change room for the more senior staff. Peace entered and removed two hats, and two pairs of gumboots, which he thought would fit them. He also found some fluorescent coats and overall tops. They donned these and stepped outside, the lamps from their helmets bobbing as they walked nonchalantly towards the mine. The hat that Peace wore was of a different colour to the rest and had something written across the front of it — *HOOF OPSIGTER*.

"That means *Chief Supervisor* in Afrikaans," Cherry had said as she saw him place it on his head.

Peace hoped the title indicated the wearer to be high up in the hierarchy and produce the respect they'd need to bluff their way past the guards or any other personnel. He felt conspicuous but hoped that they at least looked as if they belonged.

They were no more than a hundred yards from the prefabricated building when he looked across to a large open expanse where there was a wire-mesh enclosure, about two-hundred feet square, its fence over six feet high. He saw movement within and on hearing the strange whooping sound realised the animals were spotted hyena. He knew their immensely powerful jaws could crush the largest of bones and even devour them as their gastric juices were strong enough to digest the lot. A bite from a hyena was capable of severing a man's arm or leg, and in a pack when pursuing prey, they were formidable. Even lions respected them.

A pickup approached and Peace grabbed Cherry and dragged her into the shadow cast by a prefab. The pickup then skidded to a halt in front of the enclosure gate. Two armed guards were standing on the back, clasping the cattle rail erected around the vehicle's loading box. Assault rifles hung from their shoulders and both were looking down at something in the vehicle. A heated exchange between the guards and three other security personnel who had materialised when the vehicle had approached followed.

"What the hell's going on?" Peace asked, his voice barely audible.

Cherry was listening intently to what was being said and spoke only after she'd heard enough.

"It seems they've caught some Blacks on the property. The guards maintain they were snooping around, maybe thieves trying to steal something of value."

Two of the guards pushed a body from the back of the pickup. The man was a Black who was naked except for a pair of dirty white shorts. He must have already been beaten and probably tortured as he tried to shy away from his captors, his eyes wide with terror. He cried and wailed, and although Peace could not understand his yammering, it was obvious he was overcome by abject fear and pleading for his life.

Two of the men grabbed him under each arm and dragged him towards the enclosure. The man's cries seemed to agitate the hyenas and they moved closer to the wire in their strange looping gait while others slunk up and down the length of the fence. Every so often, they dipped their heads and then looked skywards, emitting a bloodcurdling whoop.

"God Almighty!" Cherry whispered. "I think they're going to put the man in the cage with the hyenas. Those men are animals!"

It appeared she was right. The steel mesh-covered gate to the enclosure was opened and the approaching hyenas were beaten back with long sticks. The guards still had a firm grasp on his arms and half-carried him to the gate, his feet dragging in the dust, and shoved him into the enclosure, quickly closing the gate behind him. He shrieked a horrible sound which seemed to rise from the depths of his soul as the hyenas tore into him, raising a cloud of dust as they danced around him, tearing at him, whooping, and squealing. The man's screams abruptly ceased and the only sounds they could hear were the whoops and snarls as the animals fought to get at the still twitching body. Peace heard Cherry suck in her breath. She lowered her head and covered her face with her hands. The snarls gradually abated, to be replaced by the sound of crunching bones and the occasional snap as the animals warned each other off. The guards and security men looked on nonchalantly, joking amongst themselves.

Cherry buried her face in his chest.

"Come, let's move while they're all still distracted," he said.

An intense hatred rose in him. He vowed he would see Van Rhyn dead, no matter what it took. Bile rose in his throat. He thought he'd seen the worst of the worst, but this capped it all. Men who did this to their fellow humans were no more than vermin and were to be treated as such. Killing them would be a pleasure. He wondered who was responsible for issuing the order that resulted in this despicable deed. There would be a reckoning.

Chapter Nine

They moved deeper into the cluster of prefabs, keeping to the shadows and away from the tunnel openings. They had to get inside the smaller tunnel, which did not appear to be used by the excavating trucks, although its entrance was guarded by two armed security guards. Nonetheless, it would be wise to be patient and observe before undertaking any action.

Peace climbed onto the roof of a prefab and hid behind a large corrugated zinc water tank, from where he watched the comings and goings from the tunnels through binoculars. The heightened vigilance of the guards was evident. Two vehicles appeared every so often — they were obviously patrolling the grounds as the occupants were armed with assault rifles.

The wind had strengthened, tugging at his clothes and bringing with it a threatening rainstorm. An exceptionally strong gust suddenly buffeted him and a large cloud of dust obscured his vision. He was no longer able to see the mine's cliff face. Here was an opportunity, he thought, so he clambered off the roof and came to stand next to Cherry.

"Come on, this is it. We'll get in under cover of the storm and dust."

She nodded. They moved off, trying their best to remain in the shadows. Soon they were at the ramp, the stairway in front of them. Most of the workers had disappeared, obviously having sought shelter, but there were still the odd individuals, probably guards, bent over protecting themselves from the flying dust and sand. The wind had now intensified.

They descended the staircase and a few others joined them as they all tried to find shelter. No one gave them a second glance. Cherry was tall, and in her smock and gumboots with the helmet covering her short hair she could easily pass for a man.

Down in the deep hollow near the cliff face the wind was not as strong and they moved towards the smaller tunnel. As they neared, Peace could see inside and was astounded at its size, which was well lit with row upon row of fluorescent lights strung along the roof. As with the hangar, access was barred by a wall of steel bars, but in this instance, a guard was stationed there too. At intervals along the wall, pockets cut into the rock face contained electrical control boxes or similar equipment.

In a deep recess in the tunnel wall before the barred entrance, they found a large toolbox and pieces of electrical equipment, including heavy duty circuit breakers and lengths of insulated cable. Obviously, electricians were still busy with work in the tunnel, no doubt doing this during the day.

"I've got an idea," said Peace. "I'm a supervisor, right? You're my assistant. We're here to work on the electrics. Let's carry some of this equipment — hang on, we better pick up some tools as well. We then simply walk through the access gate. Notice how the guard at the entrance waves the occasional man through. If we're dressed as they are, I reckon they'll let us past."

"I don't know," she said. "If we're captured, that will mean death."

"Not if we do it while this damn wind is blowing dust and sand all over the place. Nobody's going to be looking carefully at anything… I mean, you can barely open your eyes! If we are to do it, it'll have to be now." He ignored her obvious fear and picking electrical items at random, put them in her hands, and then took some himself. "Follow me," he said, and strode purposefully towards the guard who manned the gate.

The guard saw them approaching and straightened a bit, probably because of the words *HOOF OPSIGTER*[9] emblazoned on Peace's helmet. As they neared, a guard asked, "*Wat is dit nou?*[10] "

For a moment Peace was dumbstruck, and completely at loss as to what to say. He used the first, best explanatory word that came to mind. "Problem," he replied, showing the man the circuit breaker. As luck would

9. Chief Supervisor

10. What's wrong now?

have it in this instance, and with Peace at that moment ignorant of the fact, that in South Africa, spoken Afrikaans is peppered with many English words, as is English with Afrikaans. The Afrikaans for *problem* is *probleem* which was fortuitous.

The man looked at him without expression and then opened the gate and let them pass. Peace breathed a silent sigh of relief. Cherry faked a coughing spasm brought on by the dust and bent forward, partially hiding her face.

They moved away from the entrance as fast as they could. Various sub tunnels branched off the main tunnel about a hundred yards in, their entrances barred by stainless steel doors. Everything appeared spotlessly clean with no sign of dust. Peace realised that the air-conditioning and filtrations maintained a higher pressure inside than out and would contribute to this. He headed for the first electrical distribution board he saw, opened it, and busied himself pretending to inspect its innards, while Cherry stood attentively next to him. He hoped they looked the part. While they were standing there, a group of men came out from one of the tunnels jabbering amongst themselves in Afrikaans, evidently excited about something.

"Did you catch any of that?" Peace asked.

"They said something about an aircraft disappearing off the Namibian coast. That's all I heard."

That particular piece of information was of no interest to him, so he continued to pretend to be attending to something on the distribution board. He knew they had to be out of the complex before daylight and there were only a few hours left.

At the end of the tunnel was an entrance to another tunnel which had the usual steel barricade into which a smaller gate for pedestrian access was also fitted.

"Grab a couple of items. We've got to get a look in there."

Holding the circuit breaker, testing instrument and a few tools, they casually made their way to the gates and passed through without interference. Once inside they stopped, staggered at the sight before them.

The tunnel opened into a vast cavern, at least eighty yards in width, and the roof at least two storeys high. They were standing on what resembled a mezzanine floor. Two stairways led down to the main floor and between the flights was a large caged industrial elevator. Above them, a huge crane hung from a massive gantry attached to the granite ceiling and walls which ran the length of the cavern. On one side there was a curved panel, many feet in length, which contained switches, dials and numerous video terminals. Attached to the walls were international warning signs depicting radiation.

They quickly made for another electrical distribution board, located close to the main doors which they opened. They then remained there for a short while to check their surroundings. The ruse worked as it had before. Once inside, they were again surprised at what they saw. The only items on the hall floor were cylindrical missile-shaped objects resting on pneumatic wheeled metal cradles. Four had black stencilled letters on them. The fifth was different; it had Cyrillic writing on it, and a red Russian star.

A cold shudder passed through Peace as he realised what these were. He felt Cherry's fingers digging into his arm.

"My God! Those are the missing bombs!" she hissed.

Their job here was done; they'd seen enough, it was time to get out. Peace closed the distribution board. As he turned around, he saw a man approaching, dressed as they were but wearing a red hardhat with the word *HOOF BESTUURDER* emblazoned on it.

"Wat is die probleem hierso?[11] *"* the man asked.

Peace didn't understand but assumed he'd been asked what was going on.

Cherry stepped in and spoke rapidly in Afrikaans. The man's eyes widened when he realised she was a woman. He barked something at her and grabbed her by the arm. Peace made an instant decision. He knew he couldn't leave an unconscious man to be found. He rammed his pistol in the man's side.

"Be quiet and don't make a move!" he said, assuming the man could speak English. The expression on the man's face turned to one of shock.

"Who are you?" he asked.

"Just fuckin' shut up! Do exactly as I say. Walk ahead of us as though we were a group just going about our work. Make one false move or utter a wrong word, and you're a fuckin' dead man."

"You'll never get out of here alive. How did you even get in here?"

---

11. What's the problem here?

Peace prodded the man hard with the gun, and the man winced. "Move — and don't make a sound!"

Slowly they retraced their steps. It was only as they neared the tunnel entrance that they encountered people. One or two even raised their hands in greeting to the manager. Finally, they were outside and climbed the steps alongside the incline towards the prefabricated offices.

They found that the wind had subsided, although it still lifted the occasional dust cloud. When they were out of sight of others, Peace raised the silenced automatic and shot the manager in the back of the head. The man's body jerked and crumpled to the ground.

"You cold-blooded bastard! Was that necessary? That's bloody murder," Cherry blurted, her hand at her mouth and her eyes wide. He'd summarily executed the man.

"What was I supposed to do? Just hit him over the head, so he can later say he found us in the chamber that housed the nuclear weapons? Hell, he was one of the bosses — he deserved what he got. They might know somebody was here, but I doubt that they'd ever think we'd got as far as where the bombs were stored. They'd need to investigate in case it was true and the longer this is delayed, the better."

Cherry shook her head. "You're no better than they are. You people have no respect for human life."

"Jesus, just listen to yourself," he said disdainfully. "Don't be ridiculous! Look, this lot was prepared to kill millions — who's worse?"

"I was never told that we might kill in cold blood."

"Well, welcome to the new world," he murmured sarcastically and shrugged his shoulders. "Of course you were told! But you, like all of us at first, chose not to believe it. If you want to work for us, this is what the job entails; you have no choice. Now, forget it, let's move on. Our position here is compromised."

Again, using the prefabs as cover, they moved from shadow to shadow, carefully making their way towards the cuts in the fence. No rain had fallen, the clouds had been blown away and the moon was again visible.

The scrub around the airfield had not recently been cleared, and they were able to make their way undetected to the inner steel mesh fence with relative ease. Once, while amongst the prefabs, they bumped into two guards. The men did not stop them, but murmured a greeting in passing, probably because of Peace's helmet. Before leaving the cluster of prefabs, they returned to where they had changed and discarded their borrowed overalls, boots, and helmets.

Peace carefully undid the wire that held the break in the steel mesh fence together. Suddenly, out of the corner of his eye, he saw a movement in the cleared corridor beyond the fence. Two hyenas loped towards him, whooping as they approached. The animals flew at him, with only the fence stopping them. He stepped back, and as they raised their forelegs up against the fence, four rapids shots followed. They yelped and both fell to the ground. He swung around to see Cherry standing with her automatic in her hand, the silencer still attached to the barrel. She'd done the only thing possible.

"Thanks," he whispered.

He noticed that her attitude to him seemed to have softened. Whether this was out of necessity given their current circumstances, he did not know.

They clambered through the opening, not bothering to close it, dashed across the open piece of ground, and passed through the outer perimeter fence. They carefully made their way back to the hotel, being careful to avoid contact with any other people. Fortunately, the town seemed deserted. They crept into the hotel through a rear door and before entering the hotel foyer made sure no one was around to see them. They slowly approached the night-desk and found the on-duty guard asleep. The lack of security in the town was in direct contrast to the mine. Silently they passed him and made their way to their room. Hopefully, if they were questioned, no one would ever believe they'd left their room.

"I'm going to shower," she said and started to remove her clothing.

He grabbed her arm. "You can't do that. We have to be quiet — very quiet. We're still asleep; remember? Nobody's to think we were up at this ungodly hour. Just undress and get into bed. We'll shower in the morning."

"I understand." She looked at the hand that still held her arm. "Am I allowed to pee?"

He chuckled and released her arm. "Only if you do it quietly."

She returned from the bathroom and appearing oblivious of his presence, stripped to her underwear. He turned away to give her some privacy and heard her get into her bed.

"God, I hate getting into bed like this feeling unwashed," she said.

He slipped off his clothes and clad only in his Jockeys, began collecting their clothing and boots and squeezed them into a holdall, which he zipped, and put inside a cupboard. She watched him.

"Why do that?"

"I don't want any obvious evidence around. Who knows, they might snoop around tomorrow morning, or pay us an unexpected visit. Somebody's going to start investigating soon enough." He took both automatics and slid them under their pillows on the bed. "Just in case," he added.

As he made his way to his bed next to hers, she suddenly flung back her bedclothes. He saw that she was nude, noting her perfect breasts with her nipples slightly protruding, and the hint of her dark pubis.

Sweet Jesus, she stripped all the way down when my back was turned.

"So, she relents," he murmured softly to himself.

"Please, I'm still shocked and frightened. Climb in, and don't you dare refuse, because if you do then I'll never speak to you again. I'd be too embarrassed, me coming on to you like this and you rejecting me."

For a moment, he hesitated. She'd branded him as an unfeeling murderer. Why this? For the first time since he'd met her, she appeared truly vulnerable. He slid under the sheets beside her, immediately aware of the warmth and smoothness of her body against his. He thought she would turn her back to him, but she did not. To hide his surprise, he took her in his arms and kissed her, and she responded immediately.

Finally, their lips parted. "That was sudden. I thought you found me brutal and barbaric. Why the sudden change?" he whispered.

"You won't believe this, but whenever I've survived something like we've been through, it just does something to me. I know it's crazy. It's like a realisation that I'm a woman, that maybe I shouldn't be doing what's really a man's job. It's in contrast to my primal instinct of nurturing and care, if you understand what I mean. I need to be reminded that beneath this all I'm still a woman."

"I thought you said you were scared."

She giggled and snuggled close. "Damn it! I was terrified! But I'll say this, I don't think our bosses really appreciate you. You are what your colleagues believe you are — a cold-blooded, calculating killer which, of course, no one would say to your face."

He slid his hand over her body. He kissed her neck, his lips then moving down until they found her breast.

"I'll have to remember that, but then, so are you if the moment demands it," he whispered.

She moaned slightly as his lips plucked at her hardened nipple. He moved his hand down between her thighs. As his fingers found her, she gave a low groan.

At his touch, she whispered hoarsely, "See, I told you so — beneath it all, I'm a woman."

Finally, he surrendered himself to the familiar feeling of sexual euphoria.

Chapter Ten

Peace was in a deep sleep when he became aware of someone knocking at the door and it took a few seconds to glance at his wristwatch — it was just after seven.

A voice shouted, "Police! Open up immediately!"

He grabbed the bedspread, wrapped it around his waist, and made for the door, swearing loudly and prepared for a verbal confrontation with whoever had dared disturb them. "Coming!" he shouted with what he thought was the right amount of indignation. At the commotion, Cherry sat up in bed and pulled the sheet to her neck, obviously naked beneath it.

Peace flung open the door. "What the hell is the meaning of this, waking us at the bloody early hour?" It was pointless trying to pretend to be anything else but an Englishman.

Two white police officers stood in the passageway in blue uniforms, wearing shorts, long blue woollen socks to their knees, and black shoes. One was a Warrant Officer.

From their reactions it was clear that they had not expected to come upon both a very personal and embarrassing situation. He saw their looks of initial surprise and hesitation as they looked at Cherry who was clearly naked beneath the sheet she clutched to her neck. It was all too obvious what they imagined had been happening, and the officer's indecision was written over his face.

"Good morning, sir. Sorry to disturb you," the senior officer said in heavily accented broken English. "Mr and Mrs Sedgwick, I believe? Just a question or two, this is only a routine check."

Peace knew he had to play the offended hotel guest to the hilt. He purposely made a show of looking at his watch. "At bloody seven in the morning? What the hell is going on? As you can see, we're still in bed!"

They mumbled an apology, their uncertainty still evident.

"Where were you last night?" the Warrant Officer asked, doing his best to ignore Cherry on the bed.

"I was here in the hotel, of course," spat Peace. "Good God, man… You should know; there's nowhere else to go!" He knew that they would have checked with the desk first. "Have you checked with the desk?"

The officer ignored the question. "Sir, just a routine check. Sorry to have disturbed you," he said, taking a step backwards.

"Are we done?" he demanded and then not waiting for a reply muttered, "Bloody small-town morons," and slammed the door.

He waited, expecting another knock. But this did not happen.

"I think they're gone. That was a grand performance," she whispered and then dropped the sheet.

"You look absolutely ravishing," he said, "but I think it would be best if we made a quiet but hasty departure. They're bound to return soon and next time it will be more difficult. The car will be ready; the sooner we're out of this town the better."

"You're sure you don't want to…" she asked, a wicked smile on her face.

"Oh, I do, but to lose my life afterwards would be pointless. Let's save it. Go and shower, and get dressed. Do it quickly."

She was in and out of the shower in minutes. He followed her. They were soon dressed and had their bags packed. After a hearty breakfast, they collected their bags from the foyer and walked over to the garage.

The mining paraphernalia stolen from the prefabs the previous night was still in the holdall, and he made sure he also took this with him. He had checked the room carefully before leaving to make sure nothing incriminating was left behind.

The car was ready. Peace paid for the repair and for petrol. He walked into the garage forecourt shop where a newspaper poster caught his eye, the huge headlines announcing a tragic collision between two aircraft just off the northern Namibian coast. He paid the garage bill and bought cool drinks, potato crisps and a newspaper. They packed their bags into the car and left, driving slowly out of the town. This time, Cherry was at the wheel. Once the buildings were behind them, Peace settled down to read the main story in the paper.

The two aircraft that had collided were an SAAF Transall and a USAAF C141 cargo plane, which had been returning empty to the US after delivering humanitarian aid to Namibia. The details were vague and it was clear that the article included much conjecture. The report of the accident had only filtered through many hours after the collision. This was because the Transall's flight details had not been disclosed. Being privy to certain information, Peace was aware that while South Africa was technically no longer at war with Angola, a fair number of South African businesses still illegally, and for a handsome profit, supplied the UNITA movement under Savimbi at Jamba and Huambo in Angola with medicines, clothing and food. This was with the tacit backing of the Bush administration in the US and the South African government, both of whom tended to look the other way. Clandestine flights regularly left South Africa from obscure airfields in previously retired aircraft bought on the world market. Very often commercial pilots would hear South African Air Force and other pilots refusing to disclose their destination to South African air traffic control — they would merely report on entering and departing an international radio control area. This was normal procedure for these aircraft. The report said it was thought to be a million-to-one freak accident. Once word got out about the disaster, search aircraft had been dispatched, and scattered debris was discovered just off the northern Namibian coast. Rescuers had seen no sign of any life rafts or survivors.

Peace was amazed. Aircraft heights were strictly controlled. Those flying on eastern radii maintained different altitudes from those flying on western radii. The chances of a collision were near impossible. What had gone wrong? He knew it would take months before they discovered the real reasons and who was to blame.

He told Cherry what had happened as she drove.

"Somehow, I just know that the Transall that went down was the aircraft we saw leave Copperton. The bullion was on its way out of the country, hence the undisclosed destination. Bloody Van Rhyn's hiding behind a damn façade again. Now the gold's lying at the bottom of the ocean. What's he going to do?" Peace said.

"Surely he'll try to recover his gold?" surmised Cherry. "He's bound to mount such an operation immediately, certainly before the Yanks decide to send out a recovery ship. You know what they're like; they'll want to know what the cause of the accident was. They'll be after the black boxes."

Cherry had turned south at an intersection to give the impression that they were continuing their journey to the Richtersveld, but once they got to another arterial intersection, they headed back to Johannesburg.

*

Around midday, they stopped in Britstown, which was no more than a small settlement in the semi-desert.

"This is where I was born," Cherry said.

Carefully, not wanting to be offensive, he replied, "It's quaint — a village really, isn't it?"

"Be careful how you refer to my birthplace," she replied sternly but then burst out in giggles. "Actually, my father was in the South African Police and served as station-commander here. It's a dump really."

He laughed; the matter now no longer sensitive. He swivelled his head around in mock surveillance. "A dump… I agree."

They found a café with a fast-food *to go* section and drove a few miles out of the town to eat and let Peace contact the UK.

He activated the satellite phone and soon connected with VA. The greeting from Sir John was abrupt. "What the hell's been going on? I should've heard from you earlier than this."

"We found the bombs, Sir John. Five of them — one Russian, which we must assume is the missing neutron bomb." He then reported on the two bombers housed in Van Rhyn's hangar. The last bit of news really upset his boss.

"Jesus, the SA Army's high command, and certainly a few in the Air Force, must be cooperating with him and his band. God man, those people could start a nuclear war! That's not a private collection, it's a bloody air force!"

"Sir, if I may venture an opinion?"

"Your opinions and mine mean naught, but go ahead, it can't do any harm," Sir John replied irritably. Peace could hear VA's sigh of frustration that followed through the instrument.

Nevertheless, he doggedly proceeded.

"Except for a very few, I don't think any Afrikaner diehards, or rather those in high places, wish to use the bomb. They're too aware of the consequences. I reckon that if we can eliminate Van Rhyn, General Booyens, and a few others, this will fizzle out. From my interaction with Van Rhyn, it was clear that he considered this a last-ditch stand by the right-wing — it is only a small portion of the population that supports a White backlash. However, if his faction were to win, many would change sides, as it were. Therefore, the sooner the mine and the bombs are destroyed, the better."

There was a slight pause.

"Well, Peace, I suppose you're right. I'll be discussing this with the Prime Minister. I'll get back to you via the Embassy."

"Just before we ring off, something else," Peace cut in, and told the Vice Admiral about the gold he'd seen being loaded, and his belief that the Transall that had collided with the American C141 was the one containing the bullion. "Sir, I believe the gold is lying at the bottom of the sea off the Namibian coast. Damn if it doesn't get any worse than off that particular shoreline. If I'm correct, that's the notorious Skeleton Coast."

"Are you sure about this? A mid-air collision such as this is a chance in a million, especially over such a remote place."

"Miss Boxx and I are virtually certain that our assumption is correct. After all, we saw the gold being loaded onto a Transall at Copperton, and we found the discarded containers after we'd entered the complex. These certainly looked like containers which would be used for the transport of bullion — I couldn't think of anything else they may have contained. That surely says it all?"

"I have to admit, it seems to make sense. But they used the original containers to load the lead bars into, so where did these come from?"

Peace grunted. "I don't know, but be assured, the ones I saw could not have been used for little else."

"Well, maybe they had access to other containers. They would've had to in order to transport the gold." Peace heard VA sigh on the other end. He then asked, "Incidentally, how are the two of you getting on?"

Peace wondered whether he had heard a chuckle. "Surprisingly well," he replied.

The VA harrumphed. "I can imagine." Then he summarily broke the connection.

"Impolite bastard," Peace murmured to himself.

"What did he say?" Cherry queried.

He laughed. "He said I shouldn't screw you."

For a second, she appeared shocked and then realised it was a joke and playfully slapped his hand.

"Don't you dare stop doing that. I'd have to tell him."

*

They decided to spend the night in Kimberley seeing as their arrival in Johannesburg the following day was not based on time — morning versus night would make little difference. The next day, once in the city, Peace dropped Cherry off at the same casino and hotel complex where they had previously stayed. He left the car at the embassy with instructions it be returned, and then called Martin, his chauffeur, to pick him up in the Mercedes, reverting again to his cover as Lord Digby Brentwood.

Once back at the estate, he soon phoned Janet Van Rhyn and told her that he'd just returned from London where he'd been visiting friends. His cover was well thought out and prepared and had any queried him, he would have readily been able to supply an alibi — the British consul who was an acquaintance of Sir John's and had been suitably briefed.

"Digby, sweetheart, I'd love to come over but Father's had a spot of bother and he is really upset. I'd rather not leave him. However, I might possibly be able to get away later tonight, that is, of course, if you'll be home."

He smiled, not missing the sense of expectancy in her voice. Of course, he'd be home, he'd replied.

"Okay, I'll see what I can do. I do miss you."

She rang off.

He was relieved. If Van Rhyn were suspicious, his daughter would not be so forthcoming.

*

Around ten in the evening, he recognised the sound of her sports car's exhaust as she stopped in front of the house. He opened the front door and stepped out on to the landing to welcome her. She was dressed in jeans with low shoes and a cotton top over which she wore a red leather jacket. She walked straight into his arms and they kissed passionately. Then, taking her by the hand as if this was the most natural thing to do, he led her into the house. He helped her out of her jacket and thereafter prepared her usual vodka and orange juice while choosing for himself a glass of Glenfiddich on the rocks.

She took a generous swallow of her drink.

"God, do I need this! My father is in a dreadful mood. Something important went awry and it'll be difficult to fix. You certainly won't be seeing him for a while."

Subtle — no mention of what's actually wrong.

"This could also tie me up for a while," she added.

"I'm sorry to hear that. Is there anything I can do to help?"

She shook her head. "Unfortunately, you can't, but thanks."

She moved towards him, removed the whisky tumbler from his hand, and placed her hands flat on his chest.

"Let's not dwell on that which is unpleasant," she said and raised her head, looking up at him. She put her arms around his neck and drew his head down until her mouth met his, her tongue against his teeth.

His lust for her was compelling, and if he had initial misgivings, he soon forgot those in his desire for her. She was an exceptionally beautiful woman. In addition, she was highly intelligent, and clearly knew what she wanted. He also knew what he wanted — he wanted to make love to her. Minutes later, they were in his bedroom shedding their clothes.

They had hardly fallen entwined onto the bed when they were interrupted by the phone ringing. He rolled to the side and picked up the receiver.

"Brentwood."

"Hi."

He recognised Cherry's voice. "What are you doing? Are you thinking of me?" she asked teasingly.

"In fact, I was," he lied. His face remained neutral, as did his voice, but he realised he was not about to bluff his way out of this.

"Who's that?" Janet asked.

"Business," he murmured with a sinking feeling. It was the first thing that came to mind.

There was silence on the other end of the phone line. Cherry must have heard the female voice in the background.

"I heard that," Cherry hissed. "You've got a woman with you!" This was followed by a dial tone as the phone was smashed down.

"What was that about?" Janet raised her eyebrows enquiringly and appeared unperturbed.

"A business acquaintance asked whether I was already in bed. I said I was. He said he'd phone back tomorrow."

"Clever thing to do, considering the moment."

He somehow knew that he was being subtly manipulated. *I need to be careful with this one — she misses nothing. I'd be wise not to cross her seeing as she goes after exactly what she wants.*

He rolled towards her and took her in his arms. They made passionate love, as though both were trying to satisfy some urgent unspoken need.

Later, they lay quietly together, she cradled in his arm and with her arm over his chest.

"Darling, I'm sorry but I have to go away for a while. I have to be with my father. He needs to deal with a problem and insists I accompany him. I don't know how long I'll be away. We're leaving tomorrow morning so I have to go soon." Her tone was poignant.

"Don't worry yourself, I understand. Besides, I'll also be away. I've a few things I need to see to in Cape Town. Maybe we'll meet there."

"Not likely, I'm off to Namibia."

"Oh, I see."

The only reason Van Rhyn could be going to Namibia was to salvage the gold. Suddenly she added, "The family has a farm in the north of the country bordering the Etosha Pan. There is business we need to attend to."

Now, that was a surprise, he thought. He doubted whether it involved farming at all.

*

Peace woke up a few hours later as she quietly slipped out of the bed, unaware that she had woken him. He pretended to be asleep and left her to find her own way out.

Chapter Eleven

After three days of planning, he eventually arrived at the Skeleton Coast at the approximate position where the two aircraft had collided over the sea, thought to be roughly a mile or so off the coast of Namibia. The wind buffeted him as he stood on top of the rock terrace, which stretched north and south along the coast. He looked out to sea where the Atlantic rollers gathered as they prepared to launch themselves against the hostile face of Terrace Bay. The sun had passed its zenith and already the fog banks, the result of the cold Benguela Current, gathered on the western horizon over the sea. This was a near daily phenomenon, with the curtain of mist usually crossing the coastline in the hours after midnight.

Out there somewhere, no more than a mile or so from the shore, lay the wrecks of the two aircraft that had collided. No survivors had been found. He was certain that beneath the waves lay the gold.

Behind him was the desert — one of the driest in the world, windswept and bare. Access to this area was possible only by air or by four-wheel-drive vehicle. Some adventurous nature-lovers had erected three bungalows on the bluff, but these were only used by their owners in midsummer, usually during the Christmas holidays. Peace had managed to rent one through a Namibian tourist agency while the remaining two were unoccupied.

He had flown in on a chartered aircraft from Namibia's capital, Windhoek. The aircraft had deposited him and a 400cc quad-cycle on a makeshift small dirt landing strip marked out on the sand by small-whitewashed stones. He had also brought a few basic provisions to keep him for a day or so. They'd even flown in his drinking water.

They would obviously also require a decent four-wheel-drive vehicle and it was decided that Cherry would motor up the coast from Swakopmund in a Land Cruiser loaded with every piece of camping equipment and foodstuff they'd need for an extended stay. She'd be bringing a trailer behind the vehicle, complete with rubber Zodiac raft and outboard engine, air compressor and other diving paraphernalia. The first hundred miles or so of her journey would be easy, even though the roads were mere graded gravel strips. Thereafter, for 200 miles, she would be forced to follow, for a good while, well-worn vehicle tracks through the desert sand and rock. Although a coincidence, she was followed by a Namibian Wildlife Ranger in his own vehicle on his way to Terrace Bay, a very basic campsite on the coast. He would be able to assist her should she run into trouble. In the desert, two vehicles were always better than one. From Terrace Bay she would have to continue on the last leg on her own.

Peace smiled when he thought of her. To start with, after she'd discovered his dalliance with Janet Van Rhyn, she had been unapproachable — distraught that he should have slept with someone else so soon after he had been intimate with her. She lambasted him, accusing him of screwing anything that moved, as she had so eloquently put it. He felt offended, or so he claimed, and offered the explanation that his involvement with Janet had been unavoidable because of what had previously occurred, and had he not kept up the pretence it would have endangered their mission. She had scoffed at this excuse but he knew she was aware that were he confronted by a similar situation again, he'd have to play the game no matter what that may entail. Eventually she'd relented and welcomed him to her bed again, but only after she'd extracted a promise that he would not consort with that woman again, for whatever reason.

Before departing Johannesburg, he had been given access to all the most up to date information available from British Intelligence sources. The South African Air Force had not immediately disclosed the reason for the Transall aircraft being in this area, and he could imagine the consternation behind the scenes, aware that this clandestine flight had not been known to all the top brass in the Air Force. Somebody had to have a damn lot of explaining to do. Finally, it was leaked that it was a maritime reconnaissance flight

— the Air Force using Hercules C130s, DC3s and Transalls for this purpose since their old British Avro Shackletons were redundant. South Africa was unable to replace her naval reconnaissance aircraft as the country was still subject to an arms embargo, and replacement reconnaissance aircraft were not accessible. This explanation was eventually accepted by all. He, as well as the British and American Intelligence services, knew it to be a blatant lie — the Transall flight had been on no recon mission.

After the mid-air collision, the two aircraft had separated. The American investigating team had established that while the Transall had plunged straight into the sea directly below the point of impact, the C130 had continued to fly for a few miles. It managed to transmit a *mayday* distress call before it broke up, crashing into the sea and disappearing. Nobody had seen what had happened.

Peace had initially been sceptical about his part in the aircraft recovery, but it had been explained to him that the continental shelf off the Skeleton Coast was shallow and sloped very gradually. The British, who certainly had a vested interest in the gold, were not certain whether a submarine could approach close enough to launch an underwater recovery unit. Any plan to recover the gold from the surface was out of the question, as those were not international waters. Yes, the Americans had permission to enter the coastal waters since the one wrecked aircraft below the waves belonged to them, however, it was believed that they had no knowledge of any gold shipment. To have refused the Americans would have created an incident. Peace, with his rubber Zodiac and diving equipment, was vital to the plan in that he could confirm exactly where on the bottom the Transall lay and keep an eye on precisely what the South Africans were doing.

He could just make out the American salvage ship to the north where it swung on its anchor a mile or so beyond the surf line. Through the binoculars, he saw the large naval helicopter lashed to the rear helipad deck. The Americans did not consider the Transall their business, provided there was an open exchange of all information that pertained to the crash. The South African government had given them that assurance.

The problem was that the South African authorities had prohibited any approach to the position where it was said the Transall had disappeared.

Peace had been given the exact coordinates by the British Admiralty, who had obtained these from the Americans. An American NASA surveillance satellite had picked up the bright flash caused by the collision as well as the exact coordinates. A South African Navy coastal patrol boat was out there to ensure the integrity of the site, although there had been no sight of it. For all he knew, it had not yet arrived.

Peace wasn't sure what he was to do with all the diving equipment he had been given. Without a suitable vessel, nobody was going to raise tons of gold from the seabed. The coastline and seabed were treacherous and a continuous strong northerly current just aggravated the situation. Besides, the South African patrol boat would immediately investigate any suspicious activity, if it was in the vicinity.

The question was whether the South African authorities knew that the Transall had been loaded with bullion, or whether this information was limited to Van Rhyn and his political associates alone. Nobody had any idea what the South African Air Force's true involvement was.

Where the hell was Van Rhyn? Peace wondered. Surely, the man must already have put wheels in motion to recover the gold?

At that moment, a small British attack submarine was supposedly nearing the Namibian coast, having departed Gibraltar more than a week before, its destination the crash site. The Transall's position on the seabed was said to be just before the continental shelf, which rapidly fell off to the deep ocean seabed beyond. The plan was to bring the submarine close to the underwater cliff that lay a few miles offshore, and remove the gold using frogmen and submersible chariots. This had been kept so secret that he'd heard of this only just prior to his departure for the coast. He knew this would be a formidable undertaking. It intrigued him to think how Van Rhyn would go about it.

*

The next morning he rose just before the first light of dawn appeared. The coast was shrouded in fog, reducing visibility to no more than fifty yards. After an hour, the fog slowly began to disperse, allowing the sun to break through occasionally, with only a few wisps remaining. He looked out to sea and was surprised to see a large, squat ship just beyond where the sea bottom became shallower. He rushed to the bungalow to retrieve his binoculars and when he focused on it, he recognised it to be a salvage tug with the name *Johan de Waldt*, painted on the bow. He knew of the boat — it was a renowned, independently owned, ocean-salvage vessel that plied its trade in southern waters. It was certainly no government or naval vessel.

He realised that it had to be Van Rhyn who had commissioned it and its crew for his own purpose. *Damn — it has its own helicopter.* The binoculars provided by MI6 incorporated a laser rangefinder, and from the readings, he realised that the salvage ship was moored a good distance from the wreck site, probably because at that point the seabed did not afford sufficient draft, especially at low tide. This was to his advantage. The patrol boat, if it was in the vicinity, had evidently not challenged the salvage ship's presence. This again had to be Van Rhyn's doing.

*

Cherry arrived that afternoon.

They immediately sat down on the small bungalow porch that overlooked the sea, the sun already low near the horizon.

"What a trip," she said. "That was some of the most awe-inspiring scenery I've ever seen. You really get to experience the feeling of being completely alone. I know some people who would give their eye-teeth for this."

She had driven virtually non-stop and was exhausted. Peace poured her a drink and she sat back and scanned the sea.

Peace took a sip of his drink. "I'm glad you enjoyed it."

Cherry pointed at the ships on the horizon. "Whose ships are those?" she asked.

"I'm not entirely sure but I think one's American and the other either South African or Van Rhyn's," he replied.

"So, we'll be in the water tomorrow?"

"No, we must wait until the sub has arrived."

Chapter Twelve

Peace had been contacting London periodically on the satellite phone, waiting to hear whether the submarine was in position, and received his answer the day after Cherry arrived.

Previously, at the conference briefing in Pretoria, with Sir John's voice coming through the scrambler phone from London, he learned that the submarine would remain hidden, submerged on the seabed at the threshold to shallower waters, since it was too dangerous to approach any nearer to the crash site. A specially adapted submersible container had been fitted to it and bolted to the deck directly behind the conning tower, which was crammed with all the underwater equipment necessary to lift the gold bullion from the seabed. A complement of the Special Boat Service and specialised naval recovery experts were on board and they were to carry out the salvage of the gold bullion.

VA was convinced the recovery operation would encounter some resistance. In fact, he was emphatic.

He had said, "Of course, you must realise our friend Van Rhyn will make an all-out attempt to recover the bullion. Whether he mounts a recovery operation of his own or ropes in the South African Navy through his dubious connections, remains to be seen. If he uses their Special Forces from Langebaan in the Cape, you've got a problem. They were pretty active during the civil war and are combat tested and a dangerous lot. The Angolans and Cubans will vouch for that. However, in view of the sensitivity, I believe it's sure to be his own party. You can be certain that after what occurred at the mine at Copperton, he may believe we are aware of the gold on board the Transall, having put two and two together. That it departed Copperton while there were agents in his town just has to be too coincidental — he'll make the conclusion we know of the gold and must assume we'll make our own effort to recover it… So, as I mentioned to my colleagues, if you propose to join the Navy under the waves, make sure you're suitably armed, even if only with spear guns. You can be damn sure Van Rhyn's people will be… they'll be expecting trouble."

Peace had realised VA had a point and made a mental note of the warning.

VA had then given him a proposed rendezvous time when he could expect to meet the Navy's recovery crew on the seabed.

Fortunately, the coastal patrol boat had left on the arrival of the South African salvage ship, presumably because the salvage ship had government clearance and support. This supposition was confirmed to him during a satellite call to VA.

During the night, he and Cherry prepared the raft, and in the early hours of the morning, while the sea was still shrouded in mist, they launched it. This was the best time to do so, as there was little wind. A partially protected small cove enabled him to launch a light craft — no doubt the reason the owners of the bungalows had chosen this spot. However, there remained the danger of navigating through the line of surf and avoiding the reefs in deeper waters. This could only be undertaken on those days when the westwinds[12] were not blowing at storm strength trying to pound the coastline into submission.

Once out on the open sea, things proved hair-raising. He had to gun the engine intermittently to ensure they crested the waves before these broke and washed over them. From the shallow raft, the approaching waves appeared enormous, and several times the sea cascaded over the inflatable's bow, drenching them. Fortunately, the outboard engine was powerful and enabled them to double-back occasionally and outrun the surf, but each time a wave threatened to break over them, Peace could feel his heart rate speed up. Peace soon realised that Cherry knew how to handle herself in a

---

12. Those who live and visit this coastline, being predominantly Afrikaners and Germans, refer to the wind as die 'magtige westewind'. On bad days it can lift small pebbles.

boat. No doubt she had learned this during the thirteen weeks of training she did with the Special Boat Service, as part of her induction course, which was mandatory for any MI6 field operative.

Begrudgingly, she shared that during this time her name had led to much ribbing from the nearly all-male training squad. He could well believe it.

Once through the surf line and with the assistance of a sophisticated GPS, they were soon bobbing on the swells over the wreck site. Everything had been checked and double-checked before they left the shore. Peace wore a one-piece neoprene dry-suit, dubbed an FL — in a twist of humour this was diving jargon for *French Letter*. It was supposed to be watertight and if it leaked you might still live, but in cold water, there was the possibility of death from hyperthermia. This was the Benguela Current which originated in the Antarctic, and at this latitude, sea temperatures were about 10°C.

"Look, we've got a few hours before the fog begins to lift," Peace said. "I don't quite know what the lads below have in mind, but I'm going to find out."

He stuck the scuba mouthpiece between his teeth and opened the supply valve until he could hear the hiss of compressed air, then brought the face-mask down and rolled backwards into the sea. The water was freezing and plankton reduced visibility to no more than five yards. According to the depth finder, the seabed was about sixty feet below him. With the taste of compressed air in his mouth, he slowly followed the length of the weighted line, which Cherry had thrown overboard.

Eventually, the flat rocky bottom emerged out of the green murk. Interspersed with rock were patches of flat sand and clumps of green and brown seaweed. Peace, speargun in hand, was amazed at the number of fish. Small schools seemingly of every description swam before him and took little notice of the presence of this sudden and strange intruder. They had no predators, as the sharks and seals remained out at sea in pursuit of pilchard, sardine, and anchovy. Peace was well aware that the cold Benguela Current off the coast harboured very few, if any, predator sharks. Only in the warmer waters of the Indian Ocean and off the southern coastline of South Africa where shark attacks occur annually, were the homes of the tiger, Zambezi, and great white sharks to be found.

He started swimming in a circle and as he gradually widened it, he began to encounter the torn and shattered pieces of the downed Transall. He was amazed that the Americans had been able to supply the exact coordinates and marvelled at the technology that had enabled them to find the wreck.

He continued to swim in ever-widening circles, inspecting the wreckage and looking for the submarine's divers who were to rendezvous with him at the site. He saw no sign of them, nor the bullion boxes. He thought that strange. He knew that the salvage ship had to be preparing to initiate its own diving operations for he'd seen the large diving tender with its two small derricks lashed to the ship's rear deck, open to the sea with a ramp that sloped down to the water. The ship's powerful winches could launch this within minutes but he assumed they'd wait until the fog lifted.

Suddenly a dark shape loomed out of the murk. It was with relief that he recognised it as a British Navy submersible two-man craft, which resembled a torpedo with an open cockpit. Two scuba divers straddled the cockpit. He swam towards them and came alongside. They gave each other a thumbs up in greeting.

Gesturing with his hands, Peace indicated he had found no trace of the gold. One of the scuba-men pointed to the bottom and shook his head, then pointed in a northerly direction and with spread fingers showed his hands five times to Peace, probably indicating a distance of fifty yards or so. They evidently knew where the gold was. The other produced a slate on which were written coordinates; he handed this to Peace and pointed upwards.

Peace swam towards the Zodiac's mooring line, tied the slate to it, gave three strong jerks, and waited until he saw it being retrieved. He knew Cherry would realise the meaning of the new coordinates and move the raft. He wondered if the fog remained. Would she have time to do so and still allow him to come aboard before the mist lifted?

He grabbed the submersible in order to hitch a ride. Moments later, the submersible's screw started to turn and the three frogmen moved north. Moving across the seabed, he could still see wreckage, the pieces lying well spread out on the seafloor.

Suddenly, through the murk, he saw the first bullion container, and then another, and another. They were concentrated in a small area. He then saw a turbo-prop engine, the bent propeller blades still fixed to it. As they continued north, another dark shape loomed out of the translucent pea soup — it was the fuselage's nose section, which had broken off just behind the cockpit. He let go of the submersible and swam towards the cockpit that lay upright on the seabed. All the Perspex had been torn from the windows and he could just make out some movement in the interior. He suddenly realised what he was looking at. The two pilots were still strapped in their seats and wearing their light-blue short-sleeved shirts, but their exposed limbs crawled with crayfish. Already some parts of the soft tissue had been eaten away.

From the surface above him, he heard a faint drumming sound. It had to be Cherry bringing the raft to their new position. The weighted diving line appeared, snaking its way to the bottom. He saw that the two SBS divers had started to open the bullion boxes with a long crowbar and load ingots into the chariot. The salvage operation had begun, so he swam to assist them.

Soon the chariot could hold no further ingots as the ballast tanks could barely cope and the vessel was about to sink to the ocean floor. The two frogmen indicated they were about to leave. Peace showed that he understood and began his slow ascent, mindful that he needed to decompress.

Ten minutes later his head broke the surface to find the Zodiac only a few feet away. He was relieved to see the fog had still not dispersed, but knew it would not be long before the sun burned it off. He'd come up just in time.

Cherry held out a hand to help him aboard. She pulled and he kicked hard, thrusting himself out of the water. He rolled over the inflated gunwale into the boat and removed the mouthpiece and the mask.

"Quickly!" he urged. "Get the line in; we need to head back to the coast before we're seen by the *de Waldt*." He pulled his arms out of the straps to release the cylinders and looked around, but there was no sign of the salvage ship.

Cherry soon had the engine started. He told her to keep the engine noise down. With the engine just above an idle, they moved slowly towards the shore. Only when the raft approached the white waters of the shoreline did she speed up. She handled the raft superbly, positioning it in front of a swell and then racing before it as it towered behind them, starting to curl. It then broke, and a cauldron of foam chased them until it began to dissipate. She then slowed and let the remnants of the breaker pass beneath them, and followed the white line of foam rushing ahead of the Zodiac until they slipped into the cove.

"Let's get everything out of here," he said, unscrewing the lugs that held the outboard to the transom.

The engine was heavy and she helped him manhandle it to the top of the terraced ground. There, again with her assistance, he swung it onto a shoulder and carried it the seventy yards to the bungalow. They deflated the Zodiac and between them carried it to a small garage adjoining the bungalow which they squeezed it into. Within ten minutes, there was no trace of it.

A half-hour later, the sun began to break through the fog. Gradually, the salvage ship became visible, its diving tender wallowing in the swells between it and the shore. A diver's cage hung suspended above the water from a derrick. He wondered whether the divers were still below. They were in the wrong place. What was disturbing was that the helipad was empty.

"The damn chopper's gone!" he exclaimed.

"It lifted off while you were below. I heard it but never saw it in the mist — it sounded like it was heading towards land."

"I wonder where it went."

"Maybe to get supplies?"

"Could be, but I reckon it would've flown south to do that." He paused for a moment as a thought struck him. "I wonder how far it is from here to Etosha."

"God, you don't think it's gone to fetch Van Rhyn?"

"Could be." He knew Van Rhyn would want to be there when the gold was salvaged.

Peace mounted the binoculars on a tripod inside the bungalow and trained them on the salvage tender. Twice the divers came up, then the tender moved. The divers then disappeared below the surface again. He was sure they had not yet found the gold, but he knew that eventually, they were bound to stumble on the bullion containers. He had no idea what would happen after that, but VA was adamant the gold was not to fall into their hands.

Fortunately, the wind strengthened considerably in the early afternoon, making it too dangerous for the tender to work so close inshore, and it was forced to abandon its operations.

"Thank God. That'll work in our favour," he said. The submarine could continue its operations, impervious to conditions on the surface.

Cherry had prepared a mid-afternoon meal for them, even producing a chilled bottle of wine. They had just sat down to eat when suddenly they heard the unmistakable *whap-whap* of an approaching helicopter.

"Bloody hell!" Peace exclaimed.

He dropped his knife and fork, picked up the binoculars from the tripod, and moved towards the window. The helicopter flew over the bungalows at no more than a hundred feet, the sound rising to a near crescendo, and then faded as it sped out to sea towards the salvage ship. The ship's bow was pointing towards the southwest into the wind as it swung on its anchor, the stern and aft deck with the helipad clearly visible. The helicopter landed, the rotors spun to a stop and members of the ship's crew ran on deck to lash the aircraft down.

He peered through the glasses, sucked in his breath and spat an expletive.

"You won't believe it. It's that bastard Van Rhyn, and he has his daughter with him, as well as two other people. He's got two of his hyenas with him as well — they're on bloody leashes!" He had seen the ship's crew rapidly move away as the animals jumped to the deck. "It seems those damn things are his pets! If I had a rifle, I'd take him out now."

He moved away to let Cherry look through the binoculars.

"It's him all right. So, that's his daughter. I can see why you bedded her."

"It's too far away to see anybody properly, so please don't start with me, I rather we didn't fight," Peace said.

She mouthed the word *bastard* at him and spun round, disappearing through the door that led into the add-on garage to the bungalow housing the Land Cruiser and returned with a rifle in her hand.

Christ, does she want to take Janet out?

He recognised the weapon as a NATO AWM sniper's rifle fitted with a Schmidt and Bender 10x42 scope. The rifle fired .338 Lapau Magnum cartridges.

"Where'd you get that?" he asked in amazement.

"Compliments of VA. The embassy's security staff in Pretoria issued it to me. It arrived in the diplomatic pouch. I was told that VA thought that you might need it."

He was not surprised to hear this. This was Sir John's way of letting him know what he wanted without actually stating it. He'd done it before. Clearly, he wanted Van Rhyn dead.

He whistled softly and took the rifle from her. He hefted it in his hands to judge its weight — it was heavy. All sniper rifles were heavy.

"You can pick him off any time you like with that," she said. "Though I think you're only supposed to do that if all else fails, and preferably without creating a diplomatic incident."

He rolled his eyes. "Hell, that's rich coming from you. I thought you disapproved of my murderous ways. You know I can't take him out; the man's the bloody chairman of Afrikaner Goudeiendomme, for God's sake! It would lead to the biggest manhunt this country's ever seen!"

"Somehow, Geoffrey, I think it'll have to come to that. It's the only way to deal with that man. He's evil, he needs killing, and you do killing so incredibly well." She looked at him, her eyes revealing nothing.

He stared at her. For a moment, he thought she might actually approve of what he did in his job. Then he dismissed the thought. No, that couldn't be possible.

Chapter Thirteen

The next morning, before daylight, they inflated the Zodiac again, fitted the outboard motor, and launched it. Mist was drifting in from the sea on a light breeze. They sat in the raft waiting in the protection of the cove for the first indication of daylight. Cherry had insisted that she accompany him on the dive and he had relented. She also was clad in a dry-skin diving suit.

The mist began to take on a dark-grey opaque tint, indicating the onset of daylight. He started the outboard motor and manoeuvred the boat through the surf, which had calmed considerably since the previous day. He soon cut the engine, the boat drifting directly above the coordinated position recorded on the GPS. The fog still prevented them from seeing the *Johan de Waldt*, but they knew it was out there at anchor somewhere, with Van Rhyn aboard and probably directing the recovery operation. This time they dropped an anchor, intending to use its rope to guide them to the bottom. They carefully checked each other's equipment and then, one after the other, toppled backwards over the side. Following the rope, they slowly descended into the depths. Initially, it was quite dark, but in the Tropics, the transition from night to day is rapid and very soon visibility improved, allowing them to see ten or so yards ahead. There were several empty bullion canisters on the seabed. Evidently, the submarine divers had already managed to load several gold bars. He wondered if they had encountered any divers from the salvage ship,

They were surprised to see two chariots, each with two divers, loom out of the murk and knew these to be the divers from the submarine. The divers gave them a casual wave of recognition. Of course, the hi-tech equipment and periscope on the submarine would have confirmed their arrival and position. They'd timed their arrival perfectly. Once over the ingots, they dismounted and immediately began retrieving them. Peace and Cherry jumped in to help them.

Salvaging the bullion was hard work and Peace soon found that he was beginning to sweat in his dry-suit. The divers worked in two teams of three divers each; they formed a chain, handing the gold ingots one at a time from the bottom to the chariot. They'd been at the task for a while when Peace noticed another diver emerge from the grey-green murk. He had obviously spotted them, for he stopped, did an about-turn, and swam frantically away. It was pointless trying to pursue him; he was too far away to catch up.

Peace was convinced the man would return and this time with his comrades. The frogman in charge of the team clearly thought the same. He removed three of his men from the gold retrieval task and ordered them to swim ahead towards the salvage ship and to keep watch for any intruders. The rest continued loading the ingots.

Suddenly, the three submarine divers returned, swimming very rapidly. The reason for their haste was apparent a minute later when six more divers emerged, swimming abreast. They were armed with spearguns and their intention was obvious. Cherry and Peace were signalled to join their comrades to form a line and to hover over the gold below. Peace was concerned for Cherry. Professional divers were extremely fit as their jobs demanded peak physical conditioning, and Cherry was a lightweight in comparison. Even though she was trained by the SBS in hand-to-hand combat, and if attacked, could give a good account of herself, this was an entirely different situation.

As the men closed in, Peace realised the submariners had an advantage. Their guns were lethal weapons — the spears fired not by a stretched bungee rubber cord, but by a type of shotgun cartridge, giving them a far better range. He doubted whether Van Rhyn's men had anything as sophisticated. When the enemy was still ten or fifteen yards away, he heard the first thuds as the submariners fired. He and Cherry, whose guns used only thick surgical rubber similar to a catapult, had to wait.

The spears streaked through the water, with the enemy divers managing to dodge most of them, except one diver who was struck high in the chest. He dropped his speargun and grabbed the shaft that protruded from his body, his flipper-feet kicking wildly. The water around him turned pink, and he slowly sank to the bottom as the other divers continued to approach.

Peace and Cherry both fired their weapons as the divers attacked. Peace's spear struck his opponent in the stomach and the man sank slowly, legs thrashing as he tried to pull the barb free. Cherry's attacker, however, took no more than a blow to the upper arm which pierced his suit and he pushed forward to attack once more.

The divers started to grapple with one another. They had all drawn knives with eight-inch razor-sharp blades serrated on one edge. One man surged towards Peace, his knife held high, ready to strike. Peace let his own knife drop so it was suspended on the cord attached to his wrist. His empty hand then shot forward and grasped his opponent's wrist, stopping the downward thrust of the knife. He moved close and smashed the reinforced edge of his facemask into the glass of his assailant's mask. The blow dazed the man, his mask now hanging around his neck by the strap, the knife still clenched in his hand. Peace grabbed the wrist with both hands and twisted. As the man's mouth opened in pain, his mouthpiece was ejected and left a trail of bubbles, which rose towards the surface. As the knife spiralled from the man's hand, Peace deftly caught it by the hilt. In one fluid motion, he jerked it upwards through the neoprene suit just below the man's sternum. He twisted the blade round in the man's innards before pulling it out. The man was a goner. He made a few feeble movements and sank slowly to the seabed, trailing tendrils of blood.

Peace's concern was for Cherry. He swung around looking for her. She was no more than a few yards away, desperately wrestling with a diver. She was clasping both his wrists, but he was twisting about, trying desperately to free his hands. Frantically, Peace swam towards her, but knew he would be too late. The man wrenched his hand free, and when Peace was still a yard or so from him, the man lunged at her.

Peace emitted a silent scream. He thrashed his webbed feet wildly in a desperate effort to intervene. As if in slow motion, he saw the blade plunge into her left side, all the way to the hilt. He grabbed the man from behind, pulled his head back, and drove his knife into the man's neck, feeling it cut through cartilage and bone. The man immediately went limp and Peace released his grip. He looked around frantically for Cherry and found her below him, feebly kicking her feet in an attempt to rise to the surface — an automatic reaction if injured while diving. Fortunately, she still had the mouthpiece between her lips and was breathing air. He came down beside her, took her hand, and stared into her facemask. He saw the terrified look on her face and knew that she was badly hurt. Blood seeped from her side. He knew her dry-suit had to be slowly filling with blood and ice-cold seawater. The only way to save her was to get her aboard the submarine.

Out of the corner of his eye, he caught sight of one of the British divers. The man seemed to understand Peace's anguish, having seen Cherry's condition and was beckoning to Peace to bring Cherry to him. Peace did so and she feebly kicked her flippers trying to assist him.

He glanced behind him — the fight was over. He could see only one of the enemy divers, and he had two of the submarine's men around him. However, his immediate thoughts were for Cherry and whether she would make it back to the submarine.

It took a very long five minutes before it appeared in his vision. Crew were ready to assist the wounded into the airlock, but this took what seemed to be an interminable time, as compressed air had to be pumped into it to expel the seawater. Then there was another wait while the chamber was decompressed. The waiting was agony for Peace as he cradled Cherry in his arms, blood trickling from her side.

She was deathly white and her breathing was shallow. She was clearly in deep shock. He had a terrible feeling that she might also be bleeding internally. He berated himself — he should never have let her accompany him on the dive. All he could do was wait and watch blood seep from her wound and hope they'd be in time to save her. At last, he saw the lower bulkhead hatch cover's wheel beneath their feet begin to spin. It swung open and his ears popped at the pressure differentiation. Hands grasped at Cherry's limp body and she was rushed off to the infirmary.

Once on the submarine, he peeled off his diving suit, as did the others.

A man clad in navy-blue trousers and a light-blue shirt, his epaulettes indicating that he was the commander, approached Peace, and saluted him.

"I'm Captain Jefferson," he said. "I'm in command of this boat. Welcome aboard Her Majesty's submarine, *Indomitable*. You must be Commander Peace?"

"That's right. I'm glad to be aboard," he said, returning the salute then shaking the proffered hand.

"My Chief Boson's mate will find you some decent clothes. Then I'd like you to join me in my cabin. It's a bit cramped, I'm afraid, but you'll know that, having commanded a sub yourself, if I recall correctly. Don't worry about the young woman; our doctor is a first-class physician and surgeon; he'll patch her up. Let's not disturb him." Peace knew that the captain was right. His most pressing need was not to allow his worry to overtake his thought, so pushed any thought of her condition from his mind. He had to believe she was in the best of hands.

An enterprising crewman had eventually found him a standard-issue navy uniform. He was led by the Chief Boson's mate down the passageway, first through the control centre lined with computer displays manned by sailors, then through several bulkheads, where the passageway was strung with lights, and the piping and cabling fixed in bundles to the ceiling. Except for a barely perceptible hum, it was quiet. They finally arrived in front of a sliding door with the word CAPTAIN stencilled on it.

The Chief knocked and they were bidden to enter. The cabin was small and functional, containing a table with four chairs.

"Sit down, Commander. I gather from Lieutenant Hughes that you had a few worrying moments out there. I'm sorry about your colleague, Miss Boxx, but my surgeon tells me she's going to be fine. Of course, she'll need a while to mend, so she'll have to stay aboard. As for you, well, I think you need a drink. What'll it be?"

"Thanks. Whisky, please."

The captain produced a bottle and two glasses into which he poured two tots, the one intended for Peace a very generous measure.

The captain lifted his glass. "Cheers! I'm informed that you and my men gave a pretty good account of yourselves. I believe we won't be hearing about this incident on any official channels. Those on the tug, I'm told, will probably keep this to themselves as well. After all, they did salvage some bullion." He took a sip of his drink. Peace did the same.

"Have you any idea of what's going on?" Peace asked.

"Well, as you know, I've got my hydrophone specialists listening to everything. We believe only one survivor managed to make it back to the salvage ship. Now they have a tender out and we believe they've recovered your raft and taken it aboard. I have frogmen out again and they've resumed picking up the gold. Believe me, my men are ready to deal with any trouble, although the salvage boat doesn't seem to have sent down any more divers."

"This would have been a surprise for them," said Peace. "They have to be wondering where we came from. The Zodiac couldn't have accommodated six of you, so they must realise there's a submarine around, and the chariot will have been a definite giveaway."

"You're right. We'll just have to wait and see what they'll do now. Do you think they've got their government's backing?" the submarine commander asked.

Peace had no idea how well informed the submarine captain was or to what degree MI6 had taken him into their confidence. MI6 was notorious when it came to the *Need to Know* basis.

"I doubt it. After all, they stole the gold from their own country. I believe their government is investigating the theft, but you can be sure they're being hampered by others on the upper levels. I wouldn't be surprised if they didn't already know it was an inside job. Rest assured, they're not about to advertise the fact."

Peace suddenly felt very tired. At the captain's suggestion, he let the Chief lead him to the Officers' Quarters where they gave him a bunk. He was asleep within minutes.

Chapter Fourteen

He opened his eyes and glanced at his watch. It was just past midnight. He was disoriented, but then recollected where he was. It's never dark anywhere on board a submarine; there's always sufficient light to see. The faint hum of machinery also jogged his memory. Memories flooded back, and he immediately thought of Cherry and wondered how she was doing.

He rolled from the bunk and donned the navy boots they'd issued him. At a stainless-steel basin, he washed the sleep from his eyes and brushed his wet hands through his hair. He felt the stubble on his cheeks, but there was nothing he could do about that without borrowing somebody's shaving kit. And that was something he wasn't prepared to do. He ran his tongue over his teeth — they too needed brushing.

He made his way to the infirmary and entered. An orderly was sitting in a chair close to a cot, which was bolted to the floor, its sides raised. In the dim light, he recognised Cherry. Her nose and mouth were covered by a transparent plastic mask, which had an oxygen pipe attached to it. A saline drip was attached to her arm. Other pipes fed into the drip while more tubes were taped to her lower arm and wrist. A catheter emerged from the blue blanket covering her and led to a transparent bag, half-filled with dark urine. With a shock, he realised that she must have a damaged kidney — a knife stab in the side would do that. Affixed to the wall were two monitors, one emitting a beep for each heartbeat and in time with this, the line on the scope jerked into a jagged peak. Even in the dim light of the infirmary, he could see she was pale with sunken cheeks, and near blue-white lips. If an orderly was keeping a constant vigil, then her condition was obviously still serious.

"She's still in a bad way," the orderly murmured softly, apparently anticipating his question. His heart sank — clearly, she was still near critical. The captain had said she would pull through, but it seems the orderly, being a medical man, was being more cautious.

Peace nodded his head. He was consumed by an intense desire for a reckoning with the Afrikaner. He resolved that he would get that opportunity, even if he had to hatch his own plan. Abruptly, he turned and left the infirmary, overcome by an urge to put some distance between him and the suffering of this woman for whom he could do nothing to help.

He went back down the passageway towards the control centre, where he found the First Officer who had the watch. The man greeted him with a nod.

"Anything happening?" he asked.

The officer shook his head. "No, sir, all is silent. The salvage boat's still there, but it seems they're all asleep."

"Do you know whether they were able to find any of the gold?" Peace asked, patting his pocket for a cigarette, and then realising he had none.

"Can't smoke here," the officer said indicating a *No Smoking* sign on the wall. "If they did, it couldn't have been much; our chaps were out there again to stop them. I believe we've recovered most of it."

"What's going to happen now?"

"As soon as it's light, we'll be out there again."

"That's good. I don't want those bastards to get a thing," Peace said vehemently through clenched teeth, thinking again of Van Rhyn and Cherry.

Later that morning Peace was preparing to join the scuba divers and assist, but the captain intervened and would not permit it. "Look, Commander," he said, "I realise that this is your show, but really, what's the point? Let my lads deal with it, there aren't many bars left anyway. Besides, the tug's crew will probably not make another attempt."

Peace had to agree — after all, this was their boat.

During the day, the scuba divers returned with the last of the ingots. It was soon apparent that they had not salvaged all the gold; at least a third was missing. Either they were buried in the sand and seaweed, the metal detectors unable to reveal them, or more likely, Van Rhyn's men had managed to retrieve these. He thought it highly probable they would have stumbled on a few of the ingots.

He sought out the captain. "Captain, I'd like you to put me ashore this evening."

The captain raised his eyebrows at Peace's request. "Commander, is that wise? What do you propose to do?"

Peace told the captain about the hunting farm which Van Rhyn owned near the Etosha Pan in the northern part of the country, about two hundred miles from Terrace Bay. "His daughter's there and I'm sure that is where the lost ingots will land up. Besides, I've a job to do and a score to settle."

"I understand," said the captain. "How do you propose to get there? Surely not on that damned quad you've mentioned?"

Peace chuckled. "I've a vehicle as well as a few other interesting items on shore. I'll think of something. Just look after Miss Boxx, I feel responsible for her."

That wasn't quite true; he felt a good deal more than responsible, and dreaded anything else happening to her.

"By the way," he added, "if you can raise an antenna this evening, I'd like to contact London."

"I'm sure that won't be a problem."

*

Peace spent the rest of the day on the submarine, seething with impatience and waiting for nightfall. At around five in the afternoon, one of the crew operating the hydrophones reported the arrival of the helicopter on the salvage vessel. This then left an hour later. Peace knew that this had to be Van Rhyn leaving the ship, no doubt with the few ingots they'd managed to salvage. Considering the helicopter's short range, he thought it had to be making for the farm. Shortly thereafter, they heard the salvage boat raise its anchor, followed by propeller noises as it departed.

The submarine did not surface since it was still well within South African waters. However, the captain risked floating an antenna-buoy to give them immediate satellite communication. The communications officer made radio

120

contact through COMCEN, the Royal Navy's Communications Centre, who patched the call through to Sir John. Of course, the communication was scrambled.

VA started by commending Peace and Cherry for managing to salvage most of the gold and then asked where Van Rhyn was. Peace mentioned Van Rhyn flying back and forth between the salvage tug and his farm. Also, he volunteered ideas on what he thought Van Rhyn would do and that he was contemplating going after him, since he was sure Van Rhyn had to be on his Namibian farm. He told Sir John that Cherry had been seriously wounded and that she was in the sub's infirmary.

VA cleared his throat, but remained silent for a second.

"Sergeant Boxx's condition is of major concern and I'm awfully sorry to hear this. However, I'm sure she's receiving the best attention the Navy can give her. I think it's best she remains on board until the sub's returned home. Please tell her we all wish her a rapid recovery. What do you think we should do? Do you really believe going to the farm alone is a good idea?"

"Yes, sir, it is. It's clear that Van Rhyn is the kingpin — do away with him and hopefully, the pack of cards will collapse."

"You're right. Killing Van Rhyn will definitely bring them up short. Those bombs are another matter and as you say, we will have to deal with them, but how to do this without creating an international furore? However, that is something we will deal with on our side."

Seldom did VA ever imply the required demise of an enemy by using the word 'killing'; at worst he'd use the word 'eliminate'. This was definitely a new development; the man wasn't mincing his words or intentions. "What exactly do you propose to do about this man and his associates?" he then asked.

Peace proceeded to explain his plan.

"He'll have his daughter with him, you told me so," said VA. "What about her?"

Peace wondered whether he was aware of his sexual liaison with the woman. Briefly, a picture of Cherry in the infirmary came to Peace's mind, strengthening his determination. "I'll do whatever is necessary," he replied resolutely.

There was a second's silence.

"Yes, I believe you will. You've a satellite telephone. Make sure you stay in touch. Godspeed."

With that, VA ended the communication and Peace handed the instrument back to the sailor.

The captain smiled stiffly at Peace. "Well, Commander, I gather that's settled, you're going ashore. I'll have my men ferry you in an inflatable. It's already dark out there, so I doubt anyone will see you. I'd like to have my boat miles from here in deep water before daybreak. Shallow waters as treacherous as these make me nervous."

The submarine surfaced, rolling gently in the swell. Surprisingly for this area, the wind was light, but then it was past midnight. With a brief farewell and thanks, Peace left the submarine. The naval outboard attached to the stern of the submarine's Zodiac was muffled and surprisingly quiet. The helmsman expertly navigated the shallows, avoiding the incoming breakers, and deposited the boat high on the shore of the cove on the incoming wash of a small wave breaking before them. Peace jumped ashore clad only in borrowed civilian clothes. Nothing revealed that he'd just come from a British naval vessel.

Everything appeared to be as they had left it when they had last launched the Zodiac. He registered he had the whole bay and its small settlement to himself, as there was not a light to be seen.

Peace realised Van Rhyn had to know that part of the gold recovery from the seafloor had to have been directed from the shore, the Zodiac they had plucked from the ocean certainly proof thereof.

Van Rhyn did not strike him as the type to simply leave without trying to exact some sort of revenge. He wondered whether the magnate had not dropped a few men off when flying over the bungalows. Surely, he had to know the bungalows were being used as a base? They could kill anyone there, even burn the bungalows to the ground and no one would probably know for days or weeks since the place was so isolated.

Peace was not about to take a chance.

With the moon casting some light around him, he cautiously approached the bungalow, circled the structure once, and then entered armed with an automatic, a Browning Hi-Power 9x19mm Parabellum given to him by the submarine captain, in his hand. In this uninhabited remote area, doors were never locked. All was as they had left it. He purposely bent down and peered under the sofa. The sniper's rifle was still where he had hidden it. Clearly, nobody had been there.

He hesitated just before entering the kitchen as the faintest of sounds came from somewhere near the bedroom area. He froze entirely.

Moonlight shone through the open curtains in the lounge. There was no way he was going down that passage and making himself a perfect target by being backlit. Well, not until he was sure he was alone.

Keeping a wary eye on the passage, he slowly made his way to the kitchen where he knew there were three kerosene lanterns and a flashlight on the windowsill. He lit two lanterns, which cast sufficient light to illuminate the lounge and kitchen area.

Peace found a dark shadow and took up position. *Do I wait it out or flush him out?* He knew all the windows were barred, and there were only two exits — the front and back doors. Whoever was there had to use the passage.

A quarter of an hour passed and he had heard no further sounds. It was obvious he would have to flush the person out, but how?

Moments later, an idea struck him. He locked the front door and extracted the key. The door was sturdy and it would be difficult to break out through it.

In the kitchen, he used a knife to unscrew a hose-clamp around the plastic pipe from the gas-bottle to the gas stove. He opened the valve and worked the round grip on the top of the valve loose, leaving just the shaft exposed. He grabbed the pipe and pulled it off the valve, and was rewarded with the hiss of escaping gas. He quickly left the kitchen through the back door and closed it behind him.

Initially, he considered shouting a warning, not yet convinced the intruder was one of Van Rhyn's group. He was pretty sure the intruder would have realised he was up to something but, of course, probably would never have guessed he proposed blowing the building sky-high. He knew from past experience that when you have the upper hand in a stand-off, waiting was the best course of action — invariably they would make the first mistake.

A minute or so later, something unintelligible was shouted from the interior of the bungalow. This was repeated seconds later.

"English, please," Peace shouted and shifted his position but still remained close to the door.

"I'm coming out. Don't shoot!" he heard. The accent indicated the man was an Afrikaner.

"Just do everything slowly," Peace shouted back.

He watched the back door open. A man stepped out with his arms raised. He was a White, dressed in what appeared to be a khaki uniform and canvas boots. He also wore a type of pea-jacket.

Peace stepped out from behind a brick-built barbeque.

"Stop — don't move. Keep your arms raised," Peace said.

With his automatic trained on the man, he slowly walked round to his back and patted him down for weapons. He removed a military issue automatic from the man's belt-holster.

"Were you dropped off here from Van Rhyn's helicopter?"

The man did not reply and instead stared sullenly at Peace.

"Listen, you better talk," Peace said firing a shot into the ground between the man's feet.

The man instinctively jumped with a yelp. *"Moenie skiet nie!*[13] "he shouted.

Peace raised the pistol and pointed it at the man's head.

"Yes, he dropped me off. I was to wait for you to return from the sea. I was ordered to shoot you."

"Shoot me," Peace mused. "Didn't seem to work out, did it? Tell me, how many gold bars did they find?"

"Not many, about fourteen, I think," the man stammered.

For a brief moment Peace felt a feeling of satisfaction — fourteen gold bars were only a fraction of the load. That is, if the number of gold bars mentioned at the initial London briefing was correct.

"What to do now?" Peace asked.

The man was now a caricature of fear. "Are you going to kill me?"

Peace looked left and right — first at the empty sea and then the barren desert, knowing that the dune sea started a mile to the east. There really was nowhere to escape to.

---

13. Don't shoot!

"If I don't, the desert will kill you within a day or two."

Peace could see his prisoner probably thought that his last moments had arrived, since his bottom lip was quivering and his hands shaking.

"Start walking — don't look back," Peace said. "Now!"

The man turned and shuffled off, not turning around.

"If I see you again, there'll be no talking — I'll shoot immediately. You'd better remember that," Peace shouted and watched the man for five minutes until he disappeared into the darkness.

Chapter Fifteen

Peace reversed the Land Cruiser out into the open and activated the satellite phone as well as switching on the scrambler attached to it. He punched in a number that he had memorised and was soon talking to a colleague in MI6, one of those in the communications centre deep within the bowels of the Victoria Embankment in London where phone calls and transmissions were monitored around the clock.

He requested that he be given exact coordinates for the farm owned by Van Rhyn. If they did not have these on hand, they were to do whatever was necessary to get these as soon as possible. He advised his colleague that the coming and going of aircraft and helicopters would have been noticed in that area and that the whereabouts of such a farm had to be common knowledge amongst the locals as well as the rangers of the Department of Fauna and Flora at the nearby Etosha Pan Game Reserve.

Besides, the civilian flights to the farm by the Van Rhyn family would have required the air controllers in the country to know its exact coordinates. The location of a farm owned by such an affluent family could hardly be kept a secret in such a sparsely populated area. He ended by saying he would make contact again during the course of the next day.

*

He knew the general direction in which the farm lay and at first light loaded the quad cycle into the rear of the vehicle, with some difficulty. He strapped the Heckler and Koch automatic in its special holster to his thigh. Both the MP5 machine pistol that fired NATO 5.56mm calibre ammunition and the sniper's rifle rolled in a blanket, he placed on the rear seat. He thought it unlikely in this remote region and the isolated roads on which he'd be travelling that he'd be stopped and searched by any police or army patrols. He took a rug off a bed and used this to cover the weapons.

The road was no more than a track that led over a stretch of dunes, disappearing and reappearing in the undulations as it headed eastward. The sandy coastal plain then gave way to kopjes — hilly outcrops of rock dotting the desert — then into rocky terrain, all devoid of vegetation. In the distance, a good fifty miles away, he could see a range of mountains on the horizon. They were the home of the Ohahimbas, a nomadic tribe always on the move with their cattle and goats in search of grazing. He was making for Sesfontein on the Khowarib River, which would be his first stop. The only way there was to follow the track in the dry riverbed, which wound its way through the hills and mountains to the sea.

As he approached the low mountains, he often had to resort to four-wheel-drive as the sand was thick and threatened to bog down the heavy vehicle. The sun beat down relentlessly — the temperature outside the vehicle was well in the high thirties and the vehicle's air-conditioning barely able to cope.

He arrived in Sesfontein just after four in the afternoon. The settlement was no more than a small collection of a few flat-roofed buildings, which lined the road for a short distance. It had derived its name from its six fountains. The abundant water and shallow water table had created an oasis of green and trees, which was in stark contrast to the surrounding semi-desert. The country's national flag fluttered on a solitary flagpole in front of one of the buildings, which had to be the police outpost. At the sound of the vehicle, a few faces appeared in the doorways, no doubt curious to see who the new arrival was.

He climbed out of the vehicle and stretched to ease his cramped muscles. A uniformed police officer in blue shorts and tunic approached from the station.

"Dag, meneer[14], *"* he said in greeting, his dark tanned face breaking into a smile.

Peace realised that he was being greeted, and responded with a, "Good day, sir."

"Oh, you don't speak Afrikaans," said the officer in broken English. "Where are you from? I see you've come from the west, you know, the Skeleton Coast."

"Terrace Bay, actually."

"Have you got papers?"

"I have." Peace pulled the permit from his breast pocket.

"You are alone?" the man asked, clearly surprised to see that Peace was not accompanied.

"Yes, I'm alone. I'm on my way to Otjivasondo, a farm near the Etosha Park where I'm meeting a few friends. We were two, but my companion returned to Swakopmund with another crowd when she became ill. That was at Terrace on the coast."

The officer appeared satisfied with the reply and handed back his papers, wishing him a good journey. Peace drove the Land Cruiser to the petrol pumps in front of the trading store and asked the attendant to fill the tank and his spare containers.

He tried the name Van Rhyn on those in the trading store but they just looked blankly at him. Anyway, it wasn't surprising since most couldn't speak English. Afrikaans and an Ovambo dialect were the only languages spoken here. He deliberately did not ask the police officer about Van Rhyn, as this would have seemed strange coming from an overseas tourist. With the vehicle's tank and containers filled, he left, following the road east, which was in a much better condition than the track he had previously followed. It would take him to Outjo, in which vicinity he thought the Van Rhyn's farm might be.

He stopped that evening in Kamanjab, about thirty miles south of the Etosha Pan Reserve's southern border. This was bush country and it teemed with wild animals in the form of antelope, lions, cheetahs, and elephants. The

---

14. Good day, sir.

town was larger than Sesfontein and boasted a small hotel. It was a thatched building, the interior having no ceiling but rather a maze of crisscrossed creosoted poles supporting the thatch. The smell of creosote still lingered.

He needed a beer and headed to the bar. To his amazement, he saw that it dispensed a local draught. He ordered a one-litre tall glass, which was served by a huge Black dressed in a white cotton tunic shirt. Condensation from the cold beer was already beading on the glass. *Thank God! This is heaven*, he thought and glad that for once it wasn't tepid British beer. Too damn hot here! He drank deeply with relish and wiped away the white moustache of foam from his upper lip with the back of his hand.

He looked at the other occupants who he had observed on entering the bar. Two men were at the bar counter, evidently game wardens from the way they were dressed. At a nearby table sat a family — obviously new arrivals in the sun, given their complexions. They were speaking in German.

A white man dressed in khaki entered the bar through a door behind it. "Are you looking for accommodation?" he asked.

Why not, thought Peace. He booked in and paid the equivalent of four-hundred Rand in British pounds.

A little later he partook in some dinner, which was typically German with smoked warthog steaks, boiled potatoes, and red cabbage. He ate it at the bar, as did the two game wardens with whom he had struck up a conversation. Eventually, one of the men got round to asking the question he knew he would be asked, "Where are you heading?"

"To the Etosha Pan. I'm going to the Namutoni rest camp." He knew that to be on the eastern side of the saltpan.

"Be damn careful! A small herd of elephants has moved south and the cows we saw were in season. That makes them, and the bulls, unpredictable."

"I will be — don't want to tangle with them. Incidentally," Peace said, "while in Jo'burg, I met a Mr Van Rhyn. He mentioned that he had a farm near the Pan. Have you ever heard of him?"

The two men looked at each other. It seemed that the question had evoked some private communication between them.

"Yes, we know of him," said the second man. "There's a farm near Gagarus just on the Pan's southern border, maybe seventy kilometres from here, which is said to belong to the family. But I don't think you want to go there. They're not known to be friendly to visitors. The farm is fenced ten-foot high on three sides and only the side to the game reserve is open. You can't miss it — it's the only ten-foot fence around here and the farm is the largest by far in these parts. You're not planning to go there, are you? They make a point of dissuading visitors."

"No, no. I'm merely curious — he told me so much about the place."

Thankfully, they dropped the subject shortly after and reverted to the game reserve and animals.

At least he now knew where to find the farm.

Later that night, he used the satellite phone again, only to learn that MI6 had still had not found it or any coordinates. He suggested they stop the search as he had a good idea of where to go.

*

It was around midday the next day when he arrived in Gagarus. The hamlet was comprised solely of a large farmhouse with outbuildings and some huts, which appeared to be occupied by locals. He made enquiries and was told that the Van Rhyn's farm was a neighbouring property about twenty-five kilometres away. The farm was known as *Vrede*, which was Dutch for *Peace*. A local pointed out the single track that led to it and warned him of the elephants. He then babbled something in a strange language, with Peace not understanding a word and so gestured that he did not understand.

"He's telling you about the owners — they breed hyenas. He says you need to be careful," a voice behind him said.

Peace turned to confront a white man clad in khaki shorts and a shirt, his feet in calf-high boots, his socks folded down over the tops. He wore a felt bush hat with a strip of fur around the base of the crown. He had to be at least sixty, his face lined and tanned. A pair of rheumy blue eyes squinting against the sun appraised him, and there was a pipe clenched between the man's teeth. The face seemed friendly enough.

"Hi," said Peace.

"Hello." The man stuck out his hand. They shook and introduced themselves. Peace gave his name as Thornton.

"I understand you want to travel to the farm *Vrede*? I wouldn't recommend that. People out there are not known to be friendly and I know the owner is there. I heard his helicopter fly in a day or so ago. Strange things have happened there. As was said — they breed hyenas, or so rumour has it. The locals are terrified of the place as they say the hyenas are man-eaters, but then again most of us around here know the locals are superstitious."

Peace knew otherwise. "Funny that you should say so," he said. "I met one of the Van Rhyns in Johannesburg; he seemed a decent enough chap."

"Don't you believe it. People have disappeared. The police were brought in but nothing ever came of it."

"Well, that's not where I'm going. How do I get to Otjivasondo?"

The man gave him directions, and Peace drove off.

When he was within a few miles past Gagarus, he pulled off the track and drove until he found a thick copse of thorn trees, which he hoped would conceal the vehicle from passers-by. His passage spooked a small herd of kudu that had been standing in the shade of a large tree — they fled, leaping over the bush in long bounds, their corkscrew horns laid back parallel to their backs.

The terrain was flat; the outer rim of the pan from which the game reserve had derived its name was only a few miles away. The area was densely dotted with thorn trees, most only a little taller than a man, with the odd large camel-thorn tree between. At intervals, he saw the occasional baobab tree, but none very large.

It was stiflingly hot. He opened all the windows to let what little breeze there was waft through the vehicle. He let down the back of the seat, made himself as comfortable as he could, and slept.

Chapter Sixteen

Peace opened his eyes. It was late afternoon and the setting sun still emitted enough heat to make it stifling hot. Not a breath of wind was around to cool him down. He was soaked in sweat, which had even pooled in the hollow of his throat. He was annoyed; he had overslept. He should have been ready to move out.

Trying to ignore the heat, he removed the quad-cycle from the rear of the vehicle; the exertion had him breaking out with perspiration from every pore. He then stripped off his clothing, and from his haversack drew out camouflage fatigues, the material a mottled mixture of yellow, brown and grey. He put this on and pulled a cap of similar material onto his head. He slung the sniper rifle over his shoulder and let the MP5 hang from its strap around his neck. Thereafter he drank thirstily from his water bottle before hanging it from his belt. Using the GPS, he took an exact reading of his position and recorded this in the instrument.

The quad-cycle started at the first press of the button. It was powered by a four-stroke engine and fitted with an effective muffler, but he knew he would have to abandon it well before the *Vrede* homestead, as the sound of the engine would carry far in the bush. In the rapidly fading twilight, he rode back to the road and slowly made his way towards Gagarus, but ready to pull off the road should he encounter any other vehicles.

When about a mile from the Gagarus homestead, he veered off the road and slowly rode through the bush to where he thought he'd connect with the track that led from Gagarus to *Vrede*. It took a quarter hour before he came upon it, and was surprised to see it was in fair condition. He swung onto the road and slowly approached the Van Rhyn farm boundary.

From a distance, he saw the gate, barely visible in the near darkness. When he approached it, he found it wasn't actually a gate but an entrance barred by a huge cattle-grid — a rectangular concrete pit running diagonally across the road with steel poles laid longitudinally across it about four or five inches apart, designed to prevent any animal from trying to cross. This had been built between two pillars constructed of rough rock and concrete, which served as anchors for the ten-foot fence. There was no other way through the fence other than over the cattle-grid.

What the hell, he thought. He let out the clutch, drove towards the cattle gate, and crossed it with a rumble of wheels. A signboard at the entrance indicated a distance of twelve kilometres to the *Vrede* homestead. He switched on the twin headlights fitted to the front frame, keeping a careful eye on the odometer, meaning to stop and cut the engine well before reaching the house. He kept his speed down, with the engine just a tad above an idle, and the sound muted. The plan was to stop two miles from the house and proceed on foot since the house would be well lit at this early evening hour.

He saw their eyes reflected in the headlights before he actually saw the animals. It was a pride of lions just starting out on their nocturnal hunt; two females crossing the track, the one trailed by two cubs. A little further on there was another set of eyes. He thought it could be another lioness. He knew the lioness with cubs could be unpredictable and wondered whether they had ever encountered a quad-cycle before. He stopped when he saw the lioness with cubs take a few steps forward and assume a crouch position. Not wanting to provoke her any further, he killed the engine but left the lights on. The lions watched him for a few minutes and then slowly resumed their journey. He waited until he could no longer see them before restarting the quad. Carefully studying his surroundings, he made a note of his current position in case he was forced to make a hasty retreat from the farmstead. Running into the pride while trying to flee Van Rhyn and his men would be doubly dangerous.

His journey proceeded without any further hitches, although he did have to cross a few cattle-grids — the farm was obviously divided into camps. He wondered how the animals could migrate between the camps.

The terrain was flat; there was no hillock or ridge from which he could survey the surrounding bush. Again, he stopped and switched off the light and waited until his eyes had adjusted to the darkness.

The sky was clear, and the night filled with stars and the faint light of a three-quarter moon. After five minutes, he resumed his cautious journey. Now that his eyes had adjusted, the going was relatively easy, since the ground was free of rock, and the track hard-baked ground covered with a thin layer of sand. Unexpectedly, he came upon a small herd of kudu. With a few staccato barks, they immediately took flight through the bush, the sound of breaking twigs and branches continuing long after they'd disappeared. In the stillness of the night, the sound was similar to the faint crackle of gunfire.

The first sign of a light became discernible through the bush; it had to be at least a half-mile away. He would prefer to have been not quite so close, but the scattered bush had hidden the light. He stopped the quad, switched off the engine and dismounted. With the gears in neutral he pushed the quad along the track, wanting to get it as close to the farmhouse as possible should he need to make a hasty retreat.

Other lights came into view, and as he approached these, he realised they were from fires in front of small cluster bungalows — accommodation for workers, built along the road. There was movement around the fires. The lights further on were those of the homestead, and a row of windows was already lit. Clearly, the Van Rhyn family was at home.

He pushed the quad off the road and hid it behind a copse of dense bush and scrub. A high fence, reinforced with cable, surrounded the house, bungalows and gardens, no doubt to keep out predators and elephants. Here too, the entrance was rather a cattle-grid instead of an actual gate. He crossed it and walked parallel to the road, keeping the bush between him and the workers' bungalows. However, he was so close that he could clearly hear those outside their bungalows talking to one another. As he neared the house, he saw an enormous baobab tree. This was exceptionally tall and dwarfed the homestead, and was the perfect spot from which to observe the house. Luckily, a rope ladder hung down the side from above, no doubt to provide easy access to a vantage point to observe the surrounding bushveld.

Climbing while carrying the sniper's rifle and MP5 was cumbersome but he knew that he would need the weapons. Eventually, he made it to where the rope ladder had been fixed to the tree. To his surprise he found that a small platform had been built there, complete with a safety railing. He removed the weapons, placed them on the plank floor, and sat down to take a good look at his surroundings. The night was still pleasantly warm, and there was no need for any additional outer clothing, the thin material of the fatigues adequate.

The night was typical of the bushveld. There was the occasional chirr of an insect and the monotonous squeak of metal upon metal as the light breeze spun a windmill-operated water pump nearby. He could just discern the low throb of an engine — this had to be driving the generator that provided electric power to the house as Van Rhyn wasn't the type to use paraffin lamps and candles.

The faint strains of music and the sound of female laughter drifted from the house. The house was about a hundred and fifty yards away. The house's veranda stretched the entire length of the front of the house. It was ablaze with lights. A three-foot wall surrounded the porch and a fly-screen had been erected from the top of the wall to the roof, requiring anyone who approached the house to enter through a double fly-screen door that led to the actual front door. The front door stood wide open, as did another pair of French doors, further along through which he could see into a dining room. There had to be near a dozen people seated at the table. He peered through the night-glasses and recognised Lady Jocelyn and her stepdaughter Janet sitting next to each other. The others, mostly men, were unknown to him.

He carefully inspected the surrounding garden to establish how well it was guarded, but there appeared to be no sentries. The Van Rhyns obviously believed they were perfectly safe here. After all, this had been their property for many years and crime in this part of the country was seldom encountered.

Looking back at the house, he saw the diners push back their chairs and leave the table. Suddenly, the huge bulk of Van Rhyn himself appeared in the doorway that led from the dining room to the porch through a pair of French doors. He paused in the doorway where he stopped and lit a cigar, before taking a seat on a sofa on the porch. He suddenly gave a loud whistle, and from behind the house two huge dogs came rushing round the corner of the building, their gait more a slink than a run. Peace suddenly realised what they were. *Bloody hell! Those are hyenas!* Van Rhyn rose from the sofa and opened the screen door for the animals. They slunk in and nuzzled his legs. He patted each on the head.

The man was an enigma, what with tame hyenas, stolen nuclear weapons, wealth beyond the wildest dreams of most, but hell-bent on retaining power over the Blacks at any cost. Peace was certain that, if confronted with a world dominated by Blacks, Van Rhyn would not hesitate to cast the world into a new holocaust by using a nuclear bomb — even if this meant his own demise.

Fortunately, the peace talks in Namibia had been successful, the Cubans and South African forces withdrawing from conflict and the country taking the first steps towards independence. Clearly, de Klerk who was a man of vision and with him, Mandela, who was known to be a man of peace, could avoid a civil war. However, why the theft of gold and what seemed the relentless purchase of gold mining shares? What did Van Rhyn hope to achieve? Did Van Rhyn really want to control the gold mining industry in South Africa and would this not merely be the beginning of things to come? The South Africa he had grown up in was obviously the South Africa he wanted to retain. The man was a bloody megalomaniac. Van Rhyn and his kind were most certainly not open to negotiation. There was no alternative, and that was why his presence here was justified. Peace had to believe. He had seen the bombs and aircraft at Copperton.

The sound of loud voices interrupted his reverie. He focused on the veranda and was surprised to see that Margaret Langton-Van Rhyn had also stepped out onto the porch. She was casually dressed and wearing shorts. It appeared the whole family was here. He'd not expected this. That certainly complicated matters — he had no intention of stealthily entering the house and murdering Van Rhyn in the bed that he shared with his wife. That wasn't his style.

The two stood facing each other, and while he could not make out what was said, it was apparent that they were arguing — she was gesticulating and her voice was raised, while he stood stoically facing her, his arms folded across his chest, taking the occasional puff from his cigar.

Then her voice rose higher and he clearly heard her shout, "No! I won't be part of it! I won't allow myself to be associated with anything like that, and least of all with you. You're crazy! You and your people are madmen. My God, what you propose is murder! I'm not listening to this — I'm leaving right now!" She was clearly distraught.

She swung round and strode back into the house. Van Rhyn did not react, but stood peering out towards the garden, still smoking his cigar, the two hyenas at his feet. Then he appeared to come to a decision. He flicked the cigar through the screen-door where it landed on the lawn in a shower of sparks, then he turned and entered the house with the two animals following him. Finally, silence descended on the homestead, with only the occasional movement as somebody passed a lit window.

It was just past nine-thirty when he heard a car engine being fired up. This came from behind the house. Three men dressed in identical khaki bush wear stormed out of the front door, all armed with automatic rifles.

Although it was dark, it was apparent they were white men. One issued orders in Afrikaans in a loud voice. They spread themselves across the single-track road that led from behind the house, their automatic rifles at the ready. Seconds later, a Toyota Land Cruiser pickup sped round the corner, its headlights falling on the three men who immediately let off a fusillade of shots. None struck the vehicle, and it quite obvious the trio had purposely fired high above it. The vehicle skidded to a halt before them in a cloud of dust. One of the men, who appeared to be in charge, stepped forward, yanked the driver's door open, and reached inside. Peace heard the shrill scream of a woman's protests as she was dragged from the vehicle. He was shocked to see that it was Van Rhyn's stepdaughter. She had changed, and was now dressed in slacks. Two of the men grasped her by the arms, but not roughly — it seemed they were taking care not to hurt her. Van Rhyn emerged from the front of the house.

"God!" she screamed. "You let them fire at me! You're an insane bastard!"

Peace heard the loud reply. "It was harmless. They fired over your head."

Then Lady Jocelyn and Janet came running out of the house. Lady Jocelyn stood between her daughter and her husband. "What's going on? What was all that shooting about?" she screamed.

Peace thought that Lady Jocelyn seemed to have been drinking; she appeared slightly unsteady on her feet, tottering once, and her stepdaughter grabbing her to steady her.

"Mother, this madman had his men shoot at me!"

The elder woman swung round to face her husband. She said something that Peace couldn't hear, but she was obviously angry as she jerked her arm away when Van Rhyn tried to take it.

This evidently irritated him, for he raised his voice again. "Your daughter decided she was leaving us. At this critical stage, I cannot allow it."

Critical stage? Peace wondered what the man meant.

"We leave tomorrow morning for Copperton. That's final and I mean all of us!" Van Rhyn was still shouting. To the men he said, "Take her inside and keep an eye on her."

More heated exchanges followed, most of them inaudible to Peace, but eventually they all, except Van Rhyn, went back into the house. He remained, drew another cigar from the breast pocket of his shirt, and lit it. For a long while, he stood there smoking and staring into the night, the two hyenas at his side.

Peace brought the sniper's rifle slowly to his shoulder, peered through the telescopic sight, and drew a bead on the man's head. It would be quite simple; he could kill the man right here and now. Then he realised that he'd have to get down the tree, which required precious time, making a quick escape difficult. *Just bide your time*, he thought, but already a new plan was beginning to form in his mind.

Clearly, the young daughter was not the enemy; she was a victim and rather powerless, at that. What did they propose to do with her? Whatever it was, it couldn't be good.

The young woman meant nothing to Peace, but he knew that Van Rhyn would only allow those whom he could trust to be close to him, and they would have to be committed to his cause. This clearly endangered her. He didn't think the magnate would be overly concerned about his wife's view on the matter. Peace realised that he'd have to get Van Rhyn's stepdaughter out of there.

Chapter Seventeen

For the next hour, he watched the house carefully. He saw the young daughter pass a window and take a seat in front of a dressing table. When a man brought up a wicker chair and placed this near a window out on the porch, and then sat down, his assault rifle propped up against the wall, he realised that this had to be her room. He recalled Van Rhyn had ordered her to be guarded.

An hour later, he slowly climbed down the baobab tree using the ladder. He would have to abandon one of his weapons; it had to be the sniper's rifle. He hid it in some shrubbery in the garden, and then slowly circled the house, keeping a fair distance from it, and keeping a sharp lookout for guards. He was passing behind the house when his eye caught a brief reflection. He approached it stealthily and on closer examination, he realised this came from the polished fuselage of an aircraft. It was a small twin-engine executive jet, probably a Learjet, not able to seat more than eight. *This must be how they get around the country.* It was parked in front of a corrugated-iron hangar, the doors of which were closed. It was strange that the aircraft had not been parked inside for the night, then Peace remembered the helicopter. He thought it had to be in the hangar.

Suddenly, his attention was drawn to a movement he saw out of the corner of his eye and immediately focused on the source. Soon he made out it was a guard seated with his back to the hangar doors and at his feet lay a large dog. *No, wait — it's another hyena. I wonder if it'll pick up my scent if I move downwind?*

The hyena suddenly emitted a half bark, half whoop sound, and turned to face Peace's direction. At first, the guard ignored the animal's restlessness and tried to silence it, but when it continued pacing back and forth pulling on the leash, the guard stood and slowly approached, his weapon at the ready.

Peace realised there'd be no surprising the man with the animal preceding him. Then another hyena appeared, already clearly alert to his presence. If he fired the MP5 machine pistol, would others hear it? It could be fitted with a silencer, but how effective would it be firing the 5.56mm NATO ammunition? What was he to do? The guard was getting nearer, making no effort to disguise his approach. The animal strained on its leash, while the other trotted by his side.

There was a collection of various pieces of agricultural machinery in the yard behind the house. He hid behind some unrecognisable farming implement, which put him no further than a hundred yards from the hangar. Hastily, he affixed the silencer and selected single-shot fire on the firing selector. *The dogs first*, he thought. They posed the bigger danger.

He peered through the night scope and put a bullet through the leading hyena's head. It made no sound and immediately fell to the ground. For a second the guard was transfixed, but his rifle had come up to point in the general direction of Peace's hiding place. The MP5's report had been louder than he had anticipated. Fleetingly, he wondered whether anyone in the house had heard it, but he had no alternative — he had to shoot again. The shot hit the guard in the neck. The man clutched at his throat with both hands, gagging as he did so, and released his hold on the leash.

Peace swung the machine pistol round to take the hyena out, but as he was about to squeeze the trigger, a furred shape careered into him, knocking him down, the MP5 still in his hand. He could smell the animal — it was the putrid odour of rotting flesh. It lunged at his face with its vicious jaws. He dropped the rifle and grabbed it by the throat — its vile breath overpowering as it snarled and twisted its head, its lips curled back to reveal massive teeth as it tried to close its jaws on his forearms. With one hand, he grasped the chain around the animal's neck and twisted it, forcing it into a chokehold. With the other hand, he wrestled the Sig from the holster strapped to his right leg.

Although the animal had bitten his forearm, it had not managed to get it

141

between its jaws, only the flesh had been gnawed. He jammed the Heckler and Koch hard up against its side and pulled the trigger. With a muffled report, skin, blood, and bone exploded from the animal. It dropped to the ground, jerking its limbs in its final death throes. As the animal had fallen from his grasp, the chain had come away in his hand.

For a brief moment, he just lay there trying to regain his breath.

He brought the chain he'd removed from the animal's neck closer to his face. As he examined it, he noticed it was fashioned to resemble a bicycle chain. It was made of gold! Its weight was sufficient to confirm that. He got to his feet and moved to where the other fallen hyena lay. It too had a chain round its neck, and it too was gold. He realised that he had a good few thousand pounds Sterling wrapped around his hand.

God, he thought, *the man must really love these animals*! He seemed to recall that they were not the first tame hyenas he had heard of. Why anybody would want to keep an animal that stank so abominably was beyond him.

His forearm arm was bleeding, not profusely, but it needed attention. He ripped off part of the dead man's cotton shirt and tore it into strips, which he tied round his arm to staunch the bleeding. The bastard was dead and wouldn't miss his shirt. Grabbing the MP5 again, he approached the house, keeping a sharp lookout for other guards and hyenas. He slowly made his way around the house, keeping away from the porch. The lush lawn underfoot allowed him to move silently. The occupants seemed to have retired for the night even though a light was still on in one bedroom, which had two windows that overlooked the porch. It had to be the main bedroom used by Van Rhyn and his wife; the window where he had seen Margaret pass had been further along. While he thought the shots loud, it appeared no one had taken notice.

He moved away from the master bedroom towards a corner of the house. He pushed his way through the tall foliage of plants in a flowerbed bordering the veranda until he was standing next to the house's foundations, and the locked screen that enclosed the porch in front of him. From the sheath looped to his belt, he removed a hunting knife and cut first a horizontal then a vertical slit into the mesh. He folded the flap back and studied the length of the porch through the hole. There was nobody about. The guard who had previously been there had gone.

He started to worm his way through the hole, cursing silently as his weapons knocked against objects, aware that any unusual sound would immediately alert a trained ear, and Van Rhyn's men were undoubtedly well trained!

Eventually he stood upright, clutching his MP5, and gazed at the expanse of the large veranda. This was scattered with an assortment of cane furniture and glass-topped coffee tables strewn with magazines and newspapers, clearly a place where the family relaxed. The windows were the old-fashioned sash variety with wooden frames. Most of these were open, a faint breeze nudging at the drawn curtains. He approached the wall of the house and flattened himself against it, then shuffled along it towards the window that he thought belonged to Margaret's room.

Peace was one of those men who believed God only helped those who helped themselves, but on this occasion, it appeared that he was lucky; the window's sash was raised. The curtains were partially open, revealing a large gap. Another godsend.

He crouched down below the sill and listened for any sounds from within. There were none. He rose and peered through a gap in the curtains. He could just make out a large bed on which a figure lay, partially covered by a sheet. The blonde hair was a giveaway; this was indeed Margaret Langton-Van Rhyn's room. Margaret was now important to him; she had to be a source of valuable information and with her evident hostility towards Van Rhyn and his goons, she might just be the right person with whom to speak.

He placed the MP5 on the veranda's floor below the windowsill; this would be the only way he'd be leaving the room. Leaving through the bedroom's door wasn't an option. He crept over the sill, the soft rubber soles of his boots making no sound. He knew he was silhouetted against the light of the window, but she seemed fast asleep, lying partially on her side, turned slightly away from him. He moved to the bed and with one swift movement, he clamped his hand over her mouth, and pulled her against his body, ready to restrain her if she tried to struggle free. That was exactly what she did. He was surprised at her strength. She tried to force a scream through his fingers but only managed a slightly muffled squeak.

"Shut up and be quiet!" he hissed. "I won't hurt you."

She continued to squirm.

"I'm here to help! Shut up and stop struggling, otherwise I'll have to clip you," he snarled with tightly controlled emotion.

She stopped. With an arm around her neck and his hand clamped over her mouth, he reached over and switched on the dressing table light. "It's me, Lord Digby. Listen, I'm here to help you. If you understand, just nod your head. If you scream, I'll have to knock you unconscious."

He felt her trying to nod her head. Slowly he released his hand but left it an inch from her mouth. There was outrage and some bewilderment in her eyes.

"How dare you break into my room like this?" she spluttered indignantly.

He noticed that she kept her voice down.

He let her go. She remained on the bed and turned to face him, propped up on one elbow, staring at him. Her white silk nightdress gaped open, partially revealing her breasts. Involuntarily he glanced at them. She did not miss this and hastily closed the plunging neckline. "Don't be a pig!" she hissed.

He was ready with a retort but decided that this was not the moment.

"I don't need your help. What on earth are you doing here, anyway?" she asked and then hastily added, "You'd better switch off the light."

"You're in danger here," he said.

"Not as much danger as you are in now. What on earth are you doing here, sneaking around, and breaking into our house?"

"Don't give me that. I know the score. I know your stepfather has too much at stake to allow you to shoot your mouth off. I saw what happened when you tried to leave. He can't have you free to move around as you wish while you threaten to reveal his best-kept secrets."

"I didn't do that! In any case, he wouldn't dare hurt me. My mother will see to that."

Perhaps what he'd said disturbed her, for she drew the sheet around her body as if it might afford her some protection. Her blonde hair was in disarray and she'd removed her makeup, but was clearly still a very beautiful woman. She seemed older than one would expect for one still studying at university.

144

He heard the sound of approaching footsteps outside the room. Peace quickly switched off the light and ducked down behind the bed, away from the bedroom door. There was a timid knock on the door.

"Are you all right, Miss?" a male voice asked in a harsh Afrikaans accent.

"I'm fine. Just go away!"

There followed what seemed a hesitant silence, and then the sound of receding footsteps.

"That was a guard!" she whispered in his ear, so close he felt her breath.

"So I imagine," he replied with a hint of sarcasm. "Listen, you've got to come away with me. Van Rhyn will kill you. He doesn't have a choice. You obviously know too much, and from I witnessed this evening, it seems you are against whatever he's planning. I don't think he's the type who'd be unduly concerned at your mother's reaction. He's going to fly you, by force if necessary, to Copperton tomorrow morning. The place is like a fortress, you'll never get out."

"You saw what happened this evening?"

"I did."

"Copperton. I know the place. I've been there, quite often, in fact. It seems to hold an attraction for my stepfather. Lord knows why. It's an awful place in the middle of nowhere."

It was evident she knew very little about the place. She probably believed it was no more than a mine and a haven for right-wingers.

"How many guards are there here?" he asked.

"Three. One inside and two outside. One of them also keeps an eye on the aircraft and helicopter. Watch out for the hyenas."

"Rest assured, that guard is no longer a problem, neither are his hyenas."

She said nothing in response to this remark. However, he did notice her eyes widen. She was staring at the MP5 dangling from the strap around his neck and the automatic strapped to his thigh. Did she realise the man was dead, he wondered.

"You're here to kill him, aren't you?" she said. "Who are you? I don't think you're Lord Digby; you have my stepfather fooled. He spoke quite highly of you. He might believe you're Lord Digby, but I don't. In fact, I've always found you quite strange, especially after our discussion at my stepfather's house after you rudely shooed-off General Booyens' aide-de-camp."

She is smart, he thought, remembering the incident and in particular, how glad she was he'd got the man to leave them.

"Come on, we need to get out of here," he said brusquely.

"What about the guards?"

"Don't worry; we're going out of the window, the same way I came in. Get dressed, but for God's sake, be quiet! If they realise you've escaped, they'll be seriously pissed off."

She swung her legs off the bed and switched on a night-lamp.

"Don't look," she warned. He turned from her and then heard her rummaging in a chest of drawers, followed by the sound of her dressing.

"It's okay now," she said.

He turned and looked. She was wearing jeans and a dark blue knitted cotton top. She had a bag over her shoulder with a short bush jacket draped over the bag.

"Forget the bag," he said.

"No, I'm a woman. There are things I need."

"Okay," he hissed in exasperation. He grabbed her by the hand and pulled her towards the open window.

Quietly, they clambered through the window onto the porch. She pointed to the end of the veranda, indicating that it was the safest route to follow. He let her lead, but still clutched her hand. She led him around an end-corner of the veranda, and they crept along the side of the house, heading towards the back. Her soft-soled, slip-on sandals made no sound. Slowly and with great caution, she pushed open the fly-screen door. Fortunately, it opened without a sound and they passed through.

He pointed to the baobab tree. She nodded and led the way. When they reached its base, he retrieved the sniper's rifle from the nearby brush and handed it to her. "You'd better hold this. I know it's heavy, but I might just need it."

She took it from him without a word.

Suddenly, out of the corner of his eye, he detected movement. He swung round. Two hyenas were loping towards them, their intentions clear as they emitted their eerie half bark, half yowls.

146

"Shaka! Sheila!" Margaret shouted. The hyenas immediately recognised her and stopped in front of them. The female dropped to its haunches and whimpered, then rose and rubbed its body against her leg.

"My God, we're lucky. The damn thing likes you," said Peace.

The next instant the surrounds of the house were bathed in bright light as all corner security lights were switched on. The trees, bushes, and shrubs in the garden cast long black shadows. Although Peace and Margaret had moved far enough away as to be out of range of the direct beams of light, they were still sufficiently close for any movement to be detected should they step out of the shadows. He heard the fly-screen door bang shut and noticed two men emerge, both cradling military carbines, the long magazines that protruded from the rifles easily recognisable.

From inside the house, something was shouted in Afrikaans.

"They've discovered I'm missing," she said.

"Come on, it's time to run."

He pulled her in the direction of where he'd hidden the quad. The hyenas seemed confused, turning and loping towards the house, then hesitating and turning back to Margaret.

"They're calling them," she said.

The animals, alerted by the call, appeared to make a decision and with a few departing whoops bounded off towards the house. Just then, Van Rhyn stepped into the light. There was no mistaking the size of the man. He was buckling his belt. Peace grabbed the sniper's rifle from her, flicked off the safety catch, and brought it to his shoulder, swinging the crosshairs of the scope towards the Afrikaner.

Suddenly, he was struck by a blow from the side. Margaret had thrown herself at him. "No!" she hissed. "He's my mother's husband. You can't do this!"

Peace was angry. He shoved her away roughly and brought the rifle to his shoulder again. She lay sprawled on the ground, her fall raising a small cloud of dust.

"Don't be stupid!" he spat through clenched teeth. "If he knew I was out here with you, he'd be out to kill us. You still don't see it, do you? We don't count for anything around here anymore and that certainly includes you. You're a danger now!" He peered through the telescopic sight but Van Rhyn had disappeared. The opportunity was gone.

Peace swore viciously under his breath and strode off towards the cattle grid-gate. She stood and dusted herself down, then followed him. When she caught up, he turned and thrust the sniper rifle into her hands. "Take it. Now it's time to shut up and follow. Do you think you can do that?" he demanded.

His sudden show of temper subdued her. She did as he'd asked, following in his footsteps just a few feet behind. They stayed in the shadow thrown by the baobab tree, and then flitted into the shadows of other smaller trees as they moved further from the house. They were still near enough to hear engines being started and the yowl of a high-performance engine being revved. Peace realised that he was not the only one with a motorcycle or a quad. The sound gave him hope; the crackle of the cycle's two-stroke engine would drown out that made by his own machine.

Eventually, they were far enough away for him to abandon the slight detour he was making and head straight to where the quad was parked. He soon realised that she was no newcomer to the bush; she kept pace with him with practised ease. They moved nearer to the road that led from the farm, but kept a good distance from the bungalows where there was now some activity. A pickup had drawn up, and there were loud voices. They eventually made it to the fence. This was not designed to deter human intruders and after finding a strong anchor-post able to take their weight, they were able to scale it nimbly.

They were still yards from the quad when they heard the staccato bark of quads, and the rumble as these crossed the cattle-grid.

"Down!" Peace snarled, grabbed her by the arm, and pulled her down next to him, both ignoring the *duwweltjies*, those small balls of thorns the size of a marble, which painfully pierced their skin and clothing.

They heard the vehicles come to a stop a few hundred yards further along the road, their pursuers obviously having understood that they could not have gotten much further on foot. The engines were switched off. From their prone positions, they were able to see beneath the bush and trees, so they watched as some of their pursuers jumped from the rear of the pickups and spread out into the bush. The quads also entered the bush, their powerful headlamps piercing the darkness. Peace realised they would be discovered. He rose to his feet and ran towards his own quad with Margaret close behind him.

As they got to the four-wheeler, he hoped to God it would start — if it didn't, he held little hope of them escaping and they only had limited ammunition.

"Jump behind me and hang on for your life," he ordered.

She swung onto the pillion and clasped her arms around his waist. He sat with the MP5 resting across the cycle's tank and watched the approaching quads' headlights. He waited until the first was nearly upon them, and when he was able to make out the seated figure on the quad he aimed and drew a bead on the rider's chest. The sharp crack of the MP5 pierced the air. The rider arched back and tumbled backwards off the quad, the cycle rearing up on its rear wheels. The engine screamed briefly and then abruptly died, the quad dropping forward once more on its wheels, and its headlamp still on, boring a white tunnel of light through the bush ahead of it.

Peace pushed the starter button. The engine whirred and chugged twice, and then with a howl sprang to life. He opened the throttle and released the clutch, and the quad's rear tyres clawed the ground, throwing a rooster tail of sand and dust into the air. They shot off into the bush. His eyes had adjusted well to the dark and he was able to navigate with the lights off, but branches still clawed at them, scratching their faces and arms. He hoped she was better protected behind him.

He knew they had to get past the pickups blocking the road and the only way to do this was to keep to the bush. He gritted his teeth; this was going to be a wild ride. With all the swerving to avoid trees and large bushes, the quad slid from side to side. The MP5 hanging round his neck swung back and forth across the tank, banging loudly against its sides.

Suddenly the sound of rapid rifle fire split the air, clearly audible above the quad's engine. He knew they had to be those shooting blindly from the pickups. Another quad was still about a hundred yards away in full pursuit. The greater danger came from the quad chasing them as it was

149

faster — probably only having one occupant. He realised what he had to do and veered towards the road.

"Listen up!" he screamed at her. "Just keep your nerve! I'm going to have to let that quad come at us." He felt her arms tighten around his waist.

He switched the light on for a second to allow the quad driver to get a bearing on them. He then swung his vehicle around to face the oncoming quad and stopped. He flicked the MP5 to full automatic and brought it to his shoulder, and as the quad burst from the bush, he pulled the trigger. The automatic pistol chattered, spewing deadly fire He couldn't see the quad's driver, but the quad keeled over and he had a brief glimpse of the rider being flung from his saddle. He knew that his short burst of fire had been accurate.

"Another one down," he whispered through clenched teeth.

He then dropped the quad into gear, drove it over the ridge of heaped sand that separated the side of the road from the bush and shot off towards Gagarus with the headlight on, the long shaft of light boring through the dark, brightly illuminating the road ahead. He knew the pickups would be in pursuit, and on the road, they'd be a damn sight faster than the quad. If he didn't devise a plan soon, their capture, or demise, would be inevitable.

"They're after us and gaining," Margaret shouted in his ear over the roar of the wind. As if to confirm what she'd said, he heard the chatter of an automatic weapon, too distant yet to do any harm, but the knowledge that they were out to kill them gave him a hollow feeling. He would be damned though, if he'd let Van Rhyn and his horde of misfits frighten him.

"Don't worry, we'll get out of this, somehow," he replied.

Ahead of them, he saw the ground dip into an *omaramba* — a wide dry riverbed, which only receives water during the rainy season. He braked, switched off the light, and steered towards the edge of the road, where it was overhung by a large camel-thorn tree. He dismounted and led Margaret behind the tree. He had only one and a half clips of ammunition left for the MP5, but enough to do Van Rhyn's men serious harm. He wondered whether the mining magnate was with them.

As the pickups approached, he fired, knowing that the bullets would shatter the windscreen and kill anyone sitting in the cab.

The vehicle swerved, then broadsided, throwing up a massive cloud of dust and then without warning, flipped over. Two bodies were flung from the rear — they cartwheeled through the air and fell to the ground with a sickening thump. Even if they'd survived this, they would be in no condition to fight. The pickup came down on its roof, flattened the cab and rolled again, finally coming to rest on its side just off the road.

Behind him, he heard her sharp intake of breath. "My God!" she said hoarsely. "They all must be dead."

He ignored her. The MP5's magazine was empty. He took another full clip and rammed it home.

A second pickup was approaching. It slewed, and then skidded to a stop alongside the carnage. A very slight breeze had sprung up, which cleared the dust and presented Peace with an excellent target. The MP5 bucked in his hands as he sent a stream of bullets at the pickup's windscreen. He heard a shout of panic, immediately followed by a scream.

Suddenly, a man rolled out from behind the vehicle and stopped, sprawled on his stomach and propped up on his elbows, he held an automatic rifle in a classic firing position. Peace heard its loud chatter; the bullets thudded into the thorn tree, causing bark and shredded wood to fly from it. He dropped to the ground, pulling Margaret down with him. Shots whistled over their heads, and then suddenly, all was silent. *Magazine change!* Peace rose on one knee and fired a fusillade until the firing pin fell on an empty chamber. In the semi-darkness, he saw the prone figure jerk as the bullets impacted.

The MP5 was now useless as he was out of ammunition, so he dropped it. He swung a leg onto the quad and dragged Margaret behind him. As they sped down the track, Peace hoped there were none left to follow. He felt Margaret's arms wrap around him, her body hard up against his back. He realised that the last encounters had probably left her terrified.

While trying to concentrate on the road, Peace recalled the meeting in VA's office in London with the banker and the man from the Exchequer. He clearly remembered VA's words, 'We don't want you to get involved.' It was now a joke. He was already involved up to his bloody eyeballs! This mob was out to kill him and if they ever learned who he really was, it would make them only more determined.

Van Rhyn was unaware that Lord Digby was in any way involved, or so Peace hoped. However, with what had transpired, Van Rhyn was sure to accelerate any plans.

With time running out for both Peace and Van Rhyn, Peace needed to make contact with VA as soon as possible.

They made it safely back on the quad to where he had left the Land Cruiser and Peace was soon able to call London.

Sir John's instructions were explicit. He was to drive to Eros Airport in Windhoek where a private aircraft awaited them. He was given an address in Windhoek where he was to meet with MI6's people who would get them unobserved to the aircraft that would be waiting for them. They were to fly to Johannesburg's Jan Smuts Airport and would leave on the next available British Airways flight to London, where Sir John's people were to expect them. On arriving in Johannesburg, the embassy would provide passports and a holdall containing toiletries and clothing. A change of passport was necessary as Margaret could not depart the country on her original passport. It was thought that with the connections Van Rhyn had, he could well have people on the lookout. Sir John assured Peace that he would arrange for temporary but secure accommodation for Margaret in London.

Peace relayed to her only what was pertinent, that is, where they were going and where she would eventually be taken to.

"Who are you? You're certainly not the man you pretended to be!" She asked this after they had been driving for a few minutes.

"Listen, the less I say the better, but what I can divulge is that I'm a British government employee and my duties include looking after British overseas interests and British citizens, amongst a few other things," he replied.

"That, I gathered. I see you don't want to get into it any further."

"No… not now. Someone better qualified will eventually fill you in. Now try to get some sleep," he replied tersely.

"You're badly scratched and torn," she said.

He merely grunted in reply.

*

Their departure from South Africa had gone without a hitch.

Peace arrived in London just before dawn and was immediately whisked off to his mews flat and only given sufficient time to bath, change clothes, and have a quick breakfast, while his chauffeur and assistant waited patiently for him and then drove him to MI6 headquarters.

During the hours that he and Margaret had spent together, they had discussed Van Rhyn and his plans and she had come to realise precisely how horrific their plans were. She also understood the dire consequences that would have happened, had Peace not rescued her. Yes, she was concerned for her mother, but Peace assured her that it would not be long before she would see her mother again. She believed him.

The debriefing at MI6 headquarters was long and tedious. However, the good news was that, although still aboard the submarine, Cherry was making a rapid recovery and that on her arrival in Scotland would receive further treatment.

Sir John said that they had good reason to believe Peace's cover was not blown and that Van Rhyn still believed him to be Lord Digby Brentwood. It was decided that Peace would return to South Africa and continue his masquerade.

Chapter Eighteen

Peace woke. He had slept for most of the flight from London to Cape Town seated in the Business Class section, which afforded him sufficient legroom to stretch out. He realised that the aircraft had commenced its descent. The first wisps of cloud flashed over the Boeing 747's wings as it gradually lost altitude. Peace stared out of the window waiting for a break in the cloud. Suddenly, he caught his first glimpse of the sea. He knew the aircraft had to be swinging over False Bay as the pilot brought it round to line up with the runway.

He turned to look at the woman in the seat next to him.

"Not the sunny South Africa you were expecting," he said, smiling.

"Don't worry. I know it'll clear soon enough," Cherry replied.

Over a month had passed since her near-death event in the cold waters of the Atlantic off the coast of South West Africa. She had remained aboard the submarine until it had docked at Faslane in Scotland. From there she had been whisked by helicopter to the naval hospital in Glasgow, where the surgeons pronounced their satisfaction with the medical procedures carried out by the surgeon on board the submarine. She had swiftly recovered and had spent the last month getting her strength back, subjecting herself for the last ten days to a rigorous fitness regime.

For nearly a week, he and Margaret had separately undergone debriefings in VA's London headquarters where, since their arrival, he had only fleetingly seen her in passing. It was more an interrogation than a debriefing, but the analysts soon learned that Margaret had little to add to what was already known. She knew that her stepfather was strongly opposed to the release of Nelson Mandela and the recognition of the African National Congress, the party with which the Nationalist government was negotiating in an attempt to establish an acceptable transitional process to fair elections and eventual majority rule.

Only when at the *Vrede* farm had she learned that Van Rhyn proposed to lead an insurrection of right-wing whites if de Klerk went ahead with his plans to unban the forbidden ANC political movement. She, like most of the world, didn't know that America and Britain knew of the nuclear arsenal Van Rhyn had hidden at Copperton, and that he possessed the means to deliver it.

MI6 had assisted in finding secure accommodation for Margaret Langton-Van Rhyn and had enabled her to return to her studies at university under an assumed name. They were confident she could return to everyday life in London without Van Rhyn being able to trace her whereabouts. She was careful to avoid former friends and sought solace in her studies. Her accommodation arrangement was only temporary. She possessed a small fortune of her own but for security reasons could not draw from it. VA saw to it that she had adequate funds in the interim. The British government kept an eye on her, checking daily that all was well. In South Africa, the Van Rhyns had not reported their daughter missing. Before leaving South Africa, Margaret had left a message with a friend for her mother, telling her not to concern herself and that all was well. She had refused to disclose any information regarding her whereabouts.

VA had told Peace to sit tight in London. He also mentioned the government was working on a game plan in conjunction with the Americans to deal with Van Rhyn and the bombs. The South African diplomatic corps had no idea that others had misappropriated the bombs; all believed the South African nuclear arsenal had been decommissioned, but knowing otherwise, the Americans had positioned spy satellites to fly over South Africa. This had been done immediately after learning where the bombs were stored.

Peace and Cherry had resumed their intimate relationship, but not before Peace convinced Cherry that he had made no overtures to either Janet, Margaret or anyone else for that matter since the submarine incident. Nonetheless, she warned him that she, like most women, would never trust him. This pleased him, for he detected a hint of jealousy in her questioning. He had asked her about this and she had responded with a look of annoyance flashing across her face. "No, I'm not jealous," she'd replied, "but knowing you, you wouldn't have resisted a roll in the hay with her had she shown the inclination. Janet is an exceptionally beautiful woman."

He shrugged his shoulders in indifference and replied that it hadn't happened. She appeared to accept this and thereafter spent much of her time in his flat in the mews.

His flat, situated in a recently renovated building in a mews in Swiss Cottage, was spacious, with all the modern conveniences and appliances he needed. He did not know his neighbours and had no inclination to meet them, but he knew them to be a banker and a stockbroker. The fourth down towards the cul-de-sac was a Harley Street specialist doctor. Their ostentatious cars were a clear indication of their wealth. Peace wasn't a car fanatic — his interest lay in aircraft and he part owned a specially adapted De Havilland Super Chipmunk, a Canadian-built trainer aircraft. When at home he often spent his weekends at a small airfield in Kent where he tested his aerobatic skills. Of course, he did own a car, a black turbo Saab coupe, but preferred using a cab when travelling in the city. Most who knew him assumed he was attached to Naval High Command with an office in the city, his job occasionally taking him away from home. Cherry, when in his company, had quickly learned to adjust her behaviour to match his assumed persona.

When VA had said that Cherry should accompany him on his next mission to South Africa, Peace was initially resistant, although conceding that her knowledge of Afrikaans had been invaluable. He believed the mission had become too dangerous, there being no doubt that Van Rhyn and his supporters were capable of killing. He had since learned that many of them were hardened soldiers, with years of combat experience in the fight against terrorism and the extended bush war in South Africa.

VA remained adamant about his decision and stated that Cherry being a woman had no relevance on her ability to get the job done, her previous work on missions speaking volumes.

They left Cape Town's International Airport and got in a taxi. The driver was a Cape Coloured who spoke in Afrikaans. Cherry and he soon struck up a conversation, Peace not understanding a word. They had hoped for warm sunshine after London's drab weather, but this was not to be. During the night, a cold front had moved in from the southern Atlantic, bringing cold rainy weather with it. Table Mountain was shrouded in cloud and Cherry was disappointed.

Peace was returning to South Africa to resume his association with Van Rhyn. MI6 had established that Van Rhyn had no idea that Lord Digby was associated with those who had infiltrated Copperton and abducted his youngest from the farm. Had Van Rhyn investigated Lord Digby, he would have found that he had returned to London shortly after the dinner party at his Pretoria residence, and that he was due to return to Johannesburg to continue managing his growing mining share portfolio. There was no reason for Van Rhyn to suspect him. The only person who might inform on him was Margaret, but she would then be in equal danger.

Peace had let Van Rhyn know that he was returning to South Africa, and would be staying at the Mount Nelson Hotel in Cape Town. The hotel was set in a lush estate just below the slopes of Table Mountain. Its layout and décor, and the attention of the staff to their guests' needs, was redolent of the country's colonial past. While Peace and Cherry booked in, two bellhops whisked their luggage to their adjoining rooms on the top floor. These had a splendid view of Cape Town and the harbour and right across the blue waters of Table Bay to the beaches of Bloubergstrand four miles away.

Peace had insisted that the rental company again make available the chauffeur he'd used in Johannesburg, along with a Mercedes 500 or similar vehicle. Martin was to be trusted and had every reason to believe Peace was the true Lord Digby. This proved possible, but only at considerable expense. The next day Peace had found Martin waiting for him in the hotel's car park.

Immediately on his arrival in South Africa, Peace had phoned Van Rhyn. He was not available, so Peace left a message and added that he would phone Van Rhyn later. However, a phone call was received shortly thereafter, the magnate clearly elated to hear from his friend again. He insisted that Peace join him for a dinner at his estate in the Stellenbosch wine lands. When Peace mentioned his secretary, the Afrikaner laughed knowingly, as if he were aware she had to be more than just a secretary, and insisted she partner him as he wished to meet her.

Peace replaced the hotel phone on its cradle and looked up at Cherry. "Well, it seems you'll get to meet the man after all," he said.

Chapter Nineteen

As it would be a black-tie dinner, they made sure to dress appropriately. Cherry was radiant in a low-cut wine-red full-length cocktail dress with matching shoes. She wore a necklace with what appeared to be a gem, nestling in her cleavage.

"My God, you look quite regal," Peace said admiringly. "You certainly seem more than a mere secretary, I might add."

Cherry gave a snort. "Do you really believe he'll think I'm your secretary? I doubt it. That's more in line with Digby's reputation. He's known to be a notorious womaniser. Believe me, being on your arm will certainly not be out of character."

Peace had to concur, seeing as most of what he knew about the man he'd learnt from her studies. However, she also seemed to have made quite a study of him too. No wonder she'd been standoffish when he'd first met her at the embassy in Pretoria.

"Incidentally," she added, "should that Janet woman be there, don't you start with her or let her come onto you." Her eyes flashed. "You should know, I don't give a damn what VA's view is on this, if that woman starts flirting, I'll have my claws out." The look on her face told him that she was serious.

The sun was about to disappear below the horizon — it was time to go. Martin held the door open, and they slid into the backseat of the black Mercedes.

Peace wore a shoulder holster in which nestled a small KelTec P3AT, a .38 pistol that fits into a man's hand and reveals no underarm bulge. He did not believe they'd be searched or be subjected to metal detection, but even if this happened, he hoped Van Rhyn would not consider it unusual for Lord Digby to be touting a weapon. Cherry carried the small calibre KelTec P32 in a holster high on her thigh. Since they were now accepted guests, he fervently hoped they wouldn't be searched.

The short Cape twilight had set in by the time they arrived on the farm. A large Dutch-gabled house overlooked the extensive vineyards that sloped down to the small willow-lined river below. Obviously, this estate was someone's pride and joy, as the vineyards were cultivated in neat rows following the contours of the land, the grounds impeccably kept.

The car stopped at the bottom of the short flight of broad stairs that led to the porch. A man, who he presumed to be part of security, stepped forward and opened his door. Cherry was the first to emerge, followed by Peace. They climbed the stairs side-by-side.

Peace immediately noticed Van Rhyn on the wide porch, dressed in a white dinner jacket with a glass of wine in his hand, ready to greet him. He did not miss the two security guards on the porch dressed in dark suits with the ever-present white earpieces and cables leading into the collars of their shirt. He recognised one from his previous visit to Van Rhyn's Pretoria estate. Peace did not doubt that he had a firearm tucked under his armpit. All the guests were immaculately dressed, the women in full-length eveningwear. A small parking area that adjoined the driveway, brightly lit by a security light, revealed a few other chauffeur-driven cars — Peace noticed General Booyens' car with its General's standard on the vehicle's wing.

Van Rhyn extended his huge hand in greeting and his gaze then travelled up and down Cherry's body. "Your companion is truly beautiful," he said. He took her hand and brought it to his lips. "My pleasure," he whispered.

Peace climbed the steps and was met by Lady Langton-Van Rhyn. She brushed his cheek with her own. "It is so good to see you again, Lord Digby," she said. She nodded at Cherry and whispered a soft, "How do you do?" The women touched hands.

Peace saw Janet standing in the doorway. Her astounding beauty jolted him and it was hard not to show his reaction. *This woman is exquisite*. She was dressed in white, the low décolletage revealing her ample bosom and the deep valley between her breasts.

As he walked towards her, she watched his approach with a smile on her face. *Damn*, he thought, *she may as well have blurted out right here and now that he was no stranger to her*. He thought he could feel the eyes of others on him, watching his every move. This woman's effect on him was amazing — already he lusted for her. *Damn the bloody woman*.

Cherry walked next to him; her face serene. The interaction between the two was seemingly lost on her, but Peace had no doubt she had missed nothing. She stretched out her hand and smiled.

"You must be Janet Van Rhyn. Lord Digby has told me so much about you."

"Really?" said Janet, still smiling. "Told you about me? Well, that must have been interesting."

God, the woman was playing with Cherry, Peace thought.

For a second he felt Cherry stiffen, but she answered innocently, "Yes, he mentioned a previous dinner where you both met."

Peace had his hand on Cherry's back and gave her a warning pinch. She gave an almost imperceptible flinch and stepped back, grinding her heel into his foot. "Oh, I'm so sorry, Lord Digby," she said. He got the message.

They moved round to greet the other guests, mostly Afrikaners who were champions of the newly emerging Afrikaner industrial conglomerates.

As he greeted each guest, he found himself in front of General Booyens, resplendent in his military eveningwear, his aide-de-camp hovering nearby.

"Lord Digby, it's good to have you back with us," the general said, apparently truly pleased to see him.

While he was responding to the general's greeting, Peace noticed a guard outside on the lawn, slowly patrolling and cradling an automatic machine pistol. A hyena on a leash walked in front of him. Van Rhyn was obviously taking no chances. Over the last few months, Van Rhyn had had to contend with more than just a few unfortunate instances — the loss of the gold, the unknown breach of his security at Copperton, the failed salvage attempt, the death of his security personnel, and finally the abduction of his stepdaughter. He couldn't blame the man. And now, he had two cabinet ministers with their wives present for dinner. Surely, there had to be some concern for the safety of such distinguished guests.

Of course, they belonged to the hard-core right wing of the Nationalist Party who had little sympathy for de Klerk. Peace knew Van Rhyn had to be particularly cautious and thus the heavily armed guards. These could not be happy times.

Leaving Cherry in conversation with the general, he turned and advanced towards Lady Langton-Van Rhyn, who watched his approach over the rim of her cocktail glass. He noted that the cocktails were already having some effect, but the alcohol did not hide the stress the woman was clearly feeling.

"Where's your youngest?" he asked. "I so enjoyed her company in Pretoria."

For a moment, the woman was taken back, and slightly spilled her drink, bewilderment on her face.

"Oh, you mean Margaret," she said and hesitated. "The poor dear, she doesn't like the farm, and my husband and I have been spending time in the bush. She decided it wasn't for her. You know what the modern children of today are like. She decided to return to the UK. Don't forget, she still has her studies to pursue."

"You were spending time in the bush?" he asked.

"Yes, we've a farm in Namibia near the Etosha Pan. I'm sure you've heard of the place."

"Yes, I have. One of the largest game reserves in the world. Must be a lovely residence you have."

"Yes, we just love spending time there. There is no better place to unwind, but Margaret doesn't like it. She prefers lots of people and bright lights."

"I'm sorry, I'm going to miss her," he said, taking a vodka martini from an immaculately turned-out waiter.

"Me too," said Lady Langton-Van Rhyn, grabbing another cocktail from the tray.

Peace felt the presence of someone behind him and turned around. It was Cherry, with the general in tow.

"Miss Pyper tells me she is your personal secretary," said the general. "I was surprised to learn that she speaks fluent Afrikaans and like you, has little time for the Blacks. You have chosen well."

Peace laughed. "General, rest assured that if you were to meet others of my staff, you'll find them all ultra-conservative. I just wonder what you chaps are going to do about your fellow Whites who want to hand this wonderful country of yours to the Blacks. Just look at the rest of Africa — it's obvious what the final outcome will be." There was no reaction from the general, so he continued, "What truly amazed me was that you allowed the government to decommission your nuclear weapons, not to mention your chemical and biological warfare programs."

God, that's sticking my neck out!

The general's jaws clenched and his eyes hardened. "I'm surprised," he said, "that you are so well-informed. What do you propose we should have done? That we simply hand our nuclear arms development program to the new Black government when it assumes power? No, no! Can you imagine the belligerency of these people were they to have such unlimited power at their disposal? We had to get rid of the weapons."

Peace had heard enough. There was no persuading their kind that majority rule might not result in vengeance. Democracy, as the world knew and practised it, was not an option Van Rhyn and his sort in government and industry were prepared to consider. They would resist to the end, no matter what it took.

At the dinner table, Peace and Cherry found themselves seated close to Van Rhyn, who sat at its head. Janet, who appeared to have no partner, sat next to Peace, while Cherry sat on his other side. General Booyens sat opposite them with his wife, who seemed to be the typical Afrikaans housewife found so often in the country — still looking somewhat dowdy despite her long evening dress and the coiffured hair.

Peace allowed Booyens to continue their discussion on the decommissioning of the country's nuclear arsenal. Peace adopted an outrageously right-wing stance, saying that the regime should have used nuclear weapons against the Cubans and Angolans rather than negotiating with them, and that neither the Russians nor Chinese would have been likely to intervene. From the top of the table, Van Rhyn interjected saying that it was a pity Lord Digby didn't serve on the South African government. He jovially added that perhaps a few of the problems they were currently experiencing would long have been solved.

Van Rhyn's statement was greeted with some amusement.

Janet interrupted the conversation. "Come, Father, enough talk of war and atom bombs. Let us enjoy Lord Digby's company."

Peace felt her thigh being pressed against his. He furtively glanced down and saw that her dress was split along its entire left side, revealing her thigh almost all the way near to her hip. Fleetingly, his thoughts returned to when they'd had last been together, and felt a frisson of nostalgic lust. She had turned to face him, the décolletage of her dress gaping open to reveal the deep cleavage between her breasts.

"Tell me, Digby, what made you beat such a hasty retreat to London when last here?" she asked mischievously. She obviously assumed that Cherry really was no more than just his secretary. She addressed Peace as if Cherry did not exist. Neither did she hide that she was attracted to him. Cherry's composed demeanour revealed nothing, but Peace knew that she seethed.

"It was unfortunate that I had to leave so hurriedly," he replied, "but unfortunately, business demanded my presence in London."

The general interrupted, ignoring Janet's attempt to steer the conversation in another direction. He started a rant along the lines that most of those in the South African military High Command shared his sentiments — Peace knew this to be untrue — and when Peace suggested that perhaps the conscripts in the army might be unwilling to join a rebellion, the general, obviously angered, played his trump card.

"You know, as does the rest of the world, that we have the RSA-5, an intercontinental rocket — "

Peace interrupted him with a chuckle and waved his hand dismissively. "And what do you propose to arm it with? A one-ton conventional warhead capable of destroying no more than a city block?"

Silence followed his remark, during which the room seemed to crackle with tension.

"Don't believe everything you hear," the general hissed.

Peace now knew that these bastards were prepared to use the bomb.

Cherry nudged his leg with her knee, indicating that she thought this conversation was heading into dangerous territory.

Janet didn't look at him but stared at her plate as if she'd suddenly found something of interest on it, but then raised her head and said firmly, "Enough! This is a dinner! Talk about something else, please!"

The general turned to Cherry.

"Tell me, Miss Pyper," he said, speaking in Afrikaans. "What is an Afrikaner doing at the side of an English aristocrat, albeit that he is ultra-conservative as we are?"

Cherry smiled. "He advertised for a secretary. Fluent Afrikaans was a prerequisite. I applied. He pays well and provides a generous expense account. How could I refuse?"

"And your thoughts on what we've just discussed?"

"I have none. I just do what I'm told."

"Really, how interesting. Is that always the case?" Janet interjected, her voice containing a hint of sarcasm and disbelief. Cherry ignored her, not even affording her a glance.

"Clearly, you are a good person for Digby to have at his side," the general said.

The conversation now turned to everyday matters, yet the atmosphere remained tense. But Janet continued to flirt openly with Peace, obviously unconcerned by the presence of Cherry or the others.

She turned, brought her lips to his ear and whispered, "Is it to be my place or yours?"

From the corner of his eye, he could see Cherry's face and the flash of a warning that crossed over it. Had Janet noticed?

He ignored the question.

"Well?" Janet pressed him.

He had to say something. "Yours," he said.

Cherry's facial features stiffened and she appeared to visibly pale. He pressed his leg against hers to reassure her but she jerked her leg away. God, she was impossible, didn't she comprehend he had no option but to play along? Hadn't they discussed this? They had agreed that if Janet came onto him, she should keep her emotions in check. If she persisted in behaving like this, somebody was bound to realise that there was more to their relationship than that of employer and secretary.

Van Rhyn rose, indicating that dinner was over. The women got up and left for the drawing-room. Van Rhyn led the men along a short passage to his study, which was dominated by a large ornate desk and a few red, deep-buttoned leather chairs and coffee tables. Once seated, they were served a generous tot of the best South African brandy in bulbous Cognac glasses. Peace declined a cigar but accepted the brandy. All eight men then made themselves comfortable.

"Digby," Van Rhyn said. Peace noted the man had dispensed with his title, an admission of complicity, perhaps? He resolved to address Van Rhyn accordingly.

"You realise," Van Rhyn continued, "that you are seated in the midst of probably the most powerful group of Afrikaners in the country. During the last few years, we have forged the ideology on which the modern true Afrikaner movement is now founded. Of course, there are the exceptions, those who have deserted the principles of our founding fathers. However, we are not prepared to abandon them. We would rather die than succumb to a Black government. Do you understand that?"

"Of course I do, Anton." Peace launched into a tirade against British democracy, castigating the uneducated masses who had taken over the running of the country. Warming to his theme, he even expressed some sympathy with Nazi ideology.

"You're right," said Van Rhyn. "Actually, you can do something for us. British fascist groups appear to be gaining some sympathy with the masses; I believe this is a result of uncontrolled immigration, yes? Many believe the immigrants are slowly taking over your country. There are areas of London that rival Karachi in language and culture and others the Caribbean — I could go on and on. Many believe these immigrants, the non-Whites, are slowly taking over your country. We would like you to subtly advance the fascist cause in your right-wing press, and, by association, advance ours as well. You have connections in the right places which would make your intervention most effective."

Peace leaned back, slowly swirling the brandy in the goblet he held in his hand. He appeared to be giving Van Rhyn's words serious considera-tion. Then he said he was prepared to do what Van Rhyn proposed. "But I'll have to do it with discretion," he added.

At that moment there was a subtle knock on the door. It then opened. Peace recognised Van Rhyn's chief security officer, who entered and approached. He bent down to whisper in the seated industrialist's ear. Instinctively, Peace felt he was the subject of whatever the man was saying and a cold feeling of fear coursed through him. Something, somewhere, had gone awry. He saw Van Rhyn slowly nod and his features pale in obvious anger. The guard did not leave but took up position behind Van Rhyn.

Van Rhyn looked up at Peace; there was a trace of an arrogant, cruel smile on his face. "Digby, I've just received the most unfortunate news, which truly grieves me. Lately, I've experienced a few rather unfortunate incidents — interference during a salvage operation by the British Navy no less, and shortly thereafter, on our farm in Suidwes, or Namibia as you British now call it."

His eyes hardened. "We have been investigating you for some time, my friend. I now know that you are not Lord Digby Brentwood. This is distressing news, considering the matters we have discussed. What further concerns me are the many gold mining shares you've bought, financed by some outside agency. The amount of money required for this exercise must be considerable. Whoever you may be, I'm certain that your personal wealth would not permit such extravagance. It appears that you may be in the employ of the British government. My sources tell me that you are a naval officer, a Commander in fact," Van Rhyn said and then turned to his security officer and briefly whispered to him, the man then leaving the room.

Peace's face was a caricature of incredulity and affront. "Anton, is this some joke? It is preposterous — I am who I say I am." He hoped his demeanour did not reveal the mental turmoil he now felt.

"I think not. Your fingerprints are not those of the real Lord Digby. In your country he is considered a near-enemy of the state, and his fingerprints are on record." Van Rhyn sipped from his glass, obviously relishing the situation and wanting to extend it. "Yours don't match. I have this from the best authority. Not everyone in England accepts the invasion of their country by Blacks and Asians. Our friends were kind enough to tell us exactly who you are." Peace caught the inference — Van Rhyn and his band had connections in the highest of the British political establishment. "There is no point in continuing to play this stupid game," Van Rhyn said with a casual wave of his hand as if to dismiss the charade that Peace was still playing.

He knew he was sunk. The bastards would kill him and Cherry; they had no other option. Too much was at stake.

Play the game to the end. Get what you can from them.

He stared at Van Rhyn. He hoped he was still displaying a picture of quiescence, his back against the backrest of the leather chair, the brandy still in his hand, the liquid not revealing a tremor.

The man who he had thought to be Van Rhyn's main security honcho reappeared and spoke with Van Rhyn in Afrikaans.

Van Rhyn turned to look at Peace.

"Lambrecht and his men will take you away. We shan't see each other again. A pity; I thought you quite intelligent, and pleasant company. I truly believed I had an ally in you. Well, we all make mistakes, don't we?"

"Fokken veraaier![15] *"* General Booyens spat, his eyes black pools of hatred. "*Laat hulle uitvind hoe dit voel om sonder 'n valskerm uit 'n vliegtuig te spring*[16]," he hissed.

Van Rhyn smiled. "I must apologise for my friend. His hatred for the British and other lovers of Blacks knows no bounds. Jumps from aircraft without parachutes are his speciality when dealing with the enemy."

Peace had heard this before. It was rumoured the South Africans had learnt well from their fellow Portuguese colonialists in Angola and Mozambique when it came to dealing with terrorist insurgents. They left no evidence and no unmarked graves.

Peace rose from his chair and smiled at the general. "General, it's a wild horse you're riding. It'll soon throw you. History will repeat itself — a minority will eventually succumb to a majority, it is inevitable, but remember, we're not finished dealing with you and your kind."

"When you say we, do you mean the British government? My God, what can you do? You are as ineffectual as you've always been. Your country

15. Fucking traitor!

16. Let them find out what it feels like to jump from a plane without a parachute

is lost without your American friends," Van Rhyn retorted. "Take him away," he said to the guard. "Get this done, but not here — there's to be no evidence. Somewhere in the desert would be preferable."

None of the others in the room had spoken, but their expressions said everything. Lambrecht beckoned. Peace walked resignedly towards him, the general's aide-de-camp stepping aside to let him pass. As he passed, he felt a sudden stabbing pain — a hypodermic needle had been driven into his neck. The room began to reel and Lambrecht grabbed him to steady him. His vision blurred and then darkened. He felt himself falling, and Lambrecht was no longer holding him. His last sensation was of excruciating pain as his head struck the parquet floor. Oblivion followed.

Chapter Twenty

Slowly he emerged from unconsciousness, aware of a continuous drone. He didn't move. He listened, taking in his surroundings, eventually realising that he was aboard a prop-driven aircraft, strapped in a cabin seat with both hands tied or taped to the armrests. His head throbbed, probably the after-effects of the drug that had been administered, which had to account for the vile taste in his mouth.

He wanted to open his eyes but decided to wait and continued to listen intently. He heard nothing other than the aircraft's engines and the slight hiss of air. His jacket had been removed, but his braces hung loosely at his sides. He realised he still wore his dress suit and shoes. He could also smell his own rank unwashed odour. He needed a shower.

Suddenly, the aircraft bucked as it passed through a turbulent pocket of air. For a second or two he opened his eyes. He saw enough. He was aboard a multi-engine aircraft, probably capable of carrying eight or ten passengers, its interior opulent. The seat facing him was occupied by Cherry. She too was trussed to the seat, but he saw that she was awake and had seen he'd opened his eyes. A small square fold-down table separated them. He also had discerned Lambrecht across the aisle, apparently asleep. Another man sat in the seat facing him, immersed in a magazine. He realised pretending to sleep would get him nowhere, so he opened his eyes again and kept them open. The man with the magazine looked up lazily and then resumed his reading.

Peace and Cherry looked at each other. She obviously realised the serious-ness of their predicament; Booyens had made it clear that they were to be tossed out of the plane without parachutes. Who would have thought that Van Rhyn would go to such lengths to verify their bona fides and dispose of them? This surely indicated that Van Rhyn's tentacles were everywhere, both here in South Africa and in Britain. How else had he acquired this information? *It was too late to worry about that now*, Peace thought wearily.

The blinds to their window were closed. He dozed off again, wanting to let the desensitising effect of the drug wear off. He'd need his wits about him if they were to escape this situation.

The rasp of the speaker system jarred him out of his reverie. Something was said in Afrikaans, and Lambrecht rose from his seat and moved towards the cockpit where he spoke for a minute or two with the pilot of the aircraft. He leaned forward to peer out of the windscreen then returned to the cabin and spoke to his companion. They both drew their automatics, chambered a round, and approached their prisoners. Peace realised that their moment had arrived but he was powerless since both of his arms were taped to the seat's armrests. There was only one thing to do — pretend that he had not yet fully recovered from the drug.

He sat with his head still slumped forward as though he were dozing, and when Lambrecht placed a hand on his shoulder, he groggily lifted his head, slowly opened his eyes, and looked blankly at his captor who was standing over him with his weapon drawn and it pointed at him.

"What's it?" he mumbled incoherently.

"Sorry, man, time to rock 'n roll," said Lambrecht, and using his free hand, he started to unwrap the tape that bound Peace's arms to the armrest. He was careful to keep his automatic trained on him, the barrel never more than a few inches away. Lambrecht's companion was also busy doing the same with Cherry.

Peace noticed a change in the sound of the aircraft's engines and registered that the pilot was reducing speed. This would be necessary if they were to open the hatch. The aircraft also needed to descend to a lower altitude to where the pressure in the cabin was equal to the ambient pressure outside. He attempted to struggle, but did so lethargically, hoping this might indicate that he was still drugged.

But Lambrecht slapped him and spat, "Sit still!"

He slumped back into his seat. Lambrecht's gun never wavered, its hammer back. All he needed to do was pull the trigger.

The tape binding him was then removed. He sat, still with his arms resting on the armrests. "Come on, get up," Lambrecht said, grabbing him by the shoulder.

He rose unsteadily from his seat, as if still drugged and then collapsed back into the seat.

"Stand up!" Lambrecht shouted, trying to drag Peace up by his armpit. Peace noticed the other guard was bent over Cherry, trying to remove the tape from the armrest furthest away from him, requiring him to lean over her. Peace saw that she was looking at him.

He stood and then again fell back in his seat with Lambrecht struggling to keep him upright. Seizing the moment, he stuck out his hand out and swept the automatic's barrel away from him. Lambrecht reeled back, pulling the trigger, the shot deafening in the confined cabin. A low whistling sound indicated that the bullet had punctured the fuselage, allowing pressurized air to the escape.

Peace clutched Lambrecht's wrist in a vice-like grip, trying to stop him from aiming the weapon at him. With his other hand he gripped the man's clothing and jerked him towards him. Lambrecht tried to resist but Peace had his weight against Lambrecht, pressing his back against the aisle side of the seat. Peace slammed his head forward, his forehead hitting Lambrecht's nose. He felt the cartilage collapse under the powerful blow. The blow was too weak to totally incapacitate the man but gave Peace the split second's respite he needed. He twisted Lambrecht's right hand, and the automatic dropped to the floor. Peace was aware of Cherry grappling with the other guard — he too had blood streaming from his nose. Lambrecht shook his head as he tried to recover. Peace kicked him viciously in the groin and Lambrecht doubled up, emitting a howl. Peace brought his knee up violently into the man's face, further shattering the cartilage in his man's nose. Lambrecht offered no resistance for a brief moment as his hands clawed at his nose which spurted blood.

Peace tore off his braces and wrapped the stretchable white straps around

Lambrecht's neck. He forced his knee into the man's back and pulled the straps back with all his strength. The security man gagged and thrashed, trying to get his fingers under the braces. Slowly, his convulsions began to subside. It took nearly a minute before he was still. Peace released the braces and bent over the inert body, groping on the floor for the fallen automatic. His fingers finally closed around the butt.

Suddenly, a shot was fired, and he felt the air pressure as the bullet missed his cheek by a hair's breadth. He spun round to see the pilot who was still seated in his chair but twisted around, trying to aim a revolver down the aisle. At the same time, he noticed Cherry was on the floor on her back, a guard straddled over her and pistol-whipping her. Enraged, Peace shot him, almost at point-blank range. The bullet exited the man's head with an explosion of blood and brains, which splattered over Cherry, the seats and side of the fuselage.

Peace threw himself between the seats just as another shot rang out from the cockpit. Peering around the base of the seats, he saw the pilot again taking aim down the aisle. Peace fired two shots. One punched a hole through the Plexiglas windscreen, the other caught the pilot low in the shoulder, flinging him forward, even while restrained by his safety harness. Peace scrambled to his feet and charged down the aisle. The pilot had unclipped his harness and was rising from his seat, bringing his automatic round again. Peace fired again, twice. Both bullets hit the pilot in the chest, throwing him back against the control yoke and instrument panel.

The aircraft immediately began to slide off a wing, the nose dropping alarmingly and the airspeed increasing as it dove towards the ground. The automatic pilot had been disengaged by the sudden pressure exerted on the trim control switches on the yoke. He jerked the dead man off the yoke, levelled the aircraft, and re-engaged the autopilot. The aircraft began climbing back to the altitude that had last been selected. He dragged the dead pilot into the aisle and rushed to see what had happened to Cherry.

She was sprawled between the seats, the dead guard lying over her, his blood soaking her dress and pooling on the carpet floor. He had no idea what her condition was; there was so much blood he did not know if it was hers or not. Grunting with the effort, he pulled the dead man from her and dragged the body towards the back of the aisle. He lowered the backrest of one of the seats, then carefully picked her up and lay her on it.

He found a packet of wet-wipes in a locker, and with a towel taken from the toilet, he cleaned up her as best he could. The butt of the automatic had lacerated her head; the blood was seeping through her hair. He breathed a sigh of immense relief and wiped his face with a hand when he heard her groan. He returned to the cockpit, and copied their coordinates from the onboard GPS and checked these on an aeronautical map retrieved from the pilot's briefcase. He established their approximate current position and was amazed to see that they were no more than a hundred miles from Copperton.

He now had a serious dilemma. To land a South African registered aircraft with three dead people aboard anywhere in South Africa would result in immediate arrest. Noting their present position from the GPS, and recalling Sir John's instructions, it seemed Gaborone in Botswana was his best bet. This was four hundred miles away — about two hours flying time. A glance at the fuel gauges indicated the town was well within range. He worked out a track to the Botswana capital, altered course and reset the autopilot.

It would be best to land at the American-controlled airfield just outside the capital. From there he could contact the British Embassy, who could help extricate them from this near disaster or at least get Sir John to intervene. He had no idea what flight plan the dead pilot had filed. He did not attempt to contact anyone on the radio, not knowing to whom the current dialled-in frequency on the radio belonged.

About a hundred miles from Gaborone the high-frequency radio crackled, and Gaborone control came on air, complaining that they had been trying to raise him on VHF with no response. They demanded to know what his intentions were now that he was in their control area. Peace realised the airport staff had been tracking them with their state-of-the-art radar recently installed by the Americans, whose excuse for willingly financing and building this ultra-modern, high-tech airport, was to enable it to serve as an emergency airfield for the NASA Space Shuttle on re-entry. British Intelligence knew there was another, more covert reason. The Americans required a jumping-off-point for a rapid deployment force if there was ever a chance communists, or a communist-supportive socialist force, could threaten to take over in South Africa during these politically delicate times. Were this ever to be, many believed America and a few of her allies would intervene.

He requested permission to land and asked them to advise the local British Embassy of his arrival. He provided his name and special code and requested that the Embassy contact him direct on VHF frequency 124.8.

Ten minutes later, the Embassy contacted him on the radio. He asked that they make arrangements to have an ambulance standing by and to ensure the aircraft could be parked in an isolated area on landing. He did not want to mention that there were dead aboard and lastly, he didn't want the Botswana authorities first on the scene. He insisted that the Embassy's chief liaison officer — who was an undercover MI6 operative — await the plane as he would be aware of who Peace was and be able to deflect questions from the local authorities.

Once the aircraft had landed, the air traffic controller instructed Peace to taxi to an area north of the usual parking apron — this was usually reserved for military aircraft only. Peace wondered what the chief liaison officer could have said to persuade the authorities to grant them permission to park there. What was surprising was that a few soldiers, who clearly looked like British military, took up position around the aircraft to secure it.

Minutes later, an ambulance arrived and took Cherry, who had regained partial consciousness, to the American medical station on the airfield.

Peace was quickly whisked off to the Embassy in a car, accompanied by two other official vehicles. The man in the front passenger seat swung round to face Peace. Peace estimated him to be in his early thirties, and his tan tropical suit offset his African tan, making it evident he was no new arrival in the country.

"I'm Jonathan Knowles, the local British Ambassador's secretary," he said. "I should warn you of the recent developments you're about to be brought up to speed on." He laughed and offered his hand to Peace in the rear through the front seats. They shook hands. "Actually, I must admit, so am I. Obviously, you've powerful friends, if all this has been arranged for your benefit. We got a top priority message that you were on your way here," he added smiling.

Peace was thankful that none of the people he'd disturbed seemed to be annoyed.

As they left the airfield, Peace didn't miss the US Army C130 Hercules on the tarmac and the activity around its lowered rear ramp. Alongside stood an RAF Transport Vickers VC10, disgorging a troop of what had to be military personnel.

"Sir Brooke can fill you in on what's happening," said Knowles as they drove through the entrance to the Embassy. "He's the local British Ambassador, and has a direct line to MI6, or so I believe."

Peace was ushered in to the large entrance hall. The ambassador and his wife were there to greet him.

"We're glad to see you. We're sorry your colleague was hurt," the ambassador said, shaking Peace's hand vigorously. "It's extraordinary how events have suddenly accelerated around here. No doubt you're wondering what's going on, but first, you need to get out of that evening wear."

"What day is this? I was drugged and only came round an hour or so ago," Peace asked.

"Thursday, 14th of May."

"I've been out for more than a day!"

"Yes, you're right. Your people kept tabs on you and observed you being moved to the airport. It was soon evident that your captors proposed putting you on a plane to some place, but we didn't know where. At the risk of revealing ourselves, our people thought it too dangerous to intervene at that stage."

Peace was about to remark that had they intervened he would've missed all the fun on the plane. Wisely, he chose to bite his tongue. Of course, he saw VA somehow had to have had a part in this, but now was not the time to be sarcastic. Did they even know that he and Cherry were destined to make a parachute-less drop? They were lucky to be alive. Peace was so caught up in that thought, that he failed to latch on to what Knowles was saying about being observed by *his people*.

"Okay, I'll let Jonathan take over from here. It's really his show," the ambassador said.

Chapter Twenty-One

"Sir John and his team were quick to put a plan in motion. He has a rather good relationship with the Chief of the SA Air Force, General Maritz. They'd met on several occasions before and Maritz is a staunch supporter of de Klerk. Rather fortunate, I'd say. Anyway, to cut it short, when you were taken out to the aircraft, two Atlas Impalas were scrambled from Kimberley's training base and kept your aircraft under surveillance. When the aircraft began to lose speed and descend in mid-flight, they closed in but kept out of the cockpit's view. However, when the aircraft then set course for Gaborone, and the new destination was broadcast, they returned to base," the secretary said.

"Just as well, but why Gaborone? Although, we thought that if you had the choice, it would be Gaborone," the ambassador asked.

"Neutral territory. Also, there'd be no leaks — I knew the Americans had a strong presence there. Part of the airport falls under American jurisdiction as it were. American military aircraft often make a stop here."

The ambassador asked one of his staff to escort Peace to the residential block where he was shown a rather spartan room, which had the bare necessities. While he showered and shaved, another arrived with boxes and carry bags containing an assortment of suitable clothing and toiletries.

"Sir, I'm afraid you'll have to wear those evening shoes. I've been unable to find you a pair for now, but be sure, I will have done so by tomorrow lunchtime. Size eleven UK, am I right?" the staff employee said.

Peace smiled. "Not to worry. Thanks anyway, this will certainly do."

Peace had just exited the shower when the man reappeared.

"Sir Brooke asks that you join him for lunch. Dress is informal," the man said with a clear denotation that the request was not to be refused. "He said I was to tell you the Americans will be joining us."

Now, that did surprise Peace.

The luncheon was to be held indoors in one of the lesser dining rooms, and he dressed in a light-blue open-neck sport shirt and navy slacks. The colour was fortunate as it would make his evening shoes less conspicuous. When he arrived, he found the ambassador was similarly dressed. Sir Brooke was an unusually tall man with a narrow face and a crown of snow-white hair, parted and carefully combed. He was near sixty but showed no sign of body fat and was still trim. From the suntan he sported, Peace assumed the man had a penchant for the outdoors. *Probably golf*, he thought. Gaborone boasted an excellent golf course, even though it was situated in a semi-desert.

Peace entered the dining room and was surprised to see that there were others present. Two men also casually dressed were already there. Sir Brooke introduced them to him — both were American. They greeted him with firm handshakes and he realised their slight American twang was unmistakable. American spooks came first to mind — probably CIA or black ops.

The ambassador introduced them. The muscular, dark-haired American was Glen Barkly, whose eyes were dark and uncompromising. The other, Jim Croxley, was fair-haired with steel-blue eyes that appeared to portray a lesser degree of bottled-up aggression than his partner.

Everyone took their seats, with the ambassador at the head of the table and his secretary to his left.

The ambassador signalled to a steward to pour the wine. He then said, "Matters are developing rapidly in South Africa. Believe me when I tell you that the recent intervention by the two of you in Copperton was absolutely necessary."

So, the ambassador had been brought up to date, Peace thought.

The ambassador looked at Peace and the Americans. "Van Rhyn and his friends are well aware that we were closing in on them. We must assume he must now know that we are aware of his nuclear arsenal as well. You're lucky we were able to intervene and bring you here."

The secretary interrupted, "Had we not done so, I doubt whether you'd have seen another day. I believe that was bloody close!"

"You could say that. Actually, a definite understatement," Peace replied matter-of-factly. Clearly, this man had to be from London. Peace considered the secretary's words. *I wonder if he is VA's protégé or his ear-to-the-ground in these parts.* The man's actions and words indicated that he carried the necessary clout.

The man continued. "Unbeknown to many, we have maintained an extraordinary intelligence presence here, as have our American friends. Unfortunately, they had to drastically tone down their operations a good while back when they were caught using modified local civil aircraft loaded with recon cameras and the likes with which they flew some very sensitive territory." He smiled. "Of course, they got caught red-handed. Very embarrassing at the time."

"But weren't the South Africans supposed to have decommissioned their nuclear arsenal?" Peace asked.

The discussion halted when two waiters arrived and proceeded to place plates of food before those at the table.

As soon as they left, the secretary continued. "You've got to remember, this, the disclosure of the bombs and then the proposed de-commissioning was all negotiated and done under a veil of secrecy. The South Africans were paranoid. They wanted to do this in secrecy and at their own good time — the purpose of this was to publicly declare this when all was done and only when the inspectors from the Atomic Energy Association were about to do their inspection. Up to then, all would believe the country still had the bomb, ready for deployment if necessary, and therefore was not to be pressurised or messed with, particularly by the communists. Brilliant actually, because all trod warily when dealing with the South Africans. Everything had to be at their own good time."

Peace realised that in diplomatic circles, something had to be going on. Clearly, there were now two Afrikaner factions, those in favour of a move to a more democratic persuasion and political representation for all and those who wished to maintain the status quo at all costs even if this resulted in conflict. De Klerk had to know what the right-wing was trying to do. One had to wonder whether de Klerk was aware that the bombs previously held in the vaults at Pelindaba, which adjoined the nuclear research centre run by the South African Nuclear Energy Corporation, were no longer there and that only a lesser number had been decommissioned as had been instructed? Did he believe all had been decommissioned?

They all began to eat, the discussions now far removed from politics and bombs. The meal was excellent and of course, Botswana being renowned for its game and cattle-ranching, there were sumptuous, open-fire barbequed steaks — his rare just as he liked it. It was only when coffee was served that the conversation again drifted towards Van Rhyn.

The secretary resumed from where he had left off.

"The bad news is that the bombs you saw have been spirited out of Copperton on three enormous articulated trucks and well hidden under tarpaulins as ordinary cargo. Anyway, I'm also sure their contents are well disguised. The damn vehicles are already on the move and we don't know the destination but do know the direction. They're heading south, stopping only to take on fuel. This convoy is led and followed by other vehicles — most definitely there for protection," he said, unable to hide his frustration.

"The convoy's direction appears to confirm our suspicions that they're on the way to Overberg at Arniston, or Waenhuiskrans as the Afrikaners choose to refer to the place. In military circles it is referred to as the OTB, an abbreviation of the Afrikaans phrase *Overberg Toetsbaan*, the Overberg Test Range, if you like. This is the South African Defence Department's weapons systems testing facility, which includes rocket launch sites. It is near Cape Agulhas, which as you probably know, is the southernmost point of Africa. This is an area of flat sandy soil, coastal dunes, and windswept stunted vegetation — an ideal testing ground," the ambassador said. "It's actually sheep-farming country," he added as an afterthought.

The American, Jim Croxley, looked at Peace. "We've been keeping an eye on the place, satellite over flights and you probably know the rest. Over the years, they've brought in sophisticated equipment, tracking radar, optical tracking equipment, and mobile cine-theodolites. Launch sites have been erected and it was from there that the RSA-3 intermediate-range ballistic test missiles were launched. The site borders on the town of Arniston. It's a holiday resort which is very popular during the year-end holiday months, but otherwise virtually deserted except for a few die-hards and pensioners who have chosen to spend their last years away from the humdrum of normal everyday life. Actually, a damn nice place to retire. There's only one access road, which ends at Arniston. This joins Arniston and Bredasdorp, a country town with a South African Air Force base nearby."

"As you can imagine, it's an ideal place to launch rockets armed with nuclear weapons. The rockets they have were built as a joint venture with the Israelis; we know they're damn accurate," Barkly interjected.

Listening to the Americans and the ambassador, Peace knew Van Rhyn, who must surely know that his plan had been compromised, had done the unexpected. Obviously having realised the mine was under surveillance, he understood that the aircraft at Copperton could no longer be used to deliver the nukes. Christ, the bastard would launch these from on top of a rocket! Clearly, the man must have considerable pull among the disenchanted in government and the military.

"Whatever he's planning can't be too far in the future," Peace said.

"Van Rhyn has left Cape Town with his wife and daughter in tow and guess where he's staying?" The secretary hesitated for a beat but didn't wait for a reply. "At the bloody testing range. They have fabulous accommodation within the complex. It houses a private hotel of sorts, which was originally used to accommodate those Israeli scientists who assisted the South Africans with their rocket development as well as the manufacture of the nuclear weapons. Van Rhyn's helicopter landed a few hours ago, as did General Booyens'."

This seemed to be news to Sir Brooke, the ambassador, whose concern was visible on his face.

"Obviously you've been planning something?" Peace stated leaning slightly back. There was no immediate reply. "Well, gentlemen, do we have a plan?" Peace asked again with more emphasis.

Barkly smiled knowingly. "Damn right we have. My boss, the Section Chief for Southern Africa, and your Vice-Admiral amongst others, have been putting something together for quite a while. The original idea was to hit Copperton but Van Rhyn's sudden deployment of the nukes to Overberg was unexpected. You saw the aircraft and men on the apron.

They're there to help us. Unfortunately, they're now in the wrong place at the wrong time. We were going to do a drop on Copperton. The place is so isolated it would've been over before the rest of the country realised anything. Somehow, they need to be dissuaded and being as isolated as they are, we'd be surprised if the rest of the world ever heard a thing. Rest assured, Van Rhyn would have hushed it up, since he'd be the last person wishing to draw attention to themselves. All we would've had to do was explain, and… And that probably with de Klerk's blessing. It's different now," he said solemnly.

"Your Vice Admiral Sir John Whitehead has made a suggestion, which our top brass and some high-ups in government have sanctioned. Although, bloody risky, if you ask me," the ambassador said and then added, "but it might just work." He looked over at the Americans. "Our friends also seem to like the idea. Of course, President de Klerk and his right-hand men concur. You must understand, the poor man doesn't know friend from foe; his hands are tied. He sees us as their only hope against the ultra-right if they opt for force."

Ultra-right! Christ, that's putting it mildly. Van Rhyn, and his mob have to be insane.

"Why aren't there any military commanders here?" Peace asked.

"Good question. Actually, there are, but they know naught about WMDs and missiles and we're not about to tell them. They're here to create a diversion. That's all — there's to be no open conflict. They'll attend their own briefing when we're ready but there'll be nothing said about nukes," Sir Brooke said.

"What about the Botswana government?" Peace enquired.

"As far as this base is concerned, they seem to regard it as American territory and leave us alone. Sure, a few locals do work here, and they have a few liaison personnel around, but they're all rather low-key. Certainly nothing to worry about," Barkly replied. "Incidentally, American aircraft are flying in and out of here all the time. They're no novelty, if you know what I mean," he added.

"So, what's to happen?" Peace asked.

Barkly smiled. "We're going to kit some of our boys out as South African

Air Force trainees, you know, the same as the battle fatigues they use here. Make them look like conscripts who've just started their basic training. There's a basic training ground bordering the main road to Arniston, which has its own barracks. It's only occasionally used by their Air Force in Bredasdorp. A bunch of trainees suddenly arriving should raise no concern. This has happened before and there's little, if any, interaction between the Bredasdorp military and the Overberg test site. The place is still top secret. We're hoping to use our men to create a diversion."

The American paused, looking at Peace, awaiting a comment. Peace remained silent.

"This is where we the four of us come in. This includes Cherry — we'll brief her in the next few days. She's essential as none of us speaks Afrikaans, and your boss insisted that you both accompany us. Anyway, I've been told she's a professional," Barkly said.

"She is. I'll vouch for it," Peace retorted.

Barkly continued, "Great. Anyway, we're in for a high altitude drop using ram-air chutes. I understand you're all familiar with these and have undergone training. It'll be a night-drop. Our job is to find the missiles and WMDs and neutralise them and take out Van Rhyn, if that's possible. However, our bosses have agreed the WMDs and rockets are the priority."

"Surely they'll pick us up? The place is probably bristling with radar."

"No. With the CODESA talks still ongoing and progressing, the place is being mothballed. De Klerk doesn't want to rock the boat. They've shut down all intruder surveillance and stopped all development a while back already. There are supposed to be only security personnel on the site, who now seem to be working for Van Rhyn. The government, or rather let's say, de Klerk's people are not even aware of the activity now going on there. Security is now in Van Rhyn's hands — he may have replaced all of them with his own men. Remember what was said, the government doesn't want to be attracting attention to what was going on behind the scenes. The recent supposed decommissioning of the WMDs drew more than enough attention."

Croxley raised a hand from the table to draw attention. "By the way, Overberg is situated on a local air route their national carrier uses. An aircraft flying over the complex at high altitude shouldn't raise any suspicions."

Peace didn't like it. *Still too many unanswered ifs and buts.*

The secretary looked around the table. "Okay, enough of that. We'll hold several briefings before we go into action. You'll even have an opportunity to brush up on your parachuting here. We won't be moving from here for a few days yet."

Later, over drinks served on the porch, Peace soon learned that the two Americans were professionals, having seen action in Afghanistan, Columbia, and the Middle East. At least this was reassuring. They'd both been active US Navy SEALS before being press-ganged into the CIA, as they jokingly put it.

Peace had done his fair share and more for his country, first as a first officer and then as commander of an attack submarine in the Middle East, this mostly in the Persian Gulf. Following that, he'd seen considerable action in the Falklands War. It was the war in the South Atlantic that introduced him to covert operations, and it was then that he was transferred to VA's command.

Peace was not entirely happy with the developments. He didn't need anyone to remind him he was a loner. Being partnered by Cherry was bad enough. Now there were four of them. Because he was considered utterly ruthless and was known to have the tenacity of a bulldog, this had earned him a special place in what VA referred to as his 'special squad.' There were not many others like him who were afforded such discretion to kill or not kill if the situation so warranted. The thought that the mission could fail never entered his mind. This fight had to be won; there was no alternative. The understanding that they would operate as a US Seal Team left him uneasy.

Chapter Twenty-Two

It took three weeks to hone the men into a coordinated fighting force. They had spent days in the desert on route marches or crawling through the sand and rock, and marching in the dark, taking up defensive positions around some imaginary guarded complex. All were seasoned troops and the three weeks' additional training sufficient to weld them into a first-class fighting group. Peace was surprised by how well Cherry fitted in. The fact that she was a woman never became an issue, as she matched them all in every respect. Peace was impressed at how quickly she had recovered from the wound that nearly killed her. Professionalism demanded that their relationship never be allowed to come to the fore — none were to be aware of it.

All four doggedly practised their skydiving skills. First during daylight and then at night; jumping from twelve-thousand feet, free-falling to below two-thousand feet before deploying their chutes. Their proposed target was small — no more than forty yards square. They were told this was the area of the rocket-assembly hangar's roof at Overberg and that it was flat and with little in the way of air-conditioning machinery and ducting that could interfere with their parachute landing. It was considered sufficiently large for a night landing. And the building had both an external and internal staircase to the roof. If necessary, the bogus South African troops would draw the complex security's attention for a while, and give the four sufficient time to descend into the assembly hangar's interior without being observed. The bombs were said to be secured somewhere in the missile assembly building, obviously in some separate safe place and probably areas removed from the usual work zone. There was no doubt a separate guard detail would have been assigned to guard the weapons.

Finally, it was decided that a diversionary force consisting of only twenty-five of the bogus troops masquerading as Trainee South African Air Force cadets, would be flown to Swellendam, a town relatively close to Overberg and which had an airfield far enough from the town itself not to draw attention to any sudden unusual activity. The main and only runway was sufficiently long to accommodate a large Norman Islander aircraft. The proximity of a South African Air Force base nearby in Bredasdorp would hopefully justify the presence of troops in the vicinity of Overberg and prevent any suspicions, since these kinds of movements were, with any luck, a common event.

Again, through certain sympathetic connections in the South African military, two South African Army Samil all-wheel-drive canvas-canopied trucks were obtained, which would transport the troops from Swellendam to the outskirts of Overberg where they would occupy the deserted barracks. Weather conditions were a factor that had to be reckoned with; the strong winds along the coast were notorious. Assuming conditions were a go, the four agents would make their jump while the troops would immediately close in on the complex's perimeter and initiate their field manoeuvres to create the necessary diversion.

Intelligence had revealed that security around the complex in Overberg was still substantial — the perimeter fence was constantly patrolled, as were the beaches that extended outwards from the complex. Also, there were two manned observation towers. It was hoped the bogus troop exercise would draw their attention and persuade the perimeter guards to desert their usual place and move towards the perimeter fence that bordered the road, so dissuading any from entering the complex.

A standby diesel-driven electric substation had been built within the complex, which adjoined the base's workshop area. Its function was to automatically kick in if the area was to experience a power failure through the national grid. Apparently, this had happened before when the Cape experienced an unusually severe storm. If power was interrupted, circuits in the substation would close, the diesel engines would start and automatically resume supplying electrical power. The substation contained four

South African manufactured ADE V12 diesel engines, each driving a huge generator, sufficiently powerful to supply power to a medium town. The team had given much thought to sabotaging the grid and the substation. It was decided, however, that the power grid would have to be incapacitated, since the sudden and complete darkness was sure to create alarm and chaos — or so it was hoped.

Chapter Twenty-Three

All four were dressed entirely in black. The black balaclavas they wore only revealed their eyes, as the surrounding skin was blackened. Besides the Heckler and Koch USP9 with silencer strapped to his thigh, Peace cradled a Heckler and Koch MP5 machine pistol in his lap, as did his three companions. Each had chosen his favourite type of sidearm and in addition, had two concussion grenades clipped to their bulletproof vests. A slim rucksack containing a variety of explosives and timers was stationed next to each of them.

As highly trained operatives, they were all well aware that a small explosion could destroy any rocket, and even when dormant, the explosives were dangerous and highly volatile. The bombs, however, required disarmament, the nuclear trigger removed, and the weapon dismantled. This needed a degree of expertise, which was where the two CIA agents came in. However, it was considered highly unlikely the weapons were in any way armed, as they were probably all without the essential chemical explosive and the actual triggers.

The twin-engined De Havilland Twin Otter was at eleven-thousand feet, the drone of the engines loud in the barely insulated fuselage, the four passengers sitting in seats facing each other down the length of the aircraft. The inside of the plane was in darkness except for the jump light above the bulkhead door which glowed red and led to the cockpit. They'd just passed through a low-pressure weather front that lay across the country, the night sky around them blotted out by clouds, the aircraft tossed about by vertical winds and the night intermittently lit for a split second as jagged flashes of lightning rent the air. Fortunately, they'd left the storm behind and the flight now proceeded smoothly. The sky had cleared and lights dotted the land below.

Even though they were out of the path of the storm, the weather was not ideal. A moderate to strong southwester blew in from the South Atlantic bringing a cold front with it, but this was estimated to only reach the Cape in the early morning. Still, the wind would add a degree of danger to the jump. The parachute landing's approach would require perfect timing.

"Get ready!" the jumpmaster said and opened the exit hatch in the side of the fuselage. The wind roared into the fuselage with gale-force strength. The four stood, all facing rearward, each carrying out a perfunctory check of the harness of the person in front, the last having been checked by the jumpmaster. Peace took up the rear. They now clipped their rucksacks to their chests, the MP5s firmly attached to these with special hook-tape straps.

He placed his hand on Cherry's shoulder, who was standing with her back to him, facing the exit. They had jumped multiple times while at Gaborone, including four times at night, so this was no longer a novelty. But since they were now jumping into action together, the excitement and fear were palpable. He could even sense some negative emotions coming from her.

She turned to him. "Good luck," she shouted with a wink.

"You too," he yelled in return.

The flashing amber turned to a steady green.

"Go, go, go!" the jumpmaster shouted, literally shoving the first agent out of the door, the others following almost immediately.

Peace exited the fuselage door in the classic dive position with arms and legs spread.

Very rapidly, his speed increased as he plunged towards the earth, working his body and limbs to stabilise his rapid fall and to stop the slow spin his body had taken on. The wind roared in his ears even though they were covered by the thick balaclava. His pace through the cold night air soon reached the terminal velocity of one hundred and twenty miles per hour. He sought out his companions, careful to ensure that the movement of his head did not upset his horizontal stability. He had been the last out so they had to be below him.

In the thin air of the still-high altitude, the sky above consisted of a myriad of stars interspersed with broken cloud, the faint light sufficient to enable him to make out his companions, who were also dropping with arms and legs akimbo just below him as expected.

The plan was that they would freefall for about a minute and a half. He looked closely at the ground, searching for those contours of the shoreline, which he had so carefully memorised. The most important landmark would be Saxon Reef, which from this altitude could clearly be seen with its stark white contrast as the waves continuously collided with the rocks. It was a white finger against the black of the sea as it stretched miles in a southerly direction into the ocean. He believed he was facing south and confirmed this by the small compass on his wrist.

They were right on target; the testing site had to be just in front of him. He'd have to wait until nearer to the ground before he'd be able to properly distinguish it. It was agreed that the others would close in on him, but would ensure they kept at least a hundred feet from each other so to avoid being entangled in each other's chutes once these had been deployed.

As they passed through five-thousand feet, he began to make out the missile site, the perimeter fence clearly visible where the white sand had been cleared of brush to allow vehicles to patrol, creating a thin ribbon around the complex. A black strip indicated the main road to the north of the site — joining Arniston and Bredasdorp. The lights of a lone motor vehicle moved slowly along it. He made out the missile assembly hangar, its sides faintly illuminated from the lights below, and the rectangle of its roof no more than a black target. They were spot on where they needed to be. At two and half thousand feet, his chute automatically deployed, blossoming open above him, and the wide straps biting into his thighs. Using his hands, he quickly grabbed the two stabilising lines and manoeuvred his descent towards the hangar's roof.

Soon the roof loomed below, growing rapidly larger by the second. As he steered his chute towards the centre of the roof, he suddenly saw a dark shape and realised that a chute had just collapsed on the roof. They were landing into the wind and he had just enough time to pull down on the two stabilising lines he clutched in his hands, drawing the back of the square chute down — the manoeuvre dramatically killing his forward speed. He missed the black-clad parachutist already on the roof by no more than a foot or so. His rubber-soled canvas boots touched down on the roof, and he only had to run forward a few feet to steady himself. He immediately collapsed the chute's canopy around him, the black nylon material settling before his feet.

Another two distinct thuds followed as the last of the team safely landed, all successfully pulling in their parachutes. Peace was amazed that this had gone without a hitch so far. *A good start*, he thought.

Once all chutes had been gathered, all four immediately dropped prone onto the roof. Peace and Barkly crawled forward towards the edge, which was no more than a concrete sill a few inches high.

Just as they peered over the edge, they heard the distant staccato bark of automatic weapons, with another fusillade following thereafter.

"Right on time," Peace said to Barkly. "That should draw the guards' attention."

Just then, there followed the crack of a concussion grenade in the distance.

"Night manoeuvres," the American commented. "Somebody is going to be as mad as hell since nobody informed him that the South African military had planned a night exercise. Let's hope this distracts the guards."

They peered over the side and carefully inspected the area surrounding the building. There were a few people about, mostly in groups of two, but now moving towards the northern perimeter fence, no doubt anxious to discover what was going on. Hopefully, they'd all desert their usual posts out of curiosity.

The hangar had to be about one hundred and fifty feet high, but that was expected, as an RSA-4 multi-stage rocket would reach nearly to the roof with its three stages. The plan was to abseil the seaward side once they were certain all guards had moved towards the northern fence. Fortunately, there were no watchtowers on the seaward side of the complex and it was thought unlikely any would see them descending against the cement-grey concrete wall of the hangar.

Strong, but thin grey nylon ropes were quickly tied to an air-vent that rose from the concrete floor.

191

"Check your radios," Barkly said.

This only took a minute or so — the throat microphones and tiny boom microphones that were taped to the side of their mouths and the single earphone clamped to their left ears functioned perfectly.

"Peace, you first… Cherry, you follow. We'll be right behind you," Barkly said.

By this time, all rucksacks and their contents were within reach and their machine pistols hung from their necks ready for immediate use.

Four nylon ropes were slowly allowed to snake down towards the ground and Peace hoped no eagle-eyed scouts happened to be focused on the hangar at that precise moment.

Chapter Twenty-Four

Peace was about to clip his abseil harness to the rope when a movement to one side drew his attention. He turned to look and, recalling the diagrams and photographs he had studied, realised that he was looking at the *Die Herberg*, a building aptly referred to as the 'The Inn'. This was where important guests and scientists, who were mostly from Israel, were accommodated when at Overberg.

It was a two-storey building with a large central square in which a swimming pool had a place of prominence. All the lights appeared to be on — even the underwater lighting in the pool, which enhanced the sparkling blue of the water. Part of the quadrangle was taken up by a flat slate-stone floored area, which was dotted with a few terrace umbrellas, wooden veranda tables, benches, and chairs. These too were bathed in yellow light from numerous lamps on tall stands placed at random in the courtyard.

A small crowd had exited the building, their attention no doubt drawn by the intermittent gunfire beyond the security fence and towards the road that fed Arniston.

Peace quickly removed the NVD issued by the Americans from his rucksack. This was the latest state-of-the-art night vision device guaranteed to capture sufficient photons to identify an individual at long range, even in the dark of night. He brought the instrument to his eye and immediately identified Van Rhyn. He too was staring through binoculars in the direction from where the gunfire had emanated. General Booyens stood alongside him in camouflage army fatigues and to Peace's surprise, he recognised Janet standing to the man's right. There was no mistaking her mass of dark hair and the long legs in shorts with flat-heeled sandals. He recognised others who were mostly Van Rhyn's henchmen and saw two other officers in uniform. They all stood on a long balcony on the first floor that overlooked the surrounding area and had an unobstructed view of the goings on.

"Is that Van Rhyn and his crowd?" Cherry enquired softly from next to his shoulder.

"Damn right. If it isn't the bastard himself with his whole bloody entourage. I just know that him being here will complicate matters. He's bound to be wary," he snorted with obvious frustration.

"Forget him. The WMDs first," Barkly hissed forcefully. "We'll deal with his crowd later."

Peace had to resist responding, thinking that it was quite possible that Van Rhyn and his men would, in fact, be the ones who would be dealing with the four of them.

Bloody Americans — why did everything have to be reduced to an acronym? WMDs? God, just call it a bloody atom bomb!

However, Peace knew Barkly was right. This was payback time, and Van Rhyn had to die, no matter what it took. He was the driving force behind this Afrikaner movement.

As they prepared to abseil down the side, Cherry was just about to step over the small ledge to begin her descent when suddenly, Peace held out an arm and stopped her. He pointed and they all looked in the direction to where he gestured.

Two SUVs had appeared and stopped in front of the *Die Herberg*. Several people filed out of the building. He saw Van Rhyn and General Booyens were among them.

"Possibly going to find out what the hell's going on since they probably can't understand what the military is doing out there. At least I can't see any weapons," Peace said.

The vehicles drove rapidly towards the main gate and passed through. Just then, a South African Army Land Rover appeared in the distance, braking sharply next to the SUVs. South African Air Force officers alighted from the vehicle and started a discussion with those who had climbed from the SUVs. Peace was surprised to see the parties shake hands. They stood around for a few minutes, clearly having a rather in-depth conversation considering the gesticulating. The parties then returned to their vehicles where all of them, including the Land Rover, did a U-turn, and returned to the *Die Herberg* in the complex. This took a few minutes.

"Obviously, somebody's performance was quite convincing. Van Rhyn and his lot certainly appeared satisfied. It seems our bogus troops have been accepted," Barkly said.

"C'mon, let's go," Peace said, clearly impatient.

Cherry went first, her familiarity with the routine obvious as the turnbuckle on her harness drummed while she deftly let the rope slide through her fingers. She then swiftly dropped to the ground where she remained crouched. Peace immediately followed with the two Americans close behind him. The ropes had to be left but there seemed little likelihood they would be discovered.

A cemented road circled the hangar's perimeter on three sides. This was bordered by a wide swath of bare ground on its outer side on which some wild bush and scrub had taken root. The ground on the side of the hangar that faced the sea was levelled and concreted to where the ground began to fall away towards the water. Two railway lines, exceptionally wide apart, were laid in the cement and disappeared under the huge hangar doors that sealed the building. At the other end of the concrete strip and at least four hundred yards from the hangar, an illuminated steel gantry rose into the night sky, the highest point demarcated by a single red light. Beyond this structure a four-hundred-yard-wide strip of the coastal dunes commenced, which acted as a barrier to the sea. The edge of the dunes fell away directly into the sea with only a narrow beach to be seen.

No further word was spoken; they knew their objective — the interior of the hangar.

Other than the massive hangar doors through which the rocket would pass, there were only two entrances to the building — one facing the road, which they immediately dismissed as this would put them in sight of *Die Herberg,* and the two watchtowers near the road. The only other entrance they could use was that which adjoined the huge sliding doors of the hangar.

This was also a steel double door sliding entrance, but was large enough to accommodate large transport vehicles. If anything large was to be offloaded, it would be through this entrance it would pass.

Peace thought of the bombs. This had to be their objective. They noticed that the sliding doors had a small access door built into it.

Crouched low, they scurried along the building's side, one after the other, with Barkly taking the lead. On reaching the corner of the building, he signalled they should stop and all lie down on the ground. He called Peace forward. Cautiously, Peace peered round the corner. No one was to be seen, but what he did see under the huge doors was a line of light from within the hangar and he could hear the distinct whine of machinery. Somebody was using a grinder.

Croxley was immediately behind them so Peace turned.

"We're lucky. They don't seem to have been put off by the disturbance outside, so they're obviously not expecting intruders. Let's hope they stay busy," he hissed.

Croxley nodded. Barkly whispered to Peace to look again, stepping back to let him pass.

The sliding double doors were only a few feet away, the gap at the bottom about two inches through which light streamed. The light from behind the sliding door clearly outlined the small pedestrian door within it. He was about to step back to confer with Barkly when suddenly the small door opened inward, sending a bright shaft of light along the concrete apron. A man in uniform stepped over the sill, an automatic carbine with its steel stock folded back hung from his shoulder and its pistol grip held in one hand. They all tensed at the noise associated with the opening door. As the sound of booted feet approached, Peace drew back from the corner, every muscle tensed in anticipation of the man's appearance.

The man appeared around the corner and when he saw them, his eyes widened in surprise. It was obvious that the last thing he expected was to find somebody there — especially clad as they were with their weapons and bala-clavas. His reaction was immediate and he tried to raise the carbine muzzle.

Peace's movements were a blur. He stepped forward, and gripping his H&K USP9 automatic by its silencer, swung the butt of the gun down

196

at the man's head. A sickening crack rang out, followed by the man's legs folding under him as he crumpled to the concrete.

Barkly bent to examine him. "I think he's dead," he said.

"I know, I hit the bastard as hard as I could. We'll have to get rid of the body. Shove it deep into the scrub and bush over there," Peace whispered, his voice cold. He pointed at the adjoining virgin ground. Barkly and Croxley dragged the body across the rough concrete with the man's boots and clothing making a rasping sound. Cherry threw the man's weapon into the bush too.

Peace guessed that the small access door was still unlocked. They were dressed in black and if they stepped into a brightly lit hall, there'd be no mistaking them.

"Silencers," he said. The others knew what he meant — no automatic gunfire. "This'll take balls. Ready?" he enquired with a glint in his eye.

"I've got mine," Cherry retorted.

Croxley snorted at her attempt at humour but smiled.

"Here goes," Peace said with an intake of breath.

Steeling himself, he pushed against the door. There was a click and the door swung open, giving him his first glimpse of the interior. He stepped to the side and turned to flatten his profile, only part of his face visible to any on the inside. As expected, this was brightly lit by huge mercury-vapour lights strung along the top of the ceiling in rows way above them. He immediately noticed two elevated walkways attached to the side of the hangar with steel stairways at each end, both giving access to the catwalks which were about twenty feet from the ground. Now that they were inside, the sound of activity was much louder.

He soon realised there had to be a whole workforce in the hangar's interior. The catwalks were vacant, which was a relief. Had there been guards they would easily be detected, dressed as they were. Plan B would then come into effect — overrun the site by sheer force of numbers using the nearby company of fake trainee infantry. Of course, no one would then be able to contain the news of stolen bombs, the hijack of the missile-testing site, and Great Britain and the US's involvement. There was sure to follow an international uproar since South Africa was a sovereign country after all — neither the British nor the Americans had the right to be there.

There were two huge multiple-wheeled road-hauliers parked directly in front of them, one in front of the other. He could see the large but bare cradles on their loading decks and realised the cradles had to have contained the bombs. But where were they now? In the hangar or somewhere in a weapons storage bunker? The vehicles restricted his vision, but fortunately, those inside the hangar couldn't see them either. Clearly, these trucks brought the WMDs from Copperton.

"Let's slide under the rig — it's a secure place to hide for now," Croxley said dropping to his knees and crawling under the vehicle. They all followed suit and the dark shadow cast by the vehicle concealed them well. Prone as they were on the floor, they had a clear picture of what lay beyond since they were able to see under the vehicles. The hangar was a cacophony of noise with the sound of machinery, occasional shouting, and the clang of steel.

"Holy Jesus!" Peace hissed, initially overwhelmed by the sight before him.

They all swivelled their heads in response to Peace's remark. Before them, no more than a hundred feet away, stood an enormous vertical missile supported in a cradle mounted on a huge rail flatcar that straddled both sets of railway lines. Numerous lights were aimed at it, and starkly lit the huge matt white cylinder, which was about twelve feet in diameter with the orange, white and blue South African flag proudly displayed on its side. Directly below the flag, written vertically, was *Suid-Afrikaanse Lugmag*[17]. The cone of the rocket was hidden within the latticework of a massive gantry, which crowded the rocket on both sides, this being at least eighty or ninety feet high. A caged elevator shaft was stationed upwards within the gantry.

"I guess that contraption is needed to mount the nuclear warhead on top of it?" Croxley murmured, referring to the gantry.

"You're damn right — I believe they're doing just that. Van Rhyn's insane! I wonder where he's aimed the damned thing! It's an Israeli Jericho missile if I'm not mistaken, or it certainly looks as if it is," Barkly replied.

"No, no, it's a South African RSA-4. It's an ICBM multiple-stage rocket — an orbital launcher and can target anywhere in the world. The South

17. South African Air Force

African government boasted that it's accurate to within three hundred yards," Peace said. "My boss insisted that I study the South African missile arsenal," he added. "The good news is that it's a solid-fuel rocket, which you probably already know, but it's going to make one God Almighty bang when we blow it. An explosion can't trigger the warhead; the bomb's trigger mechanism is too sophisticated."

"Still, I think it too damn dangerous blowing this complex sky-high. Just think of the people we'll kill. What we need to do is kill its heart — the mission control system if you like. That's where the damn computers are and it's from there that it's armed and guided," Barkly insisted.

"And pray tell where we might find this mission control?" Peace asked sarcastically, looking around.

"That's got to be the blockhouse-like structure that appears on that reconnaissance photograph with only its top sticking out of the ground," the American replied.

Peace immediately recalled the structure. "Sorry, forgot about that. I have to admit, I don't have much compassion for any of those here, even if some are only scientists. They're about to nuke a hundred thousand or more. Nobody can tell me this lot here is not aware that a nuke is being loaded on the top of this bloody rocket. I think the idea to attack the blockhouse is dangerous. It may be a better option to go for the rocket and bombs. This place is like a box of matches in a fireworks factory," Peace said, smiling evilly.

"Apologies, you may be right. That was my damn conscience coming to the fore," Barkly whispered.

Peace smiled to himself.

Suddenly, the sound of engines cut through the air. Clearly, more than one vehicle had stopped outside the sliding doors. The small access door banged open and a few people entered the hangar. From under the rig's axles, they could only see feet. Peace noticed that some wore camouflage trousers tucked into combat boots. He had the feeling this had to be Van Rhyn and company. Those in camouflage were the officers, and it also dawned on him that the woman in sandals was Janet. The group stood for a minute just inside the hangar conversing in Afrikaans, no more than fifteen feet away from the intruders.

The group then walked further forward into the hangar and Peace breathed a sigh of relief.

"I heard what they were talking about," Cherry said, her voice close to a whisper. "They've got this thing aimed at the Cubans in southern Angola, particularly at some place called Cuito Cuanavale. Apparently, the Cubans have a large number of men and armour concentrated there. Booyens was saying that if the Cubans in Africa are scared off and there's a civil war in South Africa, the Blacks, or *kaffirs* as he referred to them couldn't rely on the Cubans for help. But Van Rhyn appears to have other ideas — he wants to drop it on some densely black populated area in the country. He believes using a nuclear weapon, even if used only against the Blacks, would scare the Cubans off in any event. General Booyens…" She shook her head unable to say more and then took a breath. "God, what a self-opinionated asshole. None of them seemed to be concerned that they'd be killing millions," she said, clearly horrified.

Peace butted in. "Never mind that, what did he eventually decide? Did you hear?"

Cherry continued, "Well, he argued that the Cubans were not a force to be underestimated and that they were just looking for an excuse to resume the conflict against South Africa. However, if they were hit with a bomb which would wipe out a good portion of Castro's expeditionary force in Angola, then he would back off… hopefully permanently."

"Well, whatever they finally decide on, we can't let it happen. We've got to take this bird out and now!" Barkly said vehemently.

"We are agreed on that. C'mon guys, let's find their little power station, and attach a few of our toys to the machinery," Croxley added with a smirk.

"Four's a crowd. If we're going to be moving around outside, I suggest you stay here while Jim and I disable the standby generators," Barkly said.

Peace agreed. The two Americans then backed off and disappeared through the access door that still stood open. Seconds later, there were the sounds of a scuffle and then a sharp cry from outside.

"Damn!" Peace exclaimed in Cherry's ear. "Van Rhyn and his people left someone with the cars. God knows what's going to happen if they return and find their guard missing." Peace assumed that the Americans had successfully dealt with the unexpected. He hoped they had got rid of the body. At least, if Van Rhyn returned, he may initially only think his man had deserted his post.

"There's little we can do about it now," she replied.

Just then, his earpiece crackled. "We ran into some schmuck outside, but he's no more."

"So we heard," Peace replied.

Cherry and Peace had taken up station behind a set of huge double wheels on the rig's trailer. The size of the shadow cast by the wheels was ideal but uncomfortable, forcing them to lie prone on their stomachs, with the massive axle over their heads. They remained silent.

Peace watched the activity within the hangar, trying to figure out where the technicians were with their launch preparations. It soon became clear that whatever bomb they'd intended to mount was already in position on the missile, since the missile's nose cone was removed and what had to be a bomb mounted on the top. Where were the other WMDs? He was sure the missile was about ready to move out of the hangar to the launch pad. All that had to be done was to replace the nose cone. Already equipment that had been used in preparation was being moved from the rail tracks. This signalled only one thing.

Again, he heard Barkly's voice in his ear. "Okay, guys, we're done here. We've splashed diesoline all over the place. When current passes to the starter motors on the diesel engines, this will trigger the detonators, and the Semtex will do the rest. Goodbye to any emergency power."

He knew what the Americans had done. They'd wired the starter motors' battery wires through a few detonators inserted in the Semtex. The moment current sped through the wires so would it pass through the detonators. *Whammo*! It was going to be a remarkable sight!

"We'll be back with you in a minute or two," Barkly said.

True to his word, the two Americans were soon crawling into position below the rig.

Peace looked at Barkly and Croxley. Barkly smiled and nodded. Peace pulled a portable walkie-talkie radio no bigger than a box of cigarettes from a pocket.

"Mike, Mike do you read?" he said speaking into the instrument. "We're ready — blow the lines."

He knew that the commanding officer of the bogus trainee troop was waiting for the instruction, having placed explosives on the pylons that carried the high-tension wires to the complex.

It was about a minute later when the hangar was suddenly cast in darkness. This was followed a second after by a massive explosion. Although those in the interior could not see the fireball, this was bright enough to briefly illuminate the exterior. They caught sight of this through the open pedestrian door, and could see corrugated iron sheets and other debris flying in all directions; the powerful shock wave collided with the massive steel doors of the hangar with a huge bang, and they rattled loudly on their rails. Those prone on the floor felt it as it surged through the small access door, pushing a cloud of dust before it.

"Good God!" Cherry exclaimed, obviously having not expected anything quite so spectacular.

The sudden darkness required night vision glasses, which they quickly extracted from their packs. They took in the bedlam, in shades of white and green, which had now taken hold on the assembly floor. The massive explosion followed by near complete darkness in the interior of the hangar left all in no doubt that something serious had gone wrong. Lamps and torches soon appeared, the cones of light stabbing through the darkness. The Semtex charges they'd been issued with were highly sophisticated, with a radio signal connecting all of them. Irrespective of when they were set, they would explode simultaneously. Peace was taking no chances that they would be found.

The other important task was to find the other nuclear bombs — they had to be somewhere in the hangar, there was nowhere else they could be.

Croxley and Barkly had, while making their way to the emergency power station, found what they thought to be a weapons or missile bunker, but this was empty and unguarded.

"As agreed, bombs first, then the rocket," Peace said. "Let's stash our packs and the machine pistols — we'll only use automatics, but make sure the silencers are attached. Get rid of the balaclavas and get out your miniature torches. What we need are those lab coats the techs are wearing. Let's find a few. There have to be change rooms and an ablution block in here somewhere. We have a few minutes; it'll take a while before they get the lights working again."

There did not appear to be many with emergency torches around them. The group moved swiftly through the confused crowd, keeping to the sides of the building avoiding any with torches. They soon found a group of rooms within the building along one side, with a sign reading *Kleedkamers.*

"This is it," Cherry said. "*Kleedkamers* — that means change rooms."

Swiftly, they entered to find the small passage leading off to two doorways.

"Let's not stand on formality," Peace said and grinned as they entered the men's room, leaving Croxley out in the passageway.

They were lucky, there were a few lab coats hanging from a row of hooks, which they quickly put on over their black jumpsuits, taking one along for Croxley. The off-white coats transformed their image, the only giveaway the black jump-boots, which no one would notice. They'd removed their balaclavas and wiped off the black grease from their faces as best they could. Their weapons were concealed under their spacious lab coats. The Semtex charges they placed in the large side pockets of their coats, since they were flat and not much bigger than a hand. Each had two grenades clipped to their chests. Unless someone looked at them closely, no one would notice the odd bulge or two.

"Find a forklift — I'm sure that's where the store area will be and no doubt the WMDs. They'd have to have used a forklift to unload them. Jim and I will go clockwise, you and Cherry the other way. Keep in contact," Barkly said.

Just then, a voice boomed around them. Somebody was using a megaphone or public-address system. The group listened intently, but it was in Afrikaans.

"This won't be easy. They're saying that they suspect sabotage and that everyone should be on the lookout. Nobody is allowed to leave the hangar; the entrance is guarded. Anybody attempting to do so will be shot on sight. It appears they believe the saboteurs are outside. There are only two entrances, the sliding doors will remain closed as will the missile rail-doors," Cherry translated.

"Okay, we still split but we'll exit as one group when we're ready. The job's twofold. Destroy the bomb's firing mechanism — Semtex charge will do the job. As we discussed, just attach it to the inner workings access plate on the bomb. This'll destroy the bomb's firing mechanism. We'll never have the time or opportunity to disarm the bombs. Only then, will we think about the rocket, okay? Remember, keep in touch."

"Are you sure the fuckin' things can't explode?" Croxley demanded with concern.

"Not possible — the explosive triggers aren't armed or have been removed but you know that, right?" Peace said.

"Just checking — what about radiation?"

"Don't worry about that — we won't be close," Peace replied.

They split. He and Cherry stuck to a demarcated walkway, which was painted on the flat concrete. They walked at a sedate pace, the beams of their torches directed in front of them, hoping that the concentrated light beams would partially blind those approaching from the front or any others trying to take a closer look at them.

They didn't have far to go. Just beyond the collection of rooms and offices, which protruded out from the side of the hangar, they found two large forklifts parked side to side. The beams of the torches could just pick out two guards with automatic carbines standing just beyond. Peace thought he could see two bombs — bulbous, elongated metal balls with large metal fins attached at one end. They rested in cradles, stacked two-high, the one stacked on the other.

"Me left, you right," Peace whispered. He withdrew his silenced automatic and fired, this immediately followed by another what seemed a hellishly loud bang. The two guards jerked like marionettes and collapsed to the concrete, one of their weapons hitting the floor with a loud clatter.

"Damn!" Peace hissed. "That was loud. It had to have been heard! Quickly, cover my back."

He moved forward.

They slunk past the two fallen guards, not sparing them a look as they

204

were surely dead. Just when the bombs were so near that he could stretch out and touch them, he was forcefully grabbed by the shoulder and spun around.

"Wie is jy?"[18] the male voice demanded in Afrikaans. Peace didn't miss the barrel pointing at his midriff. He wouldn't even have a chance to bring the automatic's barrel up since the man was watching the gun in his hand. The man would fire before he could do so.

In his other hand, he slowly brought the torch around, ready to switch it on and blind the man.

"Stop!" There was no missing the warning in the man's voice as he was sharply jabbed in the side with the carbine.

This was no technician; he was dressed in a uniform, a two-way radio clipped to his belt, an earpiece in his right ear and a microphone attached to his shirt just below his chin.

Peace wondered whether the others had heard what was transpiring. He could see no sign of Cherry within his peripheral vision.

"Ek vra weer, wie is jy?"[19] the man repeated, the beam of his torch jerking round, briefly passing the over the contents of the storage area. There was no mistaking the other bombs; these were all here bar one. Peace's mind was working at lightning speed between wondering where the other bomb could be and how to get rid of the guard when he heard the unmistakable plop of a silenced automatic loaded with subsonic cartridges being fired. The relatively slow-moving bullet struck the guard on the temple, and he actually saw the one side of the man's head bulge outwards before it exploded, spewing blood and brains. The man went down if struck by a sledgehammer. Minuscule particles of blood and flesh struck him in the face.

---

18. Who are you?

19. Again, I ask, who are you?

Chapter Twenty-Five

Cherry approached out of the darkness into the flair of the guard's fallen torch, which spread in an arc over the ground. She was still gripping the Heckler and Koch, the horizontal silencer ready to blast any other potential target into oblivion.

"Thank you," he whispered.

She smiled. "You owe me," she countered.

"Oh, I can't wait to repay you," he said with a chuckle, took her hand, and squeezed it.

They stood back to back to ensure they had all-round vision and were not about to be overwhelmed by any other surprise who could suddenly appear out of the darkness.

"Watch out, there's surely another guard. They wouldn't just leave one guard with the bombs," he said.

He pushed the transmit button on the earpiece.

"We've found the bombs, bar one, which I think is the neutron bomb. We must assume that this is already or about to be put in position on the missile. We are attaching the explosives."

"Roger that," Barkly replied.

Peace knew that the two men would now be making their way back to where the transport rig was parked, where they'd agreed they would rendezvous.

As per the plan, it would require only one explosive charge to destroy the missile, provided it was correctly placed. The damn thing was akin to a powder keg waiting for someone to light a fuse. Truly, it would be a spectacular sight.

They quickly withdrew the explosives from their pockets, each no larger than a square half-pound of butter in size, and a small liquid-crystal display device with a numbered keyboard attached apiece. These they affixed to the inspection panel of each bomb, set to explode in fifteen minutes' time. They immediately left the makeshift storage area, dodging around various crates, looking for a demarcated walkway, hoping that while clad in their coats, they did not draw attention to themselves.

Suddenly, they heard a loud rumbling. Peace soon realised it had to be the huge sliding doors being opened. A gap in the doors had hardly appeared when the rumbling stopped. There was just a small vertical slit between the doors through which the glow from the burning power station could be seen. He knew that without electricity they had to be trying to open these manually. This would take a while, since the doors were extremely heavy.

The Americans who had blown the standby power generators rendezvoused with Peace and Cherry without mishap, their only concern being the arrival of two Rooikat armoured cars. These were known to be formidable armoured vehicles with all-wheel-drive, fast in virtually any terrain, with multiple machine-guns and a 76mm turret-mounted anti-tank gun. The huge V10 diesel engine's growl could be heard distinctly above the other sounds of the hangar. The two vehicles stood just outside the access door. Obviously, these armoured vehicles had been called in to assist in finding the saboteurs. Peace had not expected Van Rhyn to have access to such sophisticated vehicles.

"I've a feeling this is going to get worse before it gets better," Croxley said, as they all lay under the same vehicle rig as before.

Peace ignored the remark. All of them had undoubtedly realised that any attack on the command blockhouse was now out of the question.

"Okay, it's time to leave. The rest of you stay here. Cherry and I will try to set the last of the explosives on that missile. Any explosion close to the external rocket fuel boosters should do."

Still dressed in their workers' coats, they slid out from beneath the rig and strode purposely down the walkway as if they had every right to be there, their weapons well concealed. He was pleased that Cherry was with him, as there was a sprinkling of women in the hangar and her presence lent them a degree of authenticity. No one would be expecting women saboteurs.

There were more lights around them now as some technicians had procured headlamps. They saw a group of men, two of whom were obviously security guards, manhandling a large portable generator into position. It looked large enough. Peace thought that if connected, it could probably illuminate the hangar's interior but nothing much else.

Suddenly there was a piercing whistle — it sounded like an English bobby. Several people began running in that direction.

Still trying to appear as nonchalant as possible, Peace whispered from the side of his mouth. "It seems that those we killed are no longer a secret. Let's move."

They speeded up their pace towards the gantry, moving past technicians with lights on the lattice walk.

As they approached the missile, Peace noted two tubes about two-thirds the length of the missile and no more than a foot and a half in diameter clamped vertically to it on opposite sides of the rocket. Peace knew that these were the booster rockets needed to get the heavily laden missile off the launch pad.

"See those tubes? We need to stick our explosive charge to at least one of them, best between the tube and the missile," Peace said.

It was not going to be that easy. The upright rocket rested in some sort of cradle, with the rocket engine's exhausts at least fifteen feet off the ground.

He then saw a ladder affixed to the gantry, which would enable a man to climb up alongside the missile, putting him near enough to squeeze the charge into the gap between the rocket and booster tube.

"Quickly! Give me a grenade!" he said to Cherry who handed it over without question.

He took it, pulled the pin, and threw it as far as he could into a collection of crates stacked alongside the hangar wall. He then grabbed her and pulled her down. A massive explosion followed together with a bright flash; the shock wave accompanied by fragmented pieces of wood blasting over them.

He dragged her to her feet. "Now!" he shouted.

They sprinted the short distance to the gantry and without checking whether he had been seen, he hauled himself up the ladder until the booster rocket's exhaust tubes were no more than two or three feet just below him.

He set the timer to go off simultaneously on a signal from those attached to the bombs and then stuffed the foam and canvas box into the small gap, making sure it was properly wedged in position.

He slid down the ladder rails like a submariner, back on the ground within seconds. There was no cry of alarm to indicate he had been seen, but Peace noticed a man come nearer with a baffled look on his face, probably trying to work out where the explosion came from. Peace saw the expression change as the man saw them. Thinking the man was about to raise the alarm, Peace never hesitated. With any sense of morality shoved somewhere in the deepest recesses of his mind, he simply pulled the trigger, the bullet hitting the man between the eyes. The shot was hardly audible above the clamour that now pervaded the hangar. The man had barely crumpled to the ground when Peace grabbed Cherry's arm and made for the exit. They didn't have more than ten minutes before the lot went up and they needed to put some distance between them and the rocket.

All other exits were barred and only the gap created between the sliding doors presented an escape route. As a few men cranked on a large handle to get the doors to open manually, the gap was now just large enough to allow a normal vehicle to pass through. Already people were hurrying out through the gap. It appeared that the explosion within the hangar had prompted the guards to allow all those inside to exit the building, completely abandoning the cordon they had placed around the entrances.

This was not the time to hesitate. Trying to blend in with the others and leaving the impression they were on some errand, they both strode purposely through the gap in the sliding doors. One of the two Rooikat armoured cars still had its engine running powerful headlights trained on the opening. They had no alternative but to walk through the bright light. Peace was very aware that their black combat boots had to be a dead giveaway.

"Stop! Don't move," someone shouted.

A cold chill passed through his body. The game was up — they weren't going to bluff or shoot their way out of this one. He reckoned there had to be still nine minutes before the explosives detonated. He stood still, knowing that any movement could lead to them being shot. Van Rhyn and his mob had to be itching for retribution, since their mission was now compromised.

No one attempted to approach them, however, and they remained standing in the stark light waiting for their adversaries to make a move. There were two or three others who had also stopped, frozen in place. At least two minutes had passed when he discerned one of the black SUVs pull up. Van Rhyn and General Booyens immediately alighted and approached Peace and Cherry.

"Well, well, if it isn't Lord Digby and his secretary. Now, why am I not surprised?" he said. He turned to the guards. "Get these bastards into the car and make sure they don't make a move. Shoot if you have to," he snarled.

Peace bit his tongue — this was not the time to make a snide remark. In the back of his mind, the now imminent explosion kept reminding him of what was about to happen. He let the guards rip the radio from his belt and ear and usher him towards the SUV where they shoved him through the door onto the backseat. Out of the corner of his eye, he saw Cherry herded to the second SUV and pushed through the rear doors.

The guards were taking no chances, and they handcuffed his wrists behind him with self-locking plastic cable ties.

"Lord Digby, or whoever you may be, I'm afraid this really is the end for you. The sooner you're dead the better and the less trouble you can cause. I'm not really interested in who you are — they say an agent from Britain? Actually, my people tell me you're Lieutenant Commander Peace of the Royal Navy and now with MI6," Van Rhyn said, his head just inside the vehicle's open door.

He turned to his henchman in the front passenger seat.

"Shoot him and dump him way out beyond the reef. I don't want his body found. That's important and please, no fuckin' mistakes. The great whites will get him," Van Rhyn spat, his hatred evident. "The sharks out there are enormous," he added, a smile of contempt on his face, this all obviously for Peace's benefit. "Oh! Give him a last cigarette. Do it away from prying eyes — I don't want all to see who and what we've found and caught. Get them away as soon as you can."

Peace kept his expression neutral and managed to show no emotion. "Sorry, don't smoke," he said. It could only be a few minutes before the charges blew. "Maybe it would be a good idea if you have a last smoke. I remember when still your guest, that you have a penchant for cigars — not Cuban, surely? It could well be your last."

"What do you mean?" Peace saw the man's cocksure expression change, as if he had just remembered something. "You bastard!" he shouted. Van Rhyn spun round and issued orders in Afrikaans; Peace not able to understand. Guards and technicians scattered as they ran for the hangar. Only Van Rhyn, his personal guards, and the two guards between whom he was sandwiched on the SUV's rear seat remained.

The explosion could give him an opportunity to escape, but without wire-cutters or a knife, he knew that any attempt would be futile. He had noticed that the two guards in the vehicle had sheath knives attached to their belts; he needed to get his hands on one of those. The man to his left had the knife attached to his right side. He was Peace's primary target; all he needed was an opportunity. He looked at the vehicle's dashboard clock — it could be no more than a minute to the explosion.

He turned to the man on his left. "Listen, buddy, there's going to be a helluva explosion soon. Maybe even in the next few seconds. I hope you don't mind if I lie down over your lap. You know, there's going to be a great deal of fire and crap flying around. I'd rather not be this close when it happens," he said nonchalantly.

"Ry, ry.[20]*"* Van Rhyn shouted to the driver. *"Skiet hom nou as julle wil. Maak net seker dat die bliksem vrek!*[21]*"*

With the engine already running, the driver put the vehicle in gear and sped off, immediately making a U-turn, gravel spurting from the tyres as they tried to find traction.

The timing devices attached to the charges were electronically connected through a short-range transmitter. A few milliseconds before the master charge exploded it would send a signal to set off all other charges, ensuring all Semtex charges exploded simultaneously.

They had not quite completed the U-turn when suddenly there was a

---

20. Drive, drive!

21. Shoot him now if you want to. Just make sure the bastard dies!

gigantic explosion, as all the multiple explosions welded into one simultaneous detonation. It was huge. The hangar doors were still partially open, and these suddenly bulged outwards and were then wrenched from their rails by some invisible force and flung away from the building as if they were mere cardboard sheets, decimating everything before them. This was followed by an enormous fireball that billowed out of the openings.

Simultaneously, the roof of the structure blew off, the explosion within the building sending bits of reinforced concrete and other burning material raining down all over the complex.

The SUVs were two score yards from the partially opened doors of the hangar. The blast's shockwave slammed into the side of the vehicle, shattering windows and actually lifting the vehicle and rolling it over, with it coming to rest on its side. This was followed by another jarring shock as something heavy collided with the SUV's underside, and the occupants were slammed into the floor as the SUV skidded on its side a short way on the ground.

Dazed and battered, Peace still managed to hold on to consciousness. He realised that this had to be his opportunity. The blast had dislodged the accumulated dust in the vehicle, and the interior was now enveloped in it. Coupled with the darkness outside, those in the interior of the vehicle were momentarily blinded.

Peace lay sprawled on top of the guard who had the sheath knife. Working by feel alone, he manoeuvred into a position where he had his hand up against the man's right side. The man didn't move — he was either dead or unconscious. He could hear the driver groaning in the front and groped with his fingers until he found the knife's hilt. He pulled but could not extract the knife. Again, he tried; still, it wouldn't slide out. He realised that it had to have some sort of restraining strap.

The dust slowly began to settle, and he could just make out dark shapes. His fingers found the strap — it was locked around the hilt of the knife with a press-stud. He unclipped it and gingerly extracted the blade. With great difficulty, he managed to insert the blade between his hands and under the plastic cable-tie, the sharp edge against the plastic, but not before he'd gouged his fingers and wrists on the razor-sharp blade. He applied pressure and the plastic parted with a snap.

Peace could see that the front windscreen of the SUV had shattered, most of it blown away. Through the gap, he detected the rocket assembly structure, or rather what was left of it. A fire raged within and smoke billowed from the top, an orange hue hanging over the building. He knew that no WMDs would be launched from here, certainly not for a long time. To re-commission the nuclear bombs, the cores of which had not exploded, would take months. He wondered what the radiation level was within the hangar. Had the explosion compromised the protective shields around the uranium?

He staggered to his feet, pulling himself up with a safety belt that dangled from the side of the SUV. He then got hold of the rear door's sill and hauled himself out, half his body now sticking out of the vehicle. He surveyed the scene around him. It was an area of horrific devastation. Other vehicles were burning, as was the brush beyond the road. He saw several bodies scattered on the ground — some lying still, some groaning and some moving. Two or three others seemed to have better survived the blast, as they staggered around disorientated, their clothing burnt and faces partially blackened.

His first concern was Cherry. He looked for the vehicle in which they'd shoved her. This had been stationed nearer to the blast, the vehicle only just in motion when all hell had broken loose. The SUV must have taken the full force of the blast; this did not bode well.

Then he spotted the vehicle. Surprisingly, it still stood upright, although the front now faced away from the hangar. The part of the outside that he could see was charred, and smoke rose from the side. He realised why it had not suffered the full force of the blast — a Rooikat armoured vehicle had partially shielded it. He wondered where Van Rhyn had been when the rocket and charges exploded.

He turned his attention back to the vehicle in which he'd been seated. The man who'd sat next to the driver had been partially flung out of the shattered armoured-glass windscreen. His carbine lay on the ground next to the vehicle, the stock folded back. Peace picked it up and thrust his head into the gaping hole that was once the windscreen, looking for an automatic. He found two, his own still with the silencer attached and a South African military issue automatic.

213

Wasting no time, he made his way to the vehicle in which he'd last seen Cherry. He could see the *Die Herberg* in the distance. All the lights appeared to be ablaze. *Maybe it did have its own standby generator.* He could see people milling around outside and already a few were climbing into a vehicle. He approached the Rooikat at a jog, keeping a lookout for Cherry but keeping within the Rooikat's blind side. He knew that those in the armoured car would be unscathed. He got to the SUV, approaching it from the side opposite to the eight-wheeler, which still had its headlights ablaze, the two horizontal cones of light penetrating the dust and smoke-filled air.

He peered into the rear window, this now a gaping hole with the glass gone. He could see her huddled on the floor, her hands clasped around her knees and her face pressed into her lap. He expected her hands to have been tied, but they were not. Part of her hair was singed and he caught that peculiar smell of it. The one guard beside her was dead — a jagged piece of steel protruded from his neck. There was blood everywhere. An artery must have been severed, his heart pumping blood from the wound until he died.

He stretched out a hand and touched her neck. She jerked away, simultaneously turning to see who it was.

For a second, she just stared at him.

"My God! You're still alive. I thought that they'd shot you," she said, the utter relief evident in her voice.

"Are you okay? Anything broken or are you hurt?"

"No! I knew the explosion was seconds away. I curled up in a ball and ignored their protests and the slaps to my head. Fortunately, they had not tied me up; they just removed all weapons. I gathered that, like you, I was to be shot and dumped, probably into the sea. From a comment made in Afrikaans by one of Van Rhyn's people, we were to become shark food," she said.

He saw that she had a raw patch on both her face and on her hands. Since these were oozing a clear liquid, she had obviously been burnt.

He assisted her as she gingerly climbed from the car. He saw the remaining guard lying prone on the rear seat. The man groaned continuously — he was clearly badly burned, as his face was raw, as was his scalp. His hair had disappeared and his eyebrows were burned away.

"When everything blew, Van Rhyn was still here," she whispered.

He could feel her fear.

"Don't concern yourself, we won't be seeing him. Besides, whatever he had planned has gone up in smoke," he replied.

"Moet dit nie glo nie![22] "

Peace spun around, simultaneously extending his arm with the automatic gripped in his hand, the hammer back. He saw Van Rhyn standing just behind the Rooikat. Gone was the usual aura of total control. He too was badly burned. Peace did not know where the man had been when the charges blew, but wherever it was had not been enough to shield him from the explosion. He was sure Van Rhyn was in great pain and close to being incapacitated.

Peace was still trying desperately to bring his weapon to bear when a single shot rang out. He felt a sharp tug on his left shoulder as the slug whistled past it, just catching the cloth on his coat.

When he saw General Booyens in his camouflaged battle fatigues with a pistol pointed at him as he emerged from behind the Rooikat, he realised that it was not Van Rhyn that had fired.

"Drop the weapon, Commander. Just look around you, it's over for you and your woman. One must surely admire your diligence and the result of your efforts, but these will cost your life," Van Rhyn said.

He slowly looked around. There were more than enough armed guards to stop him if he attempted to retaliate. To try anything now would undoubtedly mean instant death. The same applied to Cherry.

Peace dropped the weapon. "You win," he said, his words just audible.

"Get into the back of the vehicle," General Booyens ordered, indicating the open doors at the rear of the vehicle with a wave of his automatic.

Those who previously occupied the Rooikat had climbed out and were assisting those that had been hurt in the explosion and in the SUVs. Peace pushed Cherry ahead of him, and she entered first. The Rooikat was not a troop carrier but could accommodate six persons with three on each side

---

22. Don't you believe it!

facing each other. Cherry sat down to face him, followed by two guards and Van Rhyn and Booyens.

Now that they were in the vehicle and with the lights in the rear compartment on, the extent of Van Rhyn, the General, and the guards' injuries could be seen. Clearly, most were in pain, which could only get worse as the shock wore off and their injuries began to manifest themselves. They needed medical attention and Peace hoped they were all heading to the infirmary. The testing complex surely had to have one. Cherry also needed medical attention; however, he doubted they were concerned about her.

With a roar of its V10 engine, the Rooikat took off, the ride surprisingly comfortable for such a large armoured vehicle. The guards were obviously not taking any chances and sat with the muzzles of the carbines touching the sides of their prisoners.

Peace's mind reeled as he looked around him. The situation was serious and their demise could literally be minutes away. *Think, Peace, think! It would be like trying to get out of a vault to escape from here. Better to wait. But we don't have the time! Van Rhyn knows what's at stake and he'll make sure nothing sticks to him. The explosion has surely changed everything. Maybe Van Rhyn will realise that it's better not to kill us but rather use us as bargaining chips.* Peace gritted his teeth. *What the hell do I do?*

He was right; the Rooikat soon stopped. The rear doors opened, and they bustled out of the unit. They were outside a building with an illuminated, ornate board above the entrance, which read *Mediese Sentrum*. He guessed this to be the Overberg medical centre. He could hear a diesel engine and realised that the facility had a backup generator which was now providing emergency power.

If the military exercise beyond the perimeter of the testing grounds was still under way, he could hear no sounds of pretend battle — all was quiet. The only sounds emanated from the hangar, which still burned. He saw two helicopters in the sky and realised that they had to have come from the Bredasdorp Air Force base situated nearby. He wondered whether they represented friend or foe, or whether they were just a standard reaction to what had occurred.

Closely guarded, they were led into the building where he, for the first time in the bright light of the interior, realised the extent of the injuries Van Rhyn and his companions had suffered. Their hair was partially burned away in patches to near the scalp and the burns to their faces, arms, and hands were angry red blotches. Cherry was similarly burnt, if not quite so severe. Clearly, she was in pain although she showed no emotion.

He did not miss that the guard in charge of the detail was Lambrecht — the same one who had divulged his identity in Cape Town not so long ago.

Guarded by three men, they were rapidly marched into the *Die Herberg*, the interior of which resembled that of a country hotel with a reception area from which passages led out in opposite directions. It seemed strange to see such normal structures as a dining area laid out for breakfast the next morning. Finally, they were led into a small hall — bare except for two steel tables on trestles and a few steel framed chairs. The two tables were pushed together and he and Cherry were forcibly pressed down and seated behind each, a few feet apart. The guards' weapons never wavered and remained trained on them at all times.

Again, the doors that gave access to the main entrance passage opened and two men entered the hall. They were dressed in camouflage fatigues and were obviously officers of the South African Army — one a major and the other a lieutenant.

The major walked to Peace's table and leaned over until his face was inches from Peace. "I'm Major Rautenbach from Military Intelligence and this is Lieutenant Combrink" — it was immediately evident that English was not his home language as his accent was harsh and guttural — "and you're in deep shit, my friend."

"Really," Peace drawled showing no concern. "Certainly not as deep as you are. You're on the wrong side. In fact, I think you and your friends are guilty of treason. You will probably be tried and executed for exactly that reason. Quietly, of course. Your government would not want the world to know exactly what went on here, would they? They will undoubtedly tell your wife that you died in an accident and not at the end of a rope."

The major took a wild swing, landing a haymaker to the side of Peace's

217

face. The force of the blow lifted him from his chair and flung him to the floor while the major shouted, *"Fokken Engelse!*[23]*"* simultaneously.

Then the man came round and kicked him viciously in the side. *Thank God for canvas combat boots*, Peace thought, *at least the damage would be minimal*, as he curled up to protect himself as further kicks landed against his torso.

He was then bodily picked up, blood now streaming from his nose. Roughly manhandling him, they propped him back into his chair. He turned to face Cherry to give her a look of encouragement, when the lieutenant who stood leaning over the table in front of her swung his hand and slapped her viciously across the face. This too knocked her from her chair. Peace rose to intercept but had barely lifted himself from his chair when he was viciously butted from behind against the head by the folded stock of a carbine, the blow rendering him nearly unconscious. He opened his eyes to see the lieutenant grab the front of Cherry's lab coat and bodily pick her up and drop her back into the chair. Blood appeared on her face where the burnt skin on her cheek had broken.

Peace seethed with fury. "You bastard. I'll kill you for that!" he whispered hoarsely, his grey eyes like flint stone and his mouth clenched in a snarl.

The lieutenant laughed. "Who are you? Who cares — you're dead anyway or soon to be!"

The major pulled up a chair and sat.

"Unfortunately, you and your comrades have done considerable damage to our plans. However, some can be salvaged."

"Really, I don't think so," Peace replied with as much indifference as he could muster.

Again, he was thumped hard in the back with a carbine, the pain excruciating. The major patiently waited for him to recover.

"Yes, it may take a while and we still have other means," the major said. "We already know who you are, but I want to know what other plans you think you've got."

---

23. Fucking English!

"We don't know about other plans. Do you honestly believe we're privy to that? We just do as we are told. But I can elaborate on what you know by now… The Americans and British are already in Gaborone, ready to intervene should things go wrong here. There are more than the usual number of warships off your coast in the Indian and Atlantic oceans. Hell, put a foot wrong and you'll be invaded. You know that!"

"That will never happen!" the major spat.

"Do you really think the West would allow civil war to break out in your country? They've far too much invested in it," Peace said.

Just then, the doors swung open and Van Rhyn strode in followed by two of his guards. He spoke in Afrikaans, clearly issuing orders. Peace saw the shocked expression on the major's face. Something serious was obviously on the go.

Immediately plastic cable ties were produced and both had their hands bound behind their backs. The guards then herded them through the building towards the exit. Once they stepped out into the night, he realised that the Rooikat armoured cars had disappeared. Van Rhyn and General Booyens led the entourage, followed by the guards and their prisoners. An assortment of pickups and sedans stood in front of the building.

In the distance, he could distinctly hear that peculiar *thump-thump* made by an approaching helicopter. He looked in the direction from where the sound emanated and saw the flashing navigation lights of the helicopter. The guards had also heard it as Peace and Cherry were hurriedly bundled into two sedans, each sandwiched again on the rear seat between two guards. Van Rhyn slid into the passenger seat of the car in which Peace was trapped.

Already the helicopter was hovering over the helipad some two hundred yards distant, slowly settling to the ground. There was no mistaking the South African Air Force markings on the Denel Oryx helicopter. The sedans immediately drove off towards the helipad.

The small cavalcade halted close to the helicopter. As they were being bundled out of the car, shots suddenly rang out, and the man who had Peace by the left arm crumpled to the ground, as did another of the guards. Peace had immediately recognised the bark of a Heckler and Koch machine pistol; it had to be Croxley and Barkly.

Within seconds, the rest of the guards recovered from their surprise and returned fire.

Van Rhyn jammed an automatic to Peace's head. "If you don't do exactly as I say, I'll shoot you here and now! Run for the helicopter!"

Peace knew he meant every word. He ran bent doubled over, shots still ringing out. Did Croxley and Barkly know who the hell the enemy really was — the damn shots were so close! Trying to run with his hands tied was difficult and when he heard a scream behind him could not turn round.

They reached the helicopter, which had settled on the concrete square. Hands from inside grabbed him and dragged him over the sill into the interior. He saw Van Rhyn, General Booyens, and Janet being assisted aboard. That she was here surprised him as he hadn't seen her get into the car. She had not given him any sign of recognition. The helicopter's turbines immediately spooled up and the aircraft took to the air again. He noticed the navigational lights were doused, the only lighting being the eerie green of the instruments emanating from the cockpit. The noise rose to a crescendo and only when the side access-door was slid shut, did the banshee abate and become bearable. Of the people who had left in the cars only he, Van Rhyn, General Booyens, Janet, and the chief honcho guard were aboard — or so it seemed. He wondered what had happened to Cherry.

"Where are — "

That was as far as he got when he was struck a violent blow to the head, immediately losing consciousness.

Chapter Twenty-Six

The cold woke him. He lay on a bare concrete floor. The chill had penetrated his bones and had sapped the warmth from him. His muscles ached and his mouth felt as if lined with cotton wool. He had no idea how long he had been out, but the splitting headache, the foul taste in his mouth and the degree of lethargy that enveloped him, told him that he had to have been drugged again. Probably the same concoction they had administered before. He was clad only in Jockey briefs and a sweatshirt. Even his boots had been removed.

He had to warm up. With a groan, he rose gradually from the floor and stood while using a hand on the wall for support. He waited for his head to stop spinning. Slowly at first, then faster, he commenced a series of basic stretching exercises. After a few minutes, he began to feel better as his muscles loosened up and warmth returned to his body. He took stock of the room. It was small — no more than twenty by twenty feet square. It had only one small barred window, which was glazed with thick opaque glass, the vision through it so distorted that he could not make anything out. In a corner stood a bucket with a lid and a roll of toilet paper — it was functional but rudimentary. Why go to all this trouble if they wanted to kill him?

Hours later, when it began to darken outside, there was the rattle of keys at the door. Having inspected it a while ago and finding it made from thick timbers, he knew he was not going to break his way out.

Somebody shouted, "Stand back against the wall opposite the door."

Seconds later the door opened, just sufficient to allow a steel tray containing a tinplate with an ample helping of boiled potatoes with some meat stew and a stainless-steel mug of black coffee, to be slid across the threshold of the door. Two blankets were also thrown into the room. Immediately thereafter, the door was shut and locked again. The guard never entered and Peace thought that there was probably another guard covering the jailer.

What was going on? Was Cherry here and was she receiving the same treatment?

The blankets were a godsend. He immediately wrapped himself in one, using the other to create a thin mattress which enabled him to sit cross-legged with some degree of comfort. Soon he felt warmth return to his body. Using the white plastic spoon provided, he hungrily wolfed down the food on the plate and followed this with the bitter black coffee.

He woke once during the night. He heard the wind howl beyond the walls and was certain he caught something rumbling in the distance and thought this had to be thunder; he was also sure he could see vague lightning flashes dancing off the thick opaque glass of the window.

A small tracking device had been sewn into the lining of each of their jumpsuits — a precaution to enable them to be tracked. He wondered when and where his clothes had been removed. Of course, the question was whether the tracking devices had been discovered. He hoped his clothing had been removed here and would be returned to him. Without proper clothing he felt exposed, which, of course, was a way of making prisoners feel vulnerable. The whereabouts of his American colleagues also concerned him. Had they escaped?

Other than for meals, the door was never opened. He spent the day lying on his makeshift mattress. Twice he forced himself to exercise.

The day passed slowly and only the light trickling through the window revealed that night was near.

Noises from outside the door warned him that he was about to get company. As the door swung open, Lieutenant Combrink and Major Rautenbach entered, still dressed in camouflage fatigues and combat jackets. A further guard was visible in the background. They were obviously not about to take any chances, as all were armed with carbines.

222

"You're probably wondering why you haven't been shot. Well, you're now a bargaining chip. We intend to use you for that purpose," the major said, his tone and demeanour clearly expressing the hate he felt for his captive.

"So, I've some value after all," Peace replied. "How about giving me my clothes back?"

"Later. Nobody knows where you are, so don't think you can be rescued."

"You should never believe that, you being a soldier. Where's Miss Boxx?"

"She's here. In fact, next door. We've attended to her burns. They are only superficial. She'll soon heal without scars, but now, down to business. Hold out your hands." The major produced a pair of handcuffs.

Peace realised that it would be pointless to object and held out his hands while the lieutenant cuffed him.

"You're going to receive a visitor. We'll be just outside the door, so please, behave yourself. I really don't know what she sees in you," the major said with a disdainful smirk.

The two men retreated to the doorway and the major beckoned for someone to enter. Peace was astounded when Janet walked into the room. She was dressed in tight jeans with calf-high soft suede brown boots. She wore a padded anorak over a T-shirt, which told him that it was unusually cold outside. He racked his brains again trying to think where they might be. The dark hair that cascaded over her shoulder shone in the light from the passageway. Her face was a blank mask; he could not read it.

"Outside," she curtly ordered the two officers.

"Miss Van Rhyn, I don't think that's a good idea," the major said rather meekly.

Janet's eyes flashed. "Damn it, outside! We agreed I've a personal matter I want to discuss with him!"

"Okay, we'll be just outside the door if you need us." The major's reluctance was apparent. She stood there looking at the officer, waiting for him to close the door. He only pulled it against the frame, not closing it entirely.

She looked at Peace for a few seconds before she spoke. "God, Digby, or should I call you Geoffrey? For a while, I actually believed we could have had something going, then you suddenly set out to destroy my family and me. You and me… was that just a sham?"

Peace smiled ruefully. "Actually, it was with regret that I upset your father's plans. Oh, of course, it had to be done — no question about that. Even you must realise that he and his mob are lunatics. Just imagine wanting to nuke the Cubans and who knows how many others. You and I are only a subsidiary part of it. No matter what you may think, I don't bed women for whom I've no feelings. So, it was no sham."

This was not a lie. He hoped that Cherry next door had not overheard this. Actually, he was feeling slightly confused — he was locked up here, wherever here was and they were talking about relationships. Cherry was next door and his concerns for her more definitely more than just professional and here was this woman insisting on knowing whether he genuinely desired her. Who wouldn't be confused? Even though he was trained to kill, this certainly made life interesting!

For a few seconds, she just stared intently at him as if trying to penetrate some mental shield he had around him.

"Do you think this is the time to be discussing this?" he asked, while looking around the room as if to emphasise his point.

She ignored him.

"Usually, I'm immune to it, but somehow you're the first man in a long time to have wormed his way into my heart." She dropped her voice to little more than a whisper, clearly not wanting any others to hear. "I never believed my father would go this far. My stepmother has left him and returned to England. Sure, she still despises the blacks or any majority black government, but when we discovered what he and Booyens intended, we agreed it was unacceptable."

"Bit late, isn't it? It was the Cubans they wanted to bomb, wasn't it? Or maybe, those on the border of Angola with Namibia. What other plan could they've had? Even worse, drop a bomb on a black township. My God! That would kill hundreds of thousands. They're insane, the whole bloody lot of them!"

An involuntary shiver swept over him. He felt helpless, partly because of his lack of clothes but also because he was handcuffed.

"I can't tell you who. That would be crossing the line, wouldn't it? Anyway, whatever, I couldn't live with that on my conscience. If they can't use you as a negotiating tool, they're going to kill you and that woman next door. It's easy enough to dump the bodies in these mountains — you'll never be found and no one can pin a thing on them."

Peace felt a sudden stab of fear, not for himself but for Cherry. "They said they'll exchange us for something."

Janet shook her head. "They might, but in the end, I think they'll kill you," she whispered.

There was a good few feet's distance between them. She stood next to the folded blanket on the floor that served as his bed, which was against the wall just behind the door. He was near the opposite wall where he had been told to stand and not move.

"Miss Van Rhyn! Please, we must go!" the major shouted with obvious impatience from beyond the door, simultaneously pushing it slowly open.

To Peace's surprise, she quickly stepped forward to where he stood and slapped him sharply across the face, her expression now reflecting disdain and hatred. As Peace was processing the action, he realised she had dropped something to the floor at the same time. It twinkled in the light as it fell and tinkled as it struck the floor. The officers seemed not to hear. Whatever it was, he quickly moved his foot and stood on it.

She was about to exit when she stopped and turned around. "You actually deserve to die," she said. He wasn't sure whether or not she meant it, but the threat certainly seemed real. It was a convincing performance and would hopefully deceive the officers. Just before the door closed and locked behind her, he heard her say that they should give him his clothes. He was still handcuffed.

Quickly he recovered the item that she had dropped and slid it under the blanket. Minutes later, when he was sure they all had gone, he retrieved the key ring. It contained two keys held together on a wire ring. He shoved them swiftly back under the mattress while he recovered from his racing emotions of elation. Obviously, one of these had to be for the door to his room. But the other? The one was larger than the other was, but both looked clearly intended for rather complex locks. One had to be for the room next door. He realised that she'd not thought of the handcuffs. He'd have to get those off first! The officers had forgotten to, or intentionally not removed them.

A glimmer of hope passed through him. Why had she done this? However, without clothes, any attempt to escape would be foolhardy, and he realised that outside the building, it had to be close to freezing. Where on Earth had they taken him? The problem was that it was freezing in a lot of areas of South Africa at that time of the year.

Wrapped in his blanket, he dozed off. The rattle of the keys in the door woke him. The door was partially opened, letting a shaft of light stab into the room again; this was followed by a bundle of rolled-up clothing being tossed onto the floor. The door immediately closed once more.

"Compliments of Miss Van Rhyn — she didn't want you to freeze your arse off. Hot or cold, you'll still die here anyway," an unsympathetic voice said from behind the door.

He did not recognise it. *Probably one of Van Rhyn's security men*, he thought. This meant there were others. As on the previous night, the far distant throb of some engine suddenly died, the lights simultaneously dimming then going out. Clearly, the outside electrical power source had been shut down for the night and the room was plunged into deep darkness. Once his eyes adjusted, he could just make out the rectangle of the small glazed window through which starlight feebly penetrated. Five minutes later, his eyes had further adjusted and he was able to make out the room.

By feel, he removed both keys from the steel ring and with some difficulty, straightened the steel wire as best he could. He now needed to bend a ninety-degree hook into the wire. He shoved a quarter inch of the wire into the gap between the door and its frame and finally had the bend in the wire he needed. Inserting this into the cuff's lock, he picked at the innards and soon the cuffs sprang open with a click.

He then undid the bundle of clothing. These were the clothes and canvas combat boots he had been wearing when captured. He dressed and lay down on his makeshift mattress, pulling the single blanket over him. He cleared his mind of all thoughts and soon dozed off.

He suddenly woke, sure he'd heard an unusual sound. He realised that this was probably what had woken him. *Crack*! There it was again. It was the sound of some object hitting the thick glass of the window; somebody was throwing stones at the glass. He couldn't imagine who this could be, but hoped it was to be Janet. This continued for a while — maybe some sort of signal? Frightened the sound could draw a guard's attention, he rapped hard on the glass twice. It had to be heard by anyone just outside the window. No more stones struck the glass.

It took him a few minutes to grasp that it was highly probable that this was the right time to make his move. He could think of no other reason why Janet would stand outside in the freezing cold and throws stones at the window. What about the guards stationed outside the room?

He slowly inserted the largest of the keys into the lock. It fitted. Slowly he turned it, hearing the distinct click as the tumblers in the lock fell into place, the lock then opening with what he thought was an overly loud rasp. He opened the door to be greeted by a faint light that emanated from a lantern on a table in a passageway. A guard was slumped over a folding camp table, his arms and head resting on an open Playboy magazine. A military carbine lay on the table. Spittle drooled from the man's open mouth.

Peace realised the man was drugged. This too had to be Janet's work. Who else had she drugged?

He carefully picked up the guard's carbine, holding it ready to bring it down on the man's head. He shook the guard. There was no response.

Five doors led from the passageway, and two were open. Slowly, moving on rubber-soled boots, he made his way to the nearest door that was open, which was on the opposite side of the passage. This was a bathroom. He remembered hearing sounds from close by just after they shoved his meal through the doorway. This confirmed that Cherry was no further than one or two adjoining rooms from where he was kept. Were there others, he wondered? He approached the first, slowly opened the lock, and pushed the door open, but ready to slam it shut, if necessary. When just a crack was revealed, he stopped and waited. There was no sound from within. He pushed the door open to step through. As he did so, a dark shadow rushed him. He let go of the door and stepped forward right up against his attacker, thus preventing him from assailing him as his movements were restricted by the closeness. Peace immediately smelt the faintest trace of some female fragrance, which jarred his memory.

"It's me!" he hissed, groping with his hands to find her wrists, which he then grabbed in a vice-like grip.

He felt her collapse in his grasp, followed by a slight shudder as her body sagged against his. He saw that she was properly dressed; they'd also returned her clothes.

"My God," she whispered. "I've been so worried."

"Let's talk about that later. We have to get out of here. I've no idea where we are, but having travelled in a helicopter, this has to be somewhere in South Africa. Helicopters have a restricted range. But it's so damn cold here, it must be in the mountains somewhere."

The one end of the passageway ended in a wall which contained another bulletproof glass window similar to that in his cell. This meant that the only way out had to be through the door at the other end of the passageway. He removed the automatic from the drugged guard's holster and gave it to her. He knew that one shot was enough to alert the whole building, something he had to avoid at all costs. Using the dim light from the lantern, he slowly approached the other end, which was blocked by a closed door. The door responded to his touch, swinging open slowly. This revealed a combined dining room and adjoining lounge, the latter with a near burnt-out fire glowing in the hearth on the opposite wall. Two large windows were on opposite sides of the room, the heavy drapes half closed. Another man, with a carbine on the floor next to him, lay sprawled on the sofa, snoring softly. It appeared he also had been drugged. On a tray on the coffee table were the remains of his dinner.

They saw that another passageway led off the rooms, probably leading to sleeping quarters. An alcove led off to a front entrance room, and a front door was visible through the glazed doors of the walk-in room. The rooms were empty.

"Come on," he whispered with a touch of impatience and took her hand to lead her to the walk-in room. They passed through the doors without hindrance. At the front door, he checked whether it was wired to a burglar alarm but found nothing. He opened the door, to be met by a frigid blast of cold air. He could see patches of white on the ground where it was coated by a thin layer of snow. In the pale light of a half-moon that shone through a broken cloud, he could make out distant mountain peaks, which seemed to surround them. They seemed to be perched on the highest one. A short distance away stood the helicopter in which they had left Overberg, tethered by multiple cables to the ground, and the cockpit covered by a canvas. He'd probably be shot or captured before he could get it started.

Just then, he saw a movement at the corner of the house as someone stepped out of the shadows. It was a moment before recognition dawned. It was a woman, and he knew it could only be Janet Van Rhyn. She was still dressed in the parka, the hood pulled over her head casting her face in deep shadow. She approached them and her features became clear.

"The guards, were they a problem?" she asked, her eyes lingering on Cherry for a second or two before looking at him. Her face showed no emotion.

"No. What did you drug them with?"

"I don't know what it is, but it's something my father got from his army friends. They used it in Angola to incapacitate captured terrorists when flying them out of the war zone in helicopters. Very powerful, I understand."

Flown out of Angola? This struck a note. From intelligence reports, he knew better. These drugs incapacitated prisoners, and then unconscious or paralysed, they were then simply pushed out of aircraft over the sea without parachutes.

"Anyway, thank you again."

He was surprised to hear Cherry also thank her.

"Where are we?" he asked.

"High in the Drakensberg, that's why it's so cold. It's my father's mountain lodge, we're nearly at ten-thousand feet."

"How are we going to get out of here, and why are you doing this?"

"Let's just say that I'm not happy with what he and General Booyens are planning. They say you destroyed all the bombs and the rockets, but there's still one bomb left that wasn't damaged in the explosion. It'll be arriving shortly by helicopter from Overberg. It's their trump card." She turned her back on him. "Follow me," she said over her shoulder, leading the way in the dark.

"Where's your father?"

"He sleeps, as does Booyens." She paused. "If you're thinking of trying to get to them, don't. There are too many guards. They're on the other side of the house."

Peace stopped, and Cherry walked into the back of him.

"I can't leave here, not without neutralising the bomb," he said.

She swung around on the path and stared at him. "How do you…" She was clearly exasperated. "Good God, you're only one man. How do you propose to stop them and take the bomb from them?"

"I don't know, but will you help us? We need weapons," he said.

"I can't do that. You know, supply you with weapons to kill my father, because that's what you will ultimately be trying to do. I know he has succumbed to all this hatred and I realise he is wrong, but I can't let you kill him."

"I don't want to kill him. I'm just after the bomb — the final bomb in their arsenal, and it has to be the neutron bomb. Without it, their cause is lost. The whole movement will fizzle out."

Peace hoped he sounded convincing.

He knew that if he didn't kill Van Rhyn and his right-hand men, there was little hope of getting out of this alive. He knew they had similar sentiments about him, although this time, there'd be no waiting — they'd shoot immediately on sight.

Peace knew that Cherry had to understand that Janet was probably their only way out of their current predicament and wouldn't do anything that could jeopardise the assistance Janet was providing, irrespective of what her feelings were. She had not spoken since leaving the lodge other than the thank you she had uttered.

"When do you think the bomb will arrive?" Peace asked.

Janet shrugged her shoulders. "It won't come at night; it's too dangerous. Probably tomorrow morning. I overheard Booyens arrange for an SAAF Aerospatiale Puma helicopter to bring it up here. After the explosion, Overberg was taken over by the Air Force but somehow, they managed to get the bomb out without anyone being aware of it or before the Air Force, its high command still loyal to de Klerk, arrived. The testing centre is sealed. I think my father wants to stash it somewhere here until the hubbub has quietened. That's about all I know."

"Then I'll wait," he said.

"God, that's crazy! In the morning, they'll soon discover that you've escaped. He has six men here, not counting the caretaker. And he can handle a gun as well — he's ex-military. They'll be swarming all over the place."

"Three against six. I've been up against similar odds before.

"Who says I'll help?"

"You don't really have a choice, do you? They'll know you assisted us."

She remained silent for a few seconds as she thought about what he had said.

"I suppose not," she finally conceded, dropping her head in resignation.

"Right, then you'd better show me where we can get our hands on a few weapons," he said, indicating the two carbines they had taken from the guards.

"I think there are weapons in the helicopter."

They made their way over to it. Exposed out in the open, the wind howled softly around them, bringing with it the occasional flurry of snow. Peace slid the side door open and climbed in. It was dark inside. Janet handed him a mini-torch from next to the door, its narrow beam a cone of lighting dancing around the interior. He saw two carbines clipped to the inner fuselage as well as two machine pistols. Magazines containing cartridges protruded from canvas pockets of a few military weapon harnesses which hung from pegs. He saw something that he thought resembled a LAW, a light, anti-tank weapon; this was clamped to the side of the cabin by metal clips. He got up close to look at it and recognised it as an anti-tank rocket-propelled weapon manufactured by the local arms industry, a designated FT5. When loaded it was quite heavy, not something you wanted to lug around with you when you were in a hurry. It seemed quite sophisticated, complete with telescopic sight with night-vision. He looked for the projectiles to load it and realised that it was already loaded. He unclipped it from the side and then saw that the other side of the cabin had another clipped to it. This he also took. He saw the tripod-like stand to the side of the door and realised it was the mounting pedestal for a machine-gun. He swung the torch around the interior again but could not find the weapon.

He handed a machine pistol and a carbine each to Cherry and Janet in turn. "This will do," he said to them, hefting a LAW in his hands.

"Between the three of us we've got to get all this, and I mean weapons and both rocket-launchers, to a hiding place. I've a feeling we're going to need these. This bloody helicopter mounts a machine-gun but I can't see it, so hopefully, they left it behind," Peace remarked.

Nobody complained.

Then, seeing how Janet gingerly handled the carbine he added irritably, "Janet, the damn thing won't bite, just hold it for me."

He realised that should another helicopter arrive, it would have to settle on the same small piece of flat ground; there was nowhere else.

He slid the door closed and looked around carefully. There was little to use for concealment, but they had to get out of the wind. About a hundred yards away, a small outcrop of rock reached higher into the sky than the surrounding area. This was the highest point of the mountain.

"C'mon," he said, and took the lead with a LAW on each shoulder, barely managing under the load.

The outcrop was more than he hoped. If they took position behind it, they would be hidden from view from the lodge and the helicopter apron. At the same time, they'd also be out of the wind.

"What time is it?" he asked.

"Just after four," Janet replied.

He reckoned that sun up would be in about an hour and a half's time.

He found a small nook in the rocks, big enough to accommodate them. He beckoned the women closer, and they squeezed into the small area, their bodies pressed together.

"This should keep us warm enough," he said.

"Really cosy," Cherry replied with a sneer, not able to keep the sarcasm out of her voice. However, when they lay down, she made sure she lay between him and Janet. She obviously wasn't leaving anything to chance!

It had continued to snow on and off and as it became light, they awoke. They were covered in a light blanket of snow. This pleased him, as it would help conceal them.

It was some minutes later when they suddenly heard noises and raised voices from the house. Peace slowly rose, his knees stiff from the cold, and peered over the rock that separated them from the direct view to the house. He could see four dark figures outside the door of the lodge bunched together in deep conversation, with one of the figures continuously gesticulating. He thought it had to be Booyens. He also noticed that all were carrying weapons, an assortment of automatic carbines and pistols.

Thank God for the snow. At least we haven't left a trail.

Two of the men broke away from the group and made their way to the helicopter where they slid open the door and entered. Seconds later, a man reappeared and from the shouting and arm waving, Peace realised they had discovered that most of the weapons had been removed from the helicopter. The others ran from the house to join him alongside the aircraft.

Peace made a decision. If they made any movement towards where the three were hidden, he'd open fire, trying to get as many as he could. However, what disturbed him was that Van Rhyn was not to be seen.

"Where is Van Rhyn?" he asked, perplexed.

"Sorry, I lied. He's not here — he'll be coming on the helicopter," Janet said.

"Why the fuck did you do that?" Peace spat.

"I don't know — I just didn't want you going back to the house to kill people while they slept."

"Fuck! I suppose killing hundreds of thousands — all innocent and maybe most of them asleep — shouldn't concern us? Really, God help us!" Peace shook his head in horror and disbelief.

The men returned to the house; it seemed they were not about to pursue the escapees. They had probably decided to wait for back up to arrive on the helicopter. Peace was adamant they should not move so, they huddled together as they waited.

"What to do now?" Peace asked more to himself than for the others' benefit.

"There's a holiday hotel maybe forty kilometres away. Every now and then in the winter, there's enough snow to ski and a few guests arrive. Very basic, of course," Janet volunteered.

"How would we get there?" he asked.

"There's hardly a road — just a track really, not for cars but maybe scramblers."

"Walking forty k's in this terrain — pretty hazardous, I think. Isn't there any transport we could use?" Peace countered.

"No, not really, except some special motorcycles the men mess around with," she replied. "God, I've just realised, they could come after us on those bikes."

True — but if we can get hold of them, they will certainly come in handy.

"What about food and water?" Cherry asked. He knew this was not a complaint as she would suffer without saying anything, but the question affected them all.

"Food will be an issue for a while. We've got snow. But, if nature calls, you'll have to find yourselves a big rock to hide behind." The faintest chuckle escaped his lips.

Chapter Twenty-Seven

An hour later, they heard the throb of rotors in the distance. As the helicopter approached, Peace felt for the wind, checking its direction, knowing the aircraft would approach against it. This would mean that the helicopter would fly virtually directly overhead to get to the landing area. They scrambled to find a better hiding place. He positioned himself against a rock buttress and prepared an anti-tank weapon. It was a relatively easy operation — he only had to charge the scope and remove the projectile cover from the rocket-launcher.

The *whap-whap* grew louder and soon the copter came into view. He immediately recognised it — an Aerospatiale Puma, and it was an enormous target. Although still at a distance, he examined it carefully, and a cold shiver ran down his spine. The huge sliding doors were open, revealing a heavy calibre Browning .50 inch M2 machine-gun — a most formidable weapon. *Christ! So, they had the machine-gun somewhere after all — this was a bloody massacre in the making!*

A helmeted man crouched behind it, traversing the barrel from side to side just looking for an opportunity to open fire. Word must have been sent that they'd escaped with weapons. The hunt was surely on.

He dropped behind the rocks again. "Hell! This is fuckin' bad," he exclaimed under his breath.

The helicopter flew at low altitude over them, about fifty yards to their left. He took a deep breath, hefted the rocket-launcher to his shoulder, and rose until he could see over the natural parapet. The helicopter was now two hundred yards away, moving slowly forward at no more than what appeared to be a walking pace, slowly approaching the landing site. He brought his eye to the telescope, the aircraft dancing in the sights as he tried to steady it, trying to get the crosshairs onto it, his finger seeking the trigger.

Suddenly, the air was rent by the sharp staccato bark of the machine-gun. He dropped to the ground just in time; a fusillade of shots struck the rocks, showering them with splinters, the ricochets buzzing past them in all directions. He placed the rocket-launcher next to the other on the ground.

As soon as the firing stopped, he rose, and with the carbine on automatic, sent a full magazine of shots at the helicopter as it hovered a foot or two off the ground. He saw some of his shots impact, the gunner involuntary ducking down. The helicopter immediately spooled up and veered away, climbing out of range. Peace knew it must be preparing for another pass.

"Cherry!" he shouted. "Quickly, I need you!"

She rose to stand next to him.

"Switch the carbine to automatic. As he approaches, open fire and aim at the machine-gun. You're to keep him away from his gun while I'm aiming the LAW. Have you got that?"

"I think I know what to do," Cherry replied with a sigh of annoyance.

He turned to Janet. "Janet, you stay down!"

The helicopter had done a full circle and was again approaching, revealing its open side door and the machine-gun. He could see the gunner getting ready to fire, waiting to get in range and position so he could traverse the area with effective coverage.

Peace rose. "Start shooting NOW!" he bellowed.

Next to him, the carbine commenced firing. With the LAW back on his shoulder, he rose within a second, his eye glued to the scope, sweeping the sky for the helicopter. The moment the crosshairs found the aircraft, he squeezed. There was a loud whoosh. He was immediately encompassed in a pall of acrid smoke as the projectile launched from the tube and streaked across the sky towards the helicopter, leaving a trail of smoke. The pilot saw the projectile's trail and took immediate evasive action, trying to swing the aircraft round. He was nearly successful, but Peace's aim was true. The rocket slammed into the rear of the helicopter, hitting the tail-rotor. For some inexplicable reason, it did not explode, but passed straight through.

Still, Peace saw part of the helicopter's rear rotor disintegrate and the tail begin to swing. From what was happening it was evident the pilot was battling to retain control. However, this did not deter the gunner. Cherry's rifle was silent; her magazine was empty.

Peace watched the helicopter. As soon as the gunner had an open field of fire, he let loose again, the heavy .50 calibre machine-gun hammering away. Peace and Cherry dived to the ground. The bullets seemed to explode all around them.

The Aerospatiale Puma thundered past overhead. Before he could stop her, Cherry rose, the reloaded rifle at her shoulder, and she emptied another magazine at the departing aircraft and shouted, "You bastards!"

From the sounds coming from the helicopter, there seemed to be damage. It made no attempt at another pass but continued on to the makeshift helipad and soon settled.

He knew the bomb was aboard. He'd give his eyeteeth for another shot at it with the one remaining rocket-launcher, but the plane was at the extremities of the rocket-launcher's range and he was unlikely to achieve a hit. Besides, the helicopter was damaged — hopefully, it would not be flying for a while, or at least, not until repairs were carried out.

"C'mon, let's go. We've got to get out of here." He started moving in a westerly direction.

Janet grabbed his arm. "No, no. You can't go that way; we have to follow the track. This will take us to the holiday ski hotel near here — that way there's only a shepherd's hut which is occasionally used by crazy mountain hikers. You can die here in the mountains if on foot. Rather stick to the track heading to the hotel. Anyway, there's no direct track to the shepherd's place — the going will be extremely difficult cross-country. Besides, I'm not sure we'll find any help there or another means out of the mountains from that remote spot," she said firmly, pointing to where the track wound its way through the rocky outcrops.

"Okay, but where does that other track lead to?" he asked pointing at a third track that led from the lodge and disappeared over the hill.

"That's a dead-end for us — as I said, we're in Lesotho. The track leads to the Katse Dam, which they started building a few years ago. The dam has just started to fill but it's slow. It needs the summer rains. The track used to end at the river's edge, but that's already under water. My father mentioned this a few weeks ago to me. We certainly don't want to go there either," Janet declared.

He realised she knew best and probably knew the area, having undoubtedly accompanied her father on a few occasions in the past.

The track soon dipped below the horizon, hiding them from direct sight of the farmhouse. It was no more than a pathway with small rocks and stones as a bed, the rain, over the years, having washed away all soil. A four-wheel-drive vehicle could have just navigated it, but only with difficulty, as there were numerous rock shelves, parallel gullies and washed-out ditches. The scrambler motorcycles came to mind. He realised why they had these at the house.

Janet wasn't wrong when she said they would be coming after them with the motorcycles. Soon, they could hear the throb and bark of their engines as the riders manoeuvred these down the trail. As the sound grew louder, Peace turned and waited for them to come into view. The moment they appeared in the distance, silhouetted against the grey sky, he opened fire. The front rider hastily turned around and disappeared, followed by his companion.

"At least they cannot skirt around us in this terrain. It's impassable, even to a motorcycle," he said.

Well, it rather evens the odds.

He pondered the situation, hoping to find a way out of their dilemma. He knew that with the helicopter damaged, they could not fly the bomb out of there. The bomb still had to be on board, and it was not something that could simply be manhandled off the aircraft, but he was sure Van Rhyn had something in mind. He assumed Van Rhyn had to have been aboard the Aerospatiale Puma. It suddenly struck him — there was the other helicopter, the Denel Oryx job; the SAAF helicopter they had arrived on from Overberg. Surely they'd soon be using that! With a shock, he suddenly realised they could already be hauling the tarpaulin off the cockpit and getting it started.

Fortunately, both women were fit. Cherry by virtue of her profession, and Janet due to her vigorous gym schedule. There was nothing soft about either of them. While all were out of breath at this high altitude, they made good time. Now and then the motorcycles made a run at them, but their accurate return fire drove them back to either behind a ridge, rock outcrop or bend in the track.

A while later, the air again filled with the throb of a helicopter's rotors, but this now sounded different. It had to be the Denel Oryx. Soon it swung into view, those on board immediately opening fire, sending them below scurrying for shelter. Simultaneously, the two motorcycles zoomed over the horizon, approaching as fast as they could over the rough terrain.

Peace threw himself to the ground, where he discarded the second LAW he carried and brought the machine pistol to bear. He opened fire, raking the ground in front of the motorcycles, and then lifted the barrel, stitching a row of bullets horizontally across the ground, letting the motorcycles ride into the burst of fire. The riders braked hard, locking their rear-wheels, but being on a down slope, the scramblers just skidded forward. The first was lucky; he boldly threw himself from the saddle. Not so the second, who rode into a hail of bullets, two of which struck his chest. He threw up his arms and toppled backwards from the still-moving cycle.

Behind him, Peace heard the chatter of shots as those in the helicopter opened fire. He climbed to his feet and grabbed Cherry's hand, and dragged her to the ground behind a two-foot ridge of rocks, the bullets just stitching past them, the air a cacophony of *buzzes, bangs* and *whizzes* as the bullets ricocheted off the rocks.

Suddenly, next to him, he heard the sound of air driven from the lungs by a sharp blow. He turned round to see Janet collapsing to the ground, a stricken expression on her face. He rushed to her, rolled her over and immediately saw the jagged hole in her anorak. He pulled the zip down to reveal the woollen T-shirt and the blossoming circle of blood that now stained it.

"Oh my God, I've been hit," she said, her voice no more than a whisper.

He realised they could not stay where they were. The helicopter and the other scrambler would be back. Although they may not have been friends, the expression on Cherry's face told him that she too was devastated. This woman had been shot by her own kind and it would be fatal if she didn't get immediate medical attention.

Cherry helped Peace drag Janet behind a small rock ledge. He conceded there was nothing they could do for her. The bullet had penetrated a lung and they didn't even have any form of first-aid kit.

"Cherry, we've got to leave her and let them find her — they'll be here in a minute or two," Peace said. "After all, this is his daughter; he'll rush her to hospital irrespective of what she's done. He certainly isn't going to order the death of his own daughter execution-style."

"Don't leave me. He'll kill me," Janet whispered.

"Cherry, go. I'll catch up. Take the other LAW with you," he said. He wanted a few seconds alone with Janet.

Cherry seemed to understand this. She slowly rose from her haunches, backed away, returned to where the LAW lay, and then started running towards a deep gully that angled in from above to the trail that wove its way through the rocks.

The helicopter's drone had faded in the distance but then took on a more strident note. It was coming back and would soon be upon them.

Peace took Janet's hand into his own. "I'm truly sorry," he said.

She looked up into his eyes, and her expression said that she knew that he had to run if he wanted to live.

"Go," she said, "maybe my father will be kind and help me." She squeezed his hand.

He noticed that she had not coughed up any blood. Was that a good sign?

The helicopter's drone was louder. He looked up and could see it approaching. He bent and let his lips brush hers.

"Thank you," he said and ran for the protection of the gully. However, before he got there, the machine-gun began its chatter, and he imagined the impacting bullets raising chipped stone and dust as the gunner walked the shots towards him. He ran for his life. As he plunged into the vertical gap in the rocks, the walls of the gully seemed to miraculously close round him and shield him, the helicopter swooping over him as the pilot was forced to claw the aircraft skywards to avoid the rock wall. He threw himself down next to Cherry, who had rolled herself into a ball.

He could hear the helicopter but it did not return, its sound fading in the distance. Had they found Janet? Had they seen her from above? He hoped so.

"Is she going to be all right? She saved our lives," Cherry asked, her face stricken.

"I think so. Listen, you can hear it, but it's not coming closer. I hope they've found her and are airlifting her and are about to casevac her straight to hospital," he replied, hoping he was right. The woman didn't deserve to die, even Cherry believed this.

This time the distinct sound of the scrambler motorcycles distracted him. They approached again. It seemed the motorcycle of the downed rider had been retrieved and the machines were again scouring the area for them.

"We've got to backtrack," he said.

"But you said that's impossible."

"We've got to do something they'd least suspect… and that's to make our way back to the house." He forced a grin. "Straight into the lion's den — it's our only chance. But first, we've got to lose ourselves in this wilderness. They wouldn't dream of looking for us in that direction, they'd never believe we'd do that."

Cherry didn't reply but slowly picked herself up, and clutching her carbine in classic military fashion in front of her chest, prepared to move out.

"The hell with the fuckin' bomb. Let's just get out of here. Our people can get rid of it later," she said in a voice close to shrill.

"No. Cherry, later is not good enough. They could use its threat as a bargaining chip. We couldn't ignore it. Everybody would have to listen to them, never knowing whether they would use it or not. We've no choice — it's got to be destroyed now! Or at least, make sure we render it somehow unusable."

She shook her head in resignation and took up position behind him. He'd discarded all weapons except the LAW, which he carried on his shoulder, a carbine cradled in a hand, and an automatic stuck in his belt. It was a lot of equipment for a man to carry, even when taking a shortcut through the mountains.

They heard the helicopter again, both secretly hoping it had found Janet. The scramblers continued to search for them, but the terrain was now virtually impassable. They were forced to move slowly at no more than a walking pace, but now there was more than sufficient time to find ideal hiding places amongst the rocks and gullies. It was not long before they no longer heard the motorcycles.

Drinking water was not a problem. Now and then, they'd eat snow, but both suffered hunger pangs, having not eaten properly for days. The sky remained overcast, occasionally sending down a flurry of snow. He had no compass but believed they were moving in the right direction.

The area was desolate with virtually no vegetation, it being high in the Drakensberg Mountains. It was also unpopulated, which probably accounted for the deserted shepherd's hut Janet had mentioned — who would want to live here? The chances of encountering any others were almost nil. The high altitude forced them to stop and rest more often than he wanted, and every time they resumed their journey, it was more difficult to get going again.

He thought that Van Rhyn's lodge could not be far off and hoped to see it every time they topped a ridge. Cherry had rapidly tired, and he found that occasionally he had to give her a hand. At nine or ten thousand feet, if you were not used to the altitude, any exertion was excessively tiring. Fortunately, he did not find the effects quite so severe. However, the LAW bit into his shoulder and the carbine had taken on a weight of its own.

The last rock face they climbed was a near precipice, and they were forced to seek out hand-holds, their progress reduced to a crawl. For Peace, it was more difficult, as the LAW was constantly hindering him, its weight threatening to pull him down. Finally, they made it to the top and sprawled on their stomachs, both fighting for breath. They peered over the top, taking care not to create a silhouette.

"Cover your mouth with a cloth or something. Make sure your breath's vapour doesn't give our position away," he said.

"At this distance?" Cherry asked, looking at him as if she thought him ridiculous.

"Ever heard of binoculars? Russian snipers used to say it was a dead giveaway." She remained silent and did as he asked.

Chapter Twenty-Eight

The lodge was no more than two hundred yards away. The Aerospatiale Puma sat on the pad on the same spot as when it made the emergency landing. In addition to the helicopter, there was now also a Mercedes-Benz Unimog, an all-terrain truck with a load capacity, which he thought sufficient to handle the bomb. On the rear of the vehicle, he saw a hydraulic collapsible mounted on the deck behind the cab as well as hydraulically operated outriggers to steady the vehicle when loading. Two technicians were working on the helicopter's tail assembly.

Another helicopter, a small bubble-shaped Hughes, stood nearby, presumably the aircraft on which the mechanics had arrived. There was no sign of the Denel Oryx helicopter. He wondered whether it had returned from delivering any wounded, which would have included Janet, to the nearest hospital — maybe not.

It dawned on him that the neutron bomb still had to be in the Aerospatiale Puma. They probably hadn't offloaded it yet. He hoped so. How did they propose to get it off the helicopter? It then struck him; the copter had its own winch capable of lifting more than a ton. He wondered what the bomb weighed.

Of course, this hiding place high in the mountains was brilliant; nobody would look for the bomb up here and anyway, anyone who had knowledge of it would presume it was destroyed or rendered inoperative in the fire at Overberg.

Night was near; already the sky had darkened. The twilight would be short-lived. They were exhausted and Peace resolved they would not spend another night out in the freezing cold. Besides, they had to find something to eat.

He wondered whether the technicians below had any inkling of what had occurred here. Had they only been brought here to carry out repairs, oblivious of what the helicopter contained, and the purpose of it being here? He assumed they were Air Force personnel who probably thought that the big brass was on some outing in the mountains. Then again, maybe not; the damage to the helicopter had to be suspicious. Surely, there were a few visible bullet holes?

"What to do now?" Cherry asked.

"I'm not quite sure. Those two men don't pose a problem, but I see the motorcycles are back," he said and pointed towards the house where the motorcycles were parked, "so that makes four men so far. Where are the others? If the Denel Oryx doesn't return within the next hour or so, it won't be able to land. It'll be dark by then. You don't want to be flying in the dark with mountains and mist."

"Do you think they believed we escaped?"

"I think so, otherwise the motorcycles would still be out looking for us."

They saw the two mechanics unload a small portable generator and then erect a stand attached to which were large floodlights. Once the generator was started, the two floodlights starkly illuminated the area on which the helicopter stood and where the mechanics were working. The two men were engrossed in their task and took little notice of their surroundings.

"Please, Geoffrey, forget the bomb. If we get out of here, we can tell our people where it is, and they can blast this place off the planet," she pleaded. Evidently, she was convinced that they stood no chance against so many, and that Van Rhyn would kill them immediately if he had the chance.

She was beginning to irritate him. They had come this far and now she wanted to quit? He turned to face her and snarled, "Listen, woman, this is my operation and it's my decision — got that?"

She looked away and brought a hand to her forehead. "Don't be unreasonable — you know perfectly well that the odds are stacked against us. I would agree with you, but why chance it? Goodness, man, we've tremendous backup who are probably on their way. Sure, this is a sovereign country but once the local government hears the story, our chaps will be here," she pleaded.

"Cherry, please don't. These bastards are really evil. They want to kill so many. Christ, I've said that before. I will get him and get us out of here, or rather, make sure we know where this bomb eventually lands up." He turned his back on her, as if to signify that the discussion was closed.

She obviously realised it was pointless arguing with him. Just then, the front door to the lodge opened, casting a shaft of light outwards and illuminating the small cobble-stoned forecourt. Even in the late twilight, Peace immediately recognised the bulk of Van Rhyn as he stepped out into the open. He and the two who followed him out were dressed in thick anoraks and Van Rhyn was leading two large dogs on leashes. Peace recognised the dogs for what they were, which sent a shock through his system. He heard Cherry's sharp intake of breath. They weren't dogs but hyenas.

Van Rhyn had brought the damn animals with him.

"Now we daren't come out of hiding. Those fuckin' brutes' sense of smell and sight at night are incredible. Van Rhyn will soon realise something is amiss. He'll know we're close by. It's important that we remain downwind."

Peace hadn't expected the animals, and he knew there'd be no creeping up on the enemy while they were around.

The trio with the hyenas approached the helicopter and for the next hour, Peace and Cherry watched as the bomb was removed from the helicopter. This was done with the assistance of the winch and the crane on the Unimog. It was manhandled with some difficulty onto the load-bed of the truck. In the harsh light of the floodlights, Peace could clearly see the injuries Van Rhyn had sustained at Overberg. The man had to be in pain. He wondered where they proposed hiding the bomb. Surely not in the house, since there was no way of getting it into the building. There were other outer buildings, but it would be far too easy to find in these. He knew that the Unimog had to be the ideal vehicle to navigate the terrain provided it stuck to the tracks. Three tracks led from the house's surrounds. Where did they lead to? They had spotted no other buildings or settlements nearby, although they had only seen a small part of the lodge's surroundings.

It was nearly midnight by the time the loading of the bomb was complete.

It had also taken them almost an hour to secure the bomb to the vehicle. Peace saw the men were particularly meticulous about this, the bomb secured in position with multiple turnbuckle restraints and cables.

The sky had cleared; the clouds driven away by a strong wind that whistled and moaned around the crags. It was cold, and they were not properly dressed against it. They had moved and had found some shelter against the wind. Pressed closely together for warmth in a crevasse in the rocks, they spent a miserable night sleeping in short fits, the cold frequently waking them.

*

The sound of the Unimog being started woke them. They crawled forward to look and saw two men in the truck's cab, while the others, including Van Rhyn, had climbed into the Aerospatiale Puma, as it prepared for start-up.

"Where are they going?" Cherry asked, her teeth chattering.

"I don't know but I think they're going to hide the bomb. God knows where, though. Christ, but it's bloody cold!"

"The aircraft technicians are also climbing into the big helicopter," Cherry said.

Peace checked. They were all leaving, ten men in all. He wondered whether any had remained. The Denel Oryx had not returned.

The Unimog's still cold diesel engine spewed blue smoke as it started to move, slowly bouncing over the rough track that pointed northward. Shortly after, the Puma's turbines began to whine, and minutes later, it lifted in the air and swung in a northerly direction. Even Van Rhyn's pets, the hyenas, had been put on board. No smoke spiralled from the lodge and Peace was convinced all had left.

"Come on. I think they've all gone. When the truck and vehicle went, nobody came out to watch them go. Fuck, I'm starving, we need something to drink and eat. A few extra clothes would also be a godsend."

Carefully, they approached the house and when crouched next to the rough foundations, they waited for any sound that would indicate that there still were occupants. They heard nothing. Gingerly Peace opened

246

the door and listened for any sound from the interior. There was none. Slowly, he moved through the anteroom and into the lounge. The fire had nearly burned out. The few glowing embers gave off no smoke, but the room was still warm.

Five minutes later and after checking the rooms, he headed to where he thought the kitchen was, with Cherry close behind. Already the interior's heat was warming them up.

The kitchen surprised them; it was well stocked. Clearly, Van Rhyn and his collaborators lived well. They soon established that both a paraffin-operated fridge and a separate freezer contained a good supply of fresh produce and meat. The kitchen boasted a four-plate gas stove; there were still pots on the fire-rings, the contents covered with lids. Cherry lifted one.

"Oh my gosh!" she exclaimed. "Beef curry!"

She lifted the lid off another pot to find it still contained cold rice. There was more than sufficient to feed them. She lit a gas ring, mixed the curry with the rice, and placed this on the flame to warm up. A small, very low gas-fire still burned on the stove, keeping a tall, blue, enamelled coffeepot warm. They poured coffee into two used mugs, which Cherry had first rinsed, and added sugar they found on the table.

"I've a feeling that wherever they went can't be far. They were expecting to be back pretty soon. We should not overstay our welcome," Peace said.

Cherry agreed. "Whatever, let's bloody eat first."

Soon the aromatic smell of curry permeated the kitchen and when they thought the curry and rice were sufficiently warmed, they got stuck in with two spoons, eating from the same pot. They didn't speak for a few minutes, both relishing the meal. With a mouth full of curry, she looked up from the table and smiled. "Bloody hell!" she said, the sorrow and pain missing from her eyes for the first time.

He had to agree, the food was delicious. He also felt better, it was the first time she had given him a smile in a while. He finished the last of his coffee and rose from the kitchen table.

"That certainly feels better. I'd like to have stayed to catch some sleep, but I don't think it wise to stick around here. Come, it's time we left," he said and then added. "Get hold of some bread and cut it up and stick it into your pockets." His attitude softened. "Cherry, I know I've driven you hard and I believe you're an exemplary agent, other than being smart and beautiful. You know I wasn't happy when you were assigned to this caper. But I don't regret you joining me now, although I fear for you. And you know why. This is going to be over soon and we'll be the ones who walk away from this. Trust me."

Chapter Twenty-Nine

They stepped outside into the cold. The clouds were returning, although the sun was still visible in places. Hopefully, it would warm up during the day.

The motorcycles were propped up against the wall of the house. They were both identical. He recognised them as Spanish Montesa Cappra semi-trail bikes, ideal for this mountainous and rough terrain. The engines were large — 340cc two-strokes. He then realised that in the rarefied air at this altitude, the engines would not perform that well and therefore size and power would count. He had slung the LAW over his shoulder, but it was cumbersome. The carbine hung from his neck, resting on the motorcycle's slim petrol tank. He turned to look at her. After days of imprisonment and roughing it, Peace could see the traces of exhaustion on Cherry's face. But even though a lack of a comb and makeup had taken its toll on her appearance, he could still see the strength and sheer determination she displayed. He was sure he too had to be a sorry sight.

Cherry straddled the bike. "Gosh, I've not ridden one of these for a while," she said. She closed the choke, placed her foot on the kick-starter and then stomped on it with her full weight, expertly forcing the lever down. The engine immediately sprung to life, but with the two-stroke engine cold and it running rough, the exhaust spewed blue-smoke. She had the carbine in front of her hanging tight on its strap across her shoulders and resting on the motorcycle's fuel tank.

Peace's bike also started promptly.

They rode towards the track that the Unimog had taken. This was strewn with stones of all sizes, forcing them to proceed slowly in a low gear, but it was certainly a lot better and more comfortable than walking. After fifteen minutes and having travelled a little less than a mile, they began to handle the machines with more confidence. The gloves they'd removed from their black jumpsuits protected their hands against the biting cold, and the anoraks they had found helped ward off the chill. However, the sun now progressively broke through the clouds, and they began riding through intermittent patches of sunshine.

They had covered about five miles when Peace, who was leading, crested a slight rise and suddenly came across a massive expanse of water below. He immediately stopped, forcing Cherry to brake violently.

He cut the engine and pulled a hand across his throat in a cutting motion, indicating that she should do the same. They backed down the slope where they left the bikes on their side-stands. They once more approached the rise and slowly peered over the top, hoping that only their heads were visible from below and took in the scene that lay before them.

The expanse of water was enormous, at least a mile or more wide. The lake was in a steep-sided valley between the mountains and had clearly once been a gorge. The water had to be deep, a good few hundred feet at its deepest. Surprisingly, there was no vegetation around the edges of the lake.

"I reckon this must be one of the dams the South Africans built as part of the Highlands Water Project," said Cherry. "If I'm not mistaken, I think we're definitely in Lesotho. This is the main dam, but is only one of a few still to be built. I read this all somewhere. I think this could be the Katse Dam that Janet was referring to."

"It's certainly big enough. What the hell is Van Rhyn doing in Lesotho?" He knew that Lesotho, a small mountainous kingdom, was an independent state surrounded by South Africa but contained the largest rain catchment area in southern Africa. South Africa's water supply was largely dependent on the dams of its rivers.

"I don't know, but whatever it is, the bastard is ingenious. Who would come here looking for a bomb? Where on earth will he hide it? There's nothing here!"

Peace had to concede that she had a point. A WMD in Lesotho? Nobody would believe that. Did the man really want to hide the bomb in the dam?

The Unimog had stopped at the water's edge and stood on the bare rock and shale of the track, leaning over slightly towards the water due to the incline. The arroyo they had driven down continued until it disappeared into the water — it was deep-sided due to water that had eroded it as it coursed down over aeons. Surely, it had to have been quite a feat to drive the Unimog down to the water's edge. What was the man up to? Clearly, the bomb was still on the vehicle, as the shape was still covered by a tarpaulin. He saw that the dry streambed, which the vehicle had followed, disappeared into the water. At some stage, this track must have led to the bottom of the gorge. He knew that the dam had only recently started to fill some months back and was still filling. Janet had mentioned that it was still incomplete. Every week it gained a percent or so. What this equated to in terms of water-level rises per inch, he had no idea.

They saw the Aerospatiale Puma perched on a large relatively flat rock ledge that stuck out like a small plateau from the side of the valley not far from where the Unimog had stopped.

"We should have rather stolen the Hughes and flown here," she said.

This momentarily irritated him — 'we should've done this or that' — so typical of a woman.

"And where would I've put it down? There isn't anywhere that I can see, and stuck up in the air, there is no chance of a surprise attack. They'd just shoot us out of the sky," he said savagely. "They knew that the ledge could only accommodate the one helicopter."

"I suppose they are the only people who know where the bomb is." She looked up and down the gorge, but there was no sign of any habitation.

There was suddenly a distinct tremor beneath their feet, which lasted about ten seconds. Peace gave her a concerned look.

She grinned wearily. "There's nothing to be concerned about. It's seismicity."

He looked at her quizzically. "Seismicity? Jesus, that's a new one. Where did you learn that?"

"Your girlfriend of course."

He furrowed his brow but did not respond and his expression of capitulation was not lost on her. She rolled her eyes mockingly.

"For Chrissake, I read it!" she exploded. "Don't look so surprised — I'm well read, you know. The sheer weight of the water as its volume increases with the filling of the dam induces it, and that's what we felt. There have been tremors that registered 4.5 on the Richter scale." She went back to looking at the truck. "Anyway, how's he going to get the bomb off the truck? I mean, what the hell is he going to do with it here?" she added.

"Oh, the man's clever," Peace murmured, shaking his head. "He's going to hide the bomb in the dam, and as you said, they're the only ones who know where to look for it."

"But how?"

Peace snorted. "Probably just roll the truck into the water. The dam's still filling; it'll be well hidden below the surface. If we hadn't been here, nobody would've ever found it. However, we're not going to let him do that. Follow me, we have to get closer."

They abandoned the motorcycles on the track and skirted to the left, looking for cover on the sides of the gully that led to the water's edge. The slope of the arroyo was broken rock, and in places washed smooth by the flow of water over the years. It was easy to keep out of the sight of those below. Eventually, they were no more than a hundred yards or so from the Unimog.

"What are we going to do?"

He grinned, trying to conceal his concern. "You, my dear, will fire the carbine, but like a sniper, a single shot at a time. I need you to take out as many as you can. You won't get them all, they'll find cover soon enough. Van Rhyn is your prime target, but only shoot at those who give you a clear shot. We don't have much ammunition."

He handed her the carbine, which he'd unslung from round his neck. Crouched below a boulder, he lifted the LAW to his shoulder, flipped up the gun-sights, and prepared to fire.

"Now!"

They rose in unison and she immediately found a target, the sharp crack of the carbine loud in his ear. Holding the LAW rock steady, he drew a bead on the Unimog and squeezed the trigger. The rocket projectile erupted from the launch tube, the escaping gas enveloping him in a cloud of grey smoke which was blown back by the wind, but then immediately whipped away. The rocket flew true, hitting the Unimog just above the side fuel tank. The truck exploded and a huge fireball simultaneously rose into the sky, black smoke billowing and contorting above it. The echoes of the explosion rumbled up and down the valley's sides. Clearly, the truck's fuel tanks had exploded. The two men who had stood next to the vehicle disappeared in the wall of flame that had leapt outwards from the truck. They never stood a chance. Others, further away, had fallen to the ground.

In seconds, it was over. Those who had not succumbed to the explosion or to Cherry's accurate rifle fire had found cover behind the many boulders. The truck had fallen over, the bomb still secured to the load-bed but partially submerged in the water. There was no sound other than the crackle and roar of the burning vehicle. None had returned fire.

"How many did you get?" he asked.

"A definite three."

"That makes five. I'm guessing there were no more than nine in total."

Shots were fired at them, the bullets hitting the boulders and sending rock splinters flying in all directions, while the ricochets buzzed around them.

"Don't return fire, let's conserve our ammunition."

He realised that it would be pointless for the men below to stay there — the truck itself was gone; no more than a burning pyre. Their attack had been devastating and those below surely had no other option other than to flee. After all, Peace and Cherry held the high ground. Anyone coming their way could easily be picked off. They would most likely make for the Aerospatiale Puma. It still stood on the ledge unattended, about equal distance between them and the men below.

"If they make a rush to the chopper, we'll let them have it."

She nodded her head knowingly.

Other than one or two shots fired by both parties to encourage all to keep their heads down, no further firing occurred. Considering that the only knowledge of the whereabouts of the bomb rested with those below, Peace resolved that no one would be left alive to try to salvage it.

From the rocks below, a figure dressed in light-blue coveralls made a dash from behind the boulders in the general director of the helicopter. The distance was at the limit of the Heckler and Koch machine pistol range, but

Peace still fired a pattern of shots in front of the running man, the bullets eventually cutting him down like a scythe. He lay still.

"That should dissuade them from any other adventurous attempts," he said with a grim expression of satisfaction.

Chapter Thirty

Two hours passed. They removed what food they had in their pockets and ate a few mouthfuls, keeping a careful watch on those below.

They seemed to have arrived at a stalemate, and no one wanted to make the next move. Of course, Peace and Cherry could retreat along the gully, but this would serve no purpose. Peace was adamant that this had to end now — no one would be allowed to escape.

"Damn!" Cherry exclaimed.

"What is it?"

"I just saw Van Rhyn," she said, unable to conceal the fear in her voice.

Peace wasn't entirely surprised; the man seemed to have more lives than a cat.

"Where?" he asked.

"Shhh, just listen," she said. "I think I can hear an aircraft or helicopter approaching."

He listened intently. Something was certainly approaching, but he didn't think it was a helicopter, as the drone was steady without the deep throb of helicopter rotor blades. It sounded like a single-engine aircraft, and approaching from the west. Holding up a hand to shade his eyes from the sun, he soon saw the approaching dot which grew larger and recognised it to be a de Havilland Beaver, complete with floats in which small wheels could be seen. It was an amphibian.

Of course! The plane had obviously been summoned by radio, and this meant Van Rhyn had contact with the outside world. This was a blow.

The aircraft circled, losing height. He saw it extend its flaps and turn into the wind for its landing approach. It continued to lose altitude until the floats kissed the top of the wavelets on the dam, then settled, throwing up more spray. It neared the shore where Van Rhyn and his men were hidden. When about fifty yards from the shore it swung, beam on, revealing the rear double-hatch in the fuselage. They did not miss the threatening machine-gun barrel that poked through the opening. This immediately began to chatter, the shots bouncing off the rocks that sheltered them, a definite message to keep their heads down. There was no doubt they had radio contact with Van Rhyn, who must have revealed their position.

Already the survivors of the explosion were entering the water and swimming the short distance towards the floatplane. Peace wondered why. Surely, the Aerospatiale Puma would have been the best means of escape? Or had they thought it too dangerous to approach? Something didn't make sense. Four men were in the water swimming to the floatplane with two hyenas amongst them. Van Rhyn was in the lead.

When the machine-gun fire stitched its way past them, he stood and shouted, "Fire!"

The machine pistol jumped in his hands, waterspouts appearing on the water as he worked the shots towards the swimmers. Next to him, the carbine fired shot after shot. He saw a swimmer throw up an arm and roll over, then had to duck for shelter as the machine-gun's deadly track of fire again sought them out. Both hunkered down behind the rocks. The firing continued intermittently for a minute or so, but not long enough for them to rise and return fire.

The firing stopped. They looked over the boulder and saw that those who remained were already clambering aboard the floatplane. The floatplane's pilot was applying power, the aircraft turning to face into the wind. Peace saw no sign of the hyenas. Were they dead or were they already on board? The amphibian's engine was responding to the throttle and now ran at full power, the aircraft starting to surge forward.

"Run, run!" he shouted, heading towards the Aerospatiale Puma with Cherry close behind him.

He was a qualified helicopter pilot and had time on RAF Lynx helicopters. The Aerospatiale Puma's flight controls and specs were unknown to him, but comparatively speaking, its sheer size had to make it an ungainly beast. Like flying a DC3 as opposed to a Cessna Skylane or Piper Cherokee. He guessed the Beaver had to block at about a 140–150 m.p.h. indicated airspeed and the floats surely cut into her speed. The Puma was faster by a fair margin. What was the problem? Why hadn't they used it?

He pushed open the cargo door and climbed into the Puma. He heard Cherry running up behind him, grabbed her hand and pulled her aboard, both of them gasping for breath. He rushed forward and up the step into the cockpit and flung himself into the left-hand seat, his eyes simultaneously sweeping over the instruments and the controls. Basic controls were the same in all helicopters. Starting the damn thing was the problem. He needed to find the right switches! He forced himself to calm down and concentrate, and soon found the master switches, the starter controls, and fuel controls. The electric current surged through the instruments as the master switches engaged. He groaned. He realised why they hadn't used the Puma. It was virtually empty, the gauges only registering a few hundred pounds of fuel. The turbine helicopter with its two engines had a prodigious appetite; the damn thing wouldn't fly far! Certainly not to any major city.

Cherry had taken the right-hand seat. "Do you know how to fly this thing?" she asked breathlessly.

"A helicopter is a helicopter is a helicopter."

"Don't give me that Richard Burton crap! This is not a hole and you can't compare the two. Don't spout movie quotes at me, for Chrissake," she retorted angrily.

"We'll soon find out, won't we?"

He didn't mention the acute lack of fuel and pushed the thought from his mind. He couldn't let them escape. If she did read the instruments and brought up the question of fuel, he'd deal with it.

Rapidly, he went through the basic start-up procedure and soon the super large blades began to turn as power was fed to them. A minute later the helicopter lifted from the ledge, the nose pitching slightly forward as it gained momentum and speed in pursuit of the Beaver. It was a little sluggish and less responsive than the helicopters he'd previously flown. Quickly, it reached its maximum cruising speed, at least twenty to thirty miles an hour faster than a Beaver with floats. He switched on the forward-seeking radar. There were few clouds in the sky and he soon found the Beaver on the screen and turned in pursuit.

He pointed to the rear. "Try to find some ammunition for the carbine. Maybe there's something for the H&K as well."

She disappeared into the back and returned a few minutes later, smiling. "Guess what I also found besides the ammunition?" she said as she took her seat.

He shook his head but knew by the look on her face it had to be a good surprise.

"There's a small crate with rifle grenades, made exactly for the carbine we have." She indicated the carbine next to her on the floor.

"They'll come in handy if we can get close."

They were slowly closing on the Beaver. He climbed until he matched their altitude, mulling over how to attack the aircraft if he got near enough to it. He knew that Cherry would have had some helicopter training and must be able to fly those types in general use in the British Forces.

"Flown a helicopter before?" he asked.

"Of course."

Well, that was certainly matter-of-fact, he thought.

"Good, then you pilot while I try to shoot 'em down."

She did not respond but continue to stare straight ahead.

The floatplane was now in sight. The pilot seemed to have not noticed the approaching helicopter directly behind it since it was keeping its course steady. However, to get in a shot, Peace would have to bring the helicopter partially alongside so he could properly train his weapon on it. He knew they could not do this without being detected.

He got out of his seat. "Here, take the controls."

She took over his seat and adjusted it.

"Okay, come up along their right side. Let's see what damage I can do," he said, picking up her carbine.

It did not take long for her to master the controls and soon she was in complete command of the helicopter. Truly, she was a woman with many talents. They were no more than two or three hundred yards behind the

Beaver when she adjusted course slightly, holding the helicopter in a new position to avoid the vortex created by the Beaver's passage.

Peace had no idea what the rifle grenade's range was but thought the closer the better. If he recalled correctly, fifty to sixty yards had to be about the maximum range.

They finally figured out how to use the inter-crew communications gear on board the helicopter after finding the intercom earphones and mouthpieces, which they donned. They could now talk to each other, though they still had to shout.

"Starting to pass on their right," she said. The slipstream that found its way through the open cargo door was vigorously buffeting him.

Slowly, but with their speed increasing, they started to overtake the Beaver. He'd hoped they would not be spotted, but when the aircraft suddenly banked and veered left, he knew they'd been detected. The helicopter swung in unison as Cherry seemed to anticipate the plane's pilot's reaction. The superior speed of the helicopter played in their favour and soon they were moving alongside again. Again, the Beaver tried to bank away, but the helicopter's speed enabled Cherry to hold her position and even improve on it.

"God, we're running out of fuel. One of the fuel tank warning lights has started blinking!" Cherry shouted.

Peace was surprised she'd not noticed their dire fuel situation before.

"Just disregard it for another minute. The light means we've no more than about ten minutes of fuel left, so keep following the Beaver down." He hoped he sounded confident.

Meanwhile, the helicopter, with its superior speed, had caught up and was now near enough to let him use the carbine. He braced himself against the side of the loading hatch and with the rifle hard against his shoulder and hoping he was jammed rock steady, aimed at the aircraft trying to anticipate the amount of lead he would require to compensate for their speed. He imagined the distance needed, pulled the aim forward of the plane and fired. The recoil slammed into his shoulder and threw him back and he staggered, trying to keep his balance. The force of the shot had flung the barrel upwards, but still, his gaze never left the Beaver. He saw the grenade cover the distance to the plane and pass through the vertical tail plane, breaking off the top part and wrenching the vertical rudder section from its hinges. This started to bang and flap in the slipstream for a second before it was torn off. The grenade, which had passed right through, exploded thirty yards beyond the aircraft, the impact alone doing the damage. The grenade only detonated milliseconds later.

"Did you see that? The damn grenade only exploded once it was beyond the plane. It must have been a dud," Peace screamed into his mike but then realised he'd not considered the delayed fuse the grenade incorporated, which was to allow the grenade to penetrate any armour before detonating.

"I did, but look, she's in trouble."

He looked. She was right; the aircraft was in trouble. Without its vertical tail plane, it was skidding from left to right and back again. The pilot had obviously realised the problem as the plane was rapidly losing altitude. He must have been hoping to land before it plummeted to earth in a death spiral.

"What about the fuel?" Cherry shouted.

He had forgotten their fuel problem in the heat of the moment.

"Get us down, do it now!" he replied, now fearful that the engines would cut out. He didn't want Cherry to have to carry out an auto-rotation emergency if the helicopter had to descend without power. This type of emergency landing was achieved by letting the downward passage of the helicopter accelerate the freewheeling spin of the rotor. Once its spin was sufficiently fast, the aircraft's descent could be controlled by activating the collective pitch to induce a three or four second hover, and put the chopper on the ground without breaking it. The theory was great, but he was not sure whether Cherry or he could do that expertly enough with such a large helicopter — this was no trainee helicopter.

He saw a large river below, the surface on its far side flatter than that on the Lesotho side, even though it was interspersed with kopjes. They had left the jagged mountains of the Drakensberg behind.

"That's the Caledon River and on the other side, that's South African territory," she yelled.

They were still descending rapidly. The speed of the descent concerned him, but he still kept an eye on the Beaver. He didn't want to lose it.

"Never mind the damn river, just keep as close as you can to the Beaver," he shouted.

He could see the pilot of the Beaver was barely able to control the aircraft, it yawed and skidded as it descended. The moment the pilot endeavoured to reduce speed, the small piece of rudder still left became less effective, which left the pilot no option but to maintain a high-speed descent. Now they were no more than a thousand feet from the ground and it was time to find a place suitable for an emergency landing. The pilot had obviously decided on a course of action; he was bringing the plane round into the wind, the direction of which could be judged from the smoke of a bushfire in the distance.

Peace then saw where he thought the pilot would try to put the stricken aircraft down — a gravel road that wound its way through the kopjes, gently undulating, but at least relatively straight in one section for about a mile.

"Keep behind the aircraft. Don't let it get too far from us," he shouted into the microphone.

Clearly, she was doing her best. They stuck with the Beaver, the helicopter moving downwards but forwards. He realised that she had started preparing for auto-gyration. Their descent had caused the rotor to be driven like a windmill in the wind, with its revolutions ever increasing. For the moment, they'd both forgotten the aircraft in front of them, as their attention was focused on landing the helicopter in one piece. Cherry was shouting at him to brace for impact as the ground approached them rapidly. He sat down on the floor, grabbed the bulkhead that separated the cargo and cockpit areas, brought his knees up, and said a quick silent prayer.

Just when he thought it was too late, Cherry twisted the collective pitch control, causing the huge rotor blades to bite into the air and create lift. Their descent quickly slowed and their downward passage coming to a near stop. The helicopter hovered for a few seconds just above the ground and then sank the last foot or so and settled in the long grass with a slight bump.

As the rotor spooled down, he could not help himself and whispered into the microphone, "Jesus! That was close! But, sweetheart, I'll fly with you anytime — that was fuckin' brilliant!"

All he heard was her drawing in deep breaths of air; she was obviously in a semi-state of shock.

"Breathe, baby — breathe," he said.

When he'd last seen the plane, it was over the road, the pilot trying to put it down while fighting to keep the wings level with a minimum of yaw. He knew the landing would have been spectacular.

"Out, out!" he shouted at her. He grabbed the carbine and the H&K and jumped from the helicopter with her right behind him. The grass was so long that he could barely look over it. He had a good idea of the direction in which the road lay. He gave her the assault rifle and they moved off in single file, with him leading the way, brushing the long elephant grass stalks aside. It was surprisingly warm and their passage through the grass disturbed the insects, which rose in small clouds as they swiped at them.

Suddenly, they found themselves on the side of the road standing on a small border mound thrown up by a grader. They could see the aircraft a few hundred yards away. It had veered off the road, its tail high in the sky. One of the pontoons had broken off, one wing pointing skyward.

"Quick! Let's get to them before they find their wits. Hopefully, they're still dazed." He ran down the gravel road, the H&K held at the ready across his stomach. He could hear her footfalls behind him.

As they neared the aircraft, he saw that its nose had driven into the side of a deep donga, just off the road. The metal around the engine had crumpled, the propeller blades bent back, and the Plexiglas windscreen smashed. A wing was torn off. He could just make out a person seated in the plane, half sprawled over the instrument panel.

"Hurry!" he shouted. "They're still stuck in the cockpit."

She had put on a burst of speed and now ran beside him, trying to get to the wrecked plane before anyone managed to climb from it.

They were no more than fifty yards from the plane when Van Rhyn rose from the tall grass that edged the road next to the gully, a machine pistol in his hands. Peace put his hand on Cherry's shoulder and shoved with all the strength he could muster, but before she fell, the machine pistol chattered, throwing a spray of bullets at them.

Something slammed into his left side, sending him sprawling. As he fell, he saw out of the corner of his eye, Cherry's head being thrown back.

A feeling of intense fear gripped him as he realised that she'd also been hit. As he went down, he blindly fired a few shots, sufficient to make Van Rhyn dive for cover. Taking up a position to shield Cherry, he rose to one knee and again sprayed the area with bullets where he'd last seen Van Rhyn, hoping this would dissuade him from showing himself once more.

Ice-cold fear gripped him like a vice and in a near panic, he forced himself to look at her, as she sprawled on her back on the gravel. In that brief moment, he realised she was gravely wounded — shot in the chest just below the heart. He knew there had to be internal injuries. A low moan of anguish escaped his lips as he placed his arms under her and lifted her to a sitting position. She fell sideways and came to rest against him. Her breathing was shallow, and her face had turned a sickly pallor.

"You're going to be all right," he whispered, cradling her in his arms and rocking her back and forth.

She opened her eyes and stared past him, her eyes round with terror. He swung around just in time to see a hyena, its leash trailing behind it, bounding down the road towards them. Peace gave an almost inhuman howl and let Cherry go. He dropped to the ground, putting himself between the animal and Cherry. There was no time to pull his pistol from his belt. As the hyena closed on him, he quickly rose to his feet and reached out with his hands, preparing to grab the hyena by its throat as it leapt at him. Instead, and to his surprise, it veered around him and landed on Cherry.

He scrambled to get hold of the animal but it already it had its massive jaws around Cherry's neck. Desperately, he drew the automatic from his belt, but it was a futile act. The huge animal shook its head, and he distinctly heard the crack as her neck broke. The huge fangs had punctured her neck, and the first signs of blood were visible.

He shoved the barrel in the hyena's ear and pulled the trigger. The shot blew out the animal's brains in a cloud of blood and gristle. It slumped to the ground, lying half over Cherry.

A shudder rose from the depths of his soul and accompanied by an overwhelming feeling of despair and anguish he yowled in anger.

He dropped his head to his knees. He knew she was dead and another primordial wail escaped from his lips. He swung round to seek out Van

Rhyn, picking up the carbine and bringing it to his shoulder. Van Rhyn was already running towards him, no more than two hundred yards away. Tears of rage, hate and frustration blurred his vision as he tried to get the rifle's sights on the man, but some sixth sense must have warned Van Rhyn who began weaving from side to side. Peace knew he had only a few cartridges left. He pulled off only two shots. Both missed.

He heard a motor vehicle behind him and turned to see a dilapidated medium-sized truck approaching with about a dozen farmworkers on the rear with some standing and holding the roll bar behind the cab. He thought he could see others who squatted on the floor. The occupants waved to him, smiling and laughing, as was their custom. They had not yet seen the aircraft in the ditch. As the truck passed the plane, those on the back began to hammer furiously on the cab's roof, trying to get the driver's attention. By the time the vehicle stopped, it was alongside Van Rhyn. Peace's view was hampered, but he heard two shots and suddenly the crew rapidly disgorged from the truck and fled in panic into the long grass.

"Jesus!" Peace, who had begun running, screamed as he skidded to a halt on the gravel. He aimed the assault rifle and fired another two shots, but Van Rhyn was already in the truck's cab, having commandeered it at gunpoint. The engine roared and the wheels spun; gravel and dust spurted from the tyres as they sought traction.

He felt another wave of panic as it dawned on him the man was about to escape. He watched as the truck drew away. However, it was slow; Van Rhyn was clearly not able to coax much speed out of it.

"Think, think!" he cried aloud, trying to put the tragic events of the last few moments behind him. He needed to deal with Van Rhyn. The man could not be allowed to escape again.

He heard the sound of another vehicle and it came into view trailing dust. It was a surplus Army Jeep painted a bright green, a lone driver the only occupant. It drew up alongside him. Blue smoke burbled from the exhaust; the vehicle had seen better days. Behind the wheel sat an elderly man, his head covered by a shabby Stetson, wisps of grey hair peeping from beneath its brim.

"Liewe Here! Wat het hier gebeur?[24] *"* the man said, his eyes wide with alarm as he stared at the body in the ditch and the dead hyena.

"Somebody shot her. He hijacked a truck from some labourers a minute ago and has just disappeared over that rise." Peace pointed in the direction where the truck had disappeared. "Sir, I need your vehicle," he asked solemnly, but it was clear he was not to be refused.

The old man looked at him. Peace realised he must present a disturbing picture. The old farmer was seeing an unkempt, unshaven man, dressed in a filthy black jumpsuit, grasping an automatic machine pistol in one hand, and bleeding from a wound in his side. The farmer must have sensed that this was not the time to argue. Without saying a word, he slid from the seat and gestured for Peace to take the vehicle.

With an inaudible word of thanks, and now armed with both weapons, he jumped into the driver's seat, rammed the Jeep into gear, and with a jerk and cloud of blue smoke tore down the road in pursuit. The smoke might have indicated that the engine needed an overhaul, but the Jeep still managed a good turn of speed and with the accelerator pressed to the floor, he soon had the speedometer needle nudging the 60 m.p.h. mark. A large plume of dust and smoke trailed behind them.

He drove as if possessed by a demon, his whole being focused solely on seizing or killing Van Rhyn. He roared through the small gullies that bisected the road, causing the suspension to bottom out, sending jarring shocks through the vehicle. It would even become momentarily airborne when it crested any small rise in the road.

---

24. Good God! What happened here?

Chapter Thirty-One

He topped a small rise and saw the truck in the distance. Clearly, his speed was greater, and this had enabled him to catch up. Still, the Jeep's engine rattled in protest as he continued to push it to the limits.

Please God, he breathed a prayer, *let the engine hold.*

Van Rhyn must have realised that the vehicle coming up behind him was in pursuit. He swung the truck off the road onto a farm track that passed through two large stone pillars, a large signboard proclaiming that the road now entered the *Willow Ridge Guest Farm*. The board also mentioned that it was famous for its ten-thousand cherry trees.

Peace followed, the Jeep sliding sideways on the gravel as he battled to control the power-slide. He barely missed one of the stone pillars. He noticed the truck in front slow appreciably, and quickly accelerate again. He wondered why. The reason for this soon became apparent.

A deep gully loomed in front, the track disappearing into a deep ditch two or three yards wide, bordered by reeds and containing water. The approach to it was sudden and steep.

Surprised, he stomped his foot on the brake pedal. The wheels locked, the Jeep immediately slewing sideways. He fought the wheel, trying to straighten the vehicle but was only partially successful; the vehicle entered the water at a forty-five-degree angle. He was enveloped in spray. Then, with a loud bang, the rear side of the Jeep collided with something. It straightened with a vicious jerk, but the force was sufficient to throw both weapons from the open vehicle, leaving him with only Cherry's automatic. He wasn't going to stop and retrieve the weapons. Any delay might result in him losing Van Rhyn. He was determined to catch him, even if it meant killing him with his bare hands, if necessary.

The truck disappeared around a curve in the road, a copse of trees now restricting Peace's vision. As he came barrelling round the bend, he suddenly saw the truck standing stationary in the middle of the track. The sides of the road were a jumble of boulders of all sizes, barring any attempt he could make to slip past. Again, he viciously braked. The wheels locked but the tyres still skidded. He knew he'd not be able to stop in time. The rear of the truck loomed ahead. He had little option but to throw himself out of the open vehicle onto the road, and instinctively he rolled in classic parachutist's fashion to absorb the shock, trying to miss the rocks that lined the sides of the road. Simultaneously, he heard the chatter of a machine pistol and realised that Van Rhyn had set a trap for him.

Thank God, he thought. Had he been driving any slower and had he not abandoned the vehicle, the bullets might have ripped through him. Instead, they had whistled harmlessly overhead. The numbness in his side had begun to wear off and he was beginning to feel discomfort and some pain. Blood still seeped from the wound, but fortunately, less than he expected. Still, the side of the jumpsuit was drenched.

The Jeep collided with the truck with a thunderous crash, a huge cloud of dust rising into the air. He did not hesitate and despite the pain, he rolled from the road into the boulders at the side just as the machine pistol again fired, the bullets stitching a row of sand spurts past him. He pulled the automatic from his belt and removed the clip to check what was in the magazine. *Only six shots, Jesus, this is serious*. He rammed the magazine into the butt and pulled the slide back, forcing a cartridge into the chamber.

Cautiously he rose to get a better look at the vehicles. Van Rhyn had to be hiding near the vehicles waiting for him to make a move. Other than the grass swaying in the wind, nothing moved. For a few seconds, he was gripped by anxiety; this was a dangerous game of hide and seek.

He was sure Van Rhyn would think he'd try to outflank him, but would not believe he'd risk crossing the open road. However, this was precisely what Peace intended to do. But how to get across the road unscathed?

He took a fist-sized stone and threw it into the grass about twenty yards to the left of the crash site. Hopefully, Van Rhyn would turn to check the noise, thinking he was about to be attacked. As the rock clattered to the ground, Peace gritted his teeth, and in a crouched position, dashed across the road into the grass on the other side.

No shots rang out. Lying on his stomach, he remained silent but listened intently. Other than the sound of the light wind in the grass and the chirping and whistling of birds, he heard nothing suspicious. Had Van Rhyn fallen for it?

He leopard-crawled through the grass, ensuring he made a wide detour to approach the crashed vehicles from the opposite side of the road. All he had was the automatic — the sheath knife had been removed by his captors on their arrival at the lodge, and he doubted he was a match against a machine pistol even with the element of surprise in his favour.

A vision of Cherry kept coming to mind repeatedly, and he had to force himself to concentrate on his mission.

As he closed in on the edge of the road through the long grass, he peered through the stalks and carefully scrutinised the crashed vehicles. Both were so badly damaged they could not be driven. Steam hissed from the Jeep's punctured radiator and water had already pooled on the ground. The truck's rear axle had been torn from its spring-shackles on the one side. He saw no sign of Van Rhyn. Had he fled or was he hiding in the grass waiting for him to show himself? There was also the constant danger he might spray the surrounding area with bullets. Van Rhyn was the hunted and he could wait in ambush not showing himself, an advantage Peace didn't have.

Peace wondered how much ammunition Van Rhyn could still have.

Suddenly he heard a dog barking. He soon saw it; it was in the road about sixty yards down the track, its attention focused on something in the grass near a large boulder.

He jumped up, and crouching low, moved rapidly across the road. His appearance drew the dog's attention, and it now began to bark at him. It even made a half-hearted mock attack, stopping only a few feet away. Clearly, this was a dead giveaway and he cringed, expecting to hear the rifle open up. This didn't happen. He knew then that Van Rhyn must have slunk away again.

"Come here, doggie," he called, trying to coax the animal to him. At first, the dog was wary, but eventually, it slowly moved forward until close enough to allow him to put a hand out to stroke it. It gave a low growl but soon quietened, clearly happy with the attention he was giving it. He mumbled nonsensical endearments, which it seemed to appreciate while he carefully inspected the road again.

He could see from the flattened grass where Van Rhyn had concealed himself behind the boulder.

"Come, doggie, what's this," he said jabbing the ground trying to get the dog to smell the ground and catch Van Rhyn's scent. Christ, for all he knew the damn animal only responded to commands in Afrikaans! He tried, "Come doggie," again with a further display of friendliness. After ignoring him for a short while the dog finally sniffed the ground, then looked up and gazed stupidly at him, then at a large homestead in the distance, panting with its tongue out.

Still smiling, Peace said, "You fuckin' stupid dog, for Chrissake, just sniff, okay?"

All the time he kept a wary lookout, not entirely convinced that Van Rhyn had run.

Finally, the dog appeared to understand or had decided it was time to return home. It sniffed again and then moved in a circle and started to pad away, obviously following something. At that moment, he could have hugged the animal.

He followed it, occasionally having to break into a trot just to keep up. The trail the dog followed avoided the road. The ground sloped slowly away down towards what was some sort of orchard, the trees in neat rows. Beyond the orchard and at least a mile away, he could see what he thought to be a large farmstead, the main house surrounded by a host of small outbuildings. These were all perched on the banks of a small river, lined by willow trees.

It was just past midday and the sun's heat was very uncomfortable. The pace the dog set and the heat soon had him breaking out in a sweat, and he constantly had to use his sleeve to stop the perspiration from running into his eyes.

They reached the orchard, where row upon row of trees all in straight rows greeted them, the ground between them cleared. It offered little conceal-ment as the canopies were relatively high off the ground.

Slowly they moved through the trees and after a while, he thought he could hear the laughter of children. For a moment, through the trees, he thought he caught a glimpse of movement and part of a swimming pool.

I must be approaching the guest farm's swimming pool.

He could make out the buildings between the trees, and the cars and pickup trucks in an adjoining parking lot cut out of the nearby grassland. He knew it was where Van Rhyn had to be heading. The sounds distracted the dog and suddenly it deserted him, heading straight for the swimming pool, clearly attracted by the sounds of the children and the occasional scream of glee. For a moment, he thought that this might have been where the dog was heading anyway, and may not have been following Van Rhyn's trail at all.

God, then he had lost him!

He entered the car park. There was no one to be seen. Slowly he moved through the vehicles, bending down after every few steps to see whether he could see anyone's feet, but the grass was calf high, obscuring his vision. He moved from car to car and saw that some were not even locked, and several still had their keys in the ignition. Clearly, it was considered safe to do this out here in the country. He saw a large SUV and thought it just the vehicle that Van Rhyn would consider a good choice in which to make his escape. He approached it, ducking as not to be seen through the windows.

As he came alongside the driver's door, it burst open with considerable force and smashed into the side of his head. He would have been sent sprawling had he not caught hold of the top of the doorframe. However, he was still caught off-balance and the blow partially stunned him.

As the door was pushed wide open, he still clutched its frame. In the other hand, he held the automatic.

Van Rhyn spilled from the SUV. Peace tried to swing the automatic round to take a shot. Van Rhyn viciously brought his weapon down and knocked the automatic from Peace's hand, forcing him to release his grip on the doorframe as he fell, but before he struck the ground, he managed to grasp the barrel of the assault rifle. Peace realised Van Rhyn was not going to release the rifle; he had to know his life depended on it. As Peace went down, he pulled Van Rhyn with him, where they battled for control of the rifle. Van Rhyn had it by its pistol grip; the rifle's short stock was folded back, so it was now a machine pistol rather than a rifle.

Van Rhyn was heavier than Peace, and immensely strong. Peace knew that in a drawn-out fight, he would lose. He'd be overcome by the man's sheer weight. He dared not let go of the barrel. He now had both hands around it, as it pointed to the side. Suddenly, it hammered in his hands, emitting a short bark of shots, which was deafening in his ear. He had to twist his body to keep the rifle from pointing at him, causing an excruciating pain to shoot along his left side from groin to armpit. He knew that blood had to be spurting from his wound. He tried to roll, but Van Rhyn was too heavy. The huge man remained on top of him, and they both breathed heavily from their exertions. Again, Peace tried to roll, and this time had some success.

As he turned sideways, he felt his automatic under his cheek where it lay on the ground. He summoned all his strength, feinted with an intended roll to the right, and with a Herculean effort attempted a backward roll. This surprised Van Rhyn, and for a second the man relaxed his grip. Both went over, Peace rolling over on his back and head and Van Rhyn falling sideways, then rolling, finishing in a sitting position close to the vehicle's driver-side door sill. Van Rhyn's roll had not been clumsy but that of a trained paratrooper. The first thing he saw was Van Rhyn sitting with the rifle pulled close to his midriff, ready to fire. The smirk on his red and scarred face showed he knew he had the upper hand and that Peace was surely a dead man. Peace didn't even have a weapon; the automatic was too far from him.

"Jou stuk fokken Britse kak! Vrek nou![25]" the huge man hissed, a split-second away from pulling the trigger.

The vehicle's door was nearly touching Peace's side and his hand was

---

25. You piece of British shit! Die now!

against the outside of the door. He swung it as hard as he could. Van Rhyn pulled the trigger. The door hit Van Rhyn in the face but he had managed to pull off two shots, a millisecond apart. The bullets hit Peace in the left side. It was as if he'd been hit by a sledgehammer, but still, he remained sitting. The blow to the face had laid Van Rhyn flat. Peace scrambled for the automatic a few feet away and managed to get a grip on it. He swung around and pointed it at his adversary. Van Rhyn was shaking his head, still clasping the rifle. Peace's first shot hit Van Rhyn in the throat, tearing a hole in it on one side, blood immediately spurting from the wound. The second entered his right eye. The round-nosed slug blew out the back of his skull in a red mist.

Van Rhyn flopped backwards and lay on his back in the grass, his arm flung out. Peace stared at him through grey eyes of flint, devoid of emotion, and his lips in a grim line. Blood seeped from the holes in his side, the front of his jumpsuit already saturated. He still held the automatic.

"I don't know what you said, but if I had ammunition left, I'd shoot you again," Peace whispered his voice barely audible.

The job wasn't yet done.

With an immense effort, he gathered himself and rose to his feet, while hanging onto the SUV, his head reeling. Slowly his senses began to function again. He grabbed the assault rifle and removed the magazine. It had another taped to it. This was full. He threw it onto the passenger seat of the SUV and slid behind the wheel. The keys dangled from the ignition. He started the vehicle, the engine immediately catching. The SUV had an automatic transmission, so reaching over with his good right arm, he brought the T-stick back into drive and floored the accelerator. The vehicle shot into a gap between parked cars, the rear wheels throwing up grass and dust. Out of his peripheral vision, he saw a group of people approaching. He ignored them, steering the SUV towards the track that led to the main gravel road, its rear-end swaying from side to side as he fought to control it. He shot through the lodge's entrance and turned to go back to where the helicopter and aircraft had come down.

It took no more than a few minutes to get to the ditch where he saw the tail of the aircraft thrust into the air, the damaged tail plane clearly visible.

Already, he felt lightheaded. It had to be the loss of blood. He clamped his jaw, the muscles in his cheeks bulging. This wasn't over yet.

Chapter Thirty-Two

The SUV skidded to a halt. He was surprised he couldn't see anybody. Where were the farmworkers and the farmer? A little further on, he saw something covered by a piece of tarpaulin. He knew this had to be Cherry's body. A feeling of intense anguish again washed over him, but he forced this aside. He moved towards the ditch. The figure that he'd seen sprawled over the cockpit's instrument panel was no longer there. He felt his skin tingle with the first hint of alarm. He had not forgotten that this had been General Booyens. Since he'd already shoved the new magazine into the rifle, he pulled the slide back and worked a cartridge into the chamber.

He heard the unmistakable sound of helicopters and looked up. Two British Chinook helicopters moved across the sky, their roundels clearly visible, flying towards Lesotho. Had VA known all along what had transpired and where he and Cherry had been? Then why had he not lent any assistance, especially when they had been stuck in Lesotho? This could've saved Cherry's life. The callous bastard! He resolved he'd deal with him as well.

Booyens had to be around somewhere. If he didn't find him soon, he'd lose him. Besides, didn't think he could stay conscious much longer. His side hurt like hell. There seemed to be blood everywhere.

He inspected the aircraft. The two who had sat on the right side were dead. A wing strut had broken off and had pierced the passenger in the right seat in the back; this protruded through the man's chest. When the aircraft crash-landed, it had slid into the ditch, where a huge boulder had crushed the right side and killed the man in the rear seat. There was a strong smell of petrol and he realised the aircraft could go up in flames at any moment.

Peace hung on the wing strut on the left side and briefly closed his eyes, fighting off the nausea and dizziness as his head reeled. He knew he was rapidly losing blood. He had to finish this soon. He heard movement behind him, spun round, and saw the farmer. He immediately realised that the elderly man was in shock, his face pale.

"Wat op aarde gaan hier aan?[26]*"* the farmer asked with a distinctive tremor in his voice. Then he seemed to realise that Peace did not speak Afrikaans and repeated, "What on earth is going on here?" in a heavy guttural voice.

"Sir, if I told you, I'm sure you'd never believe me."

He saw the farmer's eyes dart to his assault rifle and to the blood that oozed from the punctures in his black jumpsuit.

"*Liewe aarde*[27], you're wounded; you're losing blood."

"I know, but first, where's the man that was in the aircraft, the one that was unconscious?"

"He has a broken leg; I pulled him from the plane and dragged him far enough away so if the plane exploded, he'd be all right."

"Show me."

The old man pointed to a small copse of thorn trees.

Peace took a step forward but had to stop as again a wave of light-headedness overcame him. For a moment, he stood swaying as he squeezed his eyes shut, trying to regain control. The feeling passed, and he again fell in step behind the farmer.

They got to the copse where he found Booyens propped up in the shade against the trunk of a small tree. Next to him lay a black man. Peace assumed him to be one of the farm labourers. The man was clearly dead.

"This *bliksem*[28] shot him!" the farmer blurted, seemingly close to tears. "Isaiah was my foreman; he worked for me for years. I hope they hang this bastard. Don't worry about his pistol; it's empty. He tried to shoot me but there were no bullets."

---

26. What on earth is happening here?

27. Afrikaans equivalent of "Good grief"

28. Bastard

Booyens was in great pain, as was evident by the grimace on his face as he tried to move.

"Van Rhyn's dead," Peace said.

"You killed him?"

"Yes."

"I suppose you're going to kill me, in cold-blood *nogal?*[29]"

Peace could see that the man knew he was about to be executed, but he didn't flinch.

"You suppose correctly."

"But the farmer here will be a witness, you can't do that," Booyens sneered.

"Well, that depends on how you look at it. You're no more than a fuckin' animal," Peace replied, and smiled. "And now it's time to join your boss!"

The expression on Booyens' face was one of fear as he realised that this really was the end. The assault rifle bucked in Peace's hands. The shots rang loud, each bullet jerking the general like a rag doll. With his lungs blown to shreds, the blood welled-up in Booyens' mouth and trickled down his chin.

"*My liewe Here!*[30]" the old man shouted. He stumbled backwards, trying to get away from the ghastly sight as though he feared he might be next. His heel hit a stone and he fell to the ground. He scrambled upright in an instant and turned to run.

"Stop!" Peace shouted. "I won't shoot you."

The farmer stopped. Peace lowered the rifle, but then dropped it. He swayed for a moment and finally pitched forward.

The man stood there looking at Peace, oblivious to the sound of an approaching helicopter, obviously still in a state of shock at what he had witnessed in just a short space of time. To him it must have seemed that the world had gone mad.

---

29. The word "Really?" when raised questioningly or "and even" in this context.
30. My dear God!

Chapter Thirty-Three

Peace climbed out of the taxi and paid the cab driver. For a moment he stood on the pavement and looked around at the passers-by — the bankers, stockbrokers and their clerks and secretaries as they hurried past, clearly intent on making it to the shelter of their offices before the heavens broke, showering London with the threatening rain. It all appeared so normal.

He was dressed in a dark suit but the tailor-made sling in which his left arm rested was in stark contrast, being a light grey.

As he approached, he saw the Regimental Sergeant-Major looking at him intently, and eyeing his arm in its sling. Peace knew he would notice how much thinner he was and would assume it was the result of a mission and not a skiing accident. Peace initially wanted to make an attempt at being jovial but thought better of it.

Peace stopped in front of the RSM to greet him.

"A rough one, Guv?" the RSM enquired sympathetically.

"You could say that."

"I should warn you that there's heavy brass waiting for you. You're late, you know."

"I know, but frankly, I don't give a shit. They're just a bunch of bastards, with a few limp-wristed pansies thrown in, but I'm sure you already know that."

The RSM laughed. "You're right there."

He stepped into the fore-office occupied by VA's secretary.

"Good God, Commander, you look awful," Jenny Damsby said,

obviously trying to smile to hide her shock. "Geoffrey, are you sure you should be up and about?"

"Never felt better," he lied.

He would normally flirt with her whenever he visited the Vice Admiral's office, but not today. He was in no mood for light-hearted banter.

"Geoffrey, I'm truly sorry about your partner Cherry Boxx," Miss Damsby said.

"So am I," he quietly replied, his flint-grey eyes briefly softening.

The intercom rasped. "We're waiting, Miss Damsby." The impatience in Sir John's voice was unmistakable.

"Sorry, Sir John, I'll send him through immediately." She came round from behind her desk, a rare event, and opened the door that led into VA's office.

"Good luck." She whispered this so softly he could hardly hear her.

"Come in, come in, Geoffrey," Vice Admiral Sir John Whitehead said, rising from his chair at the head of the conference table.

Being addressed by his first name by VA was significant, probably indicating that Sir John felt sorry for him and would treat him as an equal — albeit for a short while. "It's good to have you back. How's the wound, or should I rather say the wounds?"

"Well on the mend," he replied. The usual gift-boxed bottle of Glenfiddich had arrived at the Queen Elizabeth Military Hospital.

There were three others at the table. He immediately recognised the Deputy Minister of Defence, Ian Tunnecliffe. He had dealings with him before; he was one of those know-it-alls, schooled at Eton and with a degree from Oxford. Peace had been at Oxford at the same time and could recall Tunnecliffe's penchant for young black women. Chocolate was what it was usually referred to.

He had to smile as a thought crossed his mind. He wanted to ask them whether he was still so fond of chocolate. *That would put the arsehole in his bloody place.*

It would've gone down well, and VA's brief love affair with him would end immediately. He had to try hard not to grin.

The others rose and all shook hands.

"Sit, sit down, Geoffrey," Sir John said. He always repeated himself during moments like this. "Okay, down to business then."

Ian Tunnecliffe contemplated Peace for a few seconds. Clearly, he was being appraised.

"For the past few weeks, my people have been flying around stamping out fires in South Africa, Namibia, Botswana, and Lesotho. Jesus, man, couldn't you have been a little more circumspect?"

God, what a pompous arsehole. The bastard hasn't changed — he is still a sanctimonious prick. Peace stared back at Tunnecliffe, his face expressionless except a slight tic below his left eye.

"Really, Minister, I wonder what the hell you would've done with a WMD perched on a sub-orbital rocket ready to launch to God-knows-where? The bombs were destroyed, and I've learned that your clean-up operation in conjunction with President de Klerk's loyal men was successful. What more could you want?" He desperately wanted to add a few more choice expletives but decided not to. VA would have gone apoplectic — already he was showing the first signs of stress.

VA intervened, holding up a hand. "Please, gentlemen, all this has already been discussed. Suffice it to say, we're glad to see you back in one piece and I can confirm that our relationship with those countries mentioned has not been compromised. Of course, the matter concerning the WMDs was smothered; only a few know about it. Fortunately, the mishap at Overberg has been ascribed to a horrific accident. Our American operatives made it safely home, thank God. Unfortunately, many people died at Overberg, but we must accept this was unavoidable. Van Rhyn and Booyens are dead, and without them, the others are leaderless and lost." He gave Peace a brief, knowing look.

"I just wanted Geoffrey to know how difficult it is to explain away how so many people died, some with multiple bullet holes, in such obscure places as Ficksburg and the Katse Dam," Ian Tunnecliffe interjected.

Peace wanted to say that it was Ian's job to do so, but thought better of it.

Sir Norman Douglas of the Bank of England smiled at Peace. "It seems that I'm the only one who has a real appreciation of your deeds.

We got virtually all our gold back. In my eyes, that speaks volumes. All my colleagues and I can say is *Well done*."

"Oh, by the way," VA interrupted, "you've been promoted to full Commander — congratulations."

Peace remained silent.

"Well, have you any questions?" VA asked.

"In fact, I do. Any news regarding Lady Langton-Van Rhyn and her two daughters?"

"They're all well. Lady Langton, as she now prefers to be called, is trying to erase all relationships, or rather the memory of her deceased husband. She is here in London and unbelievably, has entirely divorced herself from her previous ultra-right sentiments. Janet Van Rhyn has done likewise, and you will be pleased to learn that she too recovered well from her injuries. And Margaret? She's back at Oxford, lost in her studies, and is doing her best to forget everything. Some of those men arrested by the South African Intelligence Service were interrogated. They finally squealed, which, with the assistance of de Klerk, gave us the information to round those up whom we thought represented a direct threat to political transition in South Africa."

"The bombs?"

"We, that is de Klerk's people and us, found them. Other than the nuclear core, everything else was destroyed by the fire. This included the neutron bomb, although it wasn't quite so bad, I understand. It has been retrieved from the Katse Dam. The firing systems and all the other complex bits of their systems were burned to hell. All were secretly airlifted to Pelindaba, their nuclear research station near Pretoria, where they will be completely decommissioned and destroyed."

"Miss Boxx?" Peace asked quietly, his eyes hard.

"What happened was tragic. I'm sorry, we will miss her; she was a first-class operative."

"I can vouch for that," Peace replied, his voice hard and his jaw clenched.

"Geoffrey, she was not the sacrificial lamb as you may think. We never believed we would run into the resistance we did. It got out of hand and very rapidly."

Peace didn't want to start slinging mud; he supposed his superiors had done their best.

There was little else to say. They rose to bid him goodbye, wishing him a speedy recovery.

"Have a holiday; we'll be in touch," were VA's words before he closed the door on the departing Peace.

Chapter Thirty-Four

It was two months later. Peace had spent three weeks recuperating while on holiday after the sling had been removed. He had been in no mood to socialise and sought out a quiet island in the Caribbean — eating well, sleeping late, but avoiding company and particularly, women. Cherry was still too recent a memory. There had been beautiful women around, most on holiday and some clearly out for fun, but he shunned their flirtatious advances on the beach and at the beach bar in the evenings. He drank too much and was lost in himself. This became obvious to others, who soon left him alone.

It was nine and already dark and slightly overcast when he swung the Saab into the short driveway that led to his garage and activated the automatic garage doors. A red Porsche 928S was parked on the opposite side of the mews. He noticed that the lights were on in his mews flat, although the curtains were drawn. He was surprised; his housekeeper had usually long left by this time. The flat was on the first and second floors. He climbed the staircase adjacent to the main building, which led to his landing and front door. He inserted a latchkey into the lock of the ornate wooden door.

The door swung open before he turned the lock. This was suspicious; the housekeeper could surely not be here so late, and it was already seven. Somebody had switched on his B&O hi-fi set. This would be most unlike the housekeeper — he must have a visitor.

"Is that you, Tiger?" a female voice called. This was asked in perfect English, but he still recognised the faintest of a South African twang. He had heard that voice before.

282

"I hope you've loaded your pistol," the voice added.

He didn't have an automatic with him. Contrary to what was portrayed in movies, intelligence officers didn't walk around armed when in London and off duty.

He strode through the foyer into the drawing room. A dark-haired woman sat on his sofa sipping from a martini glass. She leaned forward and placed the glass on the coffee table and with a swish of nylons, uncrossed her magnificent legs and rose to greet him with a brilliant smile. It was Janet Van Rhyn.

He could not disguise his surprise. "Good God, what are you doing here? You're the last person I expected to see, and what is it with this Tiger?" What was the reason for the visit? Was this revenge?

She walked slowly towards him. She was modestly dressed in a blue business suit but this did not disguise her allure, her black hair shimmering in the light, her perfect bosom enhanced by the narrow waist. She chuckled. "Tiger stands for cat, a very special cat with nine lives. You certainly seem to have that. Oh, you haven't answered my question, is your gun loaded?"

He was still faintly wary. "Yes, it's loaded but you haven't answered my question."

She came close, so close he could smell the scent of her perfume, a smell he remembered.

"I'm here regarding unfinished business, if you recall." Her voice had lowered and had taken on a sexy huskiness. She then stepped forward, lifted her head to his, and kissed him.

"God, I missed you so," she said. "But I waited to give you time to recover from the loss of Cherry. I hope it's not too soon. I'm truly sorry for what happened. As for my father, I now understand that you did what you had to do. They would have killed thousands, if not millions, of innocent people. In fact, somehow you even saved me from being tried as an accomplice."

He hesitated for only a moment, but then took her in his arms and kissed her.

He then held her at arms' length and studied her. "How are you?" he asked tenderly.

With her features now sombre, she replied, her voice lower, "I was lucky…

The bullet just missed my lung but I understand it was touch-and-go for a while. I'd lost a lot of blood. Had the helicopter not been there — well, that would've meant the end." She smiled. "I've a scar where you like to linger… I'm looking forward to that. Really, I'm right as rain now."

"And how did you find my place? It is supposed to be a secret," he asked.

She chuckled. "Compliments of a very good investigator I hired. He was expensive. I had your name, Royal Navy rank, and knew you were with MI6. My investigator did the rest. Incidentally, I can recommend him." She laughed and wagged a finger at him. "Never underestimate South Africans — we've also waged intelligence wars for years — sometimes, the easiest route is the best way," she remarked nonchalantly, affectionately holding a hand to his cheek.

He looked into her soft eyes, remaining silent for a moment before saying, "I should report this but I won't, simply because I'm not that difficult to find and I'm glad you did." He smiled and kissed her.

THE END